Au

Affairs

*Who could resist these gorgeous
Australian heroes?*

Three passionate novels!

In May 2007 Mills & Boon bring back
two of their classic collections, each
featuring three favourite romances
by our bestselling authors...

AUSTRALIAN AFFAIRS
The Outback Doctor by Lucy Clark
The Surgeon's Proposal by Lilian Darcy
Outback Surgeon by Leah Martyn

HIS CONVENIENT WOMAN
His Convenient Wife by Diana Hamilton
His Convenient Mistress
by Cathy Williams
His Convenient Fiancée
by Barbara McMahon

Australian Affairs

THE OUTBACK DOCTOR
by
Lucy Clark

THE SURGEON'S PROPOSAL
by
Lilian Darcy

OUTBACK SURGEON
by
Leah Martyn

MILLS & BOON®

DID YOU PURCHASE THIS BOOK WITHOUT A COVER?
If you did, you should be aware it is **stolen property** as it was
reported *unsold and destroyed* by a retailer. Neither the author nor
the publisher has received any payment for this book.

All the characters in this book have no existence outside the
imagination of the author, and have no relation whatsoever to anyone
bearing the same name or names. They are not even distantly inspired
by any individual known or unknown to the author, and all the
incidents are pure invention.

All Rights Reserved including the right of reproduction in whole or
in part in any form. This edition is published by arrangement with
Harlequin Enterprises II B.V./S.à.r.l. The text of this publication or
any part thereof may not be reproduced or transmitted in any form
or by any means, electronic or mechanical, including photocopying,
recording, storage in an information retrieval system, or otherwise,
without the written permission of the publisher.

This book is sold subject to the condition that it shall not, by way of
trade or otherwise, be lent, resold, hired out or otherwise circulated
without the prior consent of the publisher in any form of binding or
cover other than that in which it is published and without a similar
condition including this condition being imposed on the subsequent
purchaser.

MILLS & BOON and MILLS & BOON with the Rose Device
are registered trademarks of the publisher.
Harlequin Mills & Boon Limited,
Eton House, 18-24 Paradise Road, Richmond, Surrey, TW9 1SR

AUSTRALIAN AFFAIRS
© by Harlequin Enterprises II B.V. 2007

The Outback Doctor, The Surgeon's Proposal and *Outback Surgeon*
were first published in Great Britain by Harlequin Mills & Boon
Limited in separate, single volumes.

The Outback Doctor © Lucy Clark 2002
The Surgeon's Proposal © Lilian Darcy 2003
Outback Surgeon © Leah Martyn 2003

ISBN: 978 0 263 85516 6

05-0507

Printed and bound in Spain
by Litografía Rosés S.A., Barcelona

THE OUTBACK DOCTOR

by

Lucy Clark

Lucy Clark began writing romance in her early teens and immediately knew she'd found her 'calling' in life. After working as a secretary in a busy teaching hospital, she turned her hand to writing medical romance. She currently lives in South Australia with her husband and two children. Lucy largely credits her writing success to the support of her husband, family and friends.

Don't miss Lucy Clark's exciting new novel
The Surgeon and the Single Mum
**out in June 2007 from Mills & Boon
Medical Romance™**

To Pete,
My own hero.
My one true love.

CHAPTER ONE

SHE was not having fun!

Rose rested her elbow on the window-ledge and rubbed her fingers across her temple, her left hand on the steering-wheel. What had made her think that driving from Sydney to Broken Hill would be less hassle than flying and hiring a car once she arrived?

She would need to stop soon and battle the flies, due to the eighth bottle of water she'd consumed since breakfast. Drinking a lot served two purposes. She was forced to stop and revive as well as decreasing the risk of dehydrating. The weather was so stinking hot, even now, when it was approaching dusk. Well, at least there was air-conditioning in the car.

Rose heard a noise and immediately glanced in her rear-view mirror. A red sedan, with spoilers and gleaming chrome, was about to overtake her. It must be doing close to one hundred and thirty kilometres per hour as she herself was doing the State limit of one hundred.

'Idiots!' she mumbled as they roared past, the passenger in the car waving to her as they went. At this time of the evening, when the chances of hitting a kangaroo increased dramatically, speeding was the last thing on her mind. Last night, she'd made sure she'd stopped before dusk but as she was now about half an hour out of Broken Hill, she saw no point in stopping. Not if she was careful.

Rose checked the map again. Visions of using the bath-room at her father's house made her smile. Better that than a dirty, fly-ridden petrol station or worse—having to squat!

Ten minutes later, she saw the outline of a large object in the middle of the road and automatically decreased her speed. Was it a roo? She'd seen a few dead ones on the side of the road since her journey had begun and it had made her sad. Still, it was a fact of outback life—or so she'd read. No—it wasn't a roo. The silhouette was far too big.

The sun picked out a gleam of red and Rose's stomach churned. Her heartbeat accelerated and as she mentally went through a check list of what was in her medical bag, safely nestled in the back seat, she hoped she wouldn't be needing any of it.

As she neared, she saw the situation was even worse than she'd first imagined.

'Oh, no!' Rose's mouth hung open, her eyes as wide as saucers as she took in the scene before her. It was horrific!

The red car hadn't hit anything as yielding as a roo. It was on one side, the roof of the car completely buckled and hard up against the second trailer of a road train. She'd never seen a road train this close up and they were a lot longer than she'd expected. The front had hit the gravel shoulder of the road and sunk down into the drainage ditch, tipping the driver's side of the cab up so the left side was almost buried in the ground.

The trailer that was connected directly to the cab was also in the ditch but still upright. The second and third trailers were blocking the road completely. Rose swallowed the sickening jolt that had initially twisted her stomach and forced her professionalism to the fore. She picked up her mobile phone as she brought the car to a halt but found it was out of range.

'Damn!' She cut the engine and switched on her hazard lights before reaching around into the back for her medical bag and her hat. Climbing from the car, she jogged along the road towards the wreck, the hot January weather hitting her like a brick.

Dust. Petrol. Blood. Death. The smells were poignant in the air and her eyes stung with hot tears at the senseless mess before her.

As she came closer, she could see the driver of the road train lying out through the front of the cab, half in, half out of the windscreen. Dropping her bag to the ground, she grabbed hold of his wrist, checking his pulse.

She sighed with relief. It was there. It was quite strong. 'Can you hear me?' she called, but received no answer. 'I'm just going to take a quick look around and then I'll be back.'

Rose picked up her bag and headed down the road, being careful of the debris. The petrol smell became stronger as she neared the red car. She got as close as she dared, her gaze searching hard through the wreckage for the two men who'd been in there.

She could only see one—the driver—and by the way he was positioned, squashed between pieces of twisted metal, she knew he was dead. With all the broken glass around, the other person could have been thrown through the windscreen. She looked around, scanning the fairly flat vegetation for signs of life, swatting continuously at the flies.

'There.' Her heart pounded fiercely against her chest as she rushed over to where the body lay—lifeless on the fine orangey-brown dirt. He was lying face down, his legs twisted at awful angles. Just by looking at them, she could tell they were badly fractured. She dumped her bag on the ground and quickly pulled out a pair of gloves and tugged them on.

Pressing two fingers to his carotid pulse, Rose didn't like what she felt. It was thready and faint. Reaching for her medical torch, she turned his head slightly and checked his pupils. They were both sluggish.

She checked his pulse again and while her fingers were still pressed firmly to the man's neck, his pulse disappeared. 'Oh, no, you don't,' she said firmly. Turning him over, Rose checked he hadn't swallowed his tongue before grabbing an expired air resuscitation mask from her bag and placing it over the man's mouth. Tipping his head back, she pinched his nose and breathed five quick breaths into his mouth.

Finding the right spot just beneath the man's sternum, she placed one hand on top of the other and laced her fingers together before starting external cardiac compression. Rose concentrated and counted. Fifteen compressions—two breaths. She checked his pulse. Nothing. Compressions, breaths. Still no pulse. She went again and this time when she checked for a pulse she found one.

'Good,' she puffed. 'Now let's try and see what else is happening to you.' She glanced over her shoulder, thinking she'd heard something, but she couldn't see anything. Her thoughts went to the truck driver. Perhaps he'd regained consciousness. She couldn't check him just yet as this man's injuries were more urgent. As she was the only person around, she had the triage call as to which patient required immediate attention.

She checked his pupils again. They were still sluggish, the right one slightly larger than the left. Not a good sign, she thought as she felt his limbs for breaks. She checked his pulse again just as she heard the sound of a car. Thank goodness. Even if the person did nothing other than get in contact with the ambulance or Royal Flying Doctor Service, she didn't care. She wasn't on her own any more.

The pulse disappeared again and Rose groaned. She went through the motions again and was in the middle of counting her cardiac compressions when the vehicle stopped, quite close to where she was, sending dirt over her crisp white top. Rose shut both her eyes and her mouth for a few seconds while the dust settled, and when she opened them, it was to find a pair of well-worn work boots, thick socks and tanned, hairy legs in her direct line of vision. She glanced up as the man squatted down. His hat was wide and also well worn and hid most of his face.

''Struth!'

'Call for an ambulance or RFDS or something,' she muttered as he crouched down.

'Already done.'

His voice was deep and rich but she didn't have time to think about such things at the moment. 'Great. Do you know CPR?'

'Sure, but I'll just go take a look around first.'

'I need you here,' she demanded, wondering if everyone in the outback was such a sticky-beak.

'You're doing fine. I won't be long.'

'Get back here,' she called in between counts but he was gone. 'Of all my luck,' she told her unconscious patient, but returned her concentration to counting the compressions.

True to his word, the stranger came back. 'You do the breaths, I'll take over the compressions,' he stated, and simply knelt down and did as he'd said, not giving her the opportunity to say a word.

They worked together. Five compressions and then Rose blew one breath into the patient's mouth.

'One, two, three, four, five, breathe,' he kept chanting.

At the end of the next set, Rose checked for the pulse. 'Nothing,' she reported. 'Let's go again.'

'No.'

'No?'

He picked up her medical torch and checked the patient's pupils. 'Fixed and dilated. I'm calling it. Time of death...' He checked his watch.

'You can't *call* it.'

'Eighteen twenty-three,' he continued as though she hadn't spoken. 'Why not?' He stood and picked up a black bag that was just off to the right of him. She hadn't seen him put it there. She glanced at her own medical bag.

'You're a doctor?'

'Obviously.' He didn't wait for her to continue with the conversation and instead took off towards the truck driver. 'Well, come on,' he called impatiently over his shoulder, and Rose bristled as she rose to her feet and grabbed her own bag.

She supposed she shouldn't look a gift horse in the mouth. She should be glad that the one person who'd arrived to help her was probably the local doctor. Rose rushed after him, knowing the truck driver needed their attention.

'I see the driver of the red car doesn't need our expertise,' the man stated when she caught up to him.

'No. Killed himself outright.' Rose looked at the truck driver. 'He's regained consciousness.'

'What makes you say that?'

'He's moved.' The driver was now almost completely out of the cab, coming across the front of the engine.

'This is where he was when I came over to take a look. Help me get him down.'

Rose worked with the doctor, glad he was there. 'I've got some morphine in my bag so that should help him with the pain.'

'Good. Get an IV line set up, stat, then check his vital signs. Bob? Bob can you hear me? It's Dave, mate.' No reply.

'How do you know him?' Rose asked.

'He's a mate of mine,' Dave mumbled, pulling on a fresh pair of gloves and taking some scissors out of his bag before cutting Bob's navy T-shirt away. His abdomen was completely covered in blood and Dave began cleaning it up with gauze swabs. 'If he's come out through the front of the cab then he would have come over the windscreen.'

'Correct.' Rose was almost finished with the IV line. The sooner Bob got these fluids into him, the better. 'He was lying over it—half in, half out—when I first checked him.'

'Why didn't you get him out?' Dave demanded.

Rose didn't like his tone at all. 'His pulse was fine and I needed to assess the status of the other two patients. I was the only one here,' she continued, her words and body language completely defensive, 'and I made the triage call. As the other patient is now dead and Bob has clearly regained consciousness and managed to get himself out of the cab, I'd say I made the right choice.'

'All right, all right. Don't get your knickers in a twist. I was only asking.'

'No. You were criticising.'

Dave was silent for a moment. 'He's got glass in here,' he said, pulling a piece from Bob's abdomen and throwing it away, his gloved hand covered in blood. 'What's his BP?'

'Eighty over forty. That's not good.'

'No joke.'

Rose continued to check Bob's vital signs as well as running her hands expertly over Bob's limbs. 'Right femur feels fractured. That can't be helping with the blood loss.'

'Right arm doesn't look good either. He's not gonna be too thrilled when he comes around.'

'Well, at least Bob is alive.'

'Still, he isn't going to be too happy.'

'I've given him some morphine, so that should at least help with his pain.'

'Good.' Once that was done, they worked together to splint Bob's broken leg, getting him ready for when the ambulance arrived. Dave kept talking to their patient all the time, telling him everything they were doing and that he was going to make it.

'So what type of doctor are you?' Dave asked as they worked.

'Anaesthetist.'

'Rose Partridge?' he queried.

'Yes.' She was momentarily taken aback.

'Just as well you're here. The other anaesthetist left this morning and the locum isn't due to arrive until tomorrow.'

'What would you have done had I not arrived until Monday?'

'We do have people who are trained to give anaesthetics but aren't anaesthetists,' he replied matter-of-factly.

'Glad to hear it.'

He tipped his head to one side and listened. Then Rose heard it, too. Sirens. 'Let's change this dressing so he's ready for the ambos.' The cavalry was coming. Rose assisted him before doing Bob's vital signs once more.

'Pupils equal and reacting to light. BP now one hundred over fifty-five. At least those fluids being pumped into him are working.'

'Yeah, but he's still losing a lot of blood.'

When the emergency crews arrived, Rose had to admit she was impressed. They may have turned up in vehicles which weren't state of the art, like the ones in Sydney, but they were functional for what needed to be done.

Once the dressing was changed, Dave ripped off his gloves and headed over to talk to the ambulance officers, or ambos as they were more affectionately known, leaving Rose to monitor Bob. He pointed in her direction and also to where the other patient was. At least they all knew who was in charge!

'G'day.' One of the ambos brought over a stretcher. 'Dave says ya the new anaesthetist.'

'That's right,' Rose replied.

'Not the best type of welcome for ya but we're all mighty glad you're here, Doc.'

'Thank you.' Rose launched into a spiel of Bob's vital statistics as the ambos got him ready to move. When he was finally being wheeled away towards the ambulance, Rose removed her gloves and locked her bag. She was hot and sticky and as she stood to brush the dirt from her crumpled white shorts, she realised she'd have to bleach not only her shorts but her top as well as the orangey-brown dirt had well and truly settled into the fabric.

She swatted the flies away frustratedly before picking up her bag and heading back to her car. Dave jogged over and fell into step with her.

'You're going the wrong way. I need you to ride with Bob in the ambulance.'

'Why can't you?'

'I'll follow in my ute.'

'Why can't I follow in my car? I'm sure the ambos are more than capable of caring for the patient during the ride to hospital.'

'He might regain consciousness again during the drive.'

'All the more reason why you should authorise some medication for him, then.'

'But you're the anaesthetist. You'll have a better idea of what analgesics he'll need.'

Rose sighed heavily. 'Fine, I'll organise some analgesics but I'm still following in my car.'

'We can get someone else to drive it to the hospital for you.'

'Then why can't we get someone to drive your ute to the hospital? After all, if Bob starts to haemorrhage, he's going to need you on hand to deal with it.'

'Are you always this difficult to work with?' Dave asked.

Rose stumbled over a stone on the road and felt the warmth of Dave's hand immediately at her elbow, steadying her. She shrugged him off, not caring if he thought she was rude. She was hot, dirty and tired from driving for the past two days.

'You should be wearing sensible shoes, not those strappy little fashion things.'

'Well, excuse me,' she said crossly. 'I hadn't planned on assisting in a major trauma retrieval team and I'll thank you to keep your comments about the way I dress to yourself.'

'Difficult and snappy. Oh, the next six months are going to be a barrel of laughs.'

They'd reached Rose's car and she turned around to glare at him. 'Listen, Dave whoever-you-are, I have been driving for two days to get to Broken Hill. I'm hot, uncomfortable and extremely tired. Now, if you want my help then get…off…my…back!' Rose glared at him, adding emphasis to the last four words. Then she turned and opened her door, placing her medical bag carefully on the seat. Next, she took a white handkerchief from her pocket and took off her hat, wiping the perspiration from her forehead and running her fingers through her short blonde hair.

She'd half expected Dave to have gone, but when she turned around again it was to find him frowning at her as though she were some sort of alien. 'Let's check on Bob and then get to the hospital,' he said briskly, before striding off towards the ambulance.

What was the matter with him? He was a grown man and one look at Miss High and Mighty had his hormones in overdrive. So she was beautiful—he'd fallen in love with beautiful before and where had it got him? Divorced!

'Just concentrate on your patient and keep your mouth shut, Dunbar,' he mumbled.

'Talking to yaself, Dave?' one member of the emergency crews asked. They were getting ready to spray the road, dampening any petrol fumes that might ignite before they began the tedious job of cutting the body from the wreck. The young man who they'd tried to resuscitate was being taken care of by the local undertakers who'd arrived on the scene soon after the ambulance.

'Something like that. Keep up the good work,' he encouraged, but continued on his way to the ambulance. He could feel rather than see that Rose was following him, which annoyed him even more. Keep your mind on the job. That was the answer and it was the best advice he could give himself.

Once he reached the ambulance, he climbed in and assessed Bob's condition. For now, he was as stabilised as they could get him.

As Rose climbed in, Dave could smell the subtle scent of her perfume and was surprised that it wasn't as overpowering as that which most city girls usually wore. It was sleek and seductive, winding its way around him and drawing him closer. He shook his head to clear it and handed her Bob's chart.

'If you authorise some analgesics, we'll get this show on the road.'

'Certainly, Doctor,' she replied briskly, and, without waiting for her, Dave climbed from the ambulance and spoke to the ambos.

When everyone was ready, they shut the back door of the ambulance and headed back to their respective vehicles. Dave found the urge was too great and couldn't resist looking over his shoulder to where Rose hurried towards her car. Her back was ramrod straight, her arms swinging at her sides, her hips swaying slightly. The action was unintentionally provocative and once more Dave had to rein in his hormones.

He kept a close eye on her in his rear-view mirror as they followed the ambulance back into town. Her sporty Jaguar XJ-6 kept up quite nicely with the ambulance and his ute, and he couldn't help reflecting that the woman and machine complemented each other nicely.

Finally, they arrived at the hospital without the need to stop, Bob's situation remaining stable. Dave had kept in constant contact with the ambos, via the HF radio, the entire way. Now they'd arrived, it was all systems go.

As he walked in the door, he called for Carrie, one of the theatre nurses. 'Dr Rose Partridge, the new anaesthetist, is about to walk through those doors. Show her where she needs to be, changing rooms, theatres—that sort of thing.'

'No problem, Dave.'

He strode to Bob's side and asked for an update on vital signs, and was glad to hear his mate was hanging in there. 'Cross-type and match. Two units of blood, stat. Let's get him to X-ray,' Dave said as he wrote up the requests for Radiology. 'I'll be in Theatre, getting things ready. Page me when he's done.' With that he headed for the male changing rooms to get ready. Once he was changed, he walked out into the corridor, only to find Rose standing there, looking slightly lost. She was dressed in theatre scrubs.

She even looked good in baggy blue cotton, he realised, but knew he shouldn't have been surprised. She seemed the type of woman who would look good in a garbage bag. Her hair was slightly wet, indicating she'd had a quick shower to get all that dirt off her before she'd changed into the scrubs.

He stood by the door and stared.

When she turned and caught him in the act, he found he couldn't move. For what seemed like an endless moment they looked at each other, and Dave felt his breath catch in his throat. Her deep blue eyes were made brighter by the blue of the material. She was…a vision.

Rose was first to break the contact, looking down at the ground momentarily before walking off. She didn't care which direction she went but she knew she couldn't stay still any longer. With one single look, Dave had managed to increase her heartbeat so it pounded erratically against her ribs. Her knees felt like jelly and her mind seemed incapable of coherent thought.

Why should she be feeling slightly breathless just because she'd shared a look with Dave Whoever? So what if he'd made her a little breathless and light-headed with the scorching look that had seemed to reach right down into the depths of her soul? He probably looked at every woman like that. Learn from your experiences, she told herself. All men were awful and that was all there was to it.

'The heat,' she mumbled. She just wasn't used to the heat. When she finally found which theatre Bob was due to be in, she was told that the patient was still in Radiology but that Dave had asked to be paged when Bob returned. Rose frowned. Why would Dave want to know? Shouldn't the surgeon in charge be informed? The pennies started to drop and she realised that Dave *was* the surgeon and not a local GP, as she'd originally thought.

Her opinion of him grew a little—a very little. He was conceited, arrogant and dictatorial. All the qualities she'd come to expect from a surgeon. She was quite surprised she hadn't picked up on it sooner. Then again, she *had* been a little preoccupied since they'd met.

When they eventually were under way in Theatre, Rose re-evaluated her opinion of him yet again. As far as his professional attributes went, they were superb. He was casual yet direct with his staff and possessed great skill as a surgeon.

The man seemed to have many facets to his personality, at least from what she'd observed during the past few hours, and part of her was intrigued by that. She monitored the patient, keeping a close eye on the dials, forcing any personal thoughts of Dave Whoever out of her mind.

Dave methodically went through the steps to stop the bleeding, suturing off the offending arteries in the femur and removing glass from Bob's abdomen but leaving the fractured bone for the orthopod to fix. Nevertheless, he didn't close the wound until he was absolutely positive each and every piece of shattered glass had been removed.

When he was finished, Rose accompanied the patient to Recovery, ensuring that Bob didn't have any side-effects from the anaesthetic. She wrote up her notes and went to change back into her dirty clothes, longing to get to her father's house so she could have a more leisurely shower.

After she'd dressed, she returned to Recovery to find Dave sitting by Bob's bed, talking softly to his friend. She was just to the side of him so he couldn't really see her, and it gave her the opportunity to observe him further.

'Hang in there, mate,' he said softly. 'I know last year was a horrible year for you, and you didn't need this to happen, but you're going to get through it, mate. Promise.'

Rose felt her heart melt at the genuine concern Dave felt for his friend.

'I've done a first-rate job on you, mate,' he continued. 'Everything's going to be smelling of roses once we get

your orthopaedic bits taken care of. You'll be as good
as new.'

Rose continued to stare at Dave. Who was he? First
she'd thought he'd been some busybody come to gawk at
the accident. Then she'd discovered he was a doctor. Not
only a doctor but Broken Hill's resident general surgeon.

Now here he was, displaying compassion for his friend,
the friend he'd operated on and, more than likely, saved
his life. From what she could tell, Bob's internal injuries
were not a pretty sight yet Dave had systematically gone
about making sure everything was back where it was supposed to be.

It must have been extremely difficult to operate on his
friend, but when he'd been standing at the operating table
he'd been one hundred per cent professional. Rose had
never been in that type of situation before—anaesthetising
and monitoring a friend—yet she supposed that, being the
only general surgeon in Broken Hill, he would have to do
it quite often.

Thankfully, Bob's fractured femur and arm were stabilised and she wondered whether he'd be transported to
Adelaide, six hours away, for orthopaedic treatment or
whether someone at the hospital would perform the surgery.

It was all quite new to her, working in a small hospital.
She was so used to the red tape of a large teaching hospital
that she knew it might take her some time to adjust to the
way things were done in this eighty-eight-bed hospital.

As she stood by the door, watching him, Rose felt the
stirrings of admiration. It was strange. She usually took
her time to get to know new acquaintances before admiration set in—if the person was worthy of the label. Other
people usually thought her stand-offish at first, until they
discovered the real Rose lying beneath the cool exterior,
but because Julian had broken her heart and crushed her
self-confidence, Rose had built many walls around her for
protection.

'Problem?'

Rose snapped out of her reverie and realised that Dave was now looking at her.

'Uh—no problem,' she spluttered. 'I just didn't want to intrude.'

The frown in Dave's forehead deepened.

'How's he doing?' she continued as she crossed to the end of the bed and picked up the chart. She pretended to read it, knowing it was only a matter of five minutes since she'd last read it. No other changes had been made but, still, she had to do something to escape his penetrating gaze.

'Same.' He stood and walked around behind her. As he passed, Rose caught a whiff of his aftershave. It was spicy and appealing but mingled with the mild aroma of his obviously exhausting day it made for a heady combination.

He reached for the chart as Rose was about to slide it back into the holder, his arm brushing lightly against hers. The action caused shivers to run up her arm and spread throughout her body.

'Uh…' She cleared her throat. 'Excuse me.' With that, Rose turned and walked away. She didn't look back. She didn't pass Go. She didn't collect $200.

What was wrong with her? She asked herself the question over and over again as she climbed into her car and checked the map book. As she started down the road towards her father's house, Rose was determined to get control over her emotions.

She was tired. That had to be it. She'd been under a lot of stress during the past two days and even before that. During the past few months she'd had her break-up with Julian, as well as her decision to get out of Sydney. They were all factors which could contribute to her uncharacteristic behaviour towards her new colleague.

As she pulled into the driveway of her father's double brick house, Rose put all thoughts of her day behind her. Her father had been worried about her driving such a long way by herself, but she'd assured him she would be fine. If he saw otherwise in her expression, it would only cause him to worry and that was the last thing he needed. His wedding day was tomorrow. At last her father had found happiness, and she was glad he'd invited her to share it with him.

'There you are,' Beverley, her father's fiancée, said as she came out the front door and crossed to Rose's side. 'Your father and I were starting to worry.'

'Sorry,' Rose replied. 'There was an emergency. I asked someone at the hospital to call and let you know.'

'They did.' Beverley gave her a warm hug—not a gentle pat on the shoulder but a real hug. A motherly hug. To someone who'd basically grown up without a mother, these hugs were precious. 'I can't believe they've had you working at the hospital already.'

Rose smiled and shrugged. 'What else was I supposed to do?'

'What a welcome to Broken Hill!' Beverley laughed. 'We're so glad you're here.' Beverley hugged her again. 'Come inside out of the heat. We can get your bags later— right now, your father is impatient to see you.'

'How's everything going for tomorrow? All organised?' Rose asked as they walked inside, Beverley's arm linked with hers.

'I certainly hope so. Oh, Rosie, it's so silly. I've been through this before—a wedding, I mean—yet I can't believe how nervous I am.'

'Pre-wedding jitters.' Rose chuckled and patted Beverley's arm, pleased that her stepmother-to-be felt comfortable calling her Rosie. It was a pet name that only the people closest to her used. It showed her that Beverley felt comfortable and relaxed in her presence, and Rose knew this was an important factor for her father.

'Ah, the two most important women in my life,' Reg Partridge crooned as they walked into the kitchen. He took the wok off the stove and walked over to embrace his daughter. 'My beautiful Rose.' He held her possessively for a long moment before placing a kiss on her forehead. 'Your coming is an added blessing upon our marriage. Isn't that right, Bev, darling?' he asked as he held out his arm to his bride-to-be.

Rose felt a lump building in her throat and marvelled at how sentimental she was being. Then again, she hadn't seen her father for a good six months and it had been six months too long.

'I'm sorry I wasn't able to make it home for Christmas,' she told her father.

'I understand,' he said, just like he always did, and she knew he meant it. Reginald Partridge was a unique man, who accepted people for who they were. 'The bonus is that you'll be here for six months and that in itself is a present worth waiting for.' He kissed her forehead again, but when a faint hissing noise sounded, he abruptly let the two women go and rushed back to the stove to remove a lid from a bubbling saucepan.

'What are you cooking? Don't you know what the time is?' she asked, as she sat down at the island bench to watch him. It was a position she'd spent most of her life in— watching her father as he cooked. Now he was about to reap the rewards from another cookbook of his going on the shelves, the photographs having been taken by Beverley.

'I'm making beef in black bean sauce and rice, and there are spring rolls warming in the oven for the entrée. I was going to make special fried rice but we haven't been shopping so I'm missing some of the ingredients.'

'Dad—it's almost midnight.'

'I thought you might be hungry,' he said with a shrug. 'Besides, I was worried about you and you know how cooking helps me relax.'

'Never mind.' She laughed. 'It sounds and smells delicious.'

'I can't believe my good fortune, marrying a man who

likes to cook.' Beverley chuckled as she crossed to his side and kissed him.

Rose watched them and sighed with happiness. Seeing her father like this was one huge weight off her mind. He was happy—at last—and he deserved all the happiness in the world.

If only she could find such happiness, but at the moment she wasn't sure. Broken hearts took a long time to fix or, at least, she assumed this one would. A vision of Dave swam before her eyes and her heart jolted. Her uncharacteristic reaction to the man had completely thrown her, and at the moment she wasn't sure whether it was a good or bad thing.

CHAPTER TWO

THE reception was well under way when a deep voice drawled from behind her, 'What's this? The groom's daughter standing all alone in the corner?'

Even though she'd only heard that voice a few times, Rose knew immediately who it belonged to without turning around. Besides, the hairs on the back of her neck were standing on end and a wave of goose bumps had pricked their way down her arms.

'I'm watching my father and his bride,' she retorted icily, straightening her back even further. 'Not that it's any of your business.' She continued to watch her father lead Beverley around the dance floor, their arms entwined around each other.

'So true.'

'I don't recall seeing your name on the guest list.'

'It wasn't.'

'Do you always gatecrash weddings?'

'Only when there's an emergency.'

Rose turned to look at him then. It was a mistake. She hadn't realised he was *that* close. She breathed in deeply and was treated to the heady combination of spicy after-shave mingled with sweat. It must still be hot outside. 'I…er…thought there was an anaesthetist here to cover the weekend.'

'There *was*. That's the emergency.'

Rose sighed heavily. 'Isn't there anyone else? I don't officially start at the hospital until Monday.' She was cross and annoyed and it helped to dampen her other unwanted feelings. 'This is my *father's* wedding!'

'Aw, come on, Rosie,' he teased, and she widened her

gaze in surprise before bristling at the use of her nickname. 'It won't be a long operation and you know it's better if you do it rather than anyone else. Besides, your old man will be leaving soon anyway.'

'Please, don't—'

She was interrupted by the sound of the band finishing their song and people clapping.

'Ladies and gentlemen,' the MC announced, 'the bride and groom are about to depart.'

'See?' Dave said softly from behind her.

Rose looked away, becoming even more frustrated with the man. She didn't want to miss the opportunity of saying goodbye to her father and new stepmother. It would also give her an excuse to escape Dave's company.

'If you'll excuse me,' she said politely between gritted teeth, 'I'd like to go and say goodbye to my father and Beverley.'

'No need,' Dave replied, and pointed. Sure enough, her father and his blushing bride were headed straight for them.

'Dave,' her father said with delight, and heartily shook the other man's hand. 'Glad you made it after all.'

'Sorry, Reg. I'm here under false pretences. I've come to whisk your daughter away.'

Reg laughed. 'Should I ask whether your intentions are honourable?' her father joked.

'Dad!' Rose couldn't believe it. Her father was actually friends with this man?

'Only joking, Rosie.' Reg leaned over and hugged his daughter. 'I know it's probably an emergency if Dave's come to get you. He wasn't able to make it to the wedding because he was on call.' Reg turned his attention back to Dave. 'I thought you had an anaesthetist for the weekend.'

'We did. That's what I was explaining to Rosie. The locum anaesthetist *is* the emergency. Appendicitis.'

Reg chuckled. 'Always the way. Off you go, then, darling.' Reg embraced his daughter. 'Bev and I are leaving anyway.'

Rose stared, dumbfounded, at her father. It appeared he was throwing her to the wolves, or at least one of them.

'Never mind,' Beverley whispered in her ear as the two women hugged. 'Things will settle down in a week or two. Just take each day as it comes and remember that your father and I both love you.'

It was the exact thing Rose needed to hear. Beverley always seemed to know the right thing to say and Rose was immensely glad her father had married her. He needed a wife and although Rose thought she was too old to need a mother, Beverley had proved her wrong yet again. It didn't matter how old you were, it was still nice to hear that you were loved.

'Thanks,' Rose whispered back.

'Now, have you got the house keys?' Beverley fussed. 'And can you remember the controls for the air-conditioner?'

'I'll be fine,' Rose promised. 'Go. Have a good time and I'll see you in a month's time.'

'Take care of my girl.' Reg shook Dave's hand once more before kissing Rose on the cheek. 'I love you, my darling Rose.'

'I love you, too, Dad.'

'We'd better be going,' Dave said, as Reg and Beverley moved away.

'Oh, she can't go yet,' Beverley protested. 'I almost forgot. I have to throw the bouquet.'

Rose laughed uncomfortably. 'Beverley, that's an out-dated romantic tradition.'

'Well, I'm an outdated romantic traditionalist, then,' her stepmother replied good-naturedly. 'Come on,' she announced to the room. 'I need all the unmarried women in a group.'

'That's your cue, Rosie.' Dave's deep voice said from behind her, as he gave her a gentle shove.

'Don't push me,' she retorted.

'Well, hurry it up, will you? We have an appendix that's ready to perforate and you're standing there like a statue.'

'We'll do the garter toss and the bouquet at the same time,' the MC announced. 'All unmarried women over here and all unmarried men over there.'

The room was galvanised into action and soon the MC was counting to three. With both her father and Beverley standing with their backs to their respective groups, they tossed on the count of three.

Rose realised the flowers were heading for her face and instinctively put her hands up to protect herself, her fingers automatically curling around the handle of the bouquet.

Everyone clapped and cheered and then the wolf-whistling started. She turned to see what all the commotion was about and came face to face with Dave, her step-mother's garter dangling from his index finger.

Dave raised his eyebrows suggestively, which made the crowd laugh even harder. 'If you'll excuse us,' he said, and, placing his arm about her shoulders, led her out of the room. She tried not to focus on the warmth of his touch or the way her body seemed to spring instantly to life. The laughter drowned out any protests Rose might have made, but she just didn't have the energy. Besides, she felt completely and utterly humiliated and embarrassed.

'There you are, Rosie. Safely whisked away from a wedding reception.' He scanned the parking lot. 'Would you like me to unlock your car?'

'I'm more than capable,' Rose retorted. She pulled the keys from her small purse and opened the Jaguar's door.

'All right, then. I'll meet you at the hospital.'

Rose climbed behind the wheel, watching him walk away. He had nice long strides. Sure and determined—just like the rest of him. She shook her head and started the engine, glad of the reprieve from prying eyes. She drove behind Dave's ute towards the hospital, happy to follow him as otherwise she probably would have needed to stop and check the map book.

The whole day had been exhausting and she hadn't needed that extra bit of attention at the end to cap it off. Still, her dad and Beverley had enjoyed themselves and would soon be on their way to Sydney on a chartered flight. Tomorrow, they would fly to Port Douglas in Far North Queensland where they would spend four glorious, relaxing weeks by the sea. That was the one thing her father had confessed he missed the most, living in Broken Hill—the sea.

Rose refocused her thoughts into professional mode as she pulled into the hospital car park. She climbed from the car in her strapless dress of burgundy silk which Beverley had chosen for her to wear as bridesmaid.

'Let's get going, Rosie,' Dave called as he headed into the hospital. Rose bristled once again, frowning as she walked after him. Now was not the time for a conversation on her name. He was right, they had a patient to deal with and they'd already wasted more than enough time.

'Status?' Dave asked the nurse who met them at the door.

'BP is up and he's complaining of more pain.'

'What's he been given so far?' Rose enquired as they continued to walk towards Pre-op.

The nurse rattled off the list of medication and Rose mentally went through what she'd probably use.

'Go get changed, Rosie, while I check on Jim.' Dave continued walking down the corridor, effectively dismissing her.

Rose knew he was right but it was the way he'd done it—speaking to her as though she were an intolerable intern. Once she was dressed, she would go see Jim and have a chat with him before anaesthetising him. While she was doing that, Dave had time to get changed and scrubbed. She was still fuming inwardly at his dictatorial attitude as she headed towards Pre-op. As soon as she arrived, Dave gave her an update, being very specific about how long he thought the surgery might take so she knew how long to anaesthetise the patient for.

'Hello, Jim,' she said, as she looked down at the man lying on the barouche with his eyes closed. 'I'm Rose Partridge.'

'Just get on with it,' Jim growled without opening his eyes. 'I know the procedure so yadda, yadda, yadda, just do it, will ya?'

It appeared Jim wasn't too happy with the turn of events. 'Certainly,' Rose replied as she checked his chart for the vital information she'd need in order to anaesthetise him correctly. She asked him the standard set of questions which he answered in clipped tones before telling her exactly what type of drugs she should use and asking whether she wanted him to do it himself as she seemed to be taking all day about it! Rose kept her cool, knowing it was a combination of agitation, nerves and the pethidine he'd already been given.

Once Dave arrived in Theatre, everything progressed smoothly. Again, Rose was impressed with his skill. An appendicectomy was a routine operation but he performed it with such ease, always monitoring in case things went wrong. A few minutes after the small organ had been removed, it burst with little prompting inside the kidney dish.

'Perfect timing,' Dave announced to his theatre staff. His blue gaze settled on Rose briefly and she noted a twinkle in his eyes. 'Just as well you didn't take any longer to catch that bouquet at the wedding, Rosie.'

'Oh, tell us about it,' one of the nurses asked as Dave once again checked the area for any sign of leakage from the appendix.

Rose glared at him, cross that he'd brought up her personal life within the bounds of Theatre. He raised his eyebrows slightly before turning his attention back to his work.

Rose had never liked mixing business with pleasure, yet here he was doing just that. At her old hospital, she'd kept herself to herself, associating with her colleagues in a businesslike and professional manner. They didn't socialise together, they worked together—and as far as she was concerned, never the twain should meet. She didn't agree with personal relationships with colleagues as she'd seen it cause all sorts of problems.

And then there had been Julian, a small voice reminded her. Well, he hadn't been a medical professional and even though she'd met him while he'd been working at the hospital, it wasn't really the same thing.

Her friends had been gathered from her outside interests and although one or two of them might have known medical colleagues of hers, they respected her wishes and kept the two aspects of her life separate.

Now here was Dave, not only telling the staff about the events at her father's wedding but calling her Rosie in front of them, to boot! They *really* needed to talk—and soon.

Dave directed her to reverse the anaesthetic and headed off to write up his notes. Once Rose was satisfied with Jim's recovery status, she left him in the capable hands of the nurses and headed back to the change rooms. She hoped that Dave was still around as she wanted to have that chat with him.

She went back to Recovery, not sure where he might be. The nurses there thought he might have gone to the ward but instead of sending Rose on a wild-goose chase, trying to find him, they called down to the ward only to be told that he wasn't there.

'He's turned your head already, hasn't he?' one of the nurses said with a nod. 'He's a looker, that Dave. Why, if I wasn't wedded to my childhood sweetheart, I'd be giving the single females in this town a run for their money.'

'No, she's not Dave's type,' the other nurse, who was probably old enough to be Dave's mother, replied.

'Oh, Sadie,' the first nurse remarked. 'How do you know what Dave's type is or isn't?'

'She's a blonde,' Sadie replied, and Rose bristled at being talked about rather than talked to. 'And Dave doesn't go for blondes, even if she does look good in a posh dress.'

'He does so go for blondes. His wife was a blonde—wasn't she?'

'That's *why* he doesn't go for them, and she was a city slicker just like Rosie here.'

Rose was about to ask whether she needed to be here for the conversation, but the mention of Dave's wife intrigued her. So he'd been married. Was he divorced? Had his wife died? Rose wasn't sure why she found the information intriguing and in some ways she resented being told that she wasn't his type—not that she wanted to be—just that she thought, as the man was all grown up, perhaps he could decide for himself who was or wasn't his type.

'He told us how you caught Beverley's bouquet,' the first nurse continued, looking directly at Rose this time. 'And how he caught the garter. How romantic.'

'Ha! Nothing remotely romantic about young Dave,' Sadie snorted. 'He probably just did that to hurry things up. He knew he had to get back here as soon as possible.' She turned to look at Rose. 'He's not answering so I'd say he's gone home. You should do the same.'

'Ah…all right. Please, call me if you have any problems with Jim tonight, although,' Rose added as they all looked across to where he was snoring peacefully, 'I doubt it.'

As she walked out of the hospital, the heat hit her once more. Did it ever cool off in this town? She dug her keys out of her bag and headed over to where she'd parked her car. It was then she realised there was a dark silhouette leaning against it, and for one heart-stopping second she faltered. She should have asked a security guard to walk her out—then she remembered that she hadn't seen a security guard.

'It's just me.' Dave's deep voice was instantly recognisable and she shivered, not sure whether it was from fright or nervous anticipation. 'Sorry, I didn't mean to frighten you.'

Rose continued towards him, trying desperately to ignore the sudden racing of her heart. 'Is there a problem?'

'No.'

Rose stopped not far from him, now able to see him more clearly due to the lights that surrounded the car park. She couldn't get through to the driver's door because of the six feet four inches of solid male that was blocking her way. Again, she caught the scent of him and clenched her jaw. This had to stop. She didn't even know this man, let alone like him.

'Then would you mind moving, please?' She kept her tone polite and impersonal, not able to bring her gaze up to meet his but focusing on the sun-kissed skin of his upper chest that peeked out from beneath his partially unbuttoned shirt. It would have been safer to look at his eyes, she realised, and did just that.

'I sensed,' he began as he shoved his hands deep into the pockets of his shorts, 'that you wanted to talk to me.'

'And we couldn't do that inside the hospital?'

'I also sensed that you wanted privacy.'

'Then try sensing that I'm extremely tired and would like to go home.'

'Rosie.'

'Don't call me that,' she snapped. She ran her fingers through her hair. 'Sorry. It's just that the last few days have been extremely exhausting and I'm very tired.'

'Why don't you like being called Rosie?' He frowned, staying where he was. 'It suits you.'

'Whether it suits me or not is completely irrelevant. The fact that I'm not used to colleagues of mine calling me by a pet name is reason enough for you to stop it.'

He continued to frown but she saw his lips twitch. 'Actually, I don't know of any pets who are called Rosie.'

'David! Stop teasing.' She was exhausted and she didn't have time for this.

'David? Only my mother called me David,' he added with a laugh. 'It's so…formal.'

'Well, only my father calls me Rosie, which I classify as being informal.'

'Bev calls you Rosie, too.'

'That's different. She's now a member of my family.'

'Well, I'm practically that.'

'Pardon?'

'I did catch the garter after all.'

Despite her tiredness, Rose felt a smile tug at her lips. Instead, she looked down at the ground and made an attempt to push past him. Big mistake. He didn't move. She found herself pressed up against a firm, solid, male chest, his huge hands coming up to touch her arms lightly.

'We've got to stop meeting like this,' he murmured. Before she knew what was happening, he'd bent his head and brushed his lips across hers.

It was only the briefest of touches but it left her feeling breathless and desperately wanting more. Her heart was pounding furiously against her chest and the headache that had taken hold the second she'd pulled out into the Sydney traffic a few days ago vanished into thin air.

'Goodnight, Rosie,' he whispered, and in the next instant he walked away.

Rose forced herself to move. To go through the motions of getting into her car and driving back to her father's house—the house she'd be calling home for the next six months.

What had happened back there? The question was buzzing around in her mind and as she could feel the headache starting to return, she decided it wasn't worth thinking about. Dave—oh, goodness, she didn't even know his last name! Dave, with the softest lips she'd ever felt pressed against hers, could just get out of her head!

Four hours later as she tossed and turned in the unfamiliar bed, she realised it was easier said than done.

Dave wandered out onto the verandah that surrounded the old weatherboard home and stared out at the night sky. Stars twinkled down at him, making him wonder what on earth he was doing up at this hour. It was just past two o'clock and, try as he might, he'd been unable to get to sleep. And he knew why.

Rosie Partridge.

Why had he kissed her? Although it had only been fleeting, why on earth had he succumbed to the temptation and pressed his lips to hers? Sure, she was an attractive woman, but she wasn't his type.

He shook his head, trying for the umpteenth time to clear the vision of Rosie from his mind.

'Just give up, mate,' he mumbled to himself as he sat down in an old chair and stretched his legs out in front of him. Tomorrow—or, more correctly, today—was Sunday and he'd promised his brother he would help with the northern boundary fencing. That's where he'd been on Friday evening, when that horrible accident had occurred. He'd heard the crash and had all but flown to the ute where he'd driven like a madman to the scene of the accident. There, he'd found a vision in white, rendering first aid. At first, he'd thought he'd been seeing things—an angel, dressed in white? In the middle of nowhere? Instead, he'd encountered a woman as prickly as an echidna.

Dave rubbed his fingers around the back of his neck and closed his eyes. The scent of her perfume seemed to be embedded deep within his mind and she'd been here for less than forty-eight hours. How was he going to work alongside her for the next six months and keep his hands to himself?

Then he rationalised that he'd always been attracted to women who were supposedly inaccessible. That had been the initial attraction towards Mags. She'd hated that nickname and he'd used it almost constantly near the end of their disastrous marriage.

Now it appeared Rosie didn't like the nickname he used for her either. Ah…he could pick 'em, all right. The ones who looked great on the outside but weren't too pretty on the inside. Although, in Rosie's case, he wasn't too sure about that.

Dave rested his head against the wall of the house and crossed his arms over his chest. He'd thought he'd out-grown those hormonal tendencies that had him doing things he wouldn't ordinarily do—like going to Reg's wedding to pick Rosie up. Anyone could have gone but he had quickly volunteered to be the gofer and he knew why. He'd wanted to see how she'd looked all dressed up and he hadn't been disappointed with the result.

Sitting there with his eyes closed, he decided to give up fighting the inevitable and allowed different images of Rosie to drift in and out of his mind. The way she walked, with a calm confidence. The way her hips swished ever so slightly, her arms swinging loosely by her side. The way she slowly lifted her chin to meet his gaze and the way her blue eyes had looked after he'd kissed her.

He groaned in exasperation but didn't push the images away. He was only thinking about her—surely that couldn't do any harm. He was the type of man to always learn from past mistakes so there was no way he'd ever need to worry about a long-term relationship with a woman like Rosie Partridge because it simply wasn't going to hap-pen. She wasn't his type and that was all there was to it.

Yet—he'd kissed her.

He'd felt his heart leap at the wonderment and surprise in her eyes but her lips had been soft and pliant beneath his. No other woman had made his heart lurch like that before and it was a feeling he wasn't sure he wanted re-peated. He was divorced—with a child! He had responsi-bilities and they had nothing to do with Rosie Partridge.

There had to be something wrong with him. Perhaps he

was coming down with something or maybe it was due to the busy days he was putting in. Not only was he working at the hospital but he was also helping Mick out with the fencing which was in a bad state and desperately needed replacing.

He allowed his thoughts to wander even more and the next thing he knew, he felt a hand on his shoulder, shaking him awake.

'What are you doing, sleeping out here?' Mick asked, a small grin on his lips.

Dave stood and stretched. 'Just getting some fresh air. What's the time?'

'Six.'

Before his brother could quiz him further, Dave moved into the house, heading directly for the shower. When he was finished, he went to the kitchen to satisfy his growling stomach.

'How long will you be at the hospital, Dave?' Mick asked a few minutes later as he poured his brother a cup of coffee and handed it to him. Dave was just finishing his breakfast and was glad of the refill.

'Hopefully, not too long. I should be back around ten.'

Mick nodded but didn't say anything else. Dave glanced up at him, sensing there was something more. 'Spit it out.'

Mick shrugged. 'Just curious as to why you couldn't sleep last night.'

'Why?'

'Because the last time you couldn't sleep and spent the night on the verandah was not long after you separated from Mags. Is everything all right? Is Mel all right?'

Glad to have the topic off himself, Dave nodded. 'I spoke to her yesterday and she sounded fine but, then, she's six, Mick. How are six-year-olds supposed to sound?'

Mick shrugged. 'So if Mel's all right, why couldn't you sleep?'

Dave groaned and sipped his coffee. 'I just couldn't. It's

been exhausting lately. Doing my work at the hospital and then helping you out—not that I'm complaining,' he added quickly. 'I'm more than happy to help out around the farm, but I'm a doctor, Mick, and a surgeon at that.' Dave put his coffee down and held up his hands, a grin on his face. 'I need to look after these babies.'

Mick's smile increased and he nodded. 'Oh, yeah. It's a woman, all right. So who is she?'

'What? I just told you why I couldn't sleep.'

'It's that new doc, isn't it? Ah, what's-her-name. You know, Reg's daughter.'

'Rosie.' Even the way Dave said her name out loud sounded as though he were a love-struck teenager.

'That's it.' Mick was grinning from ear to ear. 'Woo-hoo. Big brother's going down for the count yet again.'

'Cut it out,' Dave warned, laughter still lighting his eyes.

'Well, if you're not interested, why don't you let me take a crack at her?'

'No way.' His words were vehement but he forced himself to relax. 'Besides, you've already got a girlfriend.'

'So?'

'Mick!' His brother knew how he felt about infidelity.

'Easy on, mate. I'm only having a lend of you. It's just she looked so gorgeous at the wedding and smiled so sweetly at me that I don't know if I'll be able to resist.' Mick's tone indicated he was teasing but Dave felt a tightening in his gut.

'Keep your distance.' Dave pointed his finger at his brother. 'She's not your type.'

'And I suppose she's yours?' Mick laughed. 'Just wait till I tell—'

'Don't you breathe a word of this to anyone,' Dave interrupted, his mirth instantly gone. 'Promise me, Mick. Besides, there's nothing really to gossip about. Understand?'

'Hey, you know I was only foolin' around.' He crossed his heart, the way they had when they'd been kids. 'You have my word,' Mick promised as he headed for the door. Before pushing open the screen door, he turned and added, 'For the moment.'

'Get out of here,' Dave growled, and sipped at his coffee. And you, he told himself sternly, get a hold of yourself. If he didn't, soon the whole town would be gossiping.

CHAPTER THREE

ROSE woke up late on Sunday morning, finally having given in to her body's need to sleep. She was glad the spare room, where she was sleeping, had its own *en suite*, complete with a bath. Her room also had a separate entry and exit. That way, when her father and Beverley returned from their honeymoon, she wouldn't wake them if she came in late from the hospital.

She wandered through to the kitchen in search of food and a hot cup of coffee. To her disgust, she only found a piece of stale bread and instant coffee. Ugh. She needed to get all of her things unpacked. Even so, she hadn't bothered to pack any special coffee because she'd presumed her father would have some. Amazingly, for someone who was a chef, her father's kitchen was basically bare. Then again, both he and Beverley had had other things on their mind than doing the grocery shopping before they'd left for their honeymoon.

Rose shuffled back to her bedroom and decided on a shower, especially as it seemed she needed to go to the shops. She took her time beneath the spray, enjoying the luxury of not rushing. That's the way her life had been for the past eighteen years since she'd started med school. Always rushing here or there. Lectures, exams, clinical sessions, operations. If it hadn't been one thing, it had been another. Now she was here she intended to relax a little.

The hospital was a whole seven-minute drive away from her father's house—rather than a forty-minute drive through peak-hour traffic, as the hospital she'd worked at in Sydney had been.

Here, in dusty, hot Broken Hill, she could relax. She

took a deep breath as though to prove it to herself and closed her eyes beneath the warm spray.

Then a vision of Dave appeared in her mind, making her tense. 'No. Relax,' she said firmly. 'Let the thoughts flow.' It was what a psychologist friend had told her before she'd left. Letting the thoughts flow would help her accept the break-up with Julian more easily. Repressing was bad. So why couldn't that work for Dave as well?

She took another breath and let the thoughts flow. He was very good-looking—tall, too. She liked tall men. Julian hadn't been as tall as Dave, she was sure of that. Last night, when Dave had brushed that brief kiss across her lips, he'd had to bend a lot further and her head had been at a different angle.

The feather-light touch of that kiss still seemed to burn on her lips and she raised her fingers to her mouth, expecting to find them hot—but they weren't. She opened her eyes and looked at the shower wall. How could one tiny kiss have such an incredible effect on her? Julian certainly hadn't affected her in this way and they'd been engaged!

'Men!' Would she ever understand them? She turned the taps off and focused her thoughts on something more practical, like what food she needed to buy. She dressed quickly and headed out to her car. It had been parked in the driveway as her father's car was in the garage, and the heat was stifling. She started the engine to get the air-conditioner working while she checked the local map Beverley had left for her, marked with places to eat, where the shopping centres were and some interesting sculptures she might want to see. Broken Hill supported a great artistic community, with outback painters capturing their own interpretation of nature's delights.

Rose glanced at the car clock and was surprised to find it was almost midday. Her stomach growled, making its sentiments known. 'Lunch, or rather brunch first, I think,' she remarked as she checked the map again, deciding on a location at which to eat.

When she pulled into the car park, she realised the place Beverley had marked was nothing more than a pub. An outback pub, she thought as she climbed from the car, her sunglasses still shielding her eyes. The food must be good—after all, her father's tastebuds were quite finicky. Determined to persevere, Rose walked up to the door, automatically swatting flies as she went.

The first thing that hit her as she walked in was the smell of beer, and stale beer at that. The second was the cool breeze from the air-conditioner. The third was the noise. It was as though the place were filled with rowdy school-children, such was the volume level. Rose frowned as her gaze adjusted to the artificial lighting.

She scanned the room, seeing big sweaty men, dressed in some sort of sports uniform, teasing and laughing with each other. Then she spotted Dave. Her lips burned again with the memory of the way he'd made her feel last night, and she shook her thoughts clear. She should have known he'd be the type of larikin to be involved in something as noisy as this. He was sitting on a chair, his elbow up on a table, his palm open in challenge. Seconds later, a victim, who had a shock of red hair, was found and mirrored Dave's position.

'Three, two, one—go!' someone shouted, and the wild cheering began again. Rose stood, mesmerised by the sight of Dave's bulging biceps and his stern concentration as the ridiculous and uncivilised contest continued. Slowly, she lifted her sunglasses from her eyes and held them loosely in her hand, now openly staring at the men and their antics. Dave was putting up a good fight and almost had his opponent's arm down.

Rose's sunglasses slipped from her fingers, bringing her back to reality. Shaking her head at being drawn under his spell, she sighed heavily and bent to pick them up.

Hoots of laughter had her straightening quickly and

glancing over at the table. Dave's blue gaze scorched right through her and for a moment she felt like a roo trapped in the headlights of an oncoming car. She held her breath before looking away.

'How could you lose?' one of the men wailed. 'You never lose.'

She risked a surreptitious glance at Dave, only to see him smiling good-naturedly at his friends as they teased him mercilessly. Dave had lost? Apparently so. She smiled to herself as she headed to the bar, glad that he wasn't so perfect.

Dave watched as Rose sat down on a bar stool. Never had he lost an arm wrestling match to a more stunning distraction. She was dressed in a flowing summer dress, the same reddish-orange colour of Uluru, which buttoned up the front and had revealed a good portion of her long legs when she'd bent to retrieve the sunglasses. It had been those long legs which had cost him his concentration.

'Dave?'

At the sound of Mick's voice, Dave quickly turned his attention back to his brother.

'Yeah?'

'Bit distracted, eh, mate?' his brother asked, his eyebrows raised suggestively. 'And I can see why.' Mick's voice was low but Dave still glared at him.

'Who is *that*?' one of the blokes asked, angling his head in Rose's direction.

Mick ruffled his friend's shock of red hair. 'She's too sophisticated for you, mate.'

'Hey. I like socistifated women,' the bloke retorted.

'Yeah, right,' one of the others chided. 'You can't even say the word right.'

'So who is she?'

'Reg Partridge's daughter.' Dave cleared his throat and looked away. 'She's the new anaesthetist at the hospital.'

'Take me in for surgery, mate. If I get to lie on that

operating table and gaze up at her, I'd be a happy man,' one of them said.

'Yeah—before she knocks you unconscious with the drugs,' Dave added. There was a round of hearty laughter.

'Dave always gets the good-lookin' ones. Mags was a definite looker,' another bloke added.

'Who slept with any bloke she met,' Mick added in defence of his brother.

'Rose is just my colleague.' Dave took a sip of his soft drink.

'Besides, she's a city slicker,' Mick stated, and some of the men nodded. In the outback, the locals stuck together, always polite but never getting too close to those who came and went with the seasons.

'How long is she here for, Dave?'

'Six months.' Dave finished off his drink. 'Well, it was a great practice game today,' he praised as he stood. 'But I've gotta get going.'

'What? You're not staying for lunch?'

'Not today.'

'But, Dave…'

'Ah, leave him,' Mick said as he slapped his brother heartily on the shoulder. 'He was up helping me with the fencing this morning before our hockey game, and he's had a few emergencies in the last few days.' Mick lowered his voice and spoke in a stage whisper. 'Besides, he's getting old now. Almost forty.'

The guys all laughed and Dave grinned at them. 'Two more years,' he told his friends. 'I need to get to the hospital and check on Bob again.'

'When are you gonna let us come and see him?'

'Maybe tomorrow.'

'Everything all right, Dave?' Mick asked, concerned.

'I'm not sure.' Dave glanced over at Rose as he spoke. She was sitting up at the bar, studying the menu. He really should mention that he might be taking Bob back to Theatre. 'I just need to check on him again. I'll see you guys later.' With that, Dave headed over to where Rose sat at the bar, trying to block out the whistles and taunts from his mates.

'Hi,' he said quietly as he leaned on the bar.

'Hello.'

He saw her nose twitch and realised he probably smelt like a wombat. He took a small step to the side, away from her. 'Can I have your mobile phone number?'

'Why?' She turned to look at him, a suspicious glint in her eyes.

'Because I'm heading to the hospital to check on Bob.' At the mention of their patient, the suspicion left her gaze. 'When I saw him this morning, he still wasn't right. One of the drains might be blocked.'

'You want to take him back to Theatre?'

'Possibility. I wanted to let you know.'

'I appreciate it.' She turned her attention back to the menu. 'I'd better decide what to order, then.'

'The hamburger is good,' he offered. 'Unlike those fast-food restaurants, this hamburger is healthy. Or, if you want something light, try their breakfast omelette. It's delicious.'

'Thanks.' When he didn't move she looked at him again. 'Something else?'

'Your mobile number?'

'The hospital has it.'

Dave pulled his mobile phone from his shorts pocket. 'I'd like it just the same. In case I need to call you away from the hospital.'

The thought of the brief kiss they'd shared jumped into her head. 'W-why?' she asked, clearing her throat, cross with herself for stuttering.

'In case there's an emergency and I'm not at the hospital,' he stated matter-of-factly.

'Oh.' She felt foolish and switched her anger towards him. How dared he make her feel this way? She rattled off her number and watched him programme it into his phone before the bartender came up to take her order.

'I'll have the fish, thank you,' she stated.

'Don't make it too big a serve,' Dave butted in. 'I might need her in Theatre soon.'

'Right you are, Dave,' was the man's reply, and Rose felt like knocking both of their heads together. Arrogant pigs.

Rose was determined to put him in his place. She might be physically attracted to him, she might have to work with him, but she didn't have to bow to his every whim. 'Was that all you wanted, Dr...?' She stopped. He'd done it again. Because she didn't know his last name, she wasn't able to put him in his place.

'What? Is there something wrong?' Dave stared at her with concern.

'No. Go see your patient and leave me to eat as much of my lunch as I have time to.' When in doubt, go for the direct dismissal. She was proud of herself for regrouping and after a few heart-stopping seconds, when she thought Dave was going to say something else, he finally turned and left her in peace, waving to his friends as he went.

She was halfway through her lunch, grudgingly acknowledging that Dave had been right to suggest a smallish portion because she was almost full, when she realised someone was standing beside her.

'G'day. I'm Mick. We met at the wedding yesterday.'

Rose forced a smile. She'd met so many people yesterday and she knew she wouldn't remember them all.

'Thought I'd give you some time to eat before coming to say g'day. Dave said he might need you at the hospital.'

'Yes,' Rose replied as she forked in another mouthful of the delicious steamed fish fillet.

Another man joined him—the one with the red hair who'd been arm-wrestling with Dave. 'G'day. I just wanted to say thanks for walking in when ya did.'

Rose frowned at him. 'What do you mean?'

'You distracted Dave.' He laughed. 'He was so busy ogling you that I managed to beat him at arm-wrestling.' He shook his head in bemusement. 'First time for everything.'

Rose wasn't quite sure how to receive this information. Surely that wasn't the way it had happened, was it? Had Dave been ogling her? She knew he must find her attractive at least, otherwise how could she explain that brief kiss last night?

So Dave had been ogling her! A small surge of feminine power shot through her but she focused her attention on the men before her.

'So, what do you gentlemen do for a living?'

'I'm a pastoralist, mainly cattle,' Mick replied. 'And this bloke is my best stockman.' He clapped his friend on the shoulder.

'And how long have you lived in Broken Hill?'

'All our lives. Dave and I were born here but our old man got work in Melbourne and a couple of other places so we moved around a bit.'

'Dave?' Rose frowned as she looked at Mick.

'Yeah. He's my brother.'

Now she could see the family resemblance. Their colouring was the same—both with dark hair, although Mick's was a bit longer than his brother's and had started to curl at the ends. Also, Mick's eyes were brown, whereas Dave's were as blue as the night sky. 'I see.' Rose put her knife and fork together on the plate, unable to finish her lunch. 'So how long since you came back to Broken Hill?'

'Ah…let's see.' Mick looked down at his hands, concentrating. 'Dave moved back here after his marriage broke up, which was about six years ago, and then I came not long after that so, yeah, about five, six years.'

Rose nodded slowly as she digested this information. He was divorced! Then that *definitely* meant he wasn't her type because she wasn't interested in divorced men. From her limited experience, they often had too much extra bag-

gage, and if there were children involved—well, it just
made matters worse. She didn't need that type of aggravation in her life. Especially as Julian had supplied her
with enough aggravation to recover from.

'Food too much for you?' Mick smiled. It wasn't as
engaging as his brother's and didn't make her heart race.

'Yes. Delicious, though.' Her mobile phone shrilled to
life. 'That will probably be your brother,' she told him as
she reached into her bag and pulled out the phone. 'Dr
Partridge,' she said automatically.

'I do need you, Rosie,' Dave's deep voice said down
the line, and Rose felt goose bumps spread over her skin.
For one fleeting moment she imagined he was saying those
words in a different context, but thankfully she came to
her senses.

'I'll be right there,' she replied, and before he could say
anything else, she disconnected the call.

'So I take it Bob needs further surgery?' Mick asked.

'It looks that way.' Rose collected her bag and slid from
the stool before taking out her purse to pay for her meal.

'Uh, allow me.' Mick pulled his wallet from his shorts.

'No, really. It's fine,' Rose insisted.

'I'd let him if I were you,' his mate added. 'Mick and
Dave have got a strong sense of um…what's it called
again? You know, that knight in shining armour thing?'

'Chivalry,' Mick supplied. 'It's called chivalry, mate.'

'Yeah, that's it.'

Rose decided she could spend more time here arguing
with the two men than it would take her to drive to the
hospital. Conceding was the only way out. 'Well, thank
you very much. I appreciate it.'

'My pleasure.' Mick's smile had a glint of teasing in it
and Rose wondered whether there wasn't something going
on here that she didn't know about.

She headed for the door and was surprised when the rest
of the men Dave had been with called goodbye to her. She

smiled shyly and waved before almost bolting through the door into the heat.

She was still smiling when she walked into the hospital.

'You look…happy,' Dave remarked as he met her in the corridor.

'Thank you. And why shouldn't I be? Your brother just bought me lunch.'

'He *what*!'

The smile vanished and Rose frowned at Dave's attitude. 'He bought me lunch. Insisted on it.'

'I can imagine,' Dave grumbled.

'What's the matter?' Rose eyed him suspiciously. 'Is there some sort of bet or something going on that I don't know about?'

'Bet? No. Just Mick being Mick.' He clenched his jaw tightly.

'Well, he was very charming.'

'He has a steady girlfriend.' Dave's voice was low and held a hint of warning. 'In fact, I wouldn't be at all surprised if they announced their engagement soon.' It was stretching the truth a little but Rosie didn't know that.

'Good for them,' Rose said without concern. 'What's that got to do with me?'

'Don't go getting any ideas on making moves on my baby brother, Rosie.'

She took offence at that. 'I never said I was going to.'

'He's not equipped to handle women like you.'

'I beg your pardon! What's that supposed to mean?' Rose stopped outside the female changing rooms and glared at him. She was pleased to see he looked apologetic and watched as he raked an unsteady hand through his hair.

'That didn't come out right. Just that you're, you know, a city slicker.'

'I'm a what?' Her voice was calm and controlled and he knew he was digging himself in deeper.

'A city slicker.'

'How would you know? You know nothing about me, David…' Oh, how she wished she knew his last name. That way, when she told him off, it would carry more clout. It was starting to drive her insane but there was no way in the world she'd ask. She had too much pride to ask him that *now*.

'So, are you trying to tell me that you're not from Sydney? I read your résumé,' he continued. He knew her credentials. Where she'd trained, what papers she'd written. That she was thirty-six and had never been married—but that was about it. It had said nothing about the way her smile could light up a room or that when her eyes were flaming with temper, as they were now, she looked vibrant.

'I came *here* from Sydney but that doesn't mean I'm a city slicker. So, before you start sticking labels on me, I suggest you check your facts first.' With that, she turned and walked into the female changing rooms, glad he couldn't follow her.

She went to the locker she'd been assigned and wrenched it open, muttering to herself.

'I'll have you know…' Dave's voice boomed as he followed her.

Rose jumped in fright. 'What are you doing in here?'

'I'm talking to you. I'll have you know it's considered rude to walk away from someone when you're having a discussion.'

'We're not having a discussion,' she all but yelled at him. 'You're in the female changing rooms and I want to get changed for surgery, or do I need to remind you that you have a patient waiting for your expert attention?'

'Don't you remind me of my responsibilities, girly.'

'Don't you ''girly'' me. My name is Rose. Not chick, bird, sheila or any other names men around here call women. Rose. R-O-S-E.'

Dave looked at her. 'Finished?'

Rose lifted her chin in defiance. 'For now.' At least her

temper was cooling but, ooh, that man could get her hot under the collar.

'Right. Let's get to Theatre and we can finish this discussion later.' He paused before adding, '*Rosie*.' There was a smirk on his face as he left her alone.

Rose was so infuriated that for the first time in her life she wanted to throw something at someone. She scowled as she went through the motions of getting changed. She didn't understand him. Not one little bit. First he was happy, then boiling mad and in the next instant he was as cool as a cucumber. Men!

She counted to ten and then, deciding that wasn't enough, counted to twenty, before leaving the changing rooms and heading to Pre-op. Bob was obviously still in pain and after Rose had spoken to him and read his chart to find out what analgesics he'd already had, she gave him a pre-med. They transported him to Theatre and started getting things set up. Dave walked in once Bob was anaesthetised and the operation began.

After an hour, Dave was ready to close, satisfied that his patient shouldn't have any further complications. He'd mentioned that the orthopaedic surgeon, Penny Hatfield, would be in Broken Hill the following morning and that Rose's services would be needed.

It was just after five o'clock when Rose headed out to her car, feeling exhausted. She frowned as she unlocked the door and climbed in, not exactly sure why she was feeling so tired.

'Probably the heat,' she mused as she started the engine and pulled out of the hospital car park. When she arrived home, she ran a warm bubble bath and sank gratefully into the tub. She rested her head back and closed her eyes.

A startling pain in her abdomen woke her up. The water was cool and her fingers were wrinkly, indicating she'd been in the water for quite some time. Rose shifted and shivered as the water moved against her skin. She sat up and started to get out of the bath, only to find that the muscles in her arms were weak and lifeless.

Another pain had her closing her eyes and holding her breath until it passed. She waited a moment before trying to get out of the bath again and this time was successful. Rose wrapped herself up in a bathrobe, the effort sapping most of her energy. After a small rest, she stumbled out of her bathroom.

She made slow progress and she leant against the wall for support, unable to believe how shaky and lifeless her legs were. What was wrong? Obviously something—but what? Rose slid down the wall onto the floor, glad her legs no longer needed to support her. Another pain gripped her and she tensed once more.

She closed her eyes and rested her head on the soft carpet, letting fatigue claim her.

'Rosie?' The call came from a distance. A place far away. Rose could hear it but she couldn't do anything about it. She was trapped. Her arms and legs were made of lead and there was nothing she could do about it.

'Rosie?' A pounding accompanied the voice and the next thing she knew she was being scooped up off the floor and placed on a comfortable bed.

The comfort only lasted for a second as the pain engulfed her. Her arms were wrapped around her waist, her eyes closed in agony.

'Rosie, here. Swallow these.' She heard the voice and knew it was one she'd heard before. It wasn't her father. It wasn't Julian—Julian had never called her Rosie. It was familiar, one she'd dreamt about. She thought hard.

'You've got food poisoning,' the voice said, and this time she recognised it as Dave's. Dave was here, taking care of her. Dave always called her Rosie.

She opened her mouth to speak but nothing came out. Instead, she concentrated on swallowing the pills, uncaring what they were. She trusted Dave. He was a doctor. He wouldn't give her anything bad. Dave always called her Rosie—and she liked it.

Dave sat by her bed, amazed at what she'd just mumbled. She *liked* it when he called her Rosie! Well, there was a turn-up for the books. He smiled to himself, feeling extremely pleased with this bit of information. And here he'd thought she didn't like him.

He stayed with her for the rest of the night, often just content to watch her sleep. She was beautiful. No doubt about that. Even though she was sick with food poisoning, she was still stunning.

He reached out and touched her forehead. She was a lot cooler now and as she'd already had her second dose of paracetamol, he knew she was over the worst. Thank goodness she hadn't been as bad as Mrs McGill, who was in hospital, her body still racked with spasms.

When the first patient had arrived at the hospital, complaining of abdominal pain, the registrar on duty had asked Dave to check her out. Then the second and third had arrived not long after. They'd managed to trace the origin of the contaminated food and had discovered it had been the fish served at the pub that afternoon.

The owner had been horrified. Dave knew he'd leave no stone unturned until he found out who was responsible for selling bad fish to him.

Dave had been in his car, heading to Rose's house, the instant they'd discovered the source. He knew she'd be all alone and his worst fears had been confirmed when he'd let himself into Reg's house, thankfully knowing where the spare key was kept.

His own stomach had lurched in anxiety when he'd seen her collapsed on the floor. He leaned over her bed and breathed in deeply, enjoying the floral scent that had wound itself around her from her bath.

During the past five and a half hours that he'd been there, Dave had helped Rosie to the bathroom and had sponged her forehead until her temperature had broken, as well as ensuring her fluids were maintained.

He'd gone into the kitchen and made himself a cup of tea and some toast, surprised to find that Reg didn't have much in his cupboards. Then again, the man had had other things on his mind. Dave smiled to himself as he remembered how happy Reg had looked on Saturday. With that image came one of Rosie dressed in her bridesmaid outfit, and with that came a tightening in his gut.

He glanced at her, sleeping peacefully. Her hair had dried all funny from lying on the pillow while still damp. Even still, she looked beautiful. Amazing. He was seeing this woman—a woman he'd known for only a few short days—at her worst and she was still beautiful.

It brought back thoughts of the way her body had looked, naked and flushed from the fever. Twice he'd had to change her clothes. The first time had been to get her out of the bathrobe, which hadn't helped in reducing her body temperature, and the second had been after the fever had broken and her body had stopped sweating.

Dave returned to the kitchen and made himself a cup of tea. It was almost two o'clock in the morning. Fatigue from his very long day was settling in and, after returning to Rosie's room, he sat in the chair, stretched his long legs out and let his head rest against the wall. Although her bed was big enough to accommodate both of them, he didn't want to risk raising her body temperature.

The sound of coughing woke him and he sat up, instantly alert but taking a few seconds to figure out where he was. He turned his head and saw Rosie lying in the bed, and memories of the night before returned. He checked the time.

'Eight o'clock!'

The sound of his voice caused her to stir and he quickly reached out a hand to rest it on her forehead. Her temperature was normal.

'Dave?' she whispered brokenly, and he reached for the glass of water with a straw that he'd put by the bed.

'I'm here, Rosie. Have a drink.' He was glad that she was aware of her surroundings. It was a good sign.

'Thank you,' she said, after swallowing a few small mouthfuls.

'How do you feel?'

'Like I've been hit by a Mack truck.'

Dave chuckled and the sound washed over her, warming her insides. 'Glad to hear it. I'm just going to ring the hospital,' he said as he started out of the room. 'I'll be back in a moment.'

Rose lay still and slowly opened her eyes. The few times she'd tried during the night, the room had been spinning on its axis. This time, though, everything seemed to be staying in its proper place.

When Dave came back into the room, she ventured a smile. 'How's everything at the hospital?'

'Settled. Five patients presented to A and E complaining of stomach pains and two of them were admitted with food poisoning.'

'How are they?' Rose asked with concern.

'One is stable, the other lady, Mrs McGill, still has a temperature.'

'Oh, dear.' Rose shifted slightly and groaned.

'What's wrong?' Dave was instantly by her side.

'My muscles ache.'

He smiled sympathetically. 'Normal, I'm afraid.' He sat in the chair. 'You were quite ill at one stage but once that passed you started to pick up.'

'Would you mind helping me to sit up?' she asked, and he was up on his feet again, assisting her. 'Thanks,' she said once she was propped up against the headboard of her four-poster bed.

He was frowning at her

'What?' she asked cautiously.

'You.' He sat on the side of her bed and met her gaze.

'I'd expected you to be…I don't know, indignant at me being here.'

Rose smiled. 'That would be ungrateful and my father raised me with better manners than that. Last night I was sick and I needed someone to take care of me. I never would have been able to cope by myself and I *am* grateful to you for coming.'

'You surprise me.'

'Because most women would feel inferior for showing their weakness?' When he nodded she continued, 'Sickness such as food poisoning isn't being weak, it's being sick. I guess a lot of people don't know the difference.'

Dave smiled, a slow, sexy smile that had her heart beating double time. 'So matter-of-fact. You're not what I expected, Rosie Partridge.' He leaned closer, placing one hand on the bed by her side.

'Is that a good thing?' Was that *her* voice so husky and seductive? She swallowed, the charged moment between them growing with each passing second.

'I'm not sure but I'm willing to find out,' Dave murmured, his lips only a hair's breadth away from her own.

'Are you going to kiss me?' Rose whispered, her gaze flicking down to his lips that were still curved into a slight smile.

'Any problems with that?'

Rose's heart was pounding so fiercely against her ribs she was certain he could hear it. She parted her lips, her breath coming out in a rush. 'Um…' Her tongue traced the contour of her lower lip, wetting it in anticipation. That brief kiss he'd pressed to her lips the other day was still firmly imprinted there. She *wanted* a repeat but…

His nose touched the tip of her own. Dave was going to kiss her. *Really* kiss her, and she wanted it more than anything in the world. As his lips moved in closer she reluctantly lifted her fingers and held them between their mouths.

Dave pulled back slightly, his gaze inquisitive.

'Let me at least brush my teeth first,' she whispered.

CHAPTER FOUR

ROSE knew she had to get out of the shower sooner or later. She couldn't hibernate in here for the entire six months of her contract, although that was exactly what she felt like doing. How could she have been so careless as to let things go so far?

Sure, she was grateful that Dave had come to look after her and she really appreciated it, but to let the man almost kiss her? Was she insane? Dave was dangerous and she'd known it from the first moment she'd seen him. Dangerous, at least, to her own equilibrium.

She reluctantly turned the taps off and took her time towelling herself dry. He was waiting for her to finish her shower before he left, to make sure she didn't have any relapses of the cramps or fever.

Rose once more had been grateful as her muscles were still quite weak, but she was feeling better than she had half an hour ago. Half an hour ago when Dave had almost kissed her!

'Keep it light. Keep it professional,' she told her reflection, before pulling on underwear and a cotton summer dress. 'The man is dangerous.' She combed her hair back, glad to be looking more herself. 'Dangerous, and don't you forget that.'

She still remembered the look in his face when she'd asked him to leave the door to the *en suite* open but to close the door to the bedroom. His gaze had skimmed her body quickly, a puzzled frown on his face.

'I'm not good in confined spaces,' she'd added by way of explanation. In fact, it had taken her years to be in a room with a door closed—or in a car without feeling mildly claustrophobic.

He'd nodded, still looking confused, but had acceded to her wishes. She sat on the bed for a few minutes, realising how weak she felt. Just to shower and dress had knocked the stuffing out of her.

Taking a deep breath, she stood and walked to the family room where she thought Dave might be waiting. He wasn't there. She listened for a moment but couldn't hear anything. Had he gone? Perhaps once he'd heard the water stop, he'd left. She felt a momentary sense of loss at the thought and then a flood of relief. If he'd left, then she wouldn't have to worry about facing him right now, especially after that intense moment before she'd stopped the kiss.

Heading into the kitchen to make herself a cup of tea, Rose stopped short in the doorway when she saw him standing with his back to her, looking out the window over the sink. Her stomach contracted, and it had nothing to do with the food poisoning. Her mouth went dry and she instinctively put a hand out to lean on the bench as she felt her knees go weak.

His shoulders were broad beneath the striped cotton shirt he wore. She knew from before that it would be unbuttoned, revealing a white T-shirt that was half tucked into his navy shorts. The front of the T-shirt was snug and defined his torso as though it was moulded to it.

His legs were lean and long, indicating he worked out often, although he didn't strike her as the gym type. She wondered if he helped his brother on the farm. His dark brown hair was ruffled and as his fingers combed through it again, Rose itched to follow the movement with her own hands.

She closed her eyes and shook her head, desperate to control her wayward thoughts. What had got into her? She was behaving very out of character and she knew it was all because of Dave. Dave, whose surname she still didn't know.

'Are you all right?'

At the sound of his voice, Rose opened her eyes, only to find that he'd moved and was standing in front of her, his arm coming out to steady her. Rose forced her legs to support her weight and moved out of his reach.

'I'm fine. Thank you.' She added a smile, realising the words had come out brisk and dismissive.

'You're a liar,' he contradicted. 'I can see perfectly well that you're not up to standing for too long.' He ushered her over to a stool and sat her down. 'Tea? I'm afraid that's about all there is to offer. There's not much in your father's pantry.'

'Oh, that's right,' Rose groaned. 'I was going to get some groceries yesterday after lunch but…' She shrugged, letting her words trail off.

He nodded in understanding. 'Somehow our jobs seem to get in the way of any other plans we might make.' He switched the kettle on and jangled the car keys in his pocket.

Rose took that as a hint that he'd rather leave. 'Don't worry about making me tea,' she said rather briskly. 'I can do it.'

'What about food?'

'I'm really not that hungry but I'll go out later today and get some food.'

'You'll do nothing of the kind,' he counteracted. 'Doctor's orders.'

'But I've got to anaesthetise for the orthopaedic surgeon. I have to go out so I may as well get some groceries while I'm at it.'

'You're not anaesthetising.'

'What? Why not? It's my first official day at work.'

'Not any more.'

'Have you reorganised my schedule for me?' Rose was a little indignant at his high-handed attitude.

'Rosie, you've just had food poisoning.'

'I'll be fine to anaesthetise. It's not as though I'll be standing on my feet, operating. I'll be sitting down, monitoring my dials.'

'The orthopaedic surgeon is bringing her own anaesthetist.'

'And how do you suppose she knew to do that?' she asked rhetorically.

'I called Penny last night and asked her to.'

'Do you always organise everyone at the hospital?'

He grinned, not at all concerned about her censorial attitude. 'Only when they've had food poisoning and are too stubborn to realise they're still not one hundred per cent recovered.'

At his words, Rose glared at him. 'Stubborn? You're calling *me* stubborn?'

'Are you implying that *I'm* stubborn?'

'Absolutely.'

'When?'

'When you came and took over Bob's treatment at the accident site. Oh, no, wait a minute,' she corrected. 'That wasn't stubbornness, that was arrogance.'

'Arrogance?'

'Yes. Now, stubborn—let me see. Ah, yes, when you came to my father's wedding and insisted upon me accompanying you. No, no, wait. That wasn't stubborn either, that was domineering.'

'What?' He stared at her with incredulity.

'How about when you warned me to keep away from Mick? Yes, now, *that* was stubbornness—or was it stupidity?' She sighed heavily. 'Oh, I give up, Dave. I guess you're all those things, and all of those attributes make up the typical Aussie bloke.'

'Well, if I'm a typical Aussie bloke, what does that make you?'

'I'm a sophisticated, modern woman, of course,' she countered quickly.

'Come off it, Rosie. You only think you're sophisticated and modern. I won't quibble with the woman part, though.' He gave her a quick perusal. 'Definitely woman.'

'Do you mind?'

'Mind what?'

'Not leering at me.'

'Oh, so now I'm a leering bloke as well.' A deep chuckle accompanied his words and Rose's skin broke out in goose bumps again. He was doing it again. Affecting her when she didn't want to be affected.

'Don't you need to get to the hospital?'

'No. Why?' He took a step closer to her. 'Are you trying to get rid of me?'

'But you have patients with, ah…food poisoning.'

'No, I don't. The GP who admitted them has patients with food poisoning.'

'Surely you're going to do a ward round. It's Monday morning. All surgeons do rounds first thing Monday morning.'

'I think you'll find things work slightly different here in the outback. I'll go in later today when things aren't so hectic.' He took another step. Rose wanted to turn tail and flee, but knew her body was still too weak. As for anaesthetising, well, she knew she could cope but she also acknowledged that it would knock her out. Dave was right—again—and she didn't like that one bit.

'Rosie? What's wrong? You've gone pale.'

'I'm fine,' she snapped. 'And don't call me Rosie.'

'Why not?'

'Because I asked.'

'But I have it on good authority that you *like* me calling you Rosie.'

'Don't be so silly.' Then she glanced up sharply. 'Whose authority?' she demanded, thinking her father might have said something.

'Yours.'

'Pardon?' Her eyes widened in surprise.

'You. You were talking in your sleep last night and you said that you liked it when I called you Rosie.'

She blushed. There was no way she could control it and she did her best to hide it. Dipping her head, she stared at the ground, trying to figure out how to get herself out of this one. 'I was delirious,' she finally retorted.

Dave closed the distance between them and slowly raised her chin until their eyes could meet. 'Yes,' he said softly. 'You were delirious, but in my experience that's when people's inhibitions are down and the truth comes out.'

Rose felt as though she were burning up inside beneath his close scrutiny. His blue gaze was probing her own, seeking a response that she knew he'd find there. She found him attractive. Immensely attractive. And it was clear that he felt the same way about her. Yet they were so wrong for each other. In fact, surely this morning had confirmed it because all they'd done since she'd walked into the kitchen had been argue.

It now looked as though he was going to follow through on his earlier impulse to kiss her, and to her surprise she realised she wanted it more than anything. There was one thing that was bothering her and as he started to lower his mouth to hers she stopped him once more.

'What is it?' The deep, husky tones washed over her. 'Your teeth look nice and clean now.'

She smiled shyly. 'Um…it's not that. It's…um…your name.'

'Sorry?'

'Your surname,' she amended. 'I don't have any idea what it is.'

'My surname?'

'Yes. Everyone I've met so far calls you Dave! No one seems to use your surname at all. I just thought that as you're about to kiss me, I…you know…might as well ask,' she said with determination.

'Absolutely. Why not?'

'I mean, we haven't really been properly introduced.'

He smiled and nodded. 'You know, you're right.' He looked down into her blue eyes, eyes that were so pretty, that radiated her intelligence and concern. 'Allow me to rectify the situation.'

Leaning closer, he softly cleared his throat. 'Rosie Partridge,' he brushed his lips gently across hers. 'Meet...' another kiss '...Dave Dunbar.'

'It's a pleasure,' she whispered against his mouth.

'Yes, it is,' he reflected, and bent his head, his lips slow and seductive on her own. Rose's head whirled with excitement and she felt her stomach churn with nervous butterflies but delighted in his touch at the same time. She sighed and closed her eyes as his mouth continued its onslaught.

His body shuddered with pleasure at her response and he pressed another gentle kiss on her lips before spreading tiny kisses down her face, around her neck to her ear. Oh, she smelled incredible, all sweet and light, and Dave felt his desire for her triple. How could someone who was so wrong for him feel so right?

And she *was* all wrong for him, he rationalised as he placed one last kiss on her lips before moving away. He'd been burnt once before and he'd vowed never to let it happen to him again. Beautiful, irresistible, gorgeous blonde women were to be avoided at all costs.

Dave watched as she slowly opened her blue eyes which were glazed with longing but held a hint of confusion. 'You need to rest,' he whispered, and then cleared his throat. Taking two huge steps back, putting some distance between them just in case he succumbed to the desire to take her in his arms and kiss her senseless.

The urgency of the emotion surprised him. All the more reason to get out of there—fast. He backed towards the door. 'I'll get someone to bring over some food for you,' he commented. 'If you rest today, you should be fine by tomorrow, but I'll call back later and see how you're doing.'

Rose watched as he continued to back away from her. What had happened? One minute he'd been kissing her and the next he was all but sprinting out. What had she done to turn him off? She bit her lip. 'You don't need to come by. I'm sure I'll be fine.' Her voice was cool and dismissive. He'd obviously found something inadequate about her and was desperate to leave. Julian had been the same, except he'd been quite open and brutal about her inadequacies, telling her to her face that she'd never make a good wife.

'I'll still come by and check,' he said firmly.

It was just the doctor in him, she told herself when her hopes started to rise again. She squashed them back into place, forcing herself to deal with the facts. He evidently regretted kissing her just now and she wanted him out of the house as fast as he apparently wanted to run.

'Well, as you let yourself in, you can let yourself out. I'll see you later, then.' She would have loved to have stood and walked away but wasn't at all sure her body would respond to her brain's signals.

'Right, then. See you later.' He stared at her for a second, his jaw clenching. In the next instant, he was gone. She listened as the back door opened and then closed with a final thud.

Rose sat there for a while, unable to move even if she'd wanted to. She balled her hands into fists, determined not to cry, but it was devastating to know that although men found her attractive, they also found something lacking in her.

It was obvious from the way Dave had retreated after those kisses that he felt the same way towards her as Julian had. Julian, who she'd thought she would end up marrying. After all, wasn't that what people expected when they became engaged?

Slowly and on wobbly legs, Rose made it back to her

bedroom and collapsed on the bed, tears rolling silently down her cheeks before she fell into a restless sleep.

When Rose went to work the next day, she wore her most professional suit, determined to keep the relationship between Dave and herself strictly business. As it turned out, she didn't see him at all. Or the next day, or the next.

She'd been grateful to Mrs Fredrick, her neighbour, who'd brought over some groceries on Monday and had stayed for a brief chat, mainly talking about her father's wedding and how wonderful it had been. Rose hadn't remembered meeting Mrs Fredrick but, then, she'd met a lot of people that day.

Dave's elective operating list alternated between Thursdays and Fridays, and this week Rose had to wait until Friday to see him. It was the first time since Monday evening, when he'd dropped in for a whole two minutes to check on her, that Rose was able to take another look at the man who had haunted her dreams since her arrival in Broken Hill.

'Feeling better, Rosie?' Dave asked as he walked onto the ward before the start of his theatre list.

'Much, thank you,' she replied lightly, and that was the extent of the personal conversation between them. On his list that morning was a five-year-old boy called Joe who had intestinal cysts that required removal. Rose and Dave went to see him together.

'Dr Rosie here is going to give you some medicine that will make you very sleepy, and when you're having a great dream, I'll fix your tummy up so you don't have any more pain.'

'Will I dreaming about swimming in the sea?' Joe asked, his eyes alive with excitement.

'Absolutely,' Dave replied, and looked at Rosie. 'Make sure you give Joe some sleepy medicine that has dreams about swimming in the sea.'

Rose raised her eyebrows but smiled politely at the boy and nodded. 'Of course.'

'Then, while you're splashing about in your dream, I'll take the sick piece of your tummy away and make sure the good bits are working real beaut. How's that sound?'

'And then I won't have a sore tummy any more?'

'Well, it will be sore for about a week or two, but after that you'll be back to your old self again.'

'Yay.' Joe clapped.

'Now, Dr Rosie just needs to check you out before giving you some special medicine.' Dave ruffled the boy's hair before stepping away, a smile lighting his face.

Rose's own smile was pasted on as she manoeuvred around to do Joe's observations. 'Poke your tongue out for me,' she said, shining the torch down his throat and pressing his tongue with a depressor. 'Say "ah".'

Joe complied and gagged a little. 'Everything looks fine,' she said, before wrapping the blood-pressure cuff around his arm. She pumped it up and listened with the stethoscope. Joe was talking to her but she needed to listen and concentrate. 'Just a minute,' she said. When she was finished, she looked at him. 'What was your question?'

'What's that thing called?'

'A sphygmomanometer.' She continued with her observations, just wanting to get it over and done with as soon as possible. She gave him a pre-med, telling him how good he was before quickly heading back to the nurses' station, sighing with relief.

'That's a big sigh,' Dave said from behind her. He leaned forward onto the counter and handed Rose Joe's case notes. 'Looking for these?'

'Yes. I just want to make some notes in them.'

'Cute kid, eh?'

'Hmm? Oh, Joe. Sure.'

'Problem?'

'No. Kids and I just don't mix, that's all. I feel…' she shrugged '…totally uncomfortable around them.'

'You don't like kids!' Dave was shocked.

'What?' Rose asked defensively. 'You look like a stunned mullet. What's so wrong with that?'

'Uh…uh…nothing.' She'd taken him completely by surprise. 'All you need to do is relax and be honest with them. They're not that difficult to deal with.'

'I haven't had a lot of contact with kids,' she replied matter-of-factly. 'Not even when I *was* a kid.'

'Why?'

'Kind of personal, don't you think? Besides, you've got a theatre list to start or we'll be running late all day.' Rose closed the case notes and slapped them up against his chest before she walked off. She was starting to shake and didn't need the third degree from Dave. Now was not the time to be dredging up old memories. She had patients to focus on.

Joe's surgery was completed without complication and Dave didn't speak to her unless it was absolutely necessary.

For the next two weeks, things didn't change. Rose's life, professionally, was great. She'd had two postcards from her father, saying that he and Beverley were having a wonderful time. The people in Broken Hill were welcoming and friendly but she still felt like an outsider. She guessed the locals saw her as a city slicker and that was that.

The following Monday, Rose was just coming out of Theatre, after anaesthetising for Penny Hatfield, the orthopaedic specialist from Adelaide, when Carrie, one of the theatre nurses, rushed up to her.

'Dave needs you in A and E, stat.'

Rose followed and was taken to the doctors' tearoom. There were several people there, all sitting down listening to Dave as he spoke.

'The Royal Flying Doctor Service will take us out to the airstrip on the property and then someone will meet us there and take us to the accident site.' He turned his head, his gaze encompassing Rose. For a split second she saw a flicker of pleasure but it was so quickly veiled that she wondered if she'd imagined it. 'Two teenagers are trapped. There appears to have been a subsidence on their property. Possibly an abandoned mine. It may still be unstable so I want everyone to exercise the utmost care.'

'Injuries?' Rose asked, her tone completely businesslike.

'Full report isn't in as no one's been able to get to them. We'll be the first medical team on the scene. Rosie—get what you'll need then come back here. You and I will head out to the airstrip together so you don't get lost. Everyone else, you've done this before, you know what to do. Let's get moving.'

Rose stood paralysed for a moment as others around her started leaving the room, talking about what they needed to do. She'd known when she'd taken this job that she might need to travel in a small aircraft, but she hadn't expected it to be this soon. The fear started to grip her heart, just as it had always done when she'd had to get on a plane—big or small.

'Something wrong, Rosie?' Dave asked, noticing she wasn't moving.

'Plane? You said we're going in a plane? H-how big is it?'

'A nine-seater. Why?'

Rose swallowed over the lump in her throat and wiped her clammy hands on her skirt. 'Ah…nothing.'

The room was now empty, except for the two of them. Dave peered at her closely before raking a hand through his hair. 'You don't like to fly, do you?'

'Not particularly,' she admitted.

'It was part of the job description. You knew you'd be flying in a light aircraft.' His tone was anything but sympathetic. In fact, he seemed rather annoyed and, truthfully, she couldn't blame him.

'I know,' she snapped, her fear being replaced by anger.

'I just hadn't expected it to be so soon.' She took a deep breath. 'I'll be fine.'

'You'd better be.' With that, he turned and headed out of the room.

Rose remained where she was, trying to control the churning in her stomach and the prickling in her eyes. Well, what had she expected? For him to say it would be all right and to hold her hand? She was a grown woman. She'd been working on her mild claustrophobia for years and had improved dramatically, but could she *really* do this?

There were no questions about it. She *had* to do this.

Straightening her shoulders, she went to get her equipment ready, forcing the overwhelming memories of the past back where they belonged. She was a professional. She could do this.

She returned to the tearoom a few minutes before Dave arrived, but it was enough to make her palms start perspiring again.

'Ready?' he asked, his tone tough.

'Yes.' Rose knew he was questioning her and she raised her chin defiantly, not wanting him to get the better of her. There were people out there, people who needed their expert help, and above all she couldn't allow herself to lose sight of that.

'Let's go.'

They headed out to the car park and climbed into Dave's ute, ever careful of her medical bag with the drugs she would need to help alleviate their patients' pain.

'So why are you afraid to fly?'

'I'm not afraid,' she countered quickly.

'No? Your body language says otherwise.'

'And tell me, Dr Freud, what does my body language tell you? Other than I'm anxious for our patients.'

'Is that why every muscle in your body is tense? Look, Rosie, I was only trying to help.'

'I don't need your help.'

'Why are you so antagonistic towards me?'

'Why shouldn't I be? Ever since I arrived in this town, all you've done is badger and pick on me.'

'Pick on *you*? You've been as prickly as an echidna. You city slickers—you're all alike. You come here, we try to make you feel welcome, perhaps ask a few questions to get to know you better, and suddenly we're being accused of badgering. Well, I'll have you know that I've never "badgered" in my life and I don't intend to start.'

'Ha. I doubt you even know what the word means.'

'It means to harass or nag.' Dave turned off the road into the RFDS car park. 'Only women nag,' he muttered as he parked.

'What?' Rose asked in disbelief. 'That's just the sort of sexist comment I'd expect from you,' she added as she climbed from the car, medical bag in tow. If she'd known where she was going, she'd have stormed off ahead of him. Instead, she had to cool her heels whilst he got out and collected his gear. 'What makes you think that the word "nag" is related only to females?'

'Because every female I know nags,' he said firmly, as he stalked ahead of her.

'Well, every male I know badgers.'

He stopped and turned to face her. 'Then I guess we're just going to agree to disagree. The only reason I asked the question in the first place was because I thought I might be able to help you, but I see it was just another wasted effort.'

'What do mean, *another*?'

'Forget it.' He continued on his way, bursting through the reception area of the building before heading out the back. 'You're just spoiling for a fight. Well, you can pick on someone else, Rosie. I won't be your whipping boy.'

'My *what*?' She noticed the strange looks from the rest of the staff who'd gathered there, but she didn't care. She was too mad with him to notice anything at the moment. 'How dare you even imply that any of this was my fault?

You definitely started this argument and then you walk away. What kind of man are you?' They were walking across the hot tarmac, heading towards the plane.

'The kind who really can't be bothered with this at the moment. Stay inside your cocoon, Miss High and Mighty. See if I care.' She watched him climb the small steps and disappear into the plane.

'There you go again. Throwing out blanket statements and then disappearing before you can be confronted with the truth,' she called out, as she mounted the steps and went after him.

Only the two of them were on the plane at that moment, and once she was inside she put her bag on the floor and turned to glare at him. It wasn't as easy as it should have been as the roof was so low that both of them had to crouch down. It was then she realised what he'd done.

She felt the blood drain from her body and her limbs start to shake. 'It's OK, Rosie. It's OK,' he said softly, as he placed his hands on her shoulders. He sat her down in a chair and looked into her eyes. 'You'll be fine. Just keep a clear head and you'll do fine.'

'I'm…I'm…' She felt her stomach clench with nervousness. Her eyes were wild with fear and her head started spinning. 'I'm on a…' Her breathing was becoming more rapid as the seconds passed.

'Breathe,' Dave instructed. 'You got this far, you can do the rest with ease.'

'I'm…I'm…'

The look of panic in her eyes had Dave cursing himself for being so uncivilised towards her, but he'd had to do something to get her onto the plane. He'd hoped their argument could have lasted a little longer—like until they'd touched down—but Rosie had become aware of her surroundings only moments after stepping onto the aircraft. Now she was hyperventilating.

He reached for a paper bag and held it over her mouth

and nose. 'Breathe,' he instructed calmly. 'Let me strap you in. Close your eyes. It'll be fine.'

'It…it won't,' she stammered, shaking her head.

Dave took her hand in his and squeezed it tight. His gaze met hers and his eyes seemed to hold her captive. 'It'll be fine,' he said again. 'I promise. Trust me, Rosie.'

It was what her father had said to her when she'd been a little girl, waking in the middle of the night after one of her horrible dreams. Thanks to the neuroses her mother had left her with, she felt doomed to deal with this mild claustrophobia for the rest of her life. But she was stronger than that and she refused to succumb to it.

'You'll be fine, Rosie,' he said again. 'Trust me.'

She nodded slightly, amazed at how he'd helped her to calm down. Slowly her breathing started to return to normal.

'Nice and calm. That's it.'

The other seven members of the medical retrieval team were starting to board and Rose kept her gaze fixed on Dave's. He monitored her during take-off, holding her hand until they landed. Even then, he undid her seat belt and helped her from the plane, giving her one of his dazzling smiles that turned her insides to mush.

'You did great,' he said softly, before calling his team to order. 'All right, everyone. Listen up.' Dave gave out instructions to the team, letting them know that once they had both patients retrieved and were ready to return to Broken Hill, there would be limited room in the King Air B200C. 'With two stretchers, we'll only have room for myself, Penny, Carrie and Rosie. All right, everyone knows their job so let's get going.'

There were two utes waiting for them at the airstrip and everyone clambered in. 'How're you doing now?' Dave yelled as he crouched down next to Rose in the back of the vehicle. The noise of the tyres on the dirt road was deafening. She was glad they were in the first ute as the tyres were also kicking up at lot of dust, almost obscuring the second ute from their vision.

'Better. Thanks. I've never travelled in a ute like this, but I guess it's the only way to transport everyone and the equipment to the site.'

'Too right,' he said with a chuckle. 'Let the wind blow through your hair—even though it's slightly longer than mine.' He laughed again and Rose smiled at him, thankful that they were out in the open again. She took a few deep breaths, knowing she had to relax and regroup so she could be of use to the patients.

'Probably best if you close your mouth, too.'

'Pardon?'

'If you're going to practise deep breathing,' he said close to her ear, 'close your mouth or you'll either get dust, bugs or both in there.'

Rose's eyes widened in surprise but she quickly closed her mouth. Dave laughed again at her reaction. As they bumped along, his arm kept brushing hers and she enjoyed the spark of excitement that spread through her every time they touched.

The land around them was almost devoid of vegetation and the orangey-brown dirt seemed to stretch on for miles. It seemed arid and depressing, although she was sure other people here would have a different view. She looked at the faces of those around her. Penny was laughing with Carrie, who was sitting beside her. The two women seemed oblivious to their surroundings or the amount of dust that was settling over them.

As she looked out again, she saw some emus in the distance. She'd never seen an emu in the wild before—only in a zoo. It was an amazing sight which made her smile. Perhaps it wasn't so depressing after all.

Finally the ute slowed down and went over a cattle grid, the jarring bumps making her teeth chatter. She looked around at her colleagues again. No one was talking now.

Everyone seemed to be concentrating on what they might find, running through different scenarios in their minds.

Once the ute stopped, Dave helped Rose out, the brief touch of his hands about her waist warming her insides. She swatted the flies away. 'Thanks.'

'No problem.' He turned and helped both Penny and Carrie as well, and she remembered his brother's remark about chivalry. People were bustling with activity, the constant swatting of flies making it almost look comical. Rose was able to focus firmly on her work, until Dave walked over with an abseiling harness for her.

'What's that for?'

'For you to put on.'

'Why? I don't need to go down there.'

He nodded. 'Yes, you do.'

Rose felt her heartbeat increase again at the thought of going down beneath the ground. She'd been out on retrievals before but they had all been inner-city accidents. None of this out in the back of beyond and down a hole! How on earth, after everything she'd been through so far, was she going to tell Dave that she couldn't do it? He already had a harness on, as did Penny.

He held up the harness—a piece of woven nylon which was supposed to support her weight as she hung on a rope. Was he mad?

When she looked up at him, she knew her face was as pale as before. 'I take it you've never abseiled before.'

Rose shook her head, unable to speak.

'Let me help you into the harness, then.'

'What? You're not mad with me?' Her words came out rather breathlessly and she watched him eye her carefully.

'Put one leg through here,' he commanded, but didn't answer her question. 'If these harnesses aren't put on correctly, we're all in trouble,' he added, knowing she'd probably be able to complete the task herself but he *wanted* to help. He *wanted* an excuse to be this close to her again.

Dave could tell she was agitated and wasn't sure

whether it was from the thought of abseiling or going into a confined space again. Probably the latter.

When Rose placed her hand on his shoulder to help herself balance, his restraint nearly broke. He should have assigned someone else the job of helping her into a harness but he hadn't been able to bear the thought of any other man getting that close to her.

There were two other females on the retrieval team but they were both busy. The past two weeks of agony, as he'd kept his distance from her, was making him forget his resolve not to touch her again. Not in a personal sense, anyway.

As he pulled the harness up her legs, he felt her hands cover his own. Thinking she wanted him to back off, he tried to pull away. She didn't move her hands.

'Rosie?' He glanced at her, only to see anguish and fear present in her eyes once more. He was beginning to realise there was a lot more to this woman than he'd originally thought. She seemed deep and complex. He knew he should probably turn and walk away but he couldn't help himself. He guessed it was his inbuilt sense of chivalry that made him want to help. That—or his attraction for her was definitely leading him astray.

'Rosie?' He swallowed over the dryness in his throat as he spoke her name again.

She opened her mouth to speak but found she couldn't. Instead, she shook her head. All he could think of was pressing his lips to hers but the fear in her eyes stopped him. She needed reassurance and although he thought that was a fantastic way to reassure someone, she might not be of the same opinion.

'You'll be fine,' he continued, his tone soft and reassuring. 'I'll go first, which means I'll be down on the bottom, helping to control your descent. Unfortunately, the hole is too narrow for both of us to go down side by side, but you'll be fine. Trust me.'

'I do,' she whispered. 'But it's not only the abseiling. It's the…the…'

'The confines of the hole? It'll be all right. Those kids need you, Rosie. Focus on them and how much you can help them. That's why you became a doctor in the first place—to help people. They need pain relief and you're the only one who can figure out exactly what they need. I'm counting on you. We're all counting on you and I know you'll come through for me, just like you did for the plane ride.'

He continued to secure the harness and reluctantly removed his hands from beneath hers. They were standing so close that if he'd just leaned down slightly, he'd be able to claim her lips with his. He was aching to do it but the last thing she needed now was to be frightened further, and he knew for a fact that the kiss he wanted to give her would be anything but reassuring and gentle. He wanted to plunder her mouth with his, which made his earlier chivalry seem like a lie.

The thought of kissing her caused him to lose sight of everything but his growing need for the woman before him. He knew how she tasted and the knowledge had driven him insane for the past couple of weeks. Rosie Partridge seemed to be one woman who refused to leave his dreams, so in the end he'd given up trying to force her out. At least that way he got some sleep, even if he did wake up frustrated.

'Rosie,' he murmured, his voice deep with desire. He edged forward so their noses were almost touching.

'Dave?' Penny called out, and he immediately stepped away from Rose. 'We're almost set.'

'Be right there,' he called back. He glanced at Rose. 'Time to get you roped up. Come with me.' His tone was brisk, mainly because he was cross with himself for almost kissing her in front of the hospital staff. He headed off towards the others, leaving Rose to follow behind him. When she was there, he called everyone to attention.

'Those two kids down there need us. Let's focus on what we're here to do, people, and let's get those kids out in one piece.'

As he continued giving instructions, Rose smiled at what he'd said, feeling some of his inner strength spread throughout her. He was a good man, a good leader, and she *did* trust him.

'Ready?' he asked, turning to face her.

She nodded, concentrating her thoughts on the two teenage kids. They hadn't asked to be down there. It wasn't their fault. They needed her help and she was determined to give it to them.

'Yes,' she said weakly, but cleared her throat and tried again. 'Yes.' It was firmer this time. Dave placed his arm on her shoulder and squeezed it gently.

'Trust me, Rosie. I won't let you down.'

He gazed down into her eyes and she realised he wasn't just talking about the retrieval.

CHAPTER FIVE

THE entire time Rose was abseiling down into the dark hole, caving helmet with a light secured firmly to her head, all she concentrated on was the sound of Dave's voice. He was constantly encouraging her, telling her it was only a little bit further, and before she knew it, she stretched her foot and felt the ground beneath her.

She sagged with relief.

'Well done. Right,' Dave said into his walkie-talkie. 'Send Penny down next and then the stretcher.' He turned to look at her, keeping the light from his helmet out of her eyes. 'Unhook your rope, like I showed you, then come carefully this way,' he instructed. He shuffled to the left and as Rose turned her head to survey the cavern, she was surprised to find it bigger than she'd expected.

'Quite large, isn't it?'

'Yes.'

He knelt down beside their patients who were both currently unconscious. 'That's why I told everyone to clear the area above us. The last thing we need is another cave-in.'

Rose shuddered at his words.

'Don't think about it. We'll be fine.'

There it was again. That reassuring tone she was coming to know so well.

'I've done a quick check. Shenae, who is fourteen, has fractured both her legs and possibly her pelvis. It looks as though she was first down.'

'You know these people?' Rose asked in amazement.

'Of course. This part of the country may be large in area, but as far as the population goes we're actually quite small. Her brother, Ian, is sixteen, and it looks as though he might have fallen on top of her when he came down, which is why I'm concerned about her pelvis. Penny will probably want to take both of them back to Adelaide with her but let's get them stabilised first.'

'Right.' Rose checked Shenae's pulse and blood pressure before roughly calculating her height and weight. Dave was doing the rest of the observations, constantly calling to both patients, hoping they'd soon regain consciousness.

'I don't like Shenae's blood pressure,' Dave said. 'If her pelvis is fractured, like I suspect, then she could have a multitude of internal injuries.'

'I'll put an IV line in and start the saline going.'

'Good.' They worked well together and with the arrival of Penny, the small cavern started to feel crowded. Rose forced herself to relax and concentrate on the patients.

'You know what they say,' Penny joked. 'Three's a crowd.' She laughed but her hands were busy the entire time, feeling bones and making diagnoses. 'Shenae's pelvis doesn't feel too good.'

Rose watched as Penny looked at Dave. They exchanged a glance that was full of meaning. Rose had seen it before—a concerned look often passed between surgeons who were worried about their patients. It made her wonder how long Penny and Dave had been working together. She knew Penny lived in Adelaide and only came to Broken Hill once a week for an orthopaedic clinic and operating session, but there seemed to be...something more between them. She'd noted that Penny didn't wear any rings on her fingers but, then, she'd only seen Penny in Theatre prior to this. She wondered whether the pretty orthopaedic surgeon had designs on Dave. Rose felt her stomach twist and it had nothing to do with the confines of the space they were in.

Rose had finished inserting the IV lines in both patients, and shortly after she'd done Ian's he started to moan.

'Ian?' Dave called. 'It's Dave. Everything's going to be all right, mate.'

'Ow.' Ian continued to moan and Rose didn't blame him. The poor kid had been through the wringer.

'Take it easy,' Dave continued. 'We're going to give you something for the pain.' He nodded at Rose who took her cue. She drew up an injection of morphine and administered it. Ian's face relaxed within seconds.

'He's fractured his left femur, left tib and fib,' Penny rattled off. 'Right tib and fib and I don't like the look of his right olecranon. Does he need anything else, Rose, or will the morphine be enough for me to straighten out that elbow?'

'He should be fine.'

'Ian?' Penny said, and explained what she was about to do. Rose had used Ian's left arm for the IV, noting that the right elbow was at an odd angle. Thank goodness Penny had still been around when this call had come in.

Once Ian's elbow was back in a more normal position, Rose and Penny manoeuvred him onto the stretcher and secured him with the straps. He'd need to be taken out vertically but the stretchers were well equipped to hold the patient firmly so he didn't sustain further injuries in the process.

'Ready to move,' Penny said into the walkie-talkie, after Dave had quickly checked the ropes and knots. 'I've only done this sort of thing a few times,' Penny confided to Rose. 'Dave here seems to do it all the time.'

Dave was now crouching back by Shenae's side. 'Part of being an outback surgeon,' he replied. 'Penny, I'm not at all happy with Shenae's situation.' All three of them crowded around the patient. 'Her blood pressure still isn't good, despite the saline.'

'Open?' Penny asked.

'I think so.'

'Midazolam,' Rose responded, and administered the short-acting sedative. She hooked a stethoscope on so she could monitor Shenae's heartbeat. Without all of her usual equipment, Rose knew she was going to have to do things the old-fashioned way.

Penny and Dave prepared Shenae for an abdominal incision. They'd pulled on sterile surgical attire and draped Shenae as best they could.

'I'm just going to find the offending artery and suture it off,' Dave mumbled from beneath his mask. 'Then we'll get her out of here. If we don't…' He raised his head, his gaze meeting Rose's. She knew what he'd been about to say. They all did. This young girl was not in a good state. 'Ready, Rosie?'

'Ready,' she replied, and watched as Dave made a neat incision into Shenae's abdomen. Rose concentrated hard on her job for the duration of the operation. The seconds passed, ticking into minutes. Five minutes, ten minutes.

'That's the one,' Dave said as he and Penny worked closely together. Due to the lack of light, it had taken longer than normal but, still, they'd found it. 'All right. Let's close her up and get a dressing on this wound so we can get out of here. How's she doing, Rosie?'

Rose performed the neurological and neurovascular obs. 'Picking up nicely.'

'That's what I want to hear,' he mumbled as he concentrated on what he was doing. 'Rosie always tells me what I want to hear.' His tone was laced with humour and right now all three of them could use some.

'Is that so?' Penny queried with interest, her eyes gleaming with laughter as she glanced at Rose.

'Absolutely,' Rose agreed. 'I say things like, "Patient is anaesthetised, Doctor," and, "Patient is stabilised."'

Penny laughed. 'Those are the types of words I like to hear from my anaesthetists as well.'

'Must be a surgeon thing, then,' Rose said and Dave's rich laughter filled the cavern.

As they continued preparing Shenae for the stretcher, Rose decided grudgingly that she liked Penny. So what if the other woman was interested in Dave? Dave was nothing to Rose—except a colleague. She glanced at him and felt her stomach twist into knots again. A colleague she found attractive, she amended honestly.

They waited until Shenae had been transferred to the surface before a rope ladder was hung over the opening of the hole and lowered down to them.

Some dirt and small rocks tumbled down the hole as well and Rose gasped in fright, flattening herself against the wall. 'It's all right, Rosie,' Dave crooned as he quickly went to her side. He placed his arm around her shoulder, but as more small rocks and dirt started to fall, she buried her head into his shoulder, knocking her helmet off.

Dave grabbed the walkie-talkie with his free hand. 'What's going on?' he asked.

No response.

He waited before calling again. 'Keep away from the opening.'

More rocks started to come down and they were getting bigger. Dave pulled himself away from Rose as he helped Penny finish packing up their equipment. Rose whimpered but couldn't move. The tears, the fears—they were all starting to threaten her resolve. She could hear Dave's muffled tones as he spoke on the walkie-talkie but she couldn't listen any more.

She shut her eyes and put her fingers in her ears, trying to block out the loud pounding noise, and only belatedly realised it was her own heartbeat. The smell of the dirt filled her nostrils. Tears streamed down her cheeks as she drew her legs even closer to her chest, her body trembling with fear.

'Rosie?' Dave's arms were back around her, holding her. Cradling her. His hand stroked her hair, comforting. The sobs started to rack her body, her breath coming in gasps.

'Paper bag?' he said to Penny. 'She's hyperventilating.'

'Claustrophobia?' Penny queried as she searched

through the medical kits. 'I've got sutures, IV lines, saline, drugs, but no paper bag!'

Dave processed this information before turning his attention to Rose. 'Rosie? Sweetheart? You need to take some deep breaths. Come on, you can do it.' Dave demonstrated by taking deep breaths himself. 'You need to slow it down.' He felt Rose move beneath his arms. 'That's it, sweetheart, and another one. Nice and big. That's right. Keep going.'

Rose blocked out everything—everything except the sound of Dave's voice and the strength of his arms securely around her.

'Fantastic. You're doing a fantastic job.' He kissed the top of her head as she took another deep breath. She slowly lifted her head to look at him, her frightened blue eyes telling him how hard this was for her to do. 'And another. That's it.' He brushed his lips across hers. 'You did it. You did it.'

Rose heaved a heavy sigh and collapsed against him. 'Penny, see how the opening looks now,' he instructed. 'We need to get Rosie out of here.'

'It's stopped.'

'Check the ladder.'

'Feels strong.'

Dave spoke into the walkie-talkie. 'How's things up there now?'

'Stabilised.'

'Beauty. Rosie's coming up.'

'No.' Rose shook her head.

'Yes, sweetheart.' Dave bent and helped her over to the opening, placing her helmet back on her head. 'You can do it. The sooner you get out, the better you're going to feel. Just concentrate on where you're putting your feet and your hands on the ladder. That's what you need to focus on, Rosie. Can you do that for me?' While he'd been speaking, he'd hooked her abseiling rope back to the D-clamp attached to her harness.

He was nodding encouragingly and she copied it. 'That a girl.' He placed her hands onto the ladder. 'Up you go, Rosie. You've done an incredible job and all you need to do now is carefully climb your way out. Nothing to it,' he said more softly in her ear.

She could feel the warmth of his chest pressing into her back. 'Take a deep breath and let it out, nice and slow. You can do this, Rosie.' Rose was glad he felt so positive because right now she wondered how on earth she was supposed to find the strength to even move, let alone climb a swinging, unstable rope ladder.

She nodded, knowing her vocal cords would definitely fail her should she attempt speech. Doing as he'd said, she took a firm grip on the ladder with both hands and hauled herself up. The slight swaying sensation made her feel ill and for a second all thought was gone. The fears started to swamp her again and she wondered how she would ever get out of this tiny hole when she could barely see the light at the top.

'You can do it, Rosie.' Dave's encouraging words broke through her haze and she forced her body to carry out the instructions her brain was sending. After what seemed like an eternity, she was at the top and being helped up the last bit by two of the rescue party.

'Well done, Doc,' one of the men said.

Rose managed to control her shaking legs until she'd checked on the status of her patients before crumbling to the ground in relief. A few sobs worked their way up and she let them bubble over. She'd done it. It was over. She sat forward and stuck her head between her knees, hoping the light-headedness would pass quickly. She needed to be in control. She had patients to attend to but the feeling that she'd been spun around and shot into space refused to leave her.

She supposed she should be extremely proud of what she'd done. She'd flown in a light aircraft and had been in a very confined space. Part of her wanted to jump for joy at what she'd accomplished but she seriously lacked the energy.

The other part wanted to close her eyes and wake to find it had all been a horrible nightmare but, then, Dave's kisses could never be classified as a nightmare. A dream? A hope? Oh, yes, but never a nightmare. Even though she told herself she didn't really like him, even though they had next to nothing in common, he was a fantastic kisser and she couldn't deny it.

How long she sat there, she wasn't sure. When she raised her head, it was to see Penny climbing out of the hole. Most of the medical equipment had been sent back up and the two patients were being closely monitored by the trained staff.

Slowly, Dave materialised not long after Penny, and Rose watched as the orthopaedic surgeon spoke animatedly with him. She could hear the excitement in Penny's voice but couldn't decipher exactly what she was saying. In the next instant, Penny had flung her arms around Dave's neck and pressed her lips to his.

Rose felt as though she'd been physically hit.

Bile rose in her throat and her head started to spin again. Did Dave go around kissing all the women he worked with? Disgust, not only with him but with herself, came hard on the heels of jealousy. She should have known better. Anyone who kissed as well as he did, who could make a woman forget everything around her, didn't get to be *that* good without a lot of practice.

As Penny disengaged herself from him and headed over to the patients, Dave turned his head and met Rose's gaze across the crowded patch of land. Even though it was now well into the evening, the stars that were out and the half-moon giving them some light, Rose knew his gaze was boring into her soul.

Finally, after long seconds, he broke away. He mumbled something to someone before heading in her direction.

'Hey, how are you feeling?' His voice was soft and

caring, and Rose clenched her jaw, determined not to succumb to his charms any more.

'Fine.'

He stared at her for a moment, his gaze narrowing slightly at her clipped tone. 'Good. Glad to hear it.' He reached out a hand to rest it on her forehead but Rose jerked away from him. 'What's wrong?'

'Nothing.' She stood as though to prove her point, hoping her legs didn't let her down. 'I presume we'll be heading back a.s.a.p.?'

'Uh, yeah.' Dave frowned at her. 'You sure everything's all right?'

'Fine.' With that, she headed back to the patients. 'Status?' she asked, and received a full report from the nurses. It was a few seconds before she realised Dave had followed her and was listening intently to everything that was being said. Rose was having a hard time controlling her unwanted emotions towards him. He stood close beside her and she could feel the warmth emanating from his body. She was cross with herself for being so aware of him. It wasn't fair, especially when Penny moved to stand on the other side of him.

'Something wrong, Rose?' Carrie asked.

Rose was stunned for a moment. 'No. No everything's fine.'

'You were just frowning so hard at what I was saying I thought something must be wrong.'

'No. Just tired,' Rose offered quickly. 'It's been a very…stressful night.'

'Then let's head back to the hospital,' Dave directed. Each of the utes had a patient in the back tray. 'Rosie and I will go with Shenae. Penny, you and Carrie go with Ian.'

'Right,' Penny and Carrie replied.

'See you at the airstrip,' Dave called with a wave as he climbed in the ute next to Shenae. 'Up you get, Rosie. This part of the journey isn't so bad.'

Rose merely nodded and set about checking Shenae's

vital signs and the saline drip. Once they were on their
way and both were satisfied with Shenae's condition, Dave
sat down next to the stretcher, resting one arm along the
side of the ute.

'You've done such a wonderful job,' he told her.

'Thank you.'

'You sure you're feeling all right? You're acting really
weird.'

'Tired,' Rose corrected.

'So do you always speak in monosyllables when you're
tired?'

'Yes.'

'I see.' There wasn't much he could say to that and for
a while neither of them spoke. Both concentrated on
Shenae until they were closer to the airstrip. 'How do you
think you'll do, going back in the plane?'

'Fine.'

'Well, if you want to hold my hand or lean on my shoulder, just let me know,' he said with a forced smile.

'Thanks.' Again her tone was clipped and she couldn't
look at him when she spoke. She was finding it increasingly difficult to keep up her anger when he was being so
darned charming and considerate. He's not your type, he's
not your type, she kept repeating to herself.

'Rosie…' The ute came to a gentle stop. 'Take a deep
breath and you'll be fine.'

Rose knew it was going to take more than a deep breath
to wash away the feelings of his betrayal. It was quite
ridiculous when she thought about it. He'd never indicated
they were an item or anything special. All he'd done was
to kiss her a few times—that was all. Why couldn't she
get past this?

'Thanks.'

She concentrated on getting the patients transferred to
the plane, ignoring the sickening sensation as she climbed
aboard. Knowing she could focus on the patients helped
dramatically and that was precisely what she did, never

once looking directly into Dave's eyes and only speaking to him when absolutely necessary.

They were all yawning by the time the plane touched down. Penny had decided to send Ian directly back to Adelaide and had called on ahead to make the arrangements. Dave wasn't too happy with Shenae. Although she was holding her own, she would still require immediate surgery.

An ambulance ferried them back to the hospital, and the instant they walked in, Dave started barking orders. 'Blood transfusion, stat. Rose, get her anaesthetised and ready for surgery the instant she's out of Radiology. Penny, come into Theatre with me so we can patch her up before you take her on to Adelaide.'

While she had the chance, Rose went and had a quick shower before getting dressed in theatre garb, hoping she had time for a cup of tea before Shenae was back from having X-rays done.

When she arrived in Theatre, Shenae's condition had improved dramatically because of the blood she'd been receiving. Everyone was ready for Rose to anaesthetise and when Dave walked into Theatre, the scent of him flowed past her, making it difficult to concentrate for a moment.

Rose kept a close eye on her dials, forcing herself not to snatch glimpses of just how well Penny and Dave worked together. How dared he kiss her if he was involved with Penny? Just because Penny had been out of town, did he think he could use anyone as a substitute? No, not anyone—the new girl. The new girl who didn't know about his relationship with Penny. The main factor that stuck in Rose's throat was that, unlike herself, Penny was a brunette.

Stop it, she berated herself. Concentrate.

The operation went well and Dave was happy with the status of Shenae's internal injuries, as was Penny.

'I'll want the pelvic fracture to ''rest'' for a few days before I decide exactly how I want to approach it. Invasive or non-invasive remains to be seen. Her other fractures are stable and can be fixed back in Adelaide. How soon can I move her, Dave?'

'Give her an hour or two and then she's all yours,' he remarked, as Shenae was wheeled to Recovery. Rose went with her, wanting to stay with her until she either woke from the anaesthetic or was taken to Adelaide.

She stayed by the young girl's bedside until her mother was brought in to see her. Dave came with her, introducing her to Rose.

'Is she going to be all right, Dave?'

'It's not going to be easy, Libby, but at the moment she's definitely holding her own, which is a good sign.'

'But she's…she's…unconscious.'

'It's mainly due to the anaesthetic,' Rose told Libby. 'I'm hoping she'll come around before she's transferred to Adelaide.'

'But all those tubes and things.'

Rose smiled compassionately. 'I guess it does look a little scary but Shenae's doing a good job of recovering on her own. Her body's been through a terrible trauma and right now it needs time to regenerate and recover.'

'What about Ian?' Libby asked, turning her worried gaze to Dave.

'I'll call through to Adelaide and get an update for you.'

'John, my husband,' she said to Rose, 'has flown down there in our little Cessna. He called me when he got there but I haven't heard anything else.'

'I'll get a call through right away,' Dave reassured her, before walking off.

'Can I get you a cup of tea or coffee?' Rose asked, feeling empathy for the distressed mother. Libby didn't answer. Instead, she came closer to Shenae and held her daughter's limp hand.

'I feel so responsible.'

'How could you have known?' Rose asked. 'From what we've learned, no one knew that mine shaft was even on your property. It's been over a hundred and fifty years since people were mining that part of the country. You weren't to know.'

'I know, but I'm their mother. I'm supposed to look out for them. When they were little 'uns, we were always so careful of their outdoor boundaries. We had fences everywhere but now…now they're so…'

'They're so much older and you don't feel you have to watch out for them as much—and they wouldn't let you anyway. From my experience with teenagers, they know *everything* and no one, let alone parents, can tell them any different.'

Libby smiled a watery smile and nodded. 'That's true.'

'They were both taken unawares. It's not your fault, Libby, and you'll do neither Shenae nor Ian any good if you start blaming yourself. They've both been found and they're both going to recover. It won't be easy but once Shenae regains consciousness, we'll have a better idea of how her recovery will progress.'

'I have the update and it's all good news,' Dave said as he returned. 'Ian is still in Theatre but I managed to get through on the phone and Sam, the orthopaedic surgeon who's taken over Ian's care, said that everything is going like clockwork. He'll give the hospital a call once he's finished and let us know what's happening. I spoke to John as well and he said to pass on that he loves you.'

'Oh!' Libby started to cry. Dave didn't hesitate and placed a comforting arm around her shoulders.

'Cry it out, Lib. Cry it out. Your babies are doing fine.'

Rose came around to the other side of the bed to check the readings from the machines once more. 'She's coming around,' she whispered, and, sure enough, a moment or two later Shenae's eyelids started to flutter. Another moment and they were open, staring unseeingly up at the ceiling.

'Hi, there, gorgeous,' Dave crooned.

'Shenae? Shenae?' Libby queried anxiously. 'Mum's here, darling.'

'This is Rosie,' Dave introduced her to Shenae. 'She's just going to check your eyes.'

'I won't be a moment, Shenae,' Rose said softly, as she shone the medical torch briefly into the teenager's eyes. 'Pupils equal and reacting to light, as previous.'

'Mum?' Shenae whispered, but choked on the word.

'Let me give you some ice chips.' Rose quickly spooned a few into Shenae's mouth and when the girl tried to speak again, Dave told her not to worry.

'Rest now. The rest will do you good.'

'They're going to move you soon,' Libby told her. 'We're going to go to Adelaide, which is where Ian and Dad are. We're going to be together as a family and we'll get through this,' Libby told her daughter with determination. 'Ain't gonna be easy but we'll do it.'

'That's the spirit,' Dave said as they all watched Shenae drift off again. The nurses came over to perform their observations while Rose continued to monitor her patient's pain relief. An hour later, they were taken back to the airstrip and, with Penny in tow, Libby and Shenae headed off to Adelaide.

Rose had another shower at the hospital, knowing by the time she made it home, all she'd want to do would be to crawl into bed and sleep the rest of the night away. She forced her legs to work, putting one in front of the other as she walked towards her car.

'So that was Monday,' Dave said as he caught up with her. 'How are you feeling?'

'A lot better, thank you.' Her tone was polite and dismissive.

'I wanted to catch you before you left to say that I'm really proud of what you faced today. It couldn't have been easy.' Dave obviously wasn't taking the hint. Usually her body language and polite tone got the message across to most males. Obviously, Dave wasn't most males.

'It wasn't, but it's over.' She stopped at her car and unlocked the door.

'Until next time,' he pointed out. 'Rosie, I am concerned about this. It was stated on your job description that flying in a small aircraft would be necessary. Why did you even apply for this job?'

'My reasons for applying for this job have nothing to do with you. I didn't think it would be as much of a problem as it has been, but I promise I'll work on it and the next time there's a call-out, I'm sure I'll be fine.'

'And if you're not? I can't have my staff crumbling to pieces in an emergency situation.'

'It won't happen again,' she said with slow deliberation.

'It had better not.' His voice was firm and brooked no argument. He was a professional and he did his job accordingly. 'I'm responsible for the retrieval team and it's a job I take seriously.'

'And rightly so.'

'Then take this as a warning, Rose. If what happened today happens again, I will have no hesitation in terminating your contract here at Broken Hill Hospital. Understood?'

'Perfectly,' she replied, fighting the lump that was rising in her throat and the angry tears that threatened to spill over her lashes. There was no way in the world she'd let Dave have the satisfaction of seeing her this upset.

With a brisk nod, he turned and strode away. Rose climbed numbly into her car, knowing full well that he'd meant every word he'd said. Not because of the tone of his voice, or his body language, but because he'd called her Rose.

CHAPTER SIX

DAVE dropped into a chair at the kitchen table and slumped forward. He felt like a first-class heel for bawling Rosie out like that, but she'd got him so mad with her ice-maiden attitude he'd felt like throttling her.

He sat up and shook his head in disbelief. One minute she'd been smiling at him and the next snarling. Perhaps it had just been delayed shock? She'd been through enough and he didn't blame her if she felt a little overwrought. Maybe that's all it had been and she'd simply been venting her frustrations at her own inadequacy on him.

He allowed himself to believe it whilst he stood and grabbed a long cool beer from the fridge, accidentally kicking against a chair on his way back to the table. He only drank light beer as he never knew when he'd be needed at the hospital or at an emergency, but right now the coolness of the liquid was what he wanted most.

'Can't you keep it down?' Mick mumbled from the doorway. 'It's after three in the morning.'

'Sorry, bro'.'

'Tough night?'

'Yeah. I suppose you've heard,' Dave said. The locals had an amazing grapevine. In fact, it was worse than any hospital he'd worked in previously. The thought made him smile. Their concern was always genuine and they could always be relied upon to help out in any emergency. Here in the outback, it was often man against the elements.

'Yep. Libby and John's kids. How are they doing?'

'They'll get through.'

'Both off to Adelaide?'

'Yes. Thankfully Penny had just finished her operating

list when the call came in so she was able to come out on retrieval with us.'

'She's back in Adelaide now?'

'Yes.'

'Sam will be pleased. Oh, hey, did you manage to get that piece of artwork Penny was after?'

'Yes. She was ecstatic when I told her, and Sam will love it when she gives it to him.'

'Yeah. Hope my wife is as devoted as Penny is to Sam. How did you get the artist to part with it? I thought it wasn't supposed to be for sale?'

'Let's just say he owed me a favour or two,' Dave replied, tapping the side of his nose.

'Most of the people in this district owe you a favour or two.'

'Happens when you save their lives.'

'And now you've got Libby and John to add to the list.'

'It would seem that way.' Dave grinned at his brother before finishing his beer. 'Think I'm about done in.'

'I guess this means you won't be getting up in two more hours to give me a hand with the cattle?'

'You've got it, little brother.' Dave smiled at him and headed towards his room.

'Hey—I almost forgot,' Mick added as he trailed after him. 'Mags called.'

Dave stopped in his tracks at the mention of his ex-wife and turned to face his brother, all traces of humour gone from his face. 'What does she want?'

Mick hesitated.

'Spit it out.'

'All right, but don't shoot the messenger.'

Dave nodded.

'She said she's getting married on Saturday and wants you to know she'll be putting Mel into an exclusive boarding school so the fees will be more expensive than before.'

'What? While she's on her honeymoon? It's school holidays! How long is she going away for?'

Mick shrugged. 'Not sure, but from what she said, it sounds as though it's going to be quite a few months. Her new husband, Julian Moncrief, will be working overseas for a while.'

'Mags is marrying *Julian*?' Dave was astounded and then wondered why he should be surprised.

'They deserve each other. Two peas in a pod.'

'How can you say that, Mick? You only met him once.'

'Twice,' Mick corrected. 'And he was a creep both times.'

'The first would have been at our wedding. When was the second?'

'When I came to Sydney one time. It wasn't long before you and Mags separated.'

'Why don't I remember?'

'You were working all sorts of hours, trying desperately to block out Mags's continual manipulations. I remember you came home one night—aw, it was probably around three or four in the morning and you were dead-dog tired. We sat on the floor on your very expensive rug and just talked. Mags came out just after five and told us both to shut up or get out.'

Dave nodded. '*That* I remember. Soon, I was back here on the farm.'

'Where you belong, mate.'

'Exactly. So when did you see Julian again?'

'He picked Mags up for work. She said her car was on the blink and as his office was across the road from hers, he was…you know…"helping her out".'

Dave didn't miss the underlying meaning. 'Typical.'

'Surprised?'

'I knew about 'em, mate. I confronted her, she didn't deny it, we separated. I'm also sure Julian wasn't the only one.'

'Hurt?'

'Way past it, bro'.' Dave thought for a moment. 'Julian was married then.'

'To his first wife?'

Dave nodded. 'Perhaps you're right, Mick. Perhaps they do deserve each other.'

'And good riddance to them.'

'Yeah, but what about Melody? She's my daughter, too. If Mags thinks she's going to dump Mel into a boarding school, she's got another think coming!'

'What else should she do?'

'Mel can come here.'

'To the farm?' Mick asked. 'It's no place for a kid, Dave. You know that. The last few times Mel has been here, she's been miserable.'

'No, she hasn't.'

'Yes, she has, Dave. If you want Mel to come here for a few months, you'll need to move closer to town.'

'We're only twenty minutes from the town centre and this is my home, too.'

'Mel needs to be with other kids her own age, and if she's coming here to live for a while, it'll take you for ever to get her to school in the morning before you're due at the hospital.'

Dave nodded and rubbed his fingers along his temple 'What exactly did Mags say?'

'She said she'd be putting Mel into the school in the next few days as she had too much to concentrate on with the wedding.'

'This is *so* like her.' Dave slapped his hand against his thigh. 'She fought for custody of Melody when I would have had her at the drop of a hat but, no, Margaret had to have everything *her* way and couldn't possibly have people thinking she wasn't a good mother. This isn't being a good mother and I object to not having a say in what happens to my own daughter. I won't pay those fees.'

'Why not?'

'Because Melody's coming to Broken Hill and that's final.'

'You think that's wise? You know, to rip her out of her environment?'

'She's six years old, Mick. Kids adapt. You and I adapted when our dad walked out on us.'

'Yeah, but we had Mum. We still had a constant in our lives.'

'Don't you remember what mum was like when he left? She fell to pieces,' Dave growled. 'She crumbled into a woman half her previous size and never fully recovered. That's not the point. I won't let Margaret dictate like this. Melody is *my* daughter, too, and I'll go to court if I have to. I'll do whatever it takes, but I will not have my daughter thrust aside in some snotty boarding school, growing up with the belief that neither of her parents wanted her. *I* want her and, believe me, mate, I'm going to get her.'

'What are you going to do?'

'I'll call Mags first thing in the morning and arrange to fly up there in the next few days to pick Melody up.'

'That's the Dunbar fighting spirit,' Mick added, then stopped and looked thoughtfully at his brother. 'You don't think this is what Mags originally wanted? That she'd want you to get on your high horse and demand to take Mel?'

Dave felt his anger rise at Mick's question. He was right. Mags was more than likely manipulating him again. Well, if she wanted to play the game, then it was going to be played by his rules. 'If she persists in going through with this, I'm going to file for full custody and I'll fight her with everything I've got.' He clenched his jaw in determination. 'Mel is my daughter and I love her, Mick. She may not like coming to the farm but I know for a fact that she also loves me.'

'And me! I'm her favourite uncle.'

'You're her only uncle, Mick.'

His brother grinned at him. 'You'll need to get a nanny as well. Or a housekeeper or something. You work such odd hours, mate, you've got to think about Mel's needs.'

Anger surged through Dave at the way his ex-wife still

managed to get to him. 'I can't believe Mags would be so…so… Ugh!' He thumped his fist into the wall and was surprised when it went straight through the old plaster-board.

'That was smart,' Mick remarked ironically, as Dave cradled his hand. 'Get it under some water.'

'It's fine.'

'Don't be a drongo, Dave.'

'I am not an unintelligent, stupid fool.'

'Yeah? Then stop acting like one!'

Dave stormed past his brother, knowing he was right. He shoved his hand under the tap and rinsed it carefully, pleased to see he'd only grazed the skin in a few places. Other than that, all phalanges and the metacarpus seemed to be unbroken.

'How's it look?'

'It'll be fine.'

'You're lucky.'

'Yeah.' He pushed passed Mick and headed to his room. 'Thanks for passing on the message. I'll think about what you've said.'

'Once you get custody of Mel, you shouldn't need to see Mags again.'

'Hadn't thought of that. Maybe she'd want access visits?'

'You think so?'

'Anything's possible with Mags. I've learned never to underestimate that woman. She's capable of anything. It might suit her in years to come to fight for custody of Melody again.'

'Mel's a smart girl, Dave. Hopefully, by then she'll be able to make up her own mind. After all, she's a Dunbar!'

'That she is. Thanks, bro'.' Dave shut his door and lay down on his bed, staring up at the ceiling. What had happened to his well-ordered life? In the last few weeks, it was as though his world had started to spin on an uneven axis.

First Rosie had come along, invading his dreams. Her sweet, pliant lips so delicious to kiss, but that had been before she'd turned into the ice queen. He still had no idea what had happened there.

Now there was Melody. His gorgeous little girl with her long blonde hair and Dunbar blue eyes. He'd seen her just a few weeks ago—at Christmas time. They'd spent the weekend together in Sydney and it had been wonderful.

Mags had seemed glad to have Mel out of the way and now he knew why. Even so, she'd never said anything about getting married again, although it was just like Mags to do things at the last minute like this.

He groaned in exasperation and turned onto his stomach, burying his head beneath the pillow, hoping to stop his mind from being so busy so he could finally get to sleep.

Women—he seemed surrounded by them and they were all a complete mystery to him.

'Morning, darl',' Sadie called as Dave headed onto the ward early Tuesday morning. He'd hardly slept a wink and had got up to help Mick, thankful for the distraction to his thoughts.

'Good morning, Sadie,' he replied, and smothered a yawn.

'What's up, darl'? You look as though you didn't sleep a wink last night.'

'I didn't.'

'What's up? You can tell me, darl'. I was one of your mum's closest friends. Go on, chew my ear.'

'Melody's coming.'

Sadie's eyebrows shot up to her greying hairline. 'Is she now? I didn't think she came in the January holidays.'

'She's coming for good.' He watched as Sadie's jaw hung open.

'You sure that's a good idea, darl'?'

'The best one I've ever had. I should have done it a long time ago.'

'What does Mags think about it?'

'I'll be calling her after ward round to tell her.' Dave slung a stethoscope around his neck as he spoke. 'Let's get the ward round done and get on with the day.'

'Right you are, darl',' Sadie said and patted him affectionately on the back.

True to his word, Dave went to his office after ward rounds and called Mags, surprised to find her awake so early. It would have been close to nine o'clock in Sydney. He didn't beat about the bush and told her up front what he wanted. When she calmly agreed, he knew for a fact that this had all been part of her plan.

'Why didn't you just come right out and say you didn't want her any more? Why can't you at least be honest about Mel?'

'Because then everyone would have thought I was a bad mother. This way, it looks as though—'

'I don't give a stuff how it looks, Mags.'

'Don't call me that. You know I hate it.'

Dave grinned, glad he'd irritated her. 'So you'll agree not to fight me for full custody of Melody?'

'I agree. In fact, my solicitor has already drawn up papers in anticipation of this. They'll be delivered to you by tonight.'

'Geez, Mags. You're…unbelievable.' Dave was completely disgusted with the woman, wondering how on earth he'd ever found her attractive in the first place. 'I'll be there on Thursday to collect her.'

'Don't bother. I've arranged for her to fly out to you.'

'By *herself*! She's six, Mags.'

'Oh, all right, then. I'll send the current nanny with her, too. Happy now? But you're paying for the flights.'

'I'm more than happy to.' Anything. He'd do anything she said at the moment if it meant he could get custody of Mel.

'Right, then. I've got to speak to the caterers.'

The line went dead and Dave looked at the receiver and

shook his head in disbelief. The woman was a piece of work! He called his brother to let him know the progress before heading off to clinic.

Once he'd got through clinic, he grabbed a quick bite of lunch, returning to his office to get his files ready for house calls. The encompassing scent of a very familiar perfume teased at his senses and he looked up to find Rose in his open doorway, her hand raised to knock.

'Good afternoon, Rosie.' He stopped his paper-shuffling, letting his gaze slowly travel over the alluring curves of her body, refreshing his memory. She was dressed in another trouser suit, this time pale blue, and she looked stunning. He could have stayed there for hours, simply watching her, but his self-control, thankfully, got the better of him. He cleared his throat and stood. 'What can I do for you?'

A *lot*! Rose worked hard at not being affected by the touch of his visual caress but she knew she was fighting a losing battle. How did the man have the power to make her knees quiver and her heart turn over with just one look? Then again, how many other women did he look at like that? The thought was enough to help pull her emotions back on track.

'I've just been told by the secretary that my house call list is the same as yours so it makes sense to go together.' When he simply stood there, staring at her as though she'd suggested they rob a bank, Rose pointed to his desk. 'Do you have all the patient files?'

'Yes.' Dave couldn't believe his luck. He got to spend the afternoon with Rosie. Beauty!

'Fine. I'll meet you at your ute.'

'We can take your car if you like.'

'What? Not intimidated by women drivers?'

'Not at all.'

'But I don't know my way around like you do.'

'I can direct you.' He shoved the files into his briefcase, picked up his medical bag, which he'd previously checked, and headed towards her. She quickly stepped out of the doorway, making room for him to pass. 'Let's get going, then.'

They walked out of the hospital together, Rose keeping her distance. She unlocked the car and opened the doors to let the heat out. Dave did the same for the passenger side. A minute later, she closed them again, swatting some flies away from her face. 'Won't take long for it to cool down,' she remarked, as she settled behind the wheel and pulled on her seat belt. Dave did the same and after she'd started the engine, she switched the air-conditioner to 'full'.

'Who's first on the list and which way do I go?' she asked, as she pulled out of the car park.

'Left. Mrs McGill.'

'Mrs McGill.' Rose nodded. 'How did she recover from her food-poisoning experience?'

'All right but it's really aggravated her intestines. I've been watching her closely since just before Christmas when she presented with abdominal pain. When she was brought in with food poisoning, I thought it might have been gallstones, but after doing an ultra sound, I discovered it wasn't.'

'Yet her abdominal pains haven't subsided?'

'Not from what her GP says. I suppose you're seeing her because of the bone cancer,' he stated.

'Yes. Unfortunately, most of the patients I visit at home have a terminal illness.'

'Take the next right turn,' he directed.

She was glad the conversation was kept to medical aspects because that way she could relax a little and enjoy being with him, rather than being forced to remember she was cross with him.

When they arrived at Mrs McGill's, it was to find her lying in bed, moaning in pain. Her husband was quite beside himself. Dave performed her obs while Rose gave her something for the pain.

'That should help,' she said softly. Soon Mrs McGill was more peaceful and started to doze. They headed out to the kitchen, Mr McGill telling them what had transpired that morning and how he'd been about to call the doctor.

'I'd like to admit her to the hospital so I can keep a closer eye on her and run some tests,' Dave said to him. 'Agreed, Rosie?'

'Yes. She can be monitored at the hospital and until the source of this pain is discovered, it'll be best for her.'

'Her oncologist is due here on Thursday so I'll make an appointment for him to stop by her bed and give her a check-up,' Dave told Mr McGill.

They organised Mrs McGill's transfer to hospital then sat down with a cool drink until the ambulance arrived. Once their patient had been handed over to the ambos, they headed to the next appointment.

Three patients later and Rose was ready to call it a day. 'It's hot, I'm tired and these flies are driving me insane,' she told Dave as they waved goodbye at their last house call. 'Which way?' she said at an intersection. 'Once I get back on the main roads, I'm OK.'

'Go right.'

'Thanks.' Rose had been impressed by his relaxed nature towards his patients and it softened her resolve a little. She couldn't let that happen. Forcing herself to concentrate on her driving, Rose worked hard to keep up her cool façade. Now that the patients were out of the way, it was the only shield she had. She was still annoyed with him. She had to remember that. A man shouldn't kiss a woman if he's already involved with another woman. It just isn't the done thing.

First Julian had thought he could do it and now Dave. She could pick them all right. As far as her taste went in men, it was lousy. She was also cross with him for ruining her sleep last night. Just when she'd thought she'd had enough sleepless nights because of him, along had come another one, leaving her feeling washed-out and cranky.

'Left here.' His deep voice broke into her thoughts and washed over her like smooth silk. Rose felt her heartbeat accelerate. Oh, why did he have to have such an effect on her? It wasn't fair. It should be illegal for a man to have such an effect on women—especially a man who was a two-timing snake!

She fixed the image of him kissing Penny firmly in her mind and clung to it, but she could feel herself losing her grip once more. The truth was, the more she saw of Dave, the more she was coming to like him. He was direct and forthright when dealing with staff and patients. He had great skill as a surgeon and as a colleague she admired him greatly. So why did he have to be such a…such a…*male*?

'Rosie,' he said when they were almost at the hospital. She'd been so wrapped in her thoughts that she jumped a little as he spoke. 'Sorry. Didn't mean to startle you.'

Rose slowed down and turned into the hospital car park, pulling into the space she'd vacated a few hours ago.

'We need to talk.' He undid his seat belt and shifted slightly to look at her.

'What about?'

'Us.'

'Dave, there *is* no us.' Rose kept the engine going, hoping he'd take the hint and get out. He didn't.

'Yes, there is, and you know it.'

She looked at him. 'Don't tell me what I know or don't know.'

'There you go again, taking what I say out of context and getting all hot-headed about it.'

'I'm not going to sit here with the engine running and have some hypothetical conversation with you because that's all a relationship between you and I would be— hypothetical. It's hot and I'm tired. Please, get out.'

'Rosie—'

'Now!'

'No. We need to talk and if I have to sit here until the morning, you're going to talk to me.'

'But people will see us toge—'

'I don't care. We need to talk. That's all there is·to it.'

He wasn't going to budge on this, she could tell. 'Fine, but…come around to my house where we can at least have some privacy.'

It was obviously an answer he could accept as without another word he got out of her car. 'See you soon, then.' He shut the door and patted the top of her roof. Rose headed off, not at all sure she'd done the right thing.

CHAPTER SEVEN

'TEA or coffee?'

'Tea, please,' he replied, as he settled onto one of the stools at her father's kitchen bench.

Rose moved around the kitchen, feeling Dave's gaze on her the entire time. 'Well?' she asked. 'Are you going to get to the point? After all, you did want to talk.'

'Not when you're in this mood.'

'David!' Her exasperation was now at overload and bubbled over when he laughed.

'All right. It's just hard to talk whilst you're flitting around the kitchen. Why don't we get our cups of tea and go sit in the lounge room?'

'What a good idea.'

'See?'

'See what?'

'I have been known to have them once in a while.'

'What?'

'Good ideas.'

Rose sighed as she handed him his tea and carried her own through to the lounge room. Her next mistake was to sit down on the sofa, thereby leaving room for Dave to come and sit beside her. She tensed for a moment but breathed a sigh of relief when he sat in the armchair opposite her.

'I'm listening,' she said, growing increasingly impatient as well as apprehensive. What was he going to say?

'Firstly, I wanted to apologise for my behaviour last night. I know yesterday evening was difficult for you to get through and you didn't really need the added stress of me bawling you out like that. I still stand by what I said—

as head of the retrieval team I must—but I could have waited to speak to you.'

'Thank you.'

'So I'm forgiven?'

Rose nodded. 'For that, but as you said, you had every right to say what you did.'

'Good.' He settled back in his chair.

'Why did you?'

'Why did I what?'

'Why did you bawl me out then and not leave it until today?'

He shifted uncomfortably in his chair and glanced away for a moment. 'I was…well…' he fumbled, and Rose was surprised. 'I was angry with you,' he finally said.

'For causing you so much trouble? I gathered at the time that you weren't that annoyed. You even said you were proud of what I'd done.'

'I was—still am,' he corrected. He leaned forward and placed his cup on the table before standing. 'It's just that…' he started to pace '…before you started to climb up the ladder out of the hole, you seemed…well… receptive to me. Then the next minute—wham!' He slammed one clenched fist into the palm of his other hand for effect. 'I'm being given the cold shoulder. I tried to talk to you, to get you to tell me what was wrong, but, no, you just froze me out. What's worse is you've been doing it ever since.'

Rose clenched her teeth at his words. Why was he talking about this? Surely he knew she must have seen Penny kissing him. He'd looked over at her directly afterwards and had seen her staring.

'So your male ego has taken a hit, eh?' Rose sipped her tea, trying to keep her cool. 'Well, what a shame that is.'

'There you go again. What have I done, Rosie? Tell me.' He walked over and sat down beside her, relieving her of her cup. He placed it on the table and took her hands in his. 'Come on, Rosie. Let's stop playing games. We both know there's this undeniable attraction between us. I know you feel it. The kisses we've shared have told me as much. I may be a little out of practice as far as women go, but I'm not completely immune to the signals.'

Rose wrenched her hands free of his. 'Out of practice? Really? That's not what it looked like to me.'

He frowned. 'What are you talking about?'

Rose stood and walked away from him. She stared unseeingly out the window. 'You and Penny.'

'What?'

'I saw you, Dave. I saw you kiss her when you both came out the hole.'

'You saw *what*? I didn't kiss Penny.'

'Yes, you did. Ask anyone who was there last night. We all saw it.'

Dave frowned as he rose to his feet, then his face relaxed and he laughed. 'Of course.'

'I really don't think this is funny.'

'Penny kissed me when we got out of the hole. Of course!' He hit his forehead as though he should have realised all of this earlier.

'That's right, and you kissed her back.'

'No. I hugged her back. Rosie,' he said laughingly, 'You've definitely got the wrong end of the stick. I'm not involved with Penny.'

'You're not? But…Penny's obviously interested in you.'

'No. Believe me, she's not. Penny is a very happily married woman.'

'She's married?'

'Yes, has been for about ten years now. Her husband, Sam Chadwick, is Head of Orthopaedics at the Adelaide hospital. He's a good friend of mine.'

'Then why was—?'

'Why was Penny kissing me?'

Rose nodded.

Dave shrugged nonchalantly. 'She was thanking me for managing to get a certain piece of artwork Sam had fallen in love with on his last trip here. The artist didn't want to part with it but I managed to persuade him. Penny wants to give it to Sam for his birthday as a surprise.'

'Oh.' Rose felt completely foolish. She knew Dave was a smart man and that he'd realise the jealousy she'd been exhibiting meant she had strong feelings for him—stronger than she'd wanted him to know about.

Dave crossed to her side and lifted her hands, drawing her closer. 'Come here, you gorgeous woman. I've been dying to kiss you for weeks. I can't wait any more, Rosie.'

His mouth was on hers within the next instant. It wasn't a soft or exploratory kiss, as they'd previously shared, but was full of hunger and passion—from both sides. It was as though the last few weeks, working together, the misunderstanding, had all taken its toll and now they were free to hold each other in their arms and take pleasure in the kiss both of them craved.

Rose brought her hands up to his head, her fingers tangling in his hair as his mouth opened over hers once more. Her heart was starting to race out of control and the blood that was pumping at a furious rate around her body was now drumming in her ears.

'Rosie,' he whispered against her lips as he broke free, gasping for breath. 'The real you is much better than any dream.' As he pressed hot kisses on her neck, he savoured the taste of her. It was a delight he could quite easily become addicted to and he quickly pushed the knowledge to the back of his mind.

'Mmm,' Rose groaned with delight, her senses being swept away by the fresh, spicy scent that wound its way around her. As he nibbled at her earlobe, a wave of goose bumps shot down her body and she savoured the sensation.

The next time his mouth met hers, his tongue traced the inner part of her lip causing all the breath to whoosh out of her. The light-headedness made her feel faint and she clung to him as she felt her knees start to give way.

Dave held onto her firmly and she was grateful for his

support. Although, Rose reflected, the hard contours of his chest which were now pressed firmly against her breasts didn't do much to settle her racing heartbeat. She felt the warmth between them, the barrier of their clothes almost non-existent.

'Rosie,' he whispered against her mouth. She liked the way her name sounded on his lips. It was as though he really cared about her and it made her feel…treasured. Whether or not it was another illusion remained to be seen, but for this brief moment Rose decided she was going to enjoy it.

She smiled up at him.

'Hmm? What's funny?'

She shook her head. 'Nothing. I'm just happy.'

'Glad to hear it.' Then, before she could say another word, he swept her off her feet and scooped her into his arms.

'What? Oh!' Rose blushed and took the opportunity to bury her head in his neck. 'You smell so good,' she murmured as he sat them down on the sofa, Rose now settled on his lap.

'So do you, sweetheart.'

'Stop it.' She giggled.

'Really?' He lifted his lips away for a fleeting second. 'No.'

He put them back. Rose closed her eyes, savouring the sensation, trying to recall whether Julian had ever taken the time to nibble at her neck. She couldn't remember. Dave shifted and she leaned back in his embrace, turning her face upwards so their lips could meet.

She sighed, her eyes fluttering closed as the gentle pressure from his mouth relaxed her. She could have stayed here for ever, safe and secure in Dave's arms.

From the sensual haze, a noise broke through. Her mind dismissed it, telling her to concentrate on nothing but Dave and the way he was making her feel.

There it was again! That noise! Her eyes snapped open and she pulled back.

'Rosie?' His voice was sluggish and filled with repressed desire. 'What's wrong?'

'Something's outside.'

Dave listened and when the noise came again he nodded. 'Probably just a bird or a possum.'

'A possum? Here?'

He smiled as he eased her into a more upright position. 'This *is* the outback, sweetheart.' He looked at her startled expression. Her eyes, which had only moments ago been filled with passion, were now as wide as saucers. 'Want to go take a look?'

'Well…uh…I don't know. Is it safe?'

'It's a possum, Rosie, not a drop bear!'

Her eyes grew even wider. 'What's a drop bear? They sound dangerous.'

Dave laughed and helped her to her feet. 'Rosie.' He shook his head sadly. 'You've been living in the city far too long. A drop bear is a tall story that was fabricated to dupe American servicemen during the Second World War.'

'What, killer koalas?' Rose's lips twitched as she saw the humour.

'Something like that. They drop out of the trees onto the shoulders of unsuspecting tourists and hug them to death.' Dave took her hand in his and led the way to the door. 'So as you're not an unsuspecting tourist, I think we'll be safe from the drop bears.' Once outside, Dave let go of her hand and Rose felt momentarily bereft. He walked into the garden and looked up at the roof.

'Just as well it's still daylight saving or we'd be out here with torches,' Dave muttered as she joined him.

'Speak for yourself. I'd be hibernating inside, hoping it came nowhere near me.'

'Aha. Over there.' Dave pointed to the drainpipe as the

possum scuttled down it and onto the verandah. It looked at them as if to say, Go on, I dare you.

'Cute, isn't it?' Dave whispered.

'You think so?' Rose wasn't quite sure. Little furry creatures weren't really her cup of tea.

'We need to watch where it goes. If it gets into your roof, it can cause all kinds of havoc.'

'What do we do? Call the fire brigade? The ranger or…or someone?' Rose gripped tightly to Dave's arm.

'Rosie? It's just a possum. Sure, it can damage property and be a pest but it's a *possum*. That's all.'

'I'll bet its claws are sharp.'

'They are.' He turned and headed over to his ute, keeping the noise down as he went.

'Wh-what are you doing?' Rose followed him, keeping a close eye on the possum.

'We'll distract it with some food and then I'll grab it.'

'*We?* Who's this *we*? I'm not going near that thing.'

Dave frowned at her. 'It's a *possum*, Rosie.'

'So? I don't mind looking at pictures of them in a book but me and furry little things just don't go together.' There was a hint of indignation in Rose's tone but she kept her gaze trained on the possum, glancing at Dave every few seconds. 'What are you going to do with it once you've caught it?'

'Let it go in the bush. I'll put it in a cardboard box and set it free on my way home.'

'I take it you've done this before.'

'Sure,' he replied matter-of-factly. He pulled out a pair of heavy-duty gloves. 'Your dad should have a box I can use in his shed. You stay here and watch it and I'll go and get the box and some food.'

'No.' Rose was by his side in an instant.

'Rosie, we need to keep an eye on it in case it moves. We need to know where it goes or it'll end up in your roof and that's when the costs start mounting up. Possum removal is high in this neck of the woods. Look, you go inside and make some possum food and *I'll* stay and watch it.'

'Possum food? I don't know what possums eat?'

'Exactly, yet you have two eyes and can watch a possum. Can't you?' Dave took a deep breath and turned to face her. 'You'll be fine.' He kissed the tip of her nose. 'Trust me.'

Rose eyed him with suspicion. The smirk on his face told her he was enjoying this and she wasn't one hundred per cent sure he wasn't pulling her leg. 'Well…what do I do if it moves?'

'Just watch it, Rosie. Watch where it goes.'

'And if it goes into the roof?'

'Then it goes into the roof and we take it from there.' Dave peeled her hand from his arm. 'You'll be fine. I'll be back before you know it.'

Rose kept her gaze on the possum, watching in her peripheral vision as Dave walked slowly to the front door and opened it. The possum moved—only slightly—towards him and for a split second Rose thought it was going to follow him into the house. 'Drop bear,' she muttered. 'More like feral furry things.'

She was growing more and more impatient with every passing second that Dave was gone. 'Come on. Hurry up,' she whispered to herself. The possum was keeping a close eye on her as well and Rose could almost see its little mouth curving into a grin. The cheeky thing was laughing at her.

'You OK?'

'Ah-h!' Rose screamed at the sound of another woman's voice. The possum moved, shooting up the drainpipe as fast as it could. Dave came bursting through the front door and raced onto the grass.

'Rosie?' he called, and then stopped dead in his tracks. 'Evening, Mrs Fredrick.' He nodded politely. He could see Rosie was trembling and walked over to pat her shoulder.

'It's all right,' he murmured, his eyes lighting with laughter.

'You OK?' Mrs Fredrick repeated. 'She all right, Dave?' she asked when she received no reply from Rose.

'Just trying to get a possum out. I think you scared poor Rosie.'

'Oh, sorry, Rosie. Didn't mean to be sneaking up on you like that.'

'She'll be fine, Mrs Fredrick.' He patted Rose's shoulder again. 'Where did the possum go?' he asked.

Rose shivered again and pointed to the drainpipe.

Dave walked to that part of the house, his expression concerned. It quickly cleared. 'No. It's all right. He's not in the roof, I can see him.' He dashed for the door. 'Let me get the food. We'll try and coax him down. Stay with Rosie, please, Mrs Fredrick.' With that, he was gone again.

'Nasty pests, these possums,' Mrs Fredrick said. 'Cute to look at and nice in their own environment but I'll tell you, they can rip the inside of your roof to shreds in no time at all. Usually it's just because they're scared, poor things, and want to get out as much as you want them out.'

Rose shuddered. 'Please, stop talking about them.'

'You don't like them?' Mrs Fredrick's eyebrows shot upwards in surprise.

'Not particularly.' Rose could feel herself calming down a fraction but she wouldn't be completely calm until that possum was long gone from the house. It appeared that Dave was going to be her knight in shining armour yet again and she wasn't going to dispute the fact one little bit. To own the truth, she rather liked it. He'd saved her from food poisoning and now a possum. A smile touched her lips as he came out of the house, holding a plate with something on it.

'What's he got?' she asked Mrs Fredrick.

'Probably some sort of fruit, soaked with wine or some other form of alcohol. Berries are the best—raspberries in vodka is one of the best ones.'

'What? Doesn't that hurt the poor animal?'

'Ah, no. Just gets them a little drunk so we can take them back to the bush without them tearing us to shreds. Concerned about the native animals, eh? There's hope for you yet.'

'I'm a doctor, Mrs Fredrick. I care about life—even if it's not human.'

'Dave would never hurt an animal. Not unless he absolutely had to.'

'What do you mean?'

'Well, out here, if you hit a roo, for example, the kindest thing you can do to the poor animal is put it out of its misery.'

'Eww!' Rose couldn't believe she was hearing this. What on earth had possessed her to come to Broken Hill in the first place? She must have been out of her mind. She knew that spending time with her dad was paramount but he was off on his honeymoon and here she was, trying to make sure a possum didn't get into the roof. Correction—here *Dave* was, making sure a possum didn't get into the roof.

He was a good man and they were *definitely* hard to come by.

She watched as Dave held the plate up towards the possum and then placed it on the ground before heading in their direction.

'What did you give it?'

'Eh?'

'The possum food. What is it?'

'Banana and scotch.'

'Oh.'

'I take it by that reply that Mrs Fredrick has been doing some explaining?' He watched as Mrs Fredrick nodded. 'Thanks. Poor Rosie here isn't used to all these non-city things that happen.'

'Most city slickers aren't.' Mrs Fredrick shook her head sadly as she spoke.

'Ah, but Dr Partridge here has told me she's not really a city slicker. She's apparently lived in the sticks.'

'Really? Where?' Mrs Fredrick asked.

'Wagga Wagga,' Rose supplied a little absent-mindedly, as the possum started to move down the drainpipe towards the food.

Dave and her neighbour laughed. 'That's not the outback, Rosie. *This*…' He spread his arms out wide. '*This* is the outback.'

'Look, he's eating it!' She said with surprise.

'Of course he is. I make the best possum food.'

'Perhaps you should think of opening a restaurant for them, then.'

'Cute. Very cute, Rosie. All right, so now we watch him and wait.'

'How long will it be before the alcohol takes effect?'

'About ten minutes or so,' he answered, and Mrs Fredrick nodded her agreement.

'So we just stand here and wait?'

'You've got it.'

'Is the box all ready?' Mrs Fredrick asked.

'It's around the back with the gloves. I'll go through the house, around and out the back and then come along the side of the house, over here.' He pointed to where the possum was now happily munching away on the banana.

'Good boy,' Mrs Fredrick replied. 'You all right now, Rosie?' she queried again.

Rose forced a smile. 'I will be, Mrs Fredrick, as soon as that possum has gone.'

'Just as well Dave was here to help out.'

Rose could tell by her neighbour's tone that she was mightily interested in what was really going on between the two of them, and Rose wasn't quite sure what she wanted people to know.

'Just as well,' she agreed mildly. 'Has it finished yet?'

'Yep. Cleaned up the plate.' Dave preened. 'Told you I make good possum food.'

Rose laughed softly. 'I'm sure it looks good on your résumé.'

'What—the possum food itself, or the fact that I can make it?' Dave chuckled.

'Well, as you've got the situation well in hand, I'll go back inside out of the heat. Have a nice evening—the pair of you,' Mrs Fredrick said with a knowing grin, before heading off towards her own home.

'Gossip out here is more potent than any hospital I've ever worked in,' Dave said quietly, as they both watched the possum.

'So I've gathered,' Rose replied.

They waited. Side by side, swatting flies, their arms brushing occasionally. Rose could feel the heat radiating from Dave and now that they were alone again she gave her senses permission to enjoy it. She shifted slightly and their hands brushed against each other. Dave didn't move away but stayed where he was.

'I'd like nothing better than to take you in my arms and kiss you goodnight, Rosie, but I think we need to protect your reputation for a little longer—at least until your father gets home.'

'How chivalrous of you.'

'Yes, I thought so.'

'Modest, too.'

'Absolutely.' Dave chuckled. 'Look.' He pointed to where the possum was starting to slump a bit. 'I think it's almost time.' He felt for her fingers and gave them a quick squeeze. 'I'm glad I came.'

'So am I.'

'Really?'

'Yes.' Rose glanced up at him. 'And not just because of the possum.'

He smiled down at her. 'Are you free for dinner tomorrow night?'

'Yes,' she replied a little hesitantly.

'What's wrong?'

'I just don't know if I want to go out in public yet. Do you know what I mean?'

'Yes. You could come out to the farm and I could rustle you up a plate of steak and egg.'

'Mmm,' she replied, pulling a sour face. 'Sounds... appetising.'

Dave laughed but as he mentioned the farm, he remembered that Melody would be arriving in two days' time. Tomorrow night would be the last time he could go out without having to worry about making babysitting arrangements. 'Yes, we definitely need to see each other tomorrow night. We have a lot to...discuss.'

Rose was glad he wanted to see her again but was slightly puzzled by the underlying vehemence in his words. Still, he was right. They *did* have a lot to discuss and she wanted to make sure he understood that whatever this was brewing between them had to be taken at a snail's pace. She wasn't going to let her heart be swept away this time. She was going to guard it and move slowly—as she should have done previously.

'Why don't you come here for dinner?'

'The neighbours will see my ute and know I'm here.'

'They already know that much,' Rose countered. 'But at least this way we won't be under a microscope.'

'Good point. All right. I'll call by after clinic. What time are you due to finish tomorrow?'

'The urology list usually finishes on time so I should be home just after five-thirty.'

'All right. Can I bring anything?'

'Yes. Any other tools you might need in case the house is ridden with other furry creatures.'

He laughed. 'You're a good sport, Rosie Partridge. That's what I like about you.' He squeezed her hand once more before finally letting go. 'Let me get this one out of here for you.'

The possum was now about to fall asleep but even so, Rose kept her distance. Dave went through the house and soon materialised around the side where the possum was, his heavy-duty gloves on his hands, the box standing by.

With little effort or struggle, he picked the dozing possum up and placed it carefully into the box. Folding the lid over, he made sure there was enough air circulating for the animal before carrying it towards his car.

Rose scooted out of the way and watched as he put the box on the front passenger seat. 'Is that a good idea?' she called.

He turned and gave her a slow but encompassing smile. She felt her insides warm at the sight. 'Worried about me? Don't be. This little fella will be asleep for the next hour at least. If I put him in the back and the box lid flies open, he might be attacked by a predator. I'll take care of him, Rosie.'

'Oh. OK. See you tomorrow.'

'Sleep sweet, Rosie.'

'You, too,' she responded. Rose turned away and walked to the front door but couldn't resist turning to watch him drive away. He tooted the horn and stuck his arm out the open window to wave. She waved back, a silly schoolgirl grin on her face.

Rose opened the door and, out of curiosity, glanced over to Mrs Fredrick's house. As she did, she saw the lace curtains fall back into place. She shook her head, surprised to find that she didn't really mind all that much. Dave made her happy and that was something she hadn't experienced in a long time.

The instant she stepped inside, the phone rang. She reached for the receiver, hoping it wasn't the hospital with an emergency.

'Hello, princess,' her father's deep voice boomed down the line. 'How are things going?'

'Oh, fine, Dad. Just fine—now.'

'What's been going on, Rosie?' She told him about the possum and how Dave had taken care of the situation. 'Just as well he was there, then,' her father said, and she noted a strangeness in his tone.

'Yes, it was.'

'Has he…you know…stopped by before?'

Rose frowned. 'Only when I had food poisoning, but I've already told you about that. Why do you want to know?'

'I think young Dave has taken a shine to you,' her father said.

Her frown changed to a smile. 'You think so?'

'Rosie.' His tone was even more curious. 'What aren't you telling me?'

'A lot of things, Dad. How's Beverley?'

'Beautiful.' Her father sighed like a man in love should. 'Simply beautiful.'

Wanting to get him off the topic of Dave and herself, Rose asked, 'So what have you been doing today? Lazing around a swimming pool, sipping cocktails?'

Reg chuckled. 'Something like that.' He then launched into a full-scale account of what they'd been doing since he'd last spoken to Rose, and while he was talking, she fixed herself some dinner, stretching the cord of the phone as far as she could. Over half an hour later, she rang off and sat down to eat her food. No sooner had she put the first forkful in her mouth than the phone rang again.

'Dr Partridge.'

'Rosie! Thank goodness.' The sound of Dave's voice warmed her right down to her toes and she forgot all about her dinner. 'I was starting to get concerned when I couldn't get through. Had you accidentally knocked the receiver off the hook?'

'No. My father called.'

'They're enjoying themselves, I hope?'

'Yes.'

'Listen, I wanted to let you know that the possum in question is now safe and back in its natural habitat.'

'And you made sure he was well hidden so he wouldn't be attacked by a dingo or something?'

'Absolutely.'

'Good.'

Dave laughed. 'You really are a mixture, aren't you?'

'A mixture of what?' she asked cautiously.

'You aren't the adventurous type at all yet your natural concern shows that you care.'

'So?' She was defensive now.

'I'm not criticising you, Rosie. I'm saying I like it. My ex-wife didn't like to venture out of her comfort zone and couldn't care less about anyone who did.'

Rose didn't miss the bitterness in his tone. 'I know what you mean,' she replied, thinking of Julian.

'Been there, experienced that?' he queried lightly.

'Yes.' Her voice was soft.

'Did he hurt you?'

'If you mean did he break my heart? I thought he had but now I'm not so sure.' If Dave had asked her that question one month ago, she would have answered in the affirmative. After tonight, with Dave's kind and caring attitude, Rose knew Julian hadn't broken her heart as she was still able to feel. 'I think he dented my ego more,' she acknowledged honestly.

'I know how that feels.' He laughed without humour.

'How about you? Did your ex-wife break your heart?'

'She gutted me from the inside, twisted me into knots and discarded me without a thought.'

'Really? When? Sorry, I didn't mean to pry, it's just that you seem so…so…well, together.'

'We divorced over six years ago, Rosie. Time is a great healer of wounds. I'm not so sure about anger but wounds—definitely.'

'You don't like her?'

'No. I can't say she's one of my favourite people.'

'Regrets?'

'We all have them, sweetheart.'

'Bitterness?'

'No. I've forgiven Mags for hurting me and for the way she disrespected our marriage vows.'

Rose grasped his meaning quickly and as she knew Dave was bound to a life of chivalry, he'd also be bound to monogamy as well.

'That doesn't mean I like her or want to spend time with her,' he added.

'Do you see her often?'

'No, but I speak to her a few times a year.'

'Why?' Rose wasn't too sure whether she should have asked the question but felt if ever she was going to pry into Dave's past, now was the time. He'd been the one to open the conversation of past relationships. Besides, if he didn't want to answer, she was sure he'd say so.

'Divorce is never easy when there's a child involved.' As Dave said the words, he held his breath. There, it was out. Rosie now knew he had a child. There was silence on the other end of the phone and he closed his eyes as he waited for her to speak. After seeing how she'd reacted with young Joe the other week, he wasn't too sure how she'd receive this news. 'Kids and I just don't mix.' That's what she'd said.

'You have a child?' she said finally, unable to believe it. A divorced man with a family. Warning bells sounded. It was on her list—her list of what to avoid at all costs—yet she was finding it increasingly difficult to adhere to *that* list. Why hadn't she heard anything about this at the hospital? Probably, she reminded herself, because she didn't listen to gossip.

'I have one child. Melody is her name and she's six years old.'

CHAPTER EIGHT

'Six?' Rose felt herself start to tremble a bit. Kids made her uncomfortable. She wasn't good with them. She was just like her mother—hopeless with children. She pushed the thoughts aside roughly. 'But I thought you'd been divorced for—' She cut herself off. 'I'm sorry, Dave. It's really none of my business.'

'I think it is, Rosie. I like you. I want to pursue a relationship with you. I don't know where it will lead but there it is, nevertheless. So let's get the past out into the open so we can move forward.' She was silent again. 'Rosie? I didn't mean to dump all of this on you straight away but isn't it better that we find things out now, rather than later? After you thinking I was involved with Penny, I don't want any other misunderstandings to surface.'

Rose listened to what he said, agreeing with him. 'Is this what you wanted to talk about tomorrow night?'

'Something like that.'

'Melody,' she said softly. 'Nice name.'

'She's a nice girl.'

She could tell Dave was smiling. He obviously thought the world of his daughter and it improved her opinion of him.

'Mags chose the name. She's the type of woman who has to have control over everything and thought a child would fit nicely into her new life. After all, a few of her friends had babies and they made it sound so special and unique. It was like a red flag to a bull and she couldn't resist.

'The conception happened during our last attempt to reconcile our marriage. Little did I know that she'd planned the entire thing.' Dave shook his head as he remembered the way Mags had used him. 'I woke up one morning and she was gone. No note. No phone call. No nothing. I contacted the solicitor, as that was the only number I had to track her down, and he informed me that Margaret saw no further need to remain in the relationship and that divorce proceedings would commence once the proper procedures had been satisfied.'

'But what about the baby?'

'She told me I was the father—after Melody's birth. I didn't even see my daughter until she was eight weeks old. By then Mags had realised that motherhood wasn't all it was cracked up to be. She hired a nanny, fought and won custody and that was that.'

'Can you be sure...? What I mean is... Is she—?'

'Is she mine? Yes. I had tests done to prove it and she's mine all right.'

Rose didn't miss the vehemence in his words. 'How often do you see her?'

'Quite a lot. I miss her like crazy but a broken marriage is just a part of our lives.'

'Must be rough, being so far away from her.'

'It is.'

'I presume they're in Sydney?'

'That's right.'

'So do you go there or does your daughter come here?'

'Both. It all depends. In fact...' Dave paused for a moment and took a deep breath '...she's coming on Thursday.'

'Thursday? *This* Thursday?'

'Yes.'

'But that's in two days' time.' Rose couldn't believe what she was hearing. She pulled the receiver away from her ear and stared at it. Who was this man? It brought back the reality that she really knew nothing about him—except for the uncharacteristic physical attraction that had flared up between them.

'I know. I was going to fly to Sydney and get her but Mags is sending her here with the current nanny.'

Rose had no idea what to say. He was divorced. He had a daughter—a daughter who was coming to town. She opened and closed her mouth like a goldfish—completely stunned by what he was saying.

'Rosie?' he said when she didn't respond. 'I know this is a lot but, as I said, I want it all out in the open.'

'How...how long will she be here for?'

He cleared his throat. 'For ever—hopefully.'

'What?'

'That is if Mags doesn't change her mind.'

'Dave, this is a lot for me to deal with.'

'I know and, fair dinkum, Rosie, I'm sorry,' he said softly, knowing he was only causing her more confusion. 'I know this is a lot for you to handle, especially as we've only just started...whatever this is that's sprung up between us. The best advice I could probably give you is to keep well away from me, but that's not what I want.'

'Why?'

'Because you're the first woman I've been remotely interested in for the last six years.'

Rose didn't know what to say. This time, though, her silence was due to overwhelming surprise. He liked her. He *really* liked her. Rose felt her insides turn to mush. He'd seen her when she'd been tired and rude, sick, gripped with fear and he *still* liked her.

'Rosie?'

'Hmm? Uh...thank you. That's really nice of you to say that but, um...that's not what I meant when I asked why.'

'What did you mean, then?'

'Why will your daughter be staying for good?'

'Because Mags is getting married again. Her wedding is this Saturday and she can't be bothered having Mel around any longer.'

'That's horrible.' Rose wasn't overly confident with

children but she knew this was a terrible thing to do to a child. 'So you offered to take her, naturally.'

'Actually, Mags was planning to put her into boarding school.'

'What? She's six years old.'

Dave smiled. Rosie really was on his wavelength. 'My sentiments exactly.'

'So you're going to apply for full custody?'

'Yes. When I told Mags I wanted custody of Mel, she told me she'd already started proceedings. The papers have been drawn up. They were supposed to have arrived to-night but obviously the courier got lost. Hopefully, I'll get them tomorrow but the waiting is starting to tear me apart. I wasn't planning on doing anything until Melody arrived but it appears Mags had other plans. Still, she has been known to change her mind in the past so until I get those papers it isn't going to be an easy ride.'

'How long are they planning to honeymoon?'

'Julian—her new husband-to-be—is in the computer business and has plans to work overseas. This is all according to Mags, so who knows how much of it is true?'

Rose almost fell off her chair. Her dinner was completely forgotten as Dave's words almost paralysed her. 'Did…did you say Julian?' Her voice was barely audible. She bit her lower lip, realising belatedly that it was trembling.

'That's right.' He heard her gasp and the tone of her voice made him sit up straighter—aware that something wasn't right. 'What's wrong? Rosie?'

'Julian Moncrief?' she whispered.

'You *know* him?'

'I was engaged to him three months ago.'

That certainly explained a lot. Dave replaced the receiver in the cradle after Rosie had quickly said she'd better go. Her tone had been full of distraught emotion and when he'd offered to come back around, she'd been adamant in her refusal. He didn't blame her. No one wanted to have their soul bared to a relative stranger like himself.

No. He and Rosie *weren't* strangers. Sure, there were things they didn't know about each other but he refused to say they were strangers. Tonight had changed that for good.

Dave stalked over to the fridge and grabbed a beer, taking it out onto the verandah. He leaned against the rail. Knowing that Julian had been a part of Rosie's past explained a lot about the woman herself. He wouldn't blame her if she avoided him simply because he was divorced. Julian had been divorced—twice.

Dave raised the beer to his lips. Knowing the type of person Julian was, he could guess how that man had behaved towards Rosie, but he knew how to fix it. He needed to show her that he wasn't like that two-timing swine. He might be divorced—just like Julian was. He might have one child—Julian had three. But, unlike Julian, he was trustworthy and wanted to be a part of his daughter's life. Julian had written off his children years ago.

There was also the problem that Rosie felt uncomfortable around children. He frowned, unsure whether he should be concerned about that. There was obviously a reason why Rosie was like this.

How could Reg have let his daughter grow up without playing with other kids? And what had happened to her mother? All he knew about Reg was that he had been divorced, never spoke about his ex-wife and had one child. Perhaps Rose's parents' divorce had emotionally scarred her in some way.

There were too many unanswered questions and it intrigued him more. A primitive protective urge came over him when he thought about Rosie. He'd helped her through food poisoning—and she'd let him. He'd helped her with her mild claustrophobia—and she'd let him. He'd helped her with the possum—and she'd let him. Yet for all that, she was still a woman who could stand on her own two feet and she'd proved that by the way she'd come through each of those situations. Everyone needed help at some point in their lives and it was refreshing to find that Rosie wasn't adverse to allowing others to help her.

Would she let him help her relax around children?

Rose finally threw back the bedcovers in disgust and headed to the shower as the clock ticked over to six a.m. What was the point of lying in bed any longer when she'd only been pretending to sleep?

She sighed as she stepped into the shower stall and turned her face up to the spray, hoping the soothing warm water would do something to relax her. 'Not good, waking up this agitated,' she mumbled to herself. She'd thought that after those wonderful kisses from Dave she might have managed a better night's sleep. 'And then he phoned.' Rose shook her head.

She had mixed emotions about the news of Julian's wedding. It was just so typical of him. He'd been married and divorced twice when she'd met him. Within two months of them starting to date, he'd proposed and, like a complete idiot, she'd been swept away by his sophistication and charm and had instantly accepted.

Then she'd discovered the truth about him. He'd started criticising the way she'd dressed and the long hours she'd spent at the hospital. He'd also told her that once they were married, he expected her to give up her career and move if he needed to move.

Being in the computer business, he needed to be mobile, he'd told her. It was important to him to have a wife who'd make a good hostess, and with her classic looks and poise, he'd decided she fitted the bill.

'He won't be faithful to you,' his first wife had told her and the second wife had confirmed. When Julian had made excuses about working late and cancelling their dinner reservations, she'd begun to suspect. Her suspicions had been confirmed when she'd followed him one evening and found he'd been meeting another woman—a woman she'd discovered was called Margaret.

When Rose had next spoken to his first wife, she'd confirmed that Margaret was a long-standing favourite of Julian's and that, regardless of who he'd been married to, Margaret had always been in the wings.

Now Rose discovered that this Margaret woman was Dave's ex-wife! He'd implied that she'd cheated on him—obviously with Julian. She shook her head, snapping herself out of the thoughts that had been spinning around all night long, and reached for the shampoo.

'Work. Concentrate on work. Julian is out of your life. You've moved on. Dave is nice. Dave likes you and Dave appears to be honest.' Rose washed her hair vigorously, speaking her thoughts out loud. 'Dave is also divorced and the father of one. You shouldn't get involved with him. He's all wrong for you. Then again, what man is really honest? Do they even exist?' She only knew one man who was honest and he'd been duped himself by a dishonest woman. 'Seems to work both ways, Dad,' she told the shower wall, and sighed heavily.

Dave had a child. This was something Rose hadn't counted on. She'd always wondered whether she was like her mother deep down inside—her mother who'd abandoned her father and herself. Rose had been just over three years old when her mother had left and when she'd questioned her father about it later, he'd said that her mother's excuse had been that she 'wasn't the maternal type'.

Her father had wanted children and her mother had obliged but had hated every minute of it. One day, she'd upped and left and Rose had never seen or heard from her again. A part of her had always been curious and her father, bless him, had answered all her questions lovingly and honestly, showing her photographs of the woman she now looked almost identical to.

Was she identical in behaviour as well? Rose had never had much to do with children in the past and she'd tried never to think about if she'd ever be a mother herself. Having grown up without one, she had no idea how they were supposed to behave. Her mother's behaviour had been appalling—according to her father—and he'd blamed himself for the way Rosie had been treated.

'Agh! Stop it,' she told herself as she switched off the taps.

After her shower, Rose decided she needed a good breakfast. 'Surely that will help improve my mood.'

The phone rang as she was in the middle of sautéing some onions for the frittata she was planning to make. She glanced at the clock as she snatched it up. At six-thirty, it could only be the hospital.

'Dr Partridge.'

'Good morning, my sweet Rosie. I just needed to hear your voice,' Dave said. His rich, deep voice washed over her and she momentarily closed her eyes, savouring the feeling.

'There you go. You've heard it. What are you doing up so early?'

'Early? I'm always up at six, sometimes earlier if Mick needs help with things. Besides,' he added in a softer tone, 'I couldn't sleep. I was worried about you.'

Rose smiled. 'Well, thank you for worrying about me, but I'm fine. Hang on a minute.' She stretched the phone cord over towards the stove. 'Don't want the onions to burn.'

'What are you cooking? Are you as good as your father?'

'I'm making breakfast frittata and, no, I'm not as good as my father...but he taught me everything I know,' she added.

'Right. Breakfast at your house. See you soon.'

Rose laughed, loving the way a few minutes talking to him had put her in a better mood. 'Dave, you can't come around for breakfast. What will the neighbours think?' It was then she heard the 'disconnected' signal. 'Dave?'

He'd hung up on her. What a cheek! 'Oh, no,' she said as she replaced the receiver. 'He's coming around!'

Rose wasn't sure what to do first. She was thankful that she'd showered and was presentably dressed, although, with Dave's easygoing nature, she doubted whether that would be of any importance to him. He *was* so different from Julian. He might be divorced, he might have a child, but he was still very different. At times like these, she had no idea how to behave.

Should she be the cool, calm sophisticate who was used to men popping in for breakfast? Should she be hard and unyielding, refusing to let him in when he arrived? 'Just concentrate on the cooking or all he's going to be turning up for is burnt offerings,' she told herself firmly.

By the time she heard his vehicle, breakfast was ready but she was nowhere near the same. What if one of the neighbours saw him? What if they thought his ute had been parked out front all night long?

What was going to happen when they saw each other again? Was it going to be awkward? No. Not with Dave. He wouldn't let it be awkward. She'd only ever had polite, predictable relationships, she realised with a start. The men she'd dated before Julian had all been professionals. Polished. Seemingly perfect. Perhaps that's what had been missing from her life? A bit of spontaneity. With Dave, she had no idea whether she was coming or going. It was a strange but not unpleasant feeling and right now, although her stomach was alive with butterflies at the thought of seeing him again, she was looking forward to it at the same time.

His coming would bring the gossips out in force but she knew there really wasn't anything she could do about the rumour mill of Broken Hill. Right now, she had a hungry man knocking loudly at her front door.

'I'm coming,' she called a little impatiently when his knocking didn't stop. She wrenched open the door and gasped with surprise as he burst through, swept her into his arms and kicked the door shut in one swift motion. Before she could say anything else, his lips were on hers, devouring them hungrily.

Rose wasn't complaining. The same urge had built within her from the moment he'd left yesterday evening and she moaned with delight as his arms tightened around her back, moulding her body to his.

Her breathing was ragged, matching his. Her body was on fire, liquid heat spreading throughout her body. How did he manage to fuel such an uncharacteristic response in her with a few simple kisses? They weren't simple, she corrected. They were the most passionate kisses she'd ever received in her life—and she *loved* them.

Finally, his mouth broke free from hers. 'You taste and smell delicious.'

Rose smiled shyly up at him. 'That's the food, silly.'

'No.' Dave was serious as he looked down into her up-turned face. 'You are one very beautiful woman, Rosie Partridge, and don't let anyone tell you differently.' He kissed her again before letting her go and taking two big steps away. 'If I don't put some distance between us, breakfast will be the last thing we'll be concentrating on this morning.'

Rose felt herself blushing and looked way. 'Is that so?' She worked hard to inject a haughty note into her tone but wasn't sure she'd succeeded. 'How do you know I'd let you do anything other than kiss me or eat the food I've cooked?' She turned away from him and headed into the kitchen.

'I should hope you wouldn't.' He chuckled as he followed her. 'I just love it when you come across all prim and proper like that.' He grabbed her from behind and held her back against his chest. He bent and nibbled at her earlobe, which sent a wave of goose bumps spreading down one side of her body. 'All I meant,' he whispered seductively, 'is that you're so…addictive, I doubt I'll ever be able to get enough of you.'

'I knew what you meant,' she told him, not entirely sure she wanted to pull away. Even if she did, would her own legs support her? 'Let's eat. I don't want you to be late for ward round. Then people will *really* start asking questions.'

'So nice to be with a woman who understands my job.' Dave reluctantly let her go and sat down on a stool.

'Your ex-wife didn't?' Rose concentrated on making sure everything was ready and pulled the frittata from beneath the grill.

'No. Mags resented my work as a doctor.'

'Then why did she marry you?'

'Good question. Apparently, it was considered fashionable to be a doctor's wife.'

'How did you meet?' She served the food up and put a plate in front of him.

'Looks and smells delicious,' he said, and took one of her hands in his. Slowly, he raised it to his lips and pressed a light kiss on her knuckles. Rose smiled, a little confused but flattered all the same. 'Thanks for letting me in.'

'How could I not?' She laughed. 'If I hadn't, I'm sure you would have knocked the door down.'

Dave laughed, before taking a bite. 'Probably. Mmm, this is great! What's in it?'

She wondered whether he was trying to avoid answering the question and decided she'd let him—for the moment. If he wanted to pursue a relationship with her, then she had the right to ask him personal questions. 'Potato, bacon, eggs, onion and sun-dried tomato—oh, and some herbs.'

'It's delicious. You *are* as good a cook as your father.'

'Thank you for saying so, even if I don't agree. I've had a lifetime of eating his cooking and somehow it always tastes better than anything I ever make. Still, he would always encourage me.'

'And that's the point. To try new things.' Dave swallowed his mouthful and looked at her, his gaze tearing a path directly to her soul.

'Is that what you're doing with me?' she asked softly. 'Trying something new?'

His fork clattered to his plate and he reached for her hand again. 'Rosie, I would never intentionally hurt you but, yes, I guess I am trying to try something new—if that makes sense. As I said, I haven't been involved with a woman since Mags so, in essence, I *am* trying something new. I'm trying to see whether this natural chemistry that exists between us is just physical or something more.'

'And if it *is* just physical?'

'We'll cross that bridge when we come to it.'

She retrieved her hand. 'That's not good enough, Dave.' Rose took a bite of her breakfast. She forced herself to chew calmly and swallow, before elaborating. 'It's only been three months since Julian broke off the engagement. You've had six years to recover from your busted relationship.'

Dave nodded. 'The situation with Julian has made you question your own judgement.'

'Yes.'

'That never goes away, Rosie. I'm *still* questioning my judgement. We should all question our judgement. It's the only way we learn. In our profession, we've learned what we need to do to save people's lives. It's our experience that helps us through in difficult times but we still question things. If we didn't and the patient wasn't a textbook case, they'd probably die. It's part of life, it's part of any relationship. I think the real problem is that for a while there we *stopped* questioning our judgement.'

He started eating again. 'You want to know how I met Mags?'

Rose didn't reply, she just forked in another mouthful and waited. If he wanted to tell her, she would listen, but she wouldn't have initially asked the question if she didn't want to know.

'She was a patient of mine. She had a badly busted appendix which perforated on the table. She was extremely ill for a while but thankfully she recovered. Once she was discharged from my care, she kept stopping by the hospital to see me. The rest, as they say, is history. How about you and Julian?'

Rose took a sip of her orange juice. 'He was supplying the hospital with new computers and devising a special program for the secretaries to use. We kept bumping into each other in the staff cafeteria and one day we sat together and had lunch. The next day, he took me out to lunch and the next thing I knew he was proposing and I'd accepted.'

'Fast.' He nodded again. 'That's the way Julian works.'

'So I gather.'

'Are you hurt that he's found someone else so soon?'

'No. His previous wives told me all about Margaret. Apparently he's been seeing her on and off for years.'

'You know his ex-wives?'

'Yes. They started calling me after our engagement was announced. At first I thought they were being vindictive— at least that's what Julian had said when I told him they'd been calling. Then I realised they were just trying to save me from what they'd been through.'

'He was at my wedding. A friend of Mags's. He was married to his first wife then. She seemed nice but I didn't see her again. Julian's the type of man who needs a pretty woman at his side who'll put up with his many indiscretions. She'll be the apple of his eye so long as she does what he wants.'

'You think Margaret fits the bill?'

He shrugged. 'They're too much alike. Both like to play the field. Both are manipulative. Good luck to them. I truly don't care. So long as I get custody of Mel, I'll be happy.'

At the mention of his daughter, Rose swallowed suddenly and started coughing. Dave patted her on the back. 'OK?'

She had a quick drink and nodded.

'I mention my daughter and you start to choke. Is

Melody going to be a problem between us?' His tone was quiet yet firm.

'She could be. I've told you, Dave. I'm just not comfortable around children.'

'Why?'

'Because that's the way I am,' she replied forcefully.

'What happened?' He gazed into her eyes and she felt as though he were touching her soul. She shivered and crossed her arms in front. 'Tell me, Rosie.'

'I…I can't,' she whispered. 'It will upset me for the rest of the day and I…I can't afford to have that happen.'

He exhaled deeply and raked his fingers through his hair. 'I see.' He looked at his now empty plate. 'That was delicious. Thank you for allowing me to come over for breakfast.' He stood and carried his plate and utensils to the dishwasher and stacked them inside.

'You're leaving?'

He groaned softly. 'I don't know what to do, Rosie. I think perhaps it's best if I did leave, for the moment.'

'Why? Are you going to say something you might regret?'

'No. It's not that. In fact, I don't know what it is. That's the truth. We seem to be going around in circles. I want to be with you and I think you want to be with me—and I don't mean that in a physical sense.'

'Ah, so you don't think what's happening between us is just physical,' she stated.

'I've never met anyone like you before, Rosie.' He came to stand behind her and placed his hands on her shoulders, kneading gently. 'You're direct, straightforward, yet you can be as cool as an ice queen when it suits you.'

'Protection,' she murmured as she closed her eyes, not only enjoying the massage but his closeness as well.

'I know. We all have our barriers. Just like the echidna. We put up our spikes whenever we're being attacked.'

'What are your barriers, Dave? Am I going to be able to break through them?'

'Do you want to break through them?' he countered quietly.

'I...I don't know.' He stopped massaging but didn't remove his hands so the warmth was still spreading down her shoulders and flooding deep within her. Her blood pumped faster around her body; her pulse mimicked the pace. 'Things have just been happening too fast but, try as I might, I just can't seem to slow them down.'

He chuckled. 'Especially when I'm barging in here, inviting myself to breakfast.'

'Did you hear me strenuously objecting?'

'Did I give you time?' He bent his head and nuzzled her neck. 'You smell incredible.' He placed light kisses on her skin and Rose closed her eyes, letting her head rest back against him. She parted her lips as her breathing increased, savouring the sensations he was evoking deep within her. 'I'm having such a hard time keeping my hands off you, Rosie. Now, that's definitely physical.'

Rose swallowed. 'I know what you mean.' She turned in his arms to face him and, placing her hands on either side of his face, brought his lips down to meet her own. She sighed with longing as he moved his mouth over hers. This was the only time she felt complete. When she was with Dave and he was kissing her. Reality seemed suspended and she wished she could live in the moment for ever.

'Sweetheart,' he groaned a few minutes later as he eased back but didn't let her go. 'It's almost half past seven and I'm due at the hospital for ward round soon.'

Rose nodded. 'So where do we go from here, Dave?'

'I'm not sure, Rosie. We'll just have to figure it out as we go along.' He bent his head and kissed her quickly. 'Do you need help cleaning up here?'

'No. I'll put it all in the dishwasher with the dishes from last night and switch it on before I go.'

'When are you leaving?'

'In about two minutes. It's Wednesday—baby day.'

'How many C-sections are there this morning?' He took a few steps away and put his hands in his shorts pockets as though he was having a hard time keeping his hands off her.

'I think there's two.'

'All right. Well, you have fun. Are we still on for dinner tonight?'

'Sure.'

'We'll talk more then.' Still keeping his hands where they were, he leaned forward again and kissed her once more. 'Sorry,' he said with that lopsided grin that always melted her heart. 'I told you I find you irresistible.'

Rose laughed. 'Thanks for stopping by.'

'I'll see myself out.'

Rose turned her attention to the sink, determined to get to the hospital as soon as possible. The sooner she got this day under way, the sooner it would be time for dinner. Dinner with Dave.

CHAPTER NINE

THE rest of the day passed in a blur as Dave anxiously counted the minutes until he would be alone with Rosie again. He hadn't been lying when he'd told her she was addictive and the more he saw of her, the harder he felt himself falling.

'What's the matter with you?' Sadie quizzed as she showed in his last patient. 'You've been as jumpy as a red roo all day long.'

'Probably getting excited about seeing his little girl to-morrow,' the patient supplied.

'Good point,' Sadie remarked, and Dave thought it safer just to smile and let them think what they wanted.

'How old is she now, Dave?' his patient asked, and she wasn't the first one to have asked that question during the course of the day. He smiled politely and murmured the correct responses, all the while trying to squash his impatience for the day to be over.

Finally, the patient was finished and as he sat down to write up the notes he heard footsteps coming down the corridor. 'What now?' he grumbled quietly. The polite smile he'd pasted onto his face changed to one of relief and genuine surprise as Rosie walked into his room and sat down opposite him.

'What a day.' She sighed.

'I know what you mean. How are you holding up?' He finished writing and closed the case notes with finality. His clinic was done!

'Nothing a good night's sleep wouldn't fix, but I don't seem to be having many of them.'

'Ah, now, that's a lie. I know for a fact that you had a

decent sleep the night you got food poisoning—well, once you stopped vomiting.'

'Yuck!' Rose grimaced and covered her face with her hands. 'Don't remind me. I must have looked awful.'

Dave stood and came around the desk to crouch down beside her chair. 'You looked amazing.'

'Amazingly awful,' she said on a laugh.

'No. Amazingly stunning,' he whispered, and the mood between them instantly changed to one of sensual delight. Dave edged in closer and raised one hand to caress her cheek. When her eyelids fluttered closed at the slight contact, that was when his restraint snapped.

'I need to kiss you,' he whispered hoarsely, his tone deep with desire.

'Ditto,' she replied, and shifted so their impatient lips could meet. She sighed into his embrace and leaned a little too heavily towards him.

'Whoa. Whoa—hang on, I'm…' Tightening his grip around her, hoping it would steady him, Dave lost his balance completely and toppled backwards, bringing Rose with him. 'Ugh!' She landed on top of him, their legs sprawled and tangled together. She started to shake. 'Rosie?' No reply. 'Rosie? Are you all right?'

Rose lifted her head, tears streaming down her face.

'Where are you hurt?' he asked instantly, not sure whether he should move her off him or not.

Rose gasped for breath and that was when he realised she wasn't crying at all but laughing instead. He relaxed back onto the floor. 'Oh! The look on your face as you went was priceless,' she said between giggles. 'Thank you, I needed that.' And she reached up and kissed him on the lips.

'Oh, fair dinkum, Dave Dunbar,' Sadie spluttered from the doorway. 'Is *this* the girlie who's had you in a tailspin all day long?'

'Uh, *now* someone calls you by your surname!' Rose mumbled in his ear, which had him chuckling. She looked up, unable to believe they'd been caught in such a compromising position. Sadie glared down at both of them, especially at her. Slowly, they untangled themselves and stood on their feet.

'Really, Dave, I expected better of you. Besides, I thought you didn't like blondes.'

'Sadie.' His voice held a hint of warning. 'You may have known me since I was born but that doesn't mean you know what I like and don't like.'

'But *she* was a blonde.'

'Yes. You're correct. *Margaret* was a blonde and so is Rosie, but apart from hair colour they are nothing alike.'

'Fine.'

Rose thought Sadie was obviously smart enough to know when to pick fights with Dave and when not to. 'I came down to tell you that you're both needed for an emergency. Hazel Fredrick is being brought in with abdominal pains.'

'Let's go, then.' He reached for Rose's hand and together they walked out.

'She wasn't too happy, was she?' Rose risked a glance over her shoulder to find Sadie glaring at her.

'Do you think I really care what Sadie or anyone else in this town thinks of whom I choose to date?'

'Uh…I don't know. Do you?'

He opened the door to the stairwell and waited for her to go first. 'No.' Their footsteps echoed as they headed down to A and E. 'Who I choose to spend time with is my business and no one else's.'

'Glad to hear it. Julian was always more concerned about what other people thought.' She went to pull open the door that led to A and E but he stopped her. He leaned in close, one hand still up against the door.

'I'm not Julian.' His tone was firm and Rose nodded. Dave bent his head and claimed her lips, his kiss more possessive than before. When he pulled back, he took her hand in his, opened the door and led her through the A and E department. People's heads turned and whispers broke out as he led her to the tearoom.

'I figured it was OK to hold your hand in public now,' he stated with a crooked smile. 'No doubt Sadie had already phoned her juicy bit of gossip around the hospital before we reached the bottom of the stairwell.'

'No doubt.' Rose shrugged. 'Nothing to be done about it now.'

'So much for trying to save your reputation.'

She smiled tiredly back at him. 'So much for dinner,' she said.

'You're right,' he groaned. 'At least you understand.'

'I'm not Margaret.'

'*Touché!*' Dave laughed. They heard the ambulance sirens and headed out to triage. 'Good evening, Mrs Fredrick,' he said as she was wheeled in to treatment room two. 'I gather you're not feeling the best.'

'Can't say I am, Dave.'

'Tell me where it hurts.'

While Dave examined Mrs Fredrick, Rose checked the ambulance notes to see what pain relief she'd already been given.

'I'd like to do an ultrasound,' Dave told his patient once he'd finished examining her. 'I think it might be gallstones and the ultrasound will confirm it.'

'Do I need an operation?' Mrs Fredrick asked, her tone worried.

'Hopefully not. Nowadays, we use a technique called lithotripsy. It's where ultrasonic shock waves shatter the stones. Once that's done, they'll be passed naturally into the bile duct and then the bowel. First of all, though, let's confirm that it is gallstones which are giving you this pain.'

Dave's diagnosis turned out to be spot on and once Mrs Fredrick's treatment had been completed, they left her to rest. Rose ensured she had sufficient medication authorised to get her through the night.

'Now we just wait and see if the stones pass by themselves. I'll be surprised if they don't.' Dave placed his arm about her shoulders as they walked out to the car park. 'Hungry?'

'Surprisingly not, but if you want something, I guess I can make us a bite of dinner.'

'I don't expect you to cook for me,' he told her as they came to stand by her car.

'I'm like my dad. Cooking relaxes me.'

'Well, in that case…' He laughed and gathered her closer, noticing the tired lines around her eyes. 'Actually, sweetheart, it's getting late and I've got a busy day tomorrow, getting things ready for when Mel and the nanny arrive.'

'Oh, yeah. That's tomorrow.' The smile disappeared from her face and her voice became flat. Why did everything have to become so complicated? It didn't matter how hard she worked to block out the fact that Dave had a daughter, it never quite worked. Reality had a way of intruding.

'Do you ever want to have any?' He kept his eyes focused on hers.

Rose swallowed nervously. 'Children?'

He nodded.

'Truthfully, Dave…I don't know.'

'I see.'

'Do you? Everything's just happened so fast, Dave. You only really kissed me properly last night. Then you tell me you have a child, and not only that but she's coming to live with you. The next bombshell was that my ex-fiancé is marrying your ex-wife. That's quite a lot to deal with in such a short space of time.'

'I know, Rosie.' He kissed her forehead and held her tight. They stood like that for a few minutes before Rose edged away.

'I don't like being rushed and right now that's exactly how I feel. Julian rushed me and it ended in pain—and before you say anything,' she continued when he opened his mouth, 'I know you're not Julian. You're very different from him. You're caring and considerate and chivalrous and…and extremely sexy, but it's as though you need to get our relationship, whatever that may be, onto a more even footing before your daughter arrives tomorrow.' She took a breath. 'I'm sorry, Dave, but I just don't feel it's possible. You're going to need to spend time with Melody when she arrives to make her feel more comfortable with the changes happening in her life. I understand this so I think, perhaps, that we should just…you know, cool it for a while.'

He was silent for a few minutes and she wondered whether she'd lost even a remote chance of a relationship with him. 'Dave,' she said softly, 'I didn't mean to go on like that. I'm telling you how I feel. I'm being honest. Isn't that what you wanted?'

'Yes.' He nodded. 'It's just not as easy to deal with as I'd anticipated.'

'What? Me not being completely comfortable with things?'

'No. A woman who actually communicates.'

She smiled. 'I could say the same about you.'

'I've heard what you've said, Rosie, and I respect it, but I can't stop seeing you. I'm at the stage that if I *don't* see you, I feel like I'm going to go insane. You're right about Mel, though. I do need to spend time with her but there's no reason why the three of us couldn't do it together.' He felt her tense beneath his arms but went on. 'I'm going to move from the farm and get a place in town. I've already looked at a few places but wanted Mel to help me choose. After all, she'll be living there, too.'

'What about the papers—from Margaret?'

'They came this morning. My solicitor's looked at them and it appears everything is going to go through uncontested and smoothly. With Mags getting married on Saturday and then leaving the country, things are moving like the proverbial freight train, but there's nothing else to do.'

Dave raised her chin slowly until their gazes met. 'I need to be with you, Rosie.' He placed a kiss on her lips. 'You're very special to me.' He kissed her again. 'I know this has been incredibly fast but...' he shrugged '...it's just the way things have turned out.' He kissed her once more before leaning his forehead against hers.

'I know Julian probably belittled your existence but don't believe anything that creep said. Cutting people down is the only way he can make himself look big. I've seen him do it, Rosie, and you're way beyond him. Believe me when I say you're a lovely person—inside and out. I've seen you with patients, I've seen you overcome your fears. You're strong and independent. It may not feel that way but you are. You took the chance to come here to Broken Hill, to give yourself a fresh start and to spend more time with your father. That tells me so much about the real you, Rosie.

This time, when he kissed her, it was slow and sensual, making her feel as though she were floating on a cloud. With the utmost certainty, his mouth moved over hers, his tongue tracing the outline of her lips before slipping between them.

His touch remained gentle yet provocative. Sweet yet electrifying. She may have been floating but desire exploded deep within her. His hands were drawing little circles on her back, causing floods of tingles to spread in every direction. Her heart was pounding fiercely against her ribs and she was positive he could hear it. She moaned with delight, threading her fingers through his hair.

Dave nearly crumbled completely as her fingers plunged through his hair, ensuring his head was kept firmly in place. The spiralling passion that he could feel building to a frenzy was becoming harder to control with every passing second. What was it about this woman and her completely uninhibited response to him? She was a natural aphrodisiac and one he was finding he couldn't get enough of. He pressed his body hard up against hers, pressing her back against her car. Her car!

Dave pulled back suddenly and looked around them.

'What's wrong?' Rosie's tone was a mixture of desire and confusion.

'Sorry, sweetheart. I just remembered where we were.' His wry grin was crooked and she felt her heart melt once more.

'I see your point,' she said, drawing in a deep breath. 'Kissing in the car park like a couple of adolescent teenagers.'

'Guess we'd better get going,' he replied, not moving away from her.

'Guess we'd better.'

'You have a really good sleep tonight. Doctor's orders. OK?'

'Why? Do I look all drawn and ugly?'

He chuckled. 'Would you believe me if I said no?' He kissed her lips again. 'You know you look beautiful, Rosie, and if you don't, take my word for it because it's true.'

She smiled. 'I guess I'll have to.'

'Here. Let me open your door for you.'

'Always the gentleman.'

'Chivalry, remember.'

'How could I forget? You and your brother seem to have it in spades. Someone in your upbringing did something right.'

'Yeah. I guess they did. Never thought of it that way before.' He kissed her again. 'Sleep sweet, Rosie—and I mean it.'

She laughed. 'I promise to do my best but with memories of kisses like the ones we've just shared, I don't know whether they're going to relax me or keep me awake!' She raised her eyebrows suggestively and laughed again when Dave groaned.

'Don't torture me. I'll call you.'

'I'd like that.'

She stepped forward and, reaching up, pressed her lips to his. 'Get in the car,' he growled. Rose smiled, glad to know she had the same encompassing effect on him as he had on her.

Finally, she pulled out of the car park and headed back to her father's house. As she drove, she thought about what they'd said tonight and was pleased with their progress. Even though she wanted to slow things down, she'd been happy to hear that Dave didn't know if he could.

He was everything she'd been looking for in a man and the thought scared the life out of her. He had a child and, although she'd come to terms with that, she still wasn't quite sure how she felt about it. 'All you need to do is to relax and be honest with them.' Rose repeated Dave's words out loud. *Was* it that easy?

Was Dave worth taking the chance on? Rose shook her head as she pulled into her father's driveway. 'Sleep?' she queried as she walked to her room. 'Ha!'

Rose dragged herself from the depths of sleep as the phone persisted in ringing. Maybe it was Dave? He'd said he'd call her. She flicked the covers back and stumbled out of bed, stubbing her toe on the wall as she rounded a corner to silence the offending instrument.

'Ow! Yes? What?'

'Rosie? Are you all right?'

'Oh, hi, Dad.' She tried to keep the disappointment from her tone. 'Yes, I'm fine. I just stubbed my toe, getting to the phone.'

'Did I wake you? Don't tell me I've got the time difference mixed up again. I thought it was about seven-thirty.'

Was it? Rose glanced at the grandfather clock that stood in the hall. 'Oh, no!' she gasped.

'What now?'

'Nothing. No, you didn't get the time wrong, Dad. I've

just slept in, that's all.' She bent down and examined her toe more closely, wincing slightly from her own light touch. It was fine.

'Really? That's not like you.'

'No,' she agreed as she realised it had been the first *really* good sleep she'd had since she'd arrived here. She took a deep breath and let it out slowly. 'Everything OK in honeymoon paradise?'

'Actually, no.'

'Dad? What's happened?' Rose was instantly alert.

'Oh, we're both fine, dear. It's the weather. It's turned bad and hasn't stopped raining. You know how unpredictable tropical weather can be at this time of year.'

'Sure. So you're coming home early?'

'Yes. We'll be back tomorrow. No point in hanging around as we were due to leave on Saturday so it's only a day early. Besides, Bev's missing everyone so we'll be back tomorrow.'

'Do you need me to pick you up from the airport?'

'No. We'll find our own way home. Well, you'd better run, princess, if you're going to make it to the hospital on time.'

'You're right. OK. See you tomorrow, Dad. Love you. Bye.' The instant she'd replaced the receiver, Rose hobbled back to her bedroom and quickly dug out some clothes. After showering and quickly drinking a glass of orange juice, she headed out the door. By the time she got to the hospital, Dave was ready to start his list.

'Sorry,' she mumbled, as she raced in and quickly changed into theatre garb. They had no time together and although she felt a little deflated, she was glad to at least be in the same room as him. Their gazes met a few times across the busy theatre and she saw the repressed desire that she knew was mirrored in her own.

Every patient she met that day, every nurse she spoke to, interns, theatre staff—everyone—gave her knowing little glances or big beaming smiles, except for Sadie who scowled at her instead. At lunch, she was sitting in the cafeteria, sipping a cup of tea, when Dave walked in. He smiled and waved at her and it was then she realised that a hush had fallen over the place.

Dave slowed his pace and stopped by her chair. 'Fine,' he said to the room. 'The rumours are true. Rosie and I are dating so now that the announcement is out of the way, would you, please, leave us alone?'

A few people clapped, others just started talking to the person next to them, but once more the place was filled with noise. 'Whew!' he said as he sat down beside her, giving her a quick peck on the lips. 'It's been a long time since I've been gossiped about.'

Rose laughed. 'Serves you right. You should have gone to greater lengths to protect my reputation. How's Mrs Fredrick this morning? She looked good when I saw her earlier but what's your professional opinion?'

'Lithotripsy appears to have been successful.'

'Excellent.' They ate lunch together then Rose's pager sounded.

'Ah. Looks as though the ophthalmology surgeon is ready to begin. I'd better go.'

Dave leaned over and kissed her again. 'How do you like being under the microscope?' he asked with a grin.

'Not very much, but I guess I'll just have to put up with it—especially after your little announcement,' she teased. 'I'll speak to you later.' With that, she left. Dave watched her go, his feelings for her increasing with every passing second.

He was really falling for her—in a big way—and he was determined to enjoy every minute of it.

'Hi, gorgeous,' Dave said, as he strode towards his daughter. She was coming out of the small aircraft which had finally come to a stop a few minutes ago.

'Hi, Dad,' she said, heaving a bag into her hand, her teddy bear tucked securely beneath her other arm. It was the bear he'd given her when he'd first seen her, and he was delighted that it was her favourite toy.

He gave her a quick hug, noting she didn't sound or look too happy. Dave glanced around. 'Where's the nanny?'

'She didn't come,' Melody told him matter-of-factly, although he thought he saw her bottom lip quiver.

'*What?*' Dave exploded, and went up the steps of the small plane to check for himself. It was empty. He looked down at Melody before coming to stand before her. He noticed she looked very worried and he quickly crouched down in front of her, bringing himself to her height. 'Have you travelled all this way by yourself?' he asked gently.

Melody's lower lip began to wobble. 'Yes.' Her eyes filled with tears and Dave found his own doing the same.

'Oh, baby.' He reached for her and brought her safely into his arms. Melody dropped the bag she was holding and buried her face into his chest. Dave held her protectively, knowing this was one female he would *always* be protective about—as was his right! 'Shh, princess. It's all right. Daddy's here.' He couldn't *believe* Margaret had done this! To let a six-year-old travel all that way by herself.

Of course, the flight attendants would have looked after her but still—how horrible. No child should ever have to go through that and he'd be damned if his daughter was ever going through something like that again.

Dave clenched his jaw in anger at his ex-wife. Thank goodness she'd signed the custody form. Now Melody was *his* daughter and he was going to protect her in any way he could, and if that meant keeping her away from her own natural mother, that's the way it would be.

'Mummy said I had to be brave. That I was a big girl now and didn't need a nanny,' Melody sobbed.

'Shh. It's all right, princess. It's all right. Daddy's here. I'll fix it,' he crooned, and stroked her long blonde hair. Slowly, her tears subsided and she stood back from him, automatically smoothing down her designer outfit. She held herself aloof, just like Mags had always done after an emotional outburst, and Dave realised he had his work cut out for him. Poor Melody didn't know how to behave any differently.

'Feeling a bit hot?'

'Yes.' She wiped at her blue eyes and nodded.

'Let's get you home and into some play clothes, eh?'

'I don't have any play clothes. Besides, my nanny—that is, my old nanny—gave me lots of school work to get done. She told me that you'd be out most of the time and that I'd have to be by myself so I may as well do some work.'

Dave looked at his daughter with incredulity. He'd never heard such nonsense but now was not the time or the place for such discussions. He shook his head slowly and bent to pick up her bag. 'Where are the rest of your bags, princess?'

Her bottom lip was still quivering as she shook her head. 'This is all there is?'

'Mummy said I wouldn't need many things out here. She gave the rest of my things away.' The tears were flowing again and Dave hoisted her up into his arms, holding her tightly as she cried yet again. The mental traumas this child had been through, and all because of her self-righteous mother. His heart melted when her own little arms came around his neck, holding him tight. He dropped the bag and stroked her hair back from her face as she cried.

'Need a hand?' one of the ladies from the air terminal asked quietly, and Dave nodded. He carried Melody to his ute. 'Come on, princess. Let's get you home.'

'It's…not…my…home.' She hiccuped between the words. 'I…don't…have one and I'm *not* a princess.'

Dave clipped her seat belt around her and rubbed his fingers gently down her cheek. 'You are a princess,

Melody. You're *my* princess and Daddy's never going to let anyone hurt you again.'

'But…but…you don't like…me.'

She couldn't have inflicted any more damage on his heart if she'd pierced it with a sword. 'What? Melody—*I love you.*'

'But…but…Mummy said you…didn't…like me and that's why…you wouldn't come and get…me.'

Dave kissed her head, holding her as she cried again. She was obviously very tired and she'd had such a terrible and emotionally draining day that he couldn't blame her for the constant tears and outbursts. He clenched his jaw again, unable to believe that Mags had said such things to her daughter. He should have flown to Sydney and collected Mel. He should have followed his gut instinct and now he was furious with himself. Why had he listened to that witch?

He took a deep breath. 'You're wrong, Melody. Mummy was wrong.' Dave could feel tears pricking at his own eyes as he gazed down at her tear-stained face. 'I *love* you, *so* much.' A tear dropped from his lashes. 'You're my precious girl and you're very, *very* special to me.' He wanted to tell her that they'd never be apart again, but he wasn't sure what else Mags had told her. He wanted to say she could rely on him for the truth and that he'd do everything he could to be a good father—but he knew it would be too much, too soon.

'Little steps,' he whispered, as he wiped her tears again. 'We'll take little steps in our new life together.'

Melody looked up at him, nodded and sniffled, her bottom lip still protruding slightly. She reached out her little hand and gently wiped away his own tears. The tender action caused the lump in his throat to swell, and his heart filled with pride at her gentleness.

There was hope.

He knew it.

He felt it.

CHAPTER TEN

ROSE wasn't surprised that she didn't hear from Dave on Thursday night as he was probably spending time with Melody. She had to face facts. There was another woman in his life now, and even though she was only six, it meant that his time would be divided between them.

She frowned. Surely she wasn't jealous of a six-year-old! From what Dave had told her, and how she knew Julian would have treated the child, Melody had obviously been through the wringer lately. Now she had to adjust to a new life here in Broken Hill with her father—but what part was Rose supposed to play?

She paced around the house once more, unable to control her thoughts. She knew she could call him. That in this day and age it was fine for women to give men a call, especially when they were dating, but she couldn't do it. She was still very uncertain about herself, thanks to Julian and the degrading way he had constantly put doubt into her mind. She could almost hear him now.

'Do you think that would be the right thing to do, Rose? Imposing on people like that? It's very rude—at least I think it's rude.'

Comments such as that had been made constantly throughout her time with him, and she wondered why she hadn't realised it had just been his way of manipulating her. How had she been so stupid?

Cross with herself, and determined not to let her silly neuroses get in the way, she took out her address book, checked Dave's number and picked up the phone. When she got to the last digit, she hung up again.

'I can't do it,' she said as she paced around the kitchen.

'Yes, you can,' she retorted, and headed back to the phone. She dialled again, forcing herself to take a deep breath and relax. She was anxious to hear his voice. Anxious to feel those tiny tingles that flooded her body when he spoke to her. Anxious to know he was nearby and thinking of her.

'Yes?' His tone was brisk.

'Dave?' Rose asked hesitantly, checking the number in her address book again. Had she dialled wrong?

'Rosie.' His voice softened marginally. 'What can I do for you?'

'Uh…' Now what? Oh, she was no good at this. 'I…uh…just wanted to see how things went. How did things go with Melody and the nanny?' She hoped the nanny was a middle-aged woman with warts on her face, rather than the red-headed beauty she'd been imagining.

'Fine.'

'Is something wrong?'

'Melody's about to go to bed but she doesn't want to sleep in the spare room. I told her she could sleep out here on the couch, but it really isn't that comfortable.'

'Um…well, why don't you let her sleep with you to-night?' she ventured. 'Surely it couldn't hurt. Just for to-night. The first night in a strange place is always uncom-fortable.'

'Yeah.' He relaxed a little. 'Good thinking. She's had a terrible time of it, poor kid.' He lowered his voice to a whisper. 'The nanny didn't come. Mel came the entire way from Sydney by herself.'

'What? What happened to the nanny?' Rose asked in stunned disbelief. Her insides twisted in horror at the thought of a six-year-old girl travelling all that way by herself.

'Mags said she didn't need a nanny.' Dave's tone was harsh and Rose didn't blame him.

'What are you going to do about tomorrow? You've got house calls and a clinic.'

He groaned. 'I'd forgotten. I have no idea.'

'What about Mick? Or his girlfriend?'

'He and his girlfriend are leaving for Adelaide in the morning. They can't cancel the trip or postpone it. They won't be back until early Saturday morning.'

'I see.' Rose thought quickly, unable to believe what she was about to do. Her heart was hammering wildly against her ribs and her throat went dry. 'Well, I'm…um…not due in Theatre—at least for tomorrow morning.' She had planned to get through some paperwork but it could always wait. Rose knew from experience that no child should ever be made to feel unwanted. 'I have a list in the afternoon, though.'

'Are you sure?' He sounded cautious. 'I appreciate the offer but if it's going to make you uncomfortable then I can make alternate arrangements.'

'I…er…want to do this, Dave. I want to help you out.' She wasn't at all sure but the caring note in his voice had helped override the fear she was starting to experience. 'Just relax and be honest, right?'

His laugh was incredulous. She'd remembered what he'd said and was willing to apply it. 'That's right. You're one remarkable woman, Rosie Partridge.'

'Thanks,' she said softly. 'Do you want me to come out to the farm?'

'Actually, I think she might appreciate getting away from the farm. It's not a great place for a kid to stay.' He looked over at his daughter, sitting primly on one of the old, uncomfortable chairs, clutching her teddy to her for dear life. She looked frightened—scared—and he wondered if she was listening to his conversation. He raked his free hand through his hair. 'I'll drop her off tomorrow morning. Right now, I'd better go.'

'All right. See you in the morning.'

'Bye.' He hung up the phone and went over to Melody. 'How about sleeping in Daddy's big bed tonight?'

'With you?' Her eyes widened as she looked at him and

for a moment he felt as though she were reaching right into his soul.

'Do you want to?' he asked slowly, and was pleased with her emphatic nod.

'I remember doing that the last time I was here and it was fun.'

Dave smiled at the way she'd instantly brightened. 'Good. Off you go, then. Get into my bed.'

He waited for her to get beneath the thin cotton sheet, the gentle whirring of the ceiling fan above them. He sat on the other side of the bed and lifted his legs on top of the sheet after kicking off his shoes. Melody shifted over and snuggled into him. Dave ran his fingers gently through her hair, his gut twisting with an overpowering and protective love.

'Daddy's got to go to work in the morning,' he said softly. 'And Uncle Mick has to go on a trip to Adelaide for the day.'

'But—'

'Shh,' he whispered. 'Just listen for a moment. I want to introduce you to…a friend of mine. Her name is Rosie and she's a doctor, just like me. We work together at the hospital but she doesn't need to come to the hospital tomorrow morning and she asked if you could go to her house to play.'

'Play?'

'Yes.' Dave wasn't sure how Rosie would cope with playing with a six-year-old but he didn't want Melody to feel unwanted. Besides, Rosie *had* offered. 'So that will be exciting, won't it?'

'I guess,' Melody replied, yawning once again.

Dave bent his head and kissed the top of hers. 'All right, princess. Time to go to sleep, and don't hog the bed like you did last time.'

Melody giggled before yawning again. 'What does "hog the bed" mean?'

'It means you take up all the room,' he explained. 'Now

shush and close your eyes.' He continued to stroke her hair, letting his thoughts wander. How would Rosie and Melody cope tomorrow? The importance of the situation penetrated him. Rosie was everything he'd ever wanted in a woman. She was intelligent, lively, spirited, direct and most of all honest. He loved the way they argued, the way she knew it was just an argument and didn't take it too seriously. He loved the way she deftly raised her chin and squared her shoulders when she was preparing to give him a piece of her mind. He smiled at the memory. They were both hotheads with tempers that sparked easily and cooled just as quickly.

They had so much in common and tomorrow he'd introduce her to the other important female in his life—his daughter. He ignored the instinct that told him it might not be as easy as he hoped.

But surely when Rosie met Melody—in person—things would be different… Wouldn't they? He knew she'd been burnt by Julian and his indifferent treatment of his own children, but *he* wasn't like that. He loved his daughter and wanted her with him.

He stopped moving his hand on Melody's hair as realisation struck. Was that it? Did Rosie want to be the only woman in his life? He'd asked her if she'd wanted children and she'd said she didn't know. What did that mean? Didn't *most* women want children?

He glanced down at his daughter who, he realised, was now asleep. His heart swelled with paternal love. How could anyone not want children? They were so…amazing. So fantastic. So humbling.

'It has to be her own childhood,' he murmured, as he carefully slid out of Melody's grasp. He walked through to the kitchen and took a beer out of the fridge. He cracked it open and took a long drink. 'What happened to her mother?'

'Talking to yourself again, bro'?' Mick asked as he walked into the room.

'Something like that.' Dave headed out to the verandah. Mick followed, sipping on a beer as well.

'Problems with Rosie?'

'Ha! When aren't there problems with women?'

'Want to talk about it?'

'She's just so…different. I'm in love with her, Mick.'

'Tell me something I *don't* know.'

'How could you know? I've only just realised it myself.'

'Hello! I live with you, remember? You've been different ever since she arrived in town. You've fallen faster than a lead balloon, and so has she. What's the problem?'

'You think Rosie loves me?' Dave couldn't help the smile of pride that filled him.

'Sure. A blind man could see that. As I said, what's the problem?'

'She doesn't like kids.'

'Are you for real?'

'Yes.'

'How do you know?'

'I asked her.' He drained his drink and leant against the verandah rail. 'I want more kids, Mick. I don't want Melody to be an only child and I want to be there from the beginning, to feel my child kick inside Rosie.'

'So she doesn't want to have kids?'

'She's not sure.' He exhaled sharply and looked up at the star-filled night. 'I've got so many unanswered questions, Mick.'

'Then why don't you find out what the answers are?'

Dave stared at his brother. 'You're right. What's the time?'

'Just after nine.'

'Look after Melody, for me, mate.' Dave stalked into the kitchen and returned a moment later with his car keys. 'I need to speak to Rosie.'

'Maybe you should call first.'

'You know me,' Dave replied as he opened the car door. 'Spontaneity at its best!'

*　　*　　*

Rose rested her head back on the edge of the bath, determined to get rid of her headache. This was her last night of peace and quiet and she was going to enjoy it with a relaxing soak. The water was like satin against her skin and the scented bubbles were enough to make her drowsy.

She refused to let herself think about the multitude of problems floating around in her head. Tonight she was going to relax and pamper herself a little. She'd taken the phone off the hook and turned out all the lights. The gentle breeze from the bathroom window ensured she didn't get too hot and the five beautiful, flickering candles gave the room a soft glow. She closed her eyes, taking her first deep relaxing breath in days.

Her worries started to slip away, which was what baths like that were designed to do. As she continued to lie there, her mind turned to Dave. She blocked out any unanswered questions she might have and just focused on how much she cared about him. He'd become so special to her in such a short time. What she'd told him about not being rushed had been absolutely true, yet in some ways it was thrilling to be so caught up with emotions the way she'd been since arriving in Broken Hill—emotions that Dave alone was responsible for.

She thought about how gorgeous he'd looked when she'd seen him arm-wrestling in the pub. Had he really been ogling her back then? Little flutterings of excitement sprang to life in her stomach as she realised he had, especially if his kisses were anything to go by.

The way his mouth felt when it met hers…it was as though they'd been designed for each other. Never had she experienced emotions of this magnitude before but, then, she'd never been in love—*really* in love—with a man.

Oh, she'd told herself she'd been in love with Julian but it was nothing compared to how she felt for Dave. She could yell at Dave. She could lose her temper. She could be at her worst and he still found her attractive. It was as though he knew she had faults and simply accepted them, rather than trying to change her.

Rose sighed as her love for him grew once more. She allowed her imagination to run wild. She and Dave were married and this was their house. After a hectic day at the hospital they'd come home together, and when it was his turn to cook he'd draw her a scented bath and tell her to unwind, bringing her in a cool glass of wine, desire sparking in his eyes. He wouldn't disturb her, though, because he'd be able to tell she just needed some time by herself.

After dinner, they'd make love, giving everything to each other. Not holding anything back. The image of Dave, lying with his legs entwined with hers, their bodies covered with the afterglow of spent passion, made her heart swell with happiness.

'Rosie?' The knock at the front door startled her from her dreams, and she realised she'd almost fallen asleep. The house was quiet and for a second she thought she'd imagined it. She'd been so caught up in her fantasies of Dave that she'd thought for a second he was here.

'Rosie?'

She hadn't imagined it. What did she do now? Her heart began to race. Why was he here? Should she pretend she was asleep or answer the door?

'Rosie?' His voice was fainter and she realised he was walking around to the back door. Then she remembered he knew where the spare key was hidden. He'd used it to get into the house the night she'd had food poisoning. Moments later she heard footsteps coming hesitantly through the house. 'Rosie? It's Dave. Is everything all right?'

If she didn't move soon, he'd be walking in to find her in the bath, yet she found herself unable to move a muscle. Her heart was drumming so loudly, the noise was reverberating in her ears. She swallowed, amazed to find her mouth suddenly dry.

'Rosie!'

It was the urgency in his tone that helped her to respond. The last thing she wanted was to worry him. 'Just a minute,' she called back as loudly as she could. The footsteps stopped, just outside her open bedroom door. The door to the *en suite* bathroom was open as well. A few more footsteps followed, but these were muffled by the carpet on the floor.

She watched as he materialised in the doorway.

'U-uh…' He faltered, stunned to find her relaxing in a bubble bath, lit only by the glow of some candles. His mouth opened at the sight of her and his eyes filled with desire. Rose swallowed, once more unable to move. They just stared at each other, the silent messages being interpreted fluently.

Dave instantly regretted not taking Mick's advice and calling before he'd just turned up on her doorstep. All rational thought disappeared from his mind as he just stared at her lying there, surrounded by white, glistening bubbles.

'If you don't mind…waiting outside my bedroom…I'll get out.' Rose was surprised to find her voice so husky but there was nothing she could do about it.

'U-uh…sure.' His legs felt as though they weighed a ton as he went out of her bedroom, closing the door behind him.

She moved in the bath, not at all surprised to discover her arms were shaky. She quickly towelled herself dry and wrapped herself up in a big bathrobe. 'All right. You can come in now.' She fiddled nervously with the end of the sash that held her robe in place.

When he opened the door, her breath caught in her throat. Oh, he was gorgeous, and she had the urge to let her fingers memorise the contours of his body in great detail.

With a few short strides, he'd crossed the room and gathered her into his arms. His mouth on hers was hot and demanding. Not that she minded. Given the direction her own thoughts had taken, it seemed appropriate he was here.

'Rosie.' Her name escaped his lips as they momentarily gasped for breath. Dave plundered her mouth, his tongue seeking and receiving a response. How did this woman do it? She had the ability to knock him beyond the black stump with one simple look. Add to that the fact that whatever scent had been in the bath water now emanated from her skin, making him lose what vestige of control he had left.

'Rosie.' He smothered her neck with tiny kisses, unable to get enough of her. 'Rosie,' he murmured again, 'I love you.'

The words were like a dousing of cold water. Rose lifted her head away from him. 'You…you…what?'

'I love you,' he repeated again, his voice filled with desire. He gazed down into her eyes, knowing that what he was about to say could be a mistake but needing to say it anyway. 'I want to marry you, Rosie.'

'Marry!' The vision she'd had of this being *their* house ran through her mind again. She brushed it away. There were still so many issues they needed to resolve—the first one being his daughter!

He'd been right. He didn't stop her as she pulled away and took a few steps backwards. 'Look, I know I'm rushing you—'

'Rushing? You give the word new meaning, David.' She was shaking all over and she wasn't quite sure what from. Was it surprise? Disbelief or rage? All of those emotions and many more were coursing through her at a rate of knots, and her earlier tranquillity had been completely shattered. The knowledge that he loved her had come as a complete shock. She hadn't expected him to feel the same way about her as she did about him. Now…now he wanted to get married?

'Why shouldn't we get married? I love you, Rosie, and

I'm sure you feel the same way.' He paused for a second. 'Don't you?'

'Dave…' Rose stopped, throwing her arms up in confusion. 'Marriage?'

'What? What's so wrong with that?' He could see her withdrawing from him and knew he'd lost her—this time. He was a man with a mission and stubborn determination to boot. He knew with an absolute certainty that he wanted to marry Rosie Partridge. 'Is it Melody?'

'Well…yes…amongst other things.'

There was that honesty—slapping him in the face again. He narrowed his gaze, determined to get to the heart of the matter. 'What happened with your mother, Rosie? Why is it that you're so afraid of children?' He watched as she straightened her spine and raised her chin, defiance gleaming in her eyes. Didn't she know she looked irresistible when she did that?

'I'm not *afraid* of them… I've just never had much to do with children, that's all. Other than treating them in my paediatric rotation, that is,' she added as an afterthought.

'What happened with your mother?' he asked again, insistently.

'She left us,' Rose blurted out. 'When I was three.'

'Do you remember her at all?'

'No, but my father has told me all about her. She wasn't at all maternal.'

'Ah, and you think you're the same.'

'Well, the children I *have* met have never taken an instant liking to me so, yes, I guess so.'

'Yet you've just told me that you haven't had too many dealings with children.'

'And now you know why.' Rose rubbed her fingers along her forehead, feeling her earlier headache returning. 'I'd really like to get to bed early tonight, Dave.'

'Kicking me out, sweetheart? Not just yet.' His gaze roved over her again. 'Put some clothes on and I'll make us a cuppa.'

'Dave, I'd really prefer that you—'

'I'll make the tea,' he said more forcefully. 'We're going to talk about this, Rosie.'

'No, we're not. You can't just come waltzing in here, laying down the law. I'm tired, Dave, and I want to go to sleep.'

'I need to know.' He stood his ground, not moving an inch.

'What? You need to know that I look *exactly* like my mother? That I'm like her in so many ways it isn't funny? I'm not maternal, Dave. When I see children, I don't feel anything for them, except a need that they grow up.'

'That's not true.'

'How would you know? You're not me.' Her eyes radiated pure disbelief at his words. 'My mother was a bad mother and I'll probably end up being just like her. She wanted a career and hated being stuck at home with a child. I'm very career-minded—just like her. I love my job. I enjoy it and I don't want to give it up.'

'No one's asking you to.'

She shook her head. 'There's more to it than that. You wanted to know why I have mild claustrophobia, so I'll tell you. At least once a week she used to lock me in my room for most of the day. It was a very small room, even for a child.' Rose's words broke on a sob. 'She sometimes even left the house, leaving me in there with only a bottle of water. She was no good with children. She didn't know how to deal with the ordinary tantrums children have, the way they expand their boundaries.

'I may not remember these things but my father has always been honest with me and answered my questions when I asked. The mild claustrophobia wasn't discovered until recently and although I'm slowly getting better, it's going to take more time.' Rose could feel the hot, angry tears pricking at her eyes.

'I have *no* idea how to deal with children but I'll tell you this. I won't allow myself to lose control the way my mother did but I can't say for certain until I put myself in that situation. Don't you see? I can't trust *myself*. To think of the permanent psychological damage that's happened to me…' She shook her head emphatically. 'I won't do that to another child. I won't do it, Dave. I won't!' The tears were now streaming down her face and she knew she'd shocked him with her outburst.

He took a few steps towards her but she held up her hands to stop him. 'Don't. Don't touch me.'

'All right. I won't.' She could hear the love in his voice when he spoke, and it only tore through her with more pain than she thought she could bear. 'But I want you to at least listen.' His eyes were filled with understanding. 'You're not like your mother, Rosie. Believe me, you're not.'

'How would you know? You've never met her. You know nothing about her, except for what I've told you.'

'Sweetheart, you *care* about kids, otherwise you wouldn't be so conscious of what your mother did and how wrong it was. You've said you don't want to inflict permanent psychological damage on a child and *that*, in itself, is proof enough that you're nothing like your mother.'

She wanted to believe him. Oh, how she desperately wanted to believe him. She brushed back the tears with an impatient hand. 'Still, what if I crack? What if I can't cope and I'm horrible…?' Her voice caught on a sob. 'I just don't know, Dave. I'm not sure.' She shook her head.

'Then why did you offer to have Melody tomorrow?'

'Because of you.'

'See? You care.'

'About *you*, Dave.'

His heart nurtured that gem. 'That's a start.' He took another step closer but she held her hands up again. He stopped. She was behaving like a caged animal and in a way he could understand it. She was fenced in by the past and now that the door was open, she wasn't sure she wanted to step through it.

'You care about me, Rosie. Doesn't that show you how different you are to your mother? She obviously didn't care about your father or she would have stayed to work things out. She would have told him that she couldn't cope all day with a child and that she wanted a career, but she didn't. You're different.'

He edged closer but she simply edged back. 'You're open, honest. You communicate.' He smiled at her, that gorgeous crooked smile that always had the ability to melt her insides. 'You sure surprised me. A female who communicates.' He was moving slowly as he talked. 'I know you offered to have Melody tomorrow because you wanted to help me out, and you have no idea how much I appreciate that.' He reached out a hand to her. 'But I would never leave Mel with you if I didn't trust you one hundred per cent.'

'Get back,' she sobbed, as she felt the wall behind her. 'Please, just go.'

'Sweetheart, I'm not going to leave you in this state.'

'Yes, you are,' she responded forcefully. 'I've listened to what you've said and now I'd like you to go.' She sniffed and wished she had a handkerchief or tissue.

Dave stood his ground, unsure whether or not to leave her. She was in such an emotional turmoil that he didn't want her to spend the rest of the night sobbing out old memories that he'd obviously triggered.

'I feel responsible.' His voice was soft but he didn't move any closer. 'I'm glad things are out in the open, Rosie. Now we can move forward.' He held her gaze for a moment before acceding. 'I'll go but only because that's what you want.' He turned and headed to the door.

Rose held her breath, not sure whether she really wanted him to go. He stopped at the door and turned to look at her.

'The other thing you need to realise is that your mother

wasn't just bad at being a parent. Rosie, what she did to you was child abuse and neglect, and I'm sure your father has spent the rest of his life feeling guilty that he didn't do something to stop it sooner.

'Take the step, sweetheart. Step into the unknown.' He smiled at her. 'I'll be there to support you all the way and catch you if you start to fall.' He blew her a kiss before walking out. 'I'll lock the door behind me,' he called.

Rose couldn't move. She listened to him leave, just as she'd listened to him arrive. Slowly, she slid down the wall, her legs unable to support her weight any longer. Was he right? Was there hope?

Fresh tears welled in her eyes and she let them fall.

CHAPTER ELEVEN

DAVE knew he had to be careful when he dropped Melody off the following morning. It wasn't going to be easy— for either Rosie or Melody—but it was a new life and if he wanted things to work out, this was going to be the place to start.

'Is she your girlfriend?' Melody asked as they pulled up outside Reg Partridge's house, her teddy bear held securely in the crook of her arm.

Dave looked down at his daughter. 'She's a girl and, yes, she's my friend.'

'Yes, but is she your *girlfriend*?'

'How do you know about these things?' he asked, slightly bewildered. 'You're only six.'

Melody shrugged. 'Mum's had lots of boyfriends that she kisses and stuff. She said that boys have girlfriends who they kiss and that's what she was.'

Dave gritted his teeth. Mags. He should have known. He took a deep breath, not wanting to lie to his daughter. 'Rosie is a very special friend.' He met his daughter's gaze. 'And, yes, we kiss. Is that OK?'

Melody thought for a moment before shrugging. 'Guess so. I want you to stay but I know you have to go to work.'

'I'll be back later to pick you up and then we can do whatever you want.'

'Can we look for a new house?'

'Hey, that was supposed to be a surprise.'

She giggled. 'Uncle Mick said that you and I are going to be moving from the farm into a house of our very own, and that I could have a room with my own bed and I could choose the colours and toys and everything.' Her face was filled with such excited anticipation even if it *hadn't* been in his plans, he would have changed them.

'When did you speak to Uncle Mick about this?'

'This morning. I woke up just before he left.'

'That was very early.'

'Yeah.' She giggled again. 'Three o'clock! I've never been up at three o'clock in the morning before. Uncle Mick told me to go back to bed just before he drove off.'

'Good ol' Uncle Mick,' Dave muttered. He reached out and cupped her cheek with his hand. She leaned into him a little, the action warming his heart. 'You're very beautiful, Melody. So very beautiful and special.' He took a deep breath. 'But right now Daddy's going to be late for clinic if we don't get a move on.'

Melody climbed from the car and waited for him so they could walk up the path together. 'I'm sure the morning will pass quickly.' He carried the bag she'd packed. 'You've got all kinds of things to do in here.'

'I guess so.'

He knocked on the door. 'You'll have fun with Rosie.' Please! Please, let them have fun together, he silently pleaded. 'Rosie's a great cook.'

'Really? She can cook?'

'Not only that but her dad writes books that tell people *how* to cook.'

'Wow!'

The door opened and Rose stood there, looking stunning in a pair of white shorts and a red summer top, a smile pasted on her face. Dave felt his insides twist with desire at seeing her there, looking very nervous. She had guts. More than anyone else he'd met. After everything she'd been through, she was willing to keep on going. He admired that.

'Hi.' She knew she sounded overly bright but she couldn't help it.

'Good morning.'

'Come on in,' she ventured.

'Thanks. Rosie, this is Melody. Mel, this is Rosie.' Dave performed the introductions. To his surprise, Rose bent down, bringing herself to eye level with Melody.

'I'm very pleased to meet you, Melody.' The child wasn't smiling and Rose faltered for a moment. She glanced up at Dave for reassurance. He nodded so she continued. 'I'm right in the middle of cooking some biscuits. Double chocolate chip.'

'Your dad's recipe?' Dave asked, his mouth instantly watering.

'Yes.' This time when she smiled at him it was genuine. She straightened. 'Come through to the kitchen. I'm almost at the stage where I'll need some help.'

'Well, *I* can't stay,' Dave replied with disgust as he put Melody's bag down and followed Rose. 'Perhaps you could help her, Mel?'

'But I've never cooked before,' the little girl said as she hesitantly followed her father, teddy still grasped firmly in her arms.

That stumped Rose. She couldn't remember a time when she hadn't been in the kitchen, helping her father cook. 'Well, there's a first time for everything. Besides, after we've made them and cooked them, we get to eat them.'

'You'd better save some for me,' Dave warned, and she realised he was serious.

She laughed. 'We'll think about it. Now go to work.' Rose was astonished with herself. She'd been so nervous about this morning, especially after what she and Dave had discussed last night, but amazingly she felt relaxed and calm at having the six-year-old for the next four or so hours. If Melody had never cooked and was interested in learning, Rose knew how they might spend their time. It wasn't going to be so bad after all.

'All right, then,' he muttered, as he held Melody's hand and walked over to the bench. 'But promise me you'll save me at least two.'

'Promise. Now, go. We'll be fine.' As she said the words, she realised she meant them. She watched as he bent to give Melody a hug and kiss, wondering whether he was going to give her one or not.

She also heard him whisper, 'Remember, Daddy loves you.' And Rose's heart filled with love for him.

Dave stood and met Rose's gaze over his daughter's head. 'You OK?' he mouthed. She nodded and smiled. Dave smiled back and blew Rose a kiss before heading to the door.

'All right. We need to sift this flour into the bowl, Melody.' She stopped. 'Do you like being called Melody or Mel?'

'Mel,' the little girl answered. 'It's my nickname that Uncle Mick and Dad call me. Dad says that everyone has to have a nickname because then it makes them feel special.'

'I guess he's right,' Rose answered, knowing she cherished the way Dave said *her* nickname.

Dave listened for a moment and released the breath he'd been unconsciously holding. Everything *was* going to be fine. He could always count on Rosie to pull through.

Three hours later, they'd made two batches of biscuits, mainly because they'd eaten all the ones from the first batch, made an upside-down pineapple cake and started on preparations for a beef wellington Rose was cooking for dinner that night. She'd made a little apron for teddy out of a hand towel and had readjusted the straps on one for Melody. Teddy had mainly watched as Melody hadn't wanted him to get too dirty and Rose had agreed, although she was almost sure she'd seen teddy sneak a biscuit or two.

'What's in the bag?' Rose asked as she hung up the drying towel. At least the kitchen was once again clean.

'Books and stuff,' Melody replied, collecting teddy from the bench and taking off his apron.

'What kind of books? Reading books?' Perhaps Rose could read Melody a story.

'Some.' She shrugged and started pulling them out.

School books, Rose realised with a frown. Well, if Dave had sent her with work to do then she guessed they had to do it, but they could at least do it somewhere more comfortable than in the kitchen.

'Why don't we go into the lounge room and sit in there?' Rose gathered up the books and Melody followed like a dutiful puppy. Rose sat down on the floor and spread the books all over the carpet. Melody gaped openly. 'What's wrong?'

'You're sitting on the carpet.'

'Sure. Try it. It's nice and soft.'

'But carpet isn't for sitting on, chairs are. Carpet is for clean feet but not dirty shoes.'

'Really?' That sounded like something Julian would have said. 'Well, I don't have dirty shoes and neither do you. This carpet is nice and soft.' Rose patted it with her hand. 'Come and try it.'

Melody came over and sat down, a small, intrigued smile on her face.

'So, which of these books do you think we should start with?'

'I don't care.'

Rose looked up and was surprised to find Melody's smile had disappeared. 'You don't have to do this if you don't want to,' she said, touching the school books lightly. 'We can always do something else.'

'Like what?'

'Um…' Now you've done it, she thought. 'What do you *like* doing?'

Melody thought. 'I like playing with dolls. I did that once at Chelsea's house.'

'Oh? Is Chelsea a friend of yours?'

Melody shook her head. 'Not really. I don't have any friends.'

'What about the girls at school?'

Melody shook her head again. 'They're not very nice. They say mean things and that I'm a baby because of teddy and that I cried when Miss Schansky took him away from me, but I'm not a baby. I'm a big girl.' There was a hint of defiance in her eyes and Rose liked it.

'Yes, you are.'

'Really? You really think so?'

'Yes, I do.'

'Mummy always says I'm too little and to get out of her way.' Melody frowned and hugged teddy close.

'What's wrong, Mel?'

Tears trembled on the little eyelashes. 'I don't think my mummy loves me.' The tears rolled over. 'She never tells me and said I was going to live with Daddy and not her but…but my daddy loves me. He told me so.'

Rose could feel her own tears threatening. Funny, she'd thought she'd cried them all out last night. 'Yes, he does,' she concurred, and pulled a tissue from her pocket. She reached over and dabbed at Melody's eyes. 'I'll tell you something special, Mel. I know exactly how you feel.'

Six-year-old eyes widened in surprise but she didn't speak.

'My mummy didn't love me either.' Saying the words out loud hurt, but the instant they were out, Rose started to feel better. She'd done it. She'd said those hateful and horrible words out loud. 'But my daddy does. He *still* does and I'm all grown up. Your daddy will love you *just* like that, too.'

Melody took the tissue out of Rose's hand and dabbed it against Rose's eyes. The action nearly brought on a fresh bout. She took a deep breath in and said, 'Now, how about we find some dolls to play with, eh?'

Melody nodded and smiled. A *real* smile and one that Rose reciprocated.

Rose almost lost track of time and if the phone hadn't rung, she would have been late for Theatre. 'Dr Partridge,' she answered.

'Hi, Rosie. How's it going?' Dave's concern wasn't lost on her. She knew how important today had been for all of them.

'Great. Really great. She's wonderful, Dave.'

He let out the breath he'd been holding. 'That's just what I needed to hear.'

'What's up?'

'I'm running late. Can you bring Mel with you to the hospital? I'll be finished by the time you get here but I'm conscious of not making you late.'

'Sure.'

'Make sure you bring my biscuits,' he reminded her.

'Would you ever let me forget? I'll put some in for Mick as well.'

'And me,' Melody added.

'Of course. All right. We'll see you soon.' She hung up and explained to Melody. 'So we need to pack up and I need to get changed for work.'

'Will you be working all night? I thought doctors worked at night.'

'Sometimes we do but not today.' Rose helped her pack up. 'My dad and his new wife are coming back from their holiday today.'

'Your dad got married again?'

'Yes.'

'So now you have a new mum?'

'Kind of. Her name is Beverley and I don't really think of her as my mum. I think of her as my friend. A good friend who really loves my dad.'

'Margaret—that's my mum—is getting married tomorrow but she didn't want me there. Julian—that's her yucky boyfriend—doesn't like me either but I don't like him. They're going on a honeymoon and I heard Margaret saying that she'd trick Daddy into letting me stay.'

'But she didn't *need* to trick him,' Rose replied. 'Your

daddy *wants* you. Remember he told you how much he loved you?'

'Yeah.' Melody's eyes registered her statements before they dimmed again. 'But I don't ever want to get married. Yuck.'

Rose didn't have time to debate the issue and it seemed as though Melody had made up her mind at any rate. No doubt she'd change it when she got older and give her father and Uncle Mick a few grey hairs with the boyfriends she'd be bringing home.

When they arrived at the hospital, Rose was running five minutes late but she made sure she said goodbye properly to Melody.

'I've had so much fun today. Thank you for coming to play, Mel.'

'Sounds as though you two girls have had a wow of a time,' Dave commented as Rose straightened. Melody instantly held out the container that was filled with biscuits.

'Look what we made, Dad.'

Dave opened the lid and took one out, biting into it immediately. 'Mmm. You girls,' he said as he swallowed his bite, 'are such good cooks. Mmm-mmm.'

Melody giggled and on that note Rose said her goodbyes and headed to Theatre.

Thankfully, the list was routine with no surprises, which she was very relieved about because, whether it was due to her bad night's sleep or playing with Melody all morning, Rose felt completely washed out.

When she arrived back at the house, she was glad to see her father and Beverley were home, her dad back in the kitchen he loved, putting the finishing touches to the dinner she'd started earlier.

While they ate, both of them chattering about their honeymoon, Rose started to unwind but couldn't suppress the yawns that kept plaguing her. 'Sorry,' she apologised as she rose from the table.

'Go to bed, dear,' Beverley said. 'You've obviously had a busy day.'

'Thanks. I think I will.' She kissed Beverley goodnight but when she went over to her father, he held her at arm's length.

'Rosie, darling, I don't want to pry, but you know I'm here for you if you need anything. To talk and things like that. Beverley, too,' he added. 'We both care about you so much and we just want you to be happy. You can count on us.'

'I know,' she said, and gave her father a big hug. 'Everything's still kind of muddled in my head and I'm too tired to try and make sense of it.'

'Well, off you go to bed, then, princess.'

'Goodnight.' Rose headed off to her room and had just closed the door when the phone rang. She groaned and then remembered that she didn't need to worry about answering it. She waited for a moment, listening for footsteps heading her way in case there was an emergency at the hospital, but after a few minutes she continued on to the bathroom to wash before bed.

Five hours later, Rose was walking quietly through to the kitchen to make herself a drink. She'd managed to sleep but had woken with a start, unable to breathe properly, her body trembling with fright.

'You all right, dear?'

She jumped as Beverley came into the room, water flying out from the kettle she was filling.

'Sorry, I didn't mean to startle you. Can't sleep?' Beverley took the kettle from Rose. 'Sit down. I'll make us a nice warm drink.'

'It's OK, I can—'

'Sit. Your father's asleep, which means I get free run of his precious kitchen.' Beverley smiled as she spoke. Once the kettle was boiling and Beverley had set out the cups, she sat down opposite Rose. 'Now, what's going on with you and Dave?'

'Oh, Beverley.' Rose slumped forward, her head resting on the bench. 'I don't know whether I'm coming or going.'

'Do you love him?'

'Yes.'

'Do you know if he loves you?'

'He says he does. He said he wants to marry me.'

'Really!' Rose lifted her head and looked into her step-mother's astonished eyes. 'This is serious.'

'Yes.'

'So what's the problem?'

Rose wasn't quite sure where to start.

'Is it his daughter? Are you afraid to take on an immediate family?'

'Oh, I don't know,' Rose wailed, and slumped forward again. 'I'm just so confused. Do I change my nice quiet lifestyle to accommodate a man and his child? Am I capable of that? Will I make a good mother?'

'Is that what's bothering you? Whether or not you'll turn out like your mother?'

Rose nodded. 'That's part of it. I'm just not good at taking chances, Beverley. I took a chance with Julian and look what happened.'

'But that was a wrong chance to take.'

'How am I supposed to know what's right and what's not?'

Beverley reached over and placed her hand on Rose's. 'You follow your heart.' The kettle boiled and soon Rose had a hot toddy in front of her. 'Sip it slowly. It's your father's recipe.' Beverley sat down again. 'I can tell you straight out, Rosie, that you're nothing like your mother. Oh, you may look like her, but in personality you are exactly like your father.'

'But how could you know? You've never—'

'Met your mother?' Beverley finished. 'Yes, I have. Of course, I had no idea she was your father's ex-wife until much later, but I knew her all right. She was my boss years ago when I lived in Sydney. She's since moved overseas to work and all I can say is good riddance to her.'

'She was in Sydney?'

'For many years.'

Rose felt even more dejected. 'She really doesn't like me, does she?' Tears stung at her eyes and Beverley quickly took her hand again.

'It's not a matter of like or dislike as far as she's concerned. She's just…' Beverley shrugged '…indifferent. Not that I'm making excuses for her.' She paused. 'I know this is easy to say and hard to do, but try not to take it personally, dear. She was indifferent to everyone she met. She has no real friends, no real relationships, except with her company, but that's who she is. So, you see, you are *nothing* like her. You aren't an icicle nor an emotional nomad. You're a woman on the brink of self-discovery, deciding whether to trust herself as well as trust others with her heart.'

Rose sipped at her drink, taking in what her stepmother had said.

'I can understand your reluctance because your father was the same. I knew from the moment I first met him, when we were discussing the photo layout for his first book, that I wanted to marry him.'

'But that was almost ten years ago.'

'That's right. Don't waste ten years of your life, Rosie. As soon as you know, do it. Get on with it now. So what if things have happened quickly? They've happened! If you love Dave, then take the chance. Trust your instincts. Listen to your heart. From what Dave has said, it seems Melody had a lovely time this morning, which proves you're nothing like your mother.'

'Dave? You've spoken to Dave?'

Beverley nodded. 'He called just as you were heading to bed. He wants me to look after Melody when he's working. I looked after her last time she came to stay and told

Dave I'd do the same whenever she came back. She's such a gorgeous child.'

Rose couldn't resist the smile that tugged at her lips when she thought of Melody. 'Yes, she is. I didn't realise you'd looked after her before.'

'Oh, yes. Moving to Broken Hill is just what Melody needs—get her away from her mother. Fancy sending a child all the way here from Sydney on her own! Poor darling. Thank goodness Dave has sense, so he called tonight to take me up on my earlier offer to help.' Beverley had a twinkle of excitement in her eyes as she continued.

'We'll fix up the spare room for her in case he works late at the hospital or has an emergency and Melody needs to stay the night. Apparently she loved cooking with you today and can't wait to do some more. Reg is looking forward to having another little girl in his kitchen, one he can pamper and teach—so it works out well for everyone.'

'It all seems well organised, then.'

'Nearly. There's one thing missing from the equation. You! Don't let this opportunity pass you by, Rosie.' Beverley squeezed her hand. 'Reach out and grab that happiness. It's just sitting there. Waiting for you. You'll be a wonderful mother for Melody and the perfect wife for Dave.'

'What if it's too late? What if he's changed his mind? What if he's decided all he needs is Melody? What if he doesn't want me any more?'

'Oh, I doubt that, dear. I doubt that very much. You know what to do. All you have to do is to follow your heart.'

The next day, Rose woke late and couldn't believe the time. 'Half past twelve!' She jumped out of bed and quickly showered. Before she'd gone back to sleep, she'd made a vow to find Dave and ask him to marry her.

Beverley was right. She had to trust her instincts and her heart. He wasn't Julian and she wasn't her mother.

They had a chance at happiness—all three of them—and she wasn't going to let it pass her by!

'Good morning,' her father said as she entered the kitchen. 'Or should I say good afternoon?'

'You shouldn't have let me sleep so late,' she told him, after kissing his cheek. She quickly poured herself a glass of orange juice and drank it, before picking up her car keys.

'I didn't want to wake you. Where are you going?'

Rose blew him a kiss. 'To ask Dave to marry me,' she said, before heading out to her car. She was running on nervous energy and as she drove out to his farm it occurred to her that he might not be there. It was the first time she'd been out that way and, after glancing at the map book a few times and doing two U-turns, she finally found it.

There were no cars in front of the house, and with the absence of Dave's ute she guessed he wasn't around. Still, she climbed out and knocked on the door but wasn't surprised when no one answered.

'The hospital,' she said, and turned the car in that direction. Again, his ute wasn't in the car park and she didn't fancy going in and asking the nurses if they knew where he was. Where else could he be? Doing house calls? Looking at houses? Visiting friends? Grocery shopping? He could be anywhere in Broken Hill or its outskirts.

She thought hard and then snapped her fingers. 'The pub.' She'd try the pub he liked, and if he wasn't there, she'd simply wait until someone turned up who knew where he was. 'You're not giving in,' she told herself sternly. 'You're going to be engaged to Dave Dunbar by the end of this day or else!'

Her hopes plummeted when she pulled into the pub car park, noticing Dave's ute was absent from there as well. She sighed as she locked up her car and headed inside. The cool air hit her and she pushed her sunglasses up to the top of her head, searching the room for the man she loved.

'G'day, Rosie,' one of the nurses called, and beckoned her over. 'How's it going?'

'Good,' Rose replied in response to the typical Australian greeting.

'Rosie.' The deep voice behind her made her heart race and she turned expectantly.

'G'day, Mick,' she murmured a moment later, her face falling.

Mick laughed. 'You've got it bad, Rosie. Real bad.'

Rose was conscious of the people around them watching her closely. 'Uh…do you know where your brother is?' she asked him quietly, hoping everyone wouldn't hear.

Mick frowned. 'Dave? Not sure. Hey!' He called at the top of his lungs. 'Has anyone seen Dave? Rosie's looking for him.'

Rose could feel herself blushing but she watched as nearly everyone shook their heads, wide grins spreading across their faces.

'Sorry. What did you want him for? Can I pass on a message?'

Rose swallowed over the lump in her throat. 'Um…er…no. I guess I'll catch up with him later.' Rose took her sunglasses off her head and was about to put them back on when Mick took her arm.

'Don't go. Stay and have a drink.' He ushered her to a table and sat down opposite her.

Rose eyed him carefully. 'Why? Why do you want me to stay?' When Mick didn't answer, she nodded slowly. 'You *do* know where he is, don't you?'

'And if I do?'

'Then tell me.'

Mick looked thoughtfully at her. 'How about we arm-wrestle for it?'

'Arm-wrestle? For what?'

'For the information.'

'What?' She frowned at him, puzzled, but his words had

stopped conversations around them and people were listening in unashamedly.

'If you win, I'll tell you where Dave is.'

'And if you win?' she queried, not sure she liked this idea at all.

'Then you have to tell me whether or not you love my brother.'

'*What?* That's none of your business.'

'That's the deal, Rosie.'

'But you'll win easily. That's not very fair.'

He nodded. 'You can use two hands.'

'Two—'

'Go on, Rosie,' one of the nurses encouraged her. 'You can take him.'

'Yeah, go on, Rosie.' Cheers went up around the place and Mick put his elbow down on the table, his palm open, waiting for hers.

Rose glanced over at the door, wondering how fast she could run. The cheering around them was starting to become louder and she even saw people passing money, placing bets.

'Come on, Rosie. You can do it, girl,' people chanted from the sidelines. 'He's a weakling. You can take him.'

Mick looked far from a weakling but as she could see no way out, she put her arm on the table, mirroring Mick's position. He clasped her hand in his and waited for the count.

'Three, two, one—go!' someone shouted, and Rose felt the instant pressure of Mick's muscles. She brought her other hand up and started to push the other way. If she lost, she'd have to confess to all these people here that she loved Dave, but if she won, then she could speak to him in private. She wrestled as though her life depended on it.

Putting all her weight behind it, Rose pushed harder and almost had Mick's hand to the table when a movement in her peripheral vision caused her to look away.

Dave! He was standing there. Watching them. Scowling

at her. Melody was by his side, holding onto his hand. Even with the scowl, the sight of him warmed her heart and made her mind go blank. She felt her heart rate increase and started to feel a little light-headed.

'Yeah!' Mick crowed, as he managed to bend her arms backwards. Everyone clapped and cheered and Rose returned her attention to what had just happened. 'All right, Rosie. Pay up.'

Before she could utter a word, Dave let go of Melody's hand, stormed over and wrenched his brother out of the chair. 'What are you doing?' he demanded roughly. 'Are you out of your mind? You could have hurt her.'

Mick grinned stupidly at his brother and Rose realised Mick wasn't at all bothered by Dave's protective behaviour. 'It's all in your honour, bro'.'

'What are you talking about?' Dave held firmly onto the collar of his brother's shirt.

'Tell him, Rosie. Time to pay up.'

Rose stood, swallowing the enormous lump that was lodged in her throat. Everyone around them went quiet.

She stared at Dave, meeting his gaze, knowing this was the man she wanted to spend the rest of her life with.

Taking a deep breath, she said clearly, 'I love you.'

Dave's gaze remained on hers as he dropped his brother's shirt. No one moved or spoke, all eyes now anxiously on Dave to see how he would react. He didn't have to say anything, not as far as Rose was concerned.

She knew that by coming here and confessing her love for him, it was sealing their future in the sweetest way possible. He'd already said that he loved her and wanted to marry her, and she was certain, by the desire that flared in the blue depths of his eyes, that he still felt that way.

Both of them stood, frozen, content just to look at each other, their hearts communicating in a language as old as time.

Dave couldn't believe it. Rosie loved him. He'd been

certain of it but to actually hear her say the words was…incredible. Like a dream come true.

He felt a little hand slip inside his and he glanced down at his daughter. Melody nodded at him then reached out and slipped her other hand through Rosie's—uniting the three of them together.

'Perfect,' Dave said softly. 'Just perfect.'

EPILOGUE

'COME on,' Dave called, as he hoisted Melody up into his arms. 'All unmarried men and women in the centre of the room.'

Rose smiled brightly at her new husband as he held out his free hand for her. She kissed the father of the bride on the cheek before heading over to Dave's side, her cream-coloured wedding gown shimmering and sparkling as she walked.

Melody's dress was made from the same material, except for a red sash around her waist which matched the colour of Beverley's matron-of-honour dress.

'Unmarried men on that side.' Dave sectioned the room off. 'Unmarried women on the other.'

Everyone was laughing and joking as people shuffled into their places. Rose was having such a wonderful day, especially as all her dreams had come true. She smiled at her new stepdaughter, now content in the knowledge that she and Melody had taken the time during the last six months to really get to know each other. She never would have thought a six-year-old girl would be one of her best friends.

'All right, princess,' Dave said softly to Melody. 'Throw the garter first.'

'Do you think she'll get him?' Rose asked quietly.

'She should do. We've been practising her throwing skills for the past month or so,' Dave mumbled. 'Can you see Uncle Mick, Mel?'

'Yep.'

'Then let's count to three.' Dave cleared his throat.

'Ready?' he called. 'One, two, three!' Melody took aim over her father's shoulder and threw the garter.

'Yes!' She punched the air with her fist. 'It got him, Dad.'

Dave and Rose turned to look. They both laughed as Mick twirled the garter around his index finger and everyone clapped.

'Ready for the next one, Mel?' Rose asked.

'Sure. This is fun.'

'All right, ladies,' Rose called. 'One, two, three!' Melody threw the bouquet over Rose's shoulder, making sure it landed firmly in Mick's girlfriend's arms.

'Woo-hoo!' she called. 'I did it.'

Dave and Rose turned to look again as Mick stared at his girlfriend. Everyone was laughing and cheering.

'Excellent throwing, Mel.' Dave kissed his daughter.

'Couldn't have done it better myself. I'm proud of you, too.' Rose kissed Melody's other cheek. The girl between them giggled happily.

They all looked at Mick who was still staring at his girlfriend, his jaw hanging open in disbelief.

'Ah, face facts, bro',' Dave called. 'The garter and flower toss never lie. Rose and I are proof of it.'

Rose leaned over and kissed her new husband on the lips. 'Absolutely, my love. Absolutely.'

THE SURGEON'S PROPOSAL

by

Lilian Darcy

Lilian Darcy is Australian, but has strong ties to the USA through her American husband. They have four growing children, and currently live in Canberra, Australia. Lilian has written over forty romantic novels, and still has more story ideas crowding into her head than she knows what to do with. Her work has appeared on bestsellers lists, and two of her plays have been nominated for major Australian writing awards. 'I'll keep writing for as long as people keep reading my books' she says. 'It's all I've ever wanted to do, and I love it.'

CHAPTER ONE

'ARE you on your mobile, Dr Calford?'

'Yes, but don't worry. I've only moved three car lengths in the last ten minutes, so I'm not exactly a danger to other road users.'

'I'm sorry, Dr Calford, I didn't catch that.'

'Never mind, Lesley.' Dylan Calford raised his voice above the background noise of peak-hour traffic. 'There's nothing that can't wait. We'll pick it up next week, OK?'

'Enjoy the wedding,' the orthopaedic clinic secretary carolled cheerfully.

Dylan swallowed the dampening response that sprang to his lips, saying instead, 'And you enjoy your weekend, Lesley.' He knew that, like most working women with a family, she deserved to.

He flipped his phone shut and concentrated on the traffic. Brisbane roads were like tangled spaghetti at the best of times, and five o'clock on a Friday afternoon was not one of those. Being January, it was a *hot* Friday afternoon, too. With the sun pouring through Dylan's front windscreen, the car's air-conditioning couldn't keep up, and he felt sticky all over.

He was already late. Didn't know why he was going to this wedding in the first place. He was cynical about weddings at the moment. He didn't altogether *want* to feel this way, but after the debacle he'd endured with Sarah... There really was something too

5

incongruous about proceeding directly from a meeting with his divorce lawyer to a ceremony designed to shackle two more innocent people together in the dubious bonds of wedlock.

'Like lambs to the slaughter,' he muttered. A crucial three metres of space opened up ahead and he was able to crawl forward far enough to turn left into a quiet side street which *should* cut through in the direction of St Lucia.

Not that Dr Alexander Sturgess remotely resembled a lamb, of course.

Traffic lights ahead. Red, naturally. Dylan had chronic bad luck with traffic. As a result, he'd learned to be alert and super-competent in the way he navigated the sprawling city. That was a plus. All the same, he would have preferred to have been one of those fortunate souls for whom green lights, empty lanes and parking spaces appeared in his path like magic.

The sun was spearing into his eyes, half blinding him and making him sleepy. He and Alex had both been in emergency surgery half the night, putting a nineteen-year-old motorbike rider back together after a horrific crash. Head injury, complicated fractures, internal injuries. It was one of those times when you didn't know whether to even hope that he would live. The metal plates and pins now keeping the young man's bones in place were the least of his problems.

As befitted a senior orthopaedic specialist and a man about to get married, Alex had then taken the rest of the day off. Dylan, in contrast, had tackled his senior's scheduled surgical list, done a three-hour fracture clinic, which had run late, made hospital rounds and met his lawyer. The man was probably on the phone with Sarah's lawyer right now, presenting the details of the proposed settlement he and Dylan had worked out together.

Would it pass muster? Dylan suspected not. Sarah apparently valued the support she'd given him during his past two years of specialist orthopaedic training more highly than he did.

'Thank God we didn't have kids!' he muttered.

Were children on the agenda for Alex and Annabelle? He imagined so. Alex would want to perpetuate the Sturgess dynasty. And Annabelle, aka Theatre Sister Annabelle Drew... Didn't she have a child already? Yes, he was sure she did. Not hers, but one she'd had dumped on her a year or so ago. Her sister's little boy, or something.

Dylan didn't know the exact circumstances. Sister Drew didn't splash her personal life around during surgery like antiseptic solution, the way some people did. She was one of the few women who, in many ways, actually suited the anachronistic title of 'Sister' that was still used for senior nurses in Australian hospitals.

She was composed, contained, warm and highly competent. Polite. Honourable. *Good.* The kind of woman men didn't swear in front of.

Except Alex, Dylan revised. Alex swore during surgery the way he used a scalpel—deliberately, and with precision.

And Annabelle laughs at dirty jokes, he thought. As long as they're actually funny.

She had a lovely laugh. It was gurgly and rich, and came from deep inside her diaphragm.

So perhaps I'm wrong about the swearing thing. Perhaps it's just me who doesn't swear in front of her. That *goodness* thing… I probably don't have the slightest idea about who she really is at all.

The thought discomfited him a little, for some reason. This marriage to Alex, for example. Unlikely, wasn't it, if Annabelle Drew was the woman Dylan believed her to be?

The light turned green and he made a little more progress before getting stopped on a steep hill, which necessitated a noisy handbrake start once the car ahead began to move. Dylan's shirt was glued to his back, and it felt far too limp for a garment he'd only put on an hour ago.

Up ahead. Was that it? At last, yes!

Except that three circuits of the parking area revealed that there were no spaces, which forced Dylan into the next street and delayed his arrival by a further five minutes.

Now I really am in a foul mood! Dylan realised. I wish I'd turned down the invitation.

But his senior colleague would have read more into this than was intended. Alex had a tendency to do that.

Dylan hurried through the entrance of the elegant function centre and asked, 'Sturgess-Drew wedding? I'm late.'

'Straight through.'

'Thanks.'

He opened one half of a double, frosted glass door, slid through the gap, narrowly avoided colliding with a potted palm directly ahead, and discovered that he'd arrived halfway through the ceremony itself. A string quartet waited patiently on a large, draped dais. Guests, seated in neat rows, listened politely as a civil marriage celebrant droned out a syrupy poem.

It was almost impossible to hear. In the front row, a little boy was squirming energetically in the arms of a rather frail-looking woman and yelling, 'No! Don't want to sit down! Don't want to sit down!' He looked to be around two years old.

There were barely any empty seats. Just one, in fact, at the end of the same short row where the little boy was refusing to sit. Dylan edged his way along the side aisle towards it, hoping Alex wouldn't notice his terrible timing.

Again, it was the kind of thing that Dr Alexander Sturgess, MB, BS, M.Sc., FRACS, FA Orth. A., would take personally. Alex never considered that other people might have vindictive ex-wives and verbose divorce lawyers, late-running clinics and bad luck with traffic.

Dylan admired Alex Sturgess as a surgeon, which was why he'd returned to Coronation Hospital to train with him after a couple of rotations in hospitals elsewhere in Queensland. As a man, however, Alex wasn't exactly a role model he strove to emulate.

Easing into the seat, Dylan could hear a little better. The celebrant intoned more flowery words about love. Alex looked as if he'd forgotten to paint an expression on his face—other than, perhaps, a faint mist of approval—and Annabelle looked very, very nervous. The pale grey suit that the groom wore was wrong. Expensive, but wrong. It made Alex's skin tone look washed out, and stressed the fact that his once blond hair was heavily greyed. He was actually a much better looking specimen of manhood than he appeared today.

Oh, shut up! Dylan told himself. Who are you, to

be this critical? Just sit through it, wish them every happiness and let them get on with it!

No.

No.

Annabelle's dress was lovely. She had resisted the current vogue for strapless wedding gowns, in which most brides looked as if they had a single, log-shaped breast plastered across their chest. Dylan suspected, too, that she had an unsuitably freckly back and shoulders. Instead, she wore some draped confection in warm cream silk.

Portrait neckline, was it called? Anyway, it gave her a classic, regal aura and made her curvy figure look perfect. Her shoulder-length dark hair was piled up in glossy curlicues and tendrils. Her brown eyes were huge. Her freckle-dappled skin looked warm and peach perfect. She wasn't beautiful, but she had *something*.

He wasn't wrong about her, Dylan decided. She was going to be miserable with Alex.

The toddler was still struggling and yelling. He was an attractive child, with brown eyes and light brown curly hair, but clearly he wasn't suited to this formal setting. The woman who held him—presumably Annabelle's mother as there was a resemblance—looked grim-faced and at the end of her rope, on the verge of giving up and carrying him out.

Dylan could hear her laboured, wheezy breathing, and remembered overhearing Annabelle talking to another nurse about 'Mum's health'. Emphysema, he thought.

Meanwhile, the little boy was ruining the occasion. Alex clearly thought so. He glared in the child's direction, then frowned tightly. The celebrant reached the meat-and-potatoes part of the ceremony. Traditional and churchy, this bit. Alex's idea? It didn't really fit, after those chintzy poems.

'If anyone here present knows any reason…'

The celebrant raised his voice, struggling to be heard above, 'Put me *down*, Gwanma!'

'May they speak now, or forever hold their peace.'

'Yes, *I* do!' Dylan muttered darkly but very distinctly. 'You're making a terrible mistake!'

They'd heard.

Not the whole congregation, but the ones who counted. Annabelle's mother and Annabelle herself. Alex. The celebrant. The bridesmaid and the best man. The first two rows of guests. Lord, had he said it that loudly?

Apparently.

It didn't help that the little boy had suddenly gone quiet. A plastic lollipop stick protruding from his mouth explained this unlikely development.

Dylan began to sweat. Again.

Alex and Annabelle had both turned in his direction. Alex was looking slack-jawed and appalled, Annabelle startled and bewildered. The bridesmaid was gulping in air, and had a hand pressed to her ribcage. The best man was staring in horror.

Even Annabelle's little boy was watching him, happily sucking on his lollipop, while 'Gwanma' looked as if she had fully expected some kind of ghastly last straw at some point during the afternoon, but hadn't thought it was going to be this.

'I'm sorry,' Dylan barked. Instinctively, he stepped forward. This was another mistake. He was standing just a foot or two from Annabelle now, and right beside her. 'I didn't mean it.' But he *had* meant it. 'It was…' a moment of indulgent madness '…a joke. It was nothing. Please, uh, carry on.'

Alex wasn't buying it. The slack jaw had hardened. The washed-out complexion had refined to white around his nostrils.

'A joke?' His voice rasped. 'That's ridiculous! People don't joke in the middle of a wedding. You have a reputation as a loose cannon in some circles, Dylan, and I've chosen to ignore it, but *this*… What do you mean by it?'

He looked from Dylan to Annabelle and back again, and the action seemed to link the two of them together, standing shoulder to shoulder, as they now were.

'Dylan? Annabelle?' His voice rose.

It was obvious that he suspected an affair. Annabelle had gone bright red. The first two rows of guests were watching in strained silence, like the audience at an amateur play in which the cast have forgotten their lines. Further back, there was whispering, as those who hadn't heard Dylan's words tried to fathom what was going on. On the string quartet's dais, the cellist let her fingers slip and the strings of her instrument squawked.

'Nothing,' Annabelle said. 'Nothing, Alex.' She clasped her hands together. The gesture could have meant either 'Believe me' or 'Forgive me'. Dylan knew it was the former, but Alex clearly wasn't so sure.

Taking another edgy step forward, which brought the billowing skirt of Annabelle's dress washing around his trouser-clad legs, Dylan said, 'Really, Alex, I'm sorry. I know what you're thinking and it's my fault, but, no, it's…' He cleared his throat. 'Nothing like that.'

Annabelle's bridal fragrance enveloped him, evocative and sweet.

'It isn't, Alex. Honestly,' she echoed. Shaking, she laid a hand on her groom's arm. From this perspective, Dylan could see the slope of her right breast where the neckline of her dress gaped a little with her movement. Too many heartbeats passed before he looked away. 'You can't possibly believe—'

'It doesn't matter what I believe,' Alex said. 'It's what other people believe, and it's fairly obvious what they'll believe about this!'

'Garbage!' Dylan put in helpfully.

'Then, please, let's just…get on with it,' Annabelle begged, ignoring him. 'The way you're reacting is only making things worse. People are whispering, and—'

'Oh, it's *my* fault?' Alex's nostrils flared again.

'No, I'm not saying that, but—'

'It's my fault,' Dylan interposed. 'That's clear. Annabelle's right. Please, just get on with it.'

But Alex had a look on his face now. It happened in surgery very occasionally if he was tired and absently asked for the wrong size of clamp or something. Most surgeons would simply correct themselves and go on, but Alex could never do that. He would doggedly proceed with a piece of equipment that was less than ideal, rather than lose face by admitting to a mistake. Fortunately, he was a good enough surgeon to carry it off, but this wasn't surgery, this was his wedding.

For heaven's sake, get over it, Dylan wanted to tell

him. Don't lose your sense of proportion. But he knew it was already too late.

'No, I won't *get on with it*,' Alex said coldly. 'Are you coming, Peter?'

'Yes,' said the best man, who had to be Alex's younger brother. He blinked, like an animal caught in a bright light. 'Yes. Right. Of course.'

Without another word, Alex spun neatly around, strode down the centre aisle and out the glass door through which Dylan had entered just a few minutes earlier. Peter hurried after him. In the dead silence that had now fallen over the assembled guests, just two sounds could be heard—the squeak of the door as it swung closed again, and the lusty sound of one little boy slurping on a red lollipop.

The silence didn't last for long.

In seconds, the sound of voices had swelled from a buzz to a roar. Annabelle's silk skirt swished against Dylan's legs again as she whirled to face him. She was furious.

'Why did you do it? A joke? You can't think I'll swallow that! It was malicious! You know Alex as well as I do, Dylan Calford. You must have known he'd take it as a personal insult or worse. *Why* did you do it!'

In hundreds of hours of working together during surgery, Dylan had never seen her brown eyes blaze that way before. Her chest was heaving. The dress had slipped a little, and one creamy shoulder was bared. Her cheeks were still fiery red. She looked electric and wild and more stunningly attractive than he'd ever have thought she could...but, then, he'd never seen her dressed for her own wedding before. A dangerous new awareness stirred inside him.

'Why?' he echoed. 'Why?'

As fast as a computer scanning its hard drive, he ran through all the possible placatory falsehoods at his disposal and rejected every one of them. He was left, therefore, with the bald truth, so he said that, aware even as he spoke the words of how inadequate they sounded.

'Because I knew you wouldn't be happy.'

Annabelle was not grateful for the insight.

In a low voice, she said, 'I wanted this marriage. I needed it. I was going to give up work and take Duncan out of child-care. He hates it, and it's not good for him. I was going to spend more time with my mother, who isn't well, who isn't going to get better, and who needs me, too.'

'Is that what marriage is—?'

She rode right over the top of him. 'I was going to relax, for once, with a man I respected and cared for—*care* for—at my side, a man who's made it clear that I'm important to him, and that we can create a good partnership together. I had faith in that partnership! How dare you impose your own shallow definition of marital happiness? And how dare you presume to make that sort of judgement about us?'

'Not Alex,' Dylan corrected. 'Just you.'

'How dare you imagine you know me that well? No wonder Alex thought we were having an affair!'

The bridesmaid squeaked and covered her mouth with her hands.

'Darling...' came a shaky, smoke-damaged voice.

Annabelle turned. 'Yes, Mum?'

'Can you take Duncan now? He won't go to anyone else, and I just...can't. I need my oxygen from the car, and my inhaler. I shouldn't have thought I could get by for so long without them.'

'Oh, Lord, Mum, I'm sorry!' Annabelle muttered. She blinked several times, and Dylan realised it was because she was fighting tears. She reached out for the little boy, but he'd had enough, lollipop notwithstanding, and wriggled immediately to the ground.

'Splore!' he said.

'No, we can't explore now, love.' She bent to him, and Dylan got a serious and spectacular view of her breasts, as smooth as ivory and as plump as fresh-baked rolls. His groin tightened unexpectedly, and he felt as if someone had barged into him and knocked him sideways. Now was not the moment to have this happen.

'Want to explore with me, Dunc?' the bridesmaid offered tentatively, just behind Annabelle.

Too late. Duncan was already off and away, through the crowds of guests, who were milling uneasily in aisles and between rows of seats. The bridesmaid followed him, way too slowly. Dylan was still rooted to the spot. For several reasons. Annabelle straightened, and a sigh escaped between her teeth.

'He'll come back, won't he?' Annabelle's mother said.

'If he doesn't head straight for the street and get mown down by a car, the little monkey-love.'

'I meant Alex.'

'Oh.' Annabelle sighed again. 'No, Mum, I don't think he will. Alex is...not the type who cools off quickly.'

'But surely he'll realise—'

'I'd better go after Duncan, Mum. Linda's had no experience with kids. I'll bring your oxygen and your inhaler, and I'll tell everyone that they're welcome to stay. You can pass the word around, too. Get the music playing, perhaps? There's no sense all this food and planning going to waste. And then I'd better phone and cancel our hotel...'

Gathering up the folds of her dress, she smiled distractedly at several guests and began to make her way down the aisle. Following her, Dylan spotted Duncan at the back of the string quartet's dais, and pointed him out to Annabelle.

Again, she wasn't grateful.

'*You* won't be staying to eat, I don't suppose,' she said. It was an order rather than a question, and her chin was raised. 'But perhaps you'd care to mention, on your way out, that cocktails and dinner are still on for those who want them?'

'Sure. Of course,' he agreed, knowing how completely inadequate it was.

He did as she'd asked, heading gradually towards the beckoning glass doors. After fielding several questions along the lines of 'What on earth did you say?' and 'Oh, was it *you*, then?' he was finally able to make his escape. He'd never been so relieved in his life.

At home, once he'd peeled off his limp clothing and had a cold shower, a message on his answering-machine awaited him.

It was from Sarah.

'I've heard your offer, and it's insulting. We're preparing a counter-offer over the weekend, and your lawyer will hear from mine on Monday.'

Am I that out of touch with reality? Dylan wondered, after he'd erased the message. We were only married for two years. I was working. She was working. We employed a cleaner. We ate take-away meals, or I cooked. We kept separate bank accounts, and split the mortgage payments. For six months of that time, I was on rotation in Townsville and we only saw each other every second weekend.

In fact, they'd been far too scrupulous about maintaining a degree of separation in their lives, he now considered. Sarah hadn't wanted to come to Townsville. Perhaps their marriage would have lasted longer, and been happier, if they'd joined themselves to each other more completely. And perhaps he would then have felt that Sarah was entitled to the top-heavy percentage of their assets that she was obviously planning to claim.

Still stewing over it, and over the wedding fiasco, he made himself some salad and one of those nutritionally challenged instant dried pasta meals that people took on camping trips. Then he bored himself with television for several hours and dropped into bed at eleven, seeking oblivion.

It didn't come. He felt like a heel and resolved to himself, I'll make it up to Annabelle. That's the least I can do.

Go and see Alex, try and explain. Cover the cost of the reception. Ring each and every guest personally. Anything. Whatever Annabelle wanted.

Had this whole mess happened because of the divorce, or because he was a really terrible person? Until things had gone pear-shaped with Sarah, he'd have said his life was in an impeccable state. Priorities in order. Heart in the right place. Career on track. Judgement damn near flawless.

Hang on, though! Had he lost that much faith in himself? Rebellion began to stir inside him.

*Annabelle Drew, I saved your backside this after-
noon, no matter how you twist your definition of marital happiness.*

Poking at his feelings a little more, he discovered,
to his surprise, that he was angry with her. Disappointed, too. Somehow, she was a woman of whom
he would have expected better. Better priorities.
Better principles. Better sense.

I *will* make it up to her, if she'll let me. But she's
wrong to blame me for this!

Rolling onto his stomach in a twisted sheet, Dylan
slept at last.

'Thank heavens that's over!' Helen Drew said to her
daughter, as the final straggle of wedding guests
headed for their cars, later than both of them had
hoped. She had her portable oxygen close beside her,
and really should have been using it more tonight.
Her breathing sounded terrible, despite the use of her
inhaler, and she looked even worse. 'You did a fabulous job, darling. I was proud of you.'

Annabelle felt her mother's arms wrap around her
like a comfortable quilt. On the dais vacated by the
departing string quartet, Duncan had fallen asleep at
last, about fifteen minutes ago. And Linda had gone,
too, thank goodness. She was a good and loyal friend,
great at helping Annabelle with tax and finance questions, but was useless, and knew it, with kids, the
elderly and sick people. Her ineffectual offers of help
had, in the end, been something of a strain.

'You mean the fact that my face felt as if it was
about to drop off didn't show from the outside?'
Annabelle said to her mother.

'Well, of course it did, but people expected that.

They knew you were upset.' Annabelle's mother hesitated for a moment. 'Life will go on, you know.'

'Oh, I know that, Mum.' Although she couldn't quite imagine it at the moment.

She felt like one of those cartoon characters who stepped off a cliff, but didn't start falling until the gravity of their situation hit home. Her mind ticked and rattled like an engine out of tune.

Cancel the hotel for this weekend. Cancel the two-week honeymoon, planned for just over a month from now, at a time when Alex had been able to make some space in his schedule. Thank goodness she hadn't handed in her notice at the hospital yet! Where was Alex right now? At home?

'And anyway, you and Alex, I'm sure, will patch things up,' Helen said. 'It would seem silly not to get married just because some idiot of a man decided to get clever during the ceremony.'

Which of those misconceptions, if any, to tackle first? Annabelle wondered.

First misconception—she and Alex weren't going to patch things up. She knew that. Their relationship was over.

He had put so much thought and time and money into making theirs a perfect, elegant wedding, befitting the strong and sensible partnership they had hoped to create together. He'd wanted a ceremony and reception that would set a benchmark for friends and colleagues to aspire to, the sort of occasion that people would talk about for years. Well, they'd achieved the latter goal! Unfortunately, not in the way he'd wanted.

And he was a very stubborn man. Slinking off next week to a sparse little ceremony in a bureaucrat's office wouldn't make the grade, even leaving out the question of Alex's loss of face.

Which Alex would never leave out. And he was probably right—people would gossip.

Second misconception—Dylan Calford wasn't an idiot.

She'd known him, on and off, for three and a half years now. In some ways, she knew him better than she knew Alex, since there wasn't such a gap in status between them. She knew what he looked like first thing in the morning, fresh from a snatched sleep in the doctors' on-call room. She knew what he ate for lunch, and the places he'd been to for holidays since his marriage. They called each other by their first names.

He was proving himself as a fine surgeon, he was good to work with, and by all scales of character measurement, he was a pretty decent man. What Annabelle knew of him, she liked—*had* liked until today—and along with the rest of the hospital staff who worked with him, she felt for him over the issue of his divorce. He wasn't quite the same person he'd been a couple of years ago. Harder. More cynical, and less patient.

And, finally, he hadn't 'decided to get clever'. He hadn't intended his words to be overheard. Possibly, he hadn't intended to speak them out loud at all.

Which means he genuinely thinks our marriage would have been a mistake.

How could something be a mistake when you needed it so badly? Annabelle knew that she and Alex weren't in love the way most couples believed themselves to be when they married. They'd talked about that, seriously and at length.

Alex had exhibited his worst qualities today—as he sometimes did in surgery—but in their private time, he was thoughtful and interesting. They respected each other. He approved of her. They could talk about plans without friction. He was a tender, undemanding lover, and he worked hard at his relationship with Duncan.

And, oh, dear Lord, she'd *needed* their marriage! She *needed* to be able to give up work for a few years in order to focus her attention on caring for her mother and Duncan. She *needed* Alex's financial support, not for herself but for the people she loved.

When they'd started going out together four months ago, it had been like being rescued from a dragon's lair by a white knight. She'd started sleeping again. She'd seen light at the end of the tunnel.

Whereas now…

Suddenly, she felt sick. Anger towards Dylan Calford rose in her throat like bile. The concern he evidently had about the dire possibility of her making a mistake in marriage, of her 'being unhappy', was a luxury she couldn't afford.

'I wouldn't have *let* it be a mistake!' she muttered to herself. 'I would have made it work, no matter what it took. I would have been happy! Imposing his cynical stance on other people just because he's having a bad divorce is unforgivably arrogant!'

'Are you angry with him?' her mother asked.

'Yes. Absolutely and utterly furious!' Annabelle said aloud.

'Don't let it get in the way when you talk.' Mum put out her hand and rested it heavily on Annabelle's arm. 'And try to talk to him soon. He acted out of pride. He'll make it up to you. I'm *sure* you can work it out.'

'Oh, Mum, no, I'm not angry with Alex. I understand why he walked out. It's Dylan Calford I'll never forgive for all this!' Annabelle said.

CHAPTER TWO

DYLAN appeared at Annabelle's house at nine-thirty the next morning.

Duncan had awoken, as usual, at six. No matter how late he stayed up, he never slept in. Right now, he was running wildly around the back garden, pushing a big toy truck, and he would barely slacken his pace all day. Annabelle often wondered what sort of a child his father had been. This active? This unstoppable? There was no one to ask about him.

'Hello,' she said coolly to Alex's registrar at the front door of her little weatherboard Queenslander.

'Uh, yeah, hi…' he answered.

'I suppose you want to come in,' Annabelle prompted him, not sure why she was taking the trouble to help him out, even to this limited extent.

She had never seen him so at a loss for words. Had never seen him dressed so casually either. His body was one hundred per cent male. Broad shoulders, strong legs, dark hair and darker eyes, football player's waist and hips. Orthopaedic surgeons had to be strong.

Since this was Brisbane in January, he wore shorts—navy blue and topped with a polo shirt subtly patterned in a beige and khaki print. He was freshly showered and shaven, and radiated an energy that was only partly physical.

He looked good, and he'd recovered his equilibrium already. He was intimidating, if she'd been in the mood to feel intimidated by anyone. Right now, she wasn't.

'Look, I won't apologise again,' he said, his tone that of a man who was sure of his ground.

'No, don't,' she agreed. 'But, please, don't stay here on the veranda. It's cooler out the back, and I need to keep an eye on Duncan.'

'Sure.' The word sharpened his slight American accent. Annabelle knew he had been here since his early teens, had been a star rugby player at Brisbane's most illustrious boys' school and held Australian citizenship, but sometimes his Chicago origins still showed.

She led the way through the house and he spoke behind her. 'But I do want to do what I can to make this whole thing less difficult for you.'

'Sure.' She turned her head and smiled as she echoed the word he'd used, but the smile didn't do much to soak up the pool of dripping sarcasm in her tone. There was nothing he could do to make this 'less difficult'!

He didn't reply, yet somehow this time his silence was much stronger than some bleating protest would have been. Her spine prickled suddenly.

They reached the back veranda, which was shaded by the riot of tropical growth that threatened to encroach upon it. Along the paved path, Duncan was still making truck sounds, while the small and securely fenced swimming pool beckoned invitingly in a patch of sunshine. Hibiscus and frangipani gave bright and sweetly scented accents of colour, and the wooden floor of the veranda was cool and smooth under Annabelle's bare feet.

From somewhere, as she invited Dylan to sit in one of the cane-backed chairs, came the thought, At least now I don't have to move. To Alex's large, air-conditioned and professionally decorated river-front house. They'd been planning to sell this place, or rent it out as an investment.

'You have a nice little place,' Dylan observed.

'I'm fond of it,' she agreed.

That was an understatement. She loved this small eighty-year-old cottage, perched on an absurd patch of land that had a cliff for a front garden and a crooked walkway of twenty-seven steps up from the street to the front door. This was one of the older areas of Brisbane, just a few kilometres from the city centre.

She didn't mention to Dylan that the mortgage on the house was stretching her finances far too thinly, now that she had child-care fees for Duncan on top of it.

Change to night shifts if I can. Mum's health is only going to get worse, but hopefully she'll have a few good years yet, and by then Duncan will be at school. As for the money...

The repetitious thoughts droned on in her head. Cutting them off, she offered, 'Would you like tea or coffee? Or something cool?'

'Coffee would be great.' The cane chair creaked a little as he shifted his weight.

'Can you keep an eye on Duncan for me while I get it?'

'Of course.'

Mad. She had been stark, raving mad to invite him in, Annabelle decided in the kitchen. He didn't particularly deserve a fair hearing, she considered, so why give him one?

Habit.

This was how she'd first become involved with Alex. He had been particularly brutal during surgery one day several months ago. Had had her on the verge of tears, which not many surgeons could have done. And he'd invited her out to dinner as an apology. 'And to prove to you that what you see in surgery is only a small part of who I am. I should probably invite the entire theatre staff in rotation!'

Although it had seemed a little out of character, she had taken the invitation at face value, and had been surprised at the ultra-expensive restaurant he'd chosen. She had been even more surprised when he'd kissed her at the end of the evening. She hadn't picked up on his intention until it had happened.

It probably hadn't been until their fourth or fifth date that she'd gone beyond the fair hearing thing and had really started to appreciate Alex for who he was. His clever mind, his knowledge of wine and food, his informed opinions and the fact that he'd made his approval of her very clear.

It had been like an audition, or a job interview. She'd realised that. He'd been making sure she was suitable. He had been impressed to discover that her mother was *that* Helen Drew, the widow of Sir William Drew, QC, and when he'd then heard from Annabelle that her father's finances had been in a disastrous state on his death several years ago, it hadn't put him off.

At the same time, Annabelle had been assessing Alex in a similar way. For a start, they'd got on well. Always had something to talk about. Never yelled at each other, if you didn't count surgery. Annabelle didn't like the way Alex behaved in surgery, but he defended himself.

'Sorry. It's bloody hard. I'm a prima donna, I know. But there's too much at stake, Annabelle, during a difficult operation. I'm going to swear if something goes wrong, and I'm going to yell at whoever's responsible. That, by the way, is never me! Don't try and get me to change.'

OK. Fair enough. She could tolerate it.

More importantly, from her point of view, Alex realised that Duncan was a permanent fixture in her life, and always took him into consideration. He was happy about supporting both of them, and understood that her mother required a huge amount of Annabelle's time and care as well. He actively preferred that she give up work.

'If you never go back at all, that's fine with me.'

This wasn't quite how she felt. She loved her career but, even leaving aside Mum's needs, Duncan just wasn't the kind of child that did well in the structured environment of a child-care centre, and she couldn't ignore that. She had begun to see unpleasant shifts in his developing personality that upset her deeply, and she knew that the overworked and underpaid child-care centre staff breathed sighs of relief when he went home each day.

Duncan had been carelessly conceived during a holiday fling with a Greek barman, carelessly brought into the world and casually abandoned by his mother, Annabelle's sister Victoria. Vic hadn't intended to abandon him permanently, of course. She'd simply left him in Annabelle's care when he was ten months old, while she went on an adventure holiday in Borneo.

'Eleven days. You don't mind, do you, Belle?'

No, she didn't mind. She loved her baby nephew, and she had days off work owing to her.

Six days into the trip, Victoria had been killed in a landslide on the side of a jungle-clad mountain. It was an exotic end to an exotic life, and a difficult start for a little boy. He deserved better, and he was going to get it in future, Annabelle had vowed.

Only now, because of Dylan Calford, he wasn't.

The electric jug boiled and she poured steaming water onto the little mounds of shiny granules at the bottom of each mug, creating a hissing sound. The coffee smelled good and rich and fresh, but unmistakably like instant. She had real ground beans, and a whiz-bang Christmas-gift coffee-machine, but wasn't going to waste either the coffee or the machine on Dylan Calford today. The coffee took longer to make that way, and might give him the mistaken impression that she wasn't furious.

'Here.'

She handed him the muddy black brew, and plonked a plate of sweet biscuits onto the coffee-table. There wasn't much room on it at the moment. Duncan was running back and forth between his toy chest and the table, depositing his trucks and cars there one by one in a long, snaking row. His sound effects were loud.

'Active little boy,' Dylan commented.

'He doesn't have ADHD,' Annabelle said.

'Did I say—?'

'A lot of people have said it. The manager of his child-care centre wanted him assessed.'

'But you didn't think it was necessary?'

'No. Because when he's with me, he's fine. Active, yes. Top-of-the-chart active, but I read up on the sub-

ject when the issue was first raised, and he doesn't
show any of the other signs of attention deficit hy-
peractivity disorder. The psychologist I finally took
him to agreed. His concentration is fully engaged
when he's interested in something. He's not aggres-
sive, unless he's handled aggressively first.' Or not
often, anyway, she revised inwardly, thinking of a
couple of recent incidents at child-care. These were
the reason she'd consulted the child psychologist, and
she'd found his ideas on the issue very sensible. She
summarised them briefly to Dylan.

'He can't express his feelings very well yet. His
language skills aren't good enough. So he gets frustrated in a situation where he's not happy, and there
have been a couple of incidents of biting and kicking
at his child-care centre. A lot of young children go
through a similar stage, and they grow out of it, if it's
handled in the right way.'

If. A big 'if', in this case, when Annabelle herself
couldn't be with him, and the staff at child-care didn't
have the resources to give him the extra attention he
needed.

Knowing she could talk for minutes on end about
Duncan, his difficulties and her feelings, she finished,
'He just likes to be on the go, to head for the horizon
and explore.'

Like Vic had. Perhaps he had received his temper-
ament from her.

'Parents usually know best,' Dylan said.

'I *am* his parent!' She glared at him. 'Or the closest
thing he's got to one, anyhow.'

'Yes, that's what I meant. You'd know, and I'm
guessing you're not influenced too much by wishful
thinking either. Or not usually.'

He frowned, and Annabelle flushed. Was that a reference to Alex and their marriage plans? It was! She'd blurted out far too much to Dylan yesterday in her anger.

'Why are you here, Dylan?' she asked him coldly.

'To make an offer. Some kind of compensation. I want to cover the cost of the reception at least.'

'Alex is the one to approach about that, although I doubt he'd accept it. *I* wouldn't!'

'And ask you if there's any other way I can make up for—'

'There isn't,' she snapped. 'Short of offering to marry me yourself.'

It had to be one of the most ill-thought-out suggestions she'd ever made, a product of fatigue and stress, and disappointment and anger, and something else she didn't have a name for. Something new. She didn't usually come out with wild statements like that.

Dylan laughed. It was a rich, confident sound. In any other circumstances, she would have wanted to join in. 'Perhaps that's exactly what I should do,' he said. 'The only thing that would really make the grade, right?'

'I didn't mean—'

'Thanks. You've made me feel better.' He was still grinning at her, his dark gaze sweeping over her like a caress. It disturbed her.

'How?'

'By proving to me that I did the right thing. The insane thing, under the circumstances, and I hadn't realised it would be the show-stopping announcement that it was, but if you could propose me as a substitute husband—'

'I wasn't serious.'

'One day later.'

'I wasn't serious!'

'Even as a joke, then doesn't that tell you—?'

'Nothing.' She shook her head sharply, clenched teeth aching. 'It was a stupid, meaningless thing to say. It doesn't tell me anything.'

'I dare you, Annabelle.' There was a light of challenge and determination in his expression now that made her uncomfortable. He was leaning forward in his seat, his strength casually apparent. 'I dare you to consider the proposition. I've got just as much to offer you as Alex does. Not exactly the same things, perhaps, but equivalent. Better, possibly, in some areas. Think about it.'

And suddenly, graphically, she was.

She was thinking about a wedding—symbol of solved problems—and a wedding night, and a bed with Dylan Calford in it. Naked. Or possibly not quite naked yet, but with some snug-fitting black stretch fabric across his groin. And smiling. The way he was smiling now, with a challenge glinting in his eyes, and a wicked, delicious expression that said, I can read your mind.

She went hot all over. My sainted aunt! She'd never thought of Dylan Calford that way before! He'd been engaged or married or absorbed in his divorce for the entire three and a half years she'd known him, and that had meant he'd been off limits. Not just in her eyes, but in his own.

He didn't give off the knowing, overtly sexual vibe that available, good-looking men so often exuded. And, anyway, they rarely encountered each other outside the demanding environment of surgery, and never away from the hospital. When they worked together, there was always too much else to think about.

Today was different. There were no patients, no colleagues. His property settlement was at the negotiation stage, with the one-year anniversary of his separation already past. The vibe was there, singing and throbbing like the strings of an instrument. Two contradictory feelings warred inside her.

The first was instinct more than thought, and insisted, You'll learn more from this than you ever learned from Alex. The second was an impatient need to reject the whole thing as dangerous, untrustworthy and insignificant.

The second feeling won.

'You don't mean it,' she told Dylan flatly.

Hardly aware of what she was doing, she wrapped her arms across her body to try and stroke away the goose-bumps that had risen on her arms. Her nipples ached, and deep inside her there was a heaviness and a heat that hadn't been there a few minutes ago. Definitely, she didn't want any of it. Not now.

'No,' he agreed. 'You're right. I don't. But you thought about it, didn't you?' His eyes were still fixed on her face.

'Not in the way you mean.'

Or, possibly, *exactly* in the way he'd meant.

Had he been aware of the vibe he'd given off? The potency of it? The delicious wickedness of it? The fact that she'd absorbed it, wrapped herself in it and reflected it right back at him? Or was he giving it off unconsciously?

'Well, think about it some more,' he said. Or, rather, *ordered*.

He took what had to be a scorching gulp of his

coffee, without apparently noticing the heat. If he had a tendency not to notice heat, that was good, a relief...and a reprieve.

'There's no need to think about it any more,' she said sharply. 'Not for a second.'

'I wonder.'

Meanwhile, Duncan had become bored with the car and truck game, and every vehicle he owned was now lined up on the coffee-table like a peak-hour traffic jam. 'Go inna pool, Mummy?' he said hopefully.

'In a little while, love,' she answered.

A swim would be great. Bruising, with the way Duncan liked to hurl himself off the edge and into her arms in the water. His eager little legs always collided painfully with her thighs as he held her tight and instinctively kicked like a frog beneath the water. But it would cool her down. The building heat in the air was extra sticky today.

Duncan had already run off in search of towels. He'd probably come back with six of them.

As soon as he had gone, Dylan asked curiously, 'He calls you that? Mummy?'

Annabelle went on the defensive at once. 'Mum and I talked about it. We agreed it would be best at this stage. He has no memory of Vic—my sister. We haven't decided when we'll tell him.'

'Tell me how it happened,' he invited quietly. 'Do you mind?'

She stifled a sigh. Sometimes she *did* mind, especially when the questions were nosy, tactless or judgmental. But somehow Dylan Calford seemed to be in her life now, since yesterday. Arrogant in his presumptions, dictatorial in his advice. She was still angry about it, yet at the same time felt her usual over-developed need to be *fair*. Beyond the arrogance, his desire to make amends as far as possible was apparently genuine.

Not that he *can* make amends, she considered inwardly. Is it the thought that counts? Aloud, she said, 'No, I don't mind. She'd gone trekking, and there was an accident. In Borneo. It was in the news. You might have read about it.'

He thought for a moment, then nodded. 'Mmm, yes, I remember now. I'm sorry, I didn't realise that was your sister.'

'I didn't want to talk about it much at work.'

'It must have been hard. For you and your mother.' They weren't flowery words, but she appreciated the depth of sincerity behind them.

'Still can't believe it sometimes,' she admitted. 'Sometimes I—' She broke off and shook her head.

Sometimes she'd hear a voice in a crowded shopping mall and instinctively turn her head because it sounded like Vic. Sometimes, with news or a funny anecdote to tell, she'd pick up the telephone and stop with her finger poised over the first digit of Vic's old phone number, her whole body frozen and a stabbing pain in her stomach.

But she didn't want to tell Dylan Calford about any of that. He didn't prompt her to finish, and she felt a small stirring of gratitude for the fact.

'And there was no father around?' he asked after a moment.

'Not one that we could trace. Vic never even told Mum and me his last name. He didn't know about Duncan and wouldn't have cared, Vic said. It was a holiday romance. She travelled a lot.'

'The adventurous type. Like her son.'

'I'm starting to see that, yes, although at the end of a long day, I always blame his father for the high energy levels!'

'How do you deal with it? How do you know that your full-time care will be better than a child-care centre?' Evidently he remembered exactly what she'd said to him yesterday.

'Because I love him. I...' she searched for the right word '...*champion* him, in a way those very nice girls—really, they're very nice—at child-care just don't have time for, with their ratio of one adult to five kids.'

'That high?'

'It's standard,' she answered. 'I believe in him, and know him well enough to bring out the best in him. I understand what he's trying to tell me, which some people don't. His speech isn't very clear yet, and that frustrates him. I have the time and care to head off his difficult behaviour, and I know when he's over-dosed on other kids and needs some time to himself. We go to the park for hours, and just run each other down as if we were two little toys in one of those battery commercials on television. He sleeps well, if an hour or two less than most kids his age. And I'm pretty fit, as a result!'

'Hmm,' Dylan said. There was a pause. 'And what will happen now?'

'He'll stay in child-care. Unless I can juggle my shifts at the hospital, which, of course, I'll try to do.'

Which doesn't deal with the mortgage. There must be some other areas where I can save. If I get an increase on my credit-card limit...

'There's no other choice? Your mother—'

'Has emphysema, as you may have realised. She's

tired and breathless, gets asthma attacks quite often, and can't do much for herself. She could sell her little unit and come and live here, yes, but she's too ill to help with Duncan, other than overnight babysitting, and really too ill to live under the same roof as such an active little boy.'

'Yes, I can understand that.'

'She loves him, but she wouldn't be happy here. Can you stop asking these questions, Dylan? Marrying Alex wasn't just about solving my current family problems. There was a lot more. You mean well. I can see that. But you're trivialising my life, and my choices. It's not helping. Don't try and help, please.'

She lifted her chin and met his gaze steadily, still far more conscious of their two bodies than she wanted to be. What was he thinking? She couldn't tell. His dark eyes were clouded and thoughtful, and he was frowning.

At that moment, Duncan ran back out to the veranda, as expected, with his arms full of towels. One dangling end was dangerously close to tripping up his eager little feet. Turning away from Dylan, Annabelle took the bundle from Duncan quickly, and asked, 'What about your cozzie? Know where that is?'

'Onna line,' he said confidently, and rushed off again, to the far corner of the crowded garden where the rotary clothesline stood, hung with pegged-up garments.

'I should go,' Dylan said, and Annabelle didn't argue. 'Please, think a little more about what I said.'

She laughed. 'The marriage proposal? You didn't mean it. I'm not going to think about it for a second.'

'You're right. I didn't mean it. But think about it

anyway.' His dark gaze collided with hers again. It seemed to trap her, making her hot.

'That doesn't make sense,' she told him.

'Probably not,' he agreed. 'Although I wonder... Maybe one day we'll both understand what it meant.'

Then he shrugged, smiled and stood up, looking long and strong and sturdy. Not at all the kind of man who should make whimsical marriage proposals that he admitted he didn't mean but still wanted her to take seriously.

'Enjoy the pool,' he said, and touched her bare shoulder.

His hand left a warm imprint there, and was gone again in a second. Annabelle's awareness of his touch was unsettling and unwanted. She took him quickly back through the house, and they got through a few last polite phrases, then she closed the door behind him and listened with relief to the confident sound of his feet as he loped down the twenty-seven steps.

She spent a shrieking half-hour in the pool with Duncan, got him dried and dressed and settled him with a video.

Then she phoned Alex.

'I was wondering when you'd call,' he said stiffly.

'It's just on eleven. I wasn't sure whether to...' She trailed off, feeling the phone line between them heavy with stony silence. She tried again, newly determined that there had to be a way to get through this. It was ridiculous to call off a marriage *permanently* because of one meaningless intrusion during the ceremony. They were both mature adults. Alex was almost forty, and she was thirty-two. 'I really wanted to talk, Alex, but I thought we both needed to cool down after last night. I'm just as angry with Dylan as you are.'

Silence.

'And if you still think I gave him any cause to make that idiotic objection, then I'm not sure what to do next, because I *didn't*, and I've told you that, and *he's* told you that…' She paused expectantly.

Silence.

'Which makes me start to wonder if you were just looking for an excuse.'

'Don't be so ridiculous.'

'So we'll get married. A small, discreet ceremony, with—'

'That's impossible. I'm not going to rehash it again.'

'Tell me what you're *feeling*, Alex!' she begged him desperately. 'Just blustering like this, stonewalling anything I say, it's not telling me anything.'

Silence.

'Shall I come over to your place, or do you want to come here?' she suggested.

Silence.

'Dylan wants to pay for the reception. I told him to talk to you about it.'

'So you've seen him? When have you seen him?'

'He came round just now. He obviously feels bad.'

'I can't believe you're defending him, and that you talked to him before you talked to me.'

'I'm not defending him.' *Am I?* 'I'm just letting you know that he'll probably phone you, too. I don't know why he came to me first.'

Silence.

'So, should we talk about—?'

'There's absolutely nothing to talk about at all,' Alex snapped. 'It's out of the question to have him pay for the reception.'

'Well, yes, that's what I thought, but since it was your money, I didn't want to—'

'And it's out of the question to talk about scheduling another ceremony. I won't get over this in a hurry, Annabelle. You're the last person I would have thought the type to trail chaos and melodrama in your wake, but now I'm wondering how many other ex-boyfriends—'

'Dylan Calford isn't an—'

'Or *would-be* boyfriends I can expect to crawl out of the woodwork. I was embarrassed to the core last night. People, no doubt, are already talking and making conjectures. And I don't even think I could look at you at the moment, Annabelle.'

The reproachful crash of the slamming phone invaded Annabelle's left ear, and stinging tears flooded her vision. Today, this hurt in a way it hadn't hurt last night. Last night she'd been angry, and in shock. Now came the full realisation that Alex had dropped her like a hot coal, as if she were tainted in some way.

He'd almost said as much. He'd called her a 'type'. Not the type to attract scandal. Not the type to compromise his reputation and his ambitions. Political ambitions. She knew he had them. President of the Australian Medical Association. Queensland State Minister for Health. But she'd believed herself to mean much more to Alex than a suitably well-bred and stain-resistant political wife, just as he meant more to her than a way out of her family problems.

Annabelle stuffed her knuckles into her mouth and sobbed wildly, until she remembered Duncan in the next room. He would be worried and confused if he saw her like this—red-eyed, swollen-nosed. He had a caring little heart, when he stood still long enough for it to show.

She heard the clatter of his feet as he bounced off the couch to come looking for her, and quickly turned to the kitchen sink to wash away the worst of the mess her face was in. By the time he appeared, she was wearing a smile.

CHAPTER THREE

ANNABELLE and Duncan reached Gumnut Playcare just as it opened, at six-thirty on Monday morning. Annabelle was rostered in Theatre with a seven o'clock start, and timing, as usual, was tight.

'Got your backpack?' she prompted Duncan, then watched as he dragged it slowly across the back seat of the car.

His little face looked sullen and closed and not at all cute.

She helped him put the backpack on, then took his hand and tried to lead him up the path to the front door, but he stalled, pulled out of her grasp and ran off to examine some interesting leaves on a nearby bush.

'We can't look at those now, love,' she told him brightly, but he ignored her. 'I'll be late,' she finished, knowing the concept—and the consequences—were meaningless to a little boy.

Since it was all too likely that either Alex or Dylan, or both of them, would be operating in Theatre Three today, she was doubly anxious to arrive on time.

''Eaves,' Duncan said. His tone was stubborn.

'I know, they're lovely leaves, but we just can't look at them now. This afternoon, OK?'

She hoped, guiltily, that he'd forget. It would be six or later before she got back here, as Mum had a doctor's appointment. Annabelle had cleaned and done laundry for her yesterday, but today, in addition, they would need to stop at the shops on the way back from the doctor. If the doctor was running late, or if she herself was late off work...

A twelve-hour day was too long for a two-year-old.

''Eaves,' he said again.

'Not now, sweetie.'

She picked him up and carried him inside, ignoring the way he wriggled and kicked. He'd been a darling all weekend, sitting rapt and attentive on the couch yesterday afternoon while Mum read to him, 'helping' to hang out the laundry. Today, she already knew he was going to be a demon.

Inside the child-care centre, once she had put him down, he streaked off and began running noisily around the room, without responding to the overly cheerful greetings of Lauren and Carly, the two staff on duty. Annabelle signed him in, unsurprised to find that he was the first name on today's page.

Just then a second child arrived—a four-year-old girl named Katie, prettily dressed and obediently holding her mother's hand. As soon as she saw Duncan, she said in a loud voice, 'That's the naughty boy who bit me, Mummy.'

Annnabelle's stomach flipped. She turned to Lauren. 'You didn't tell me...'

'There's a note in his pocket.' Lauren gestured towards the bright row of cloth 'pockets' running along the wall, where children's artwork and notes for parents were placed. Duncan's was brimming with untidily folded paintings, and Annabelle thought guiltily, When did I last remember to check it? Wednesday?

When she picked him up, she was always so keen to get out of here quickly.

'I'm sorry,' she said. 'I'll speak to him about it.'

Which would be pointless with a two-year-old, when the incident had occurred several days earlier. Katie's mother was glaring at Annabelle, however, and she felt obliged to act tough. Inside, she was crumbling.

'And it's not the first time either, I've heard,' the mother said coldly.

She was right. It wasn't.

But it only ever happened at child-care.

'Can I make an appointment to talk to you?' Annabelle asked Lauren desperately.

'This afternoon?'

'I can't today. I have other commitments.' And tomorrow wasn't any better. 'I'll have to look at my diary. Duncan, Mummy has to go, OK?'

She had to say it twice to get his attention, but when she did, he rushed over and flung his arms around her legs.

'No!'

'You have a great day, OK?'

'No. Don't go.'

'I'll see you later.' Aeons later. 'And we'll have spaghetti for dinner.'

Duncan burst into tears and clung to her legs as she dragged herself towards the door. Lauren intervened, picking him up and talking brightly about blocks and puzzles. He began to kick and struggle, and the brightness was more forced. 'We don't kick, Duncan,' she said.

The little girl's mother walked past, in the wake of a sweet-voiced and perfectly contented, 'I love you, Mummy!'

'I love you too, Katie, my sweetheart angel,' she called back. Smugly, it seemed to Annabelle.

'Just go, Annabelle. He'll be fine in two seconds,' Lauren said.

They both knew it wasn't true.

'Thanks,' Annabelle answered.

Unlocking her car, she heard the little girl's mother muttering pointedly about discipline and aggression and behaviour problems. She was still shaking and queasy as she drove out of the parking area and into the street.

The whole of today's list in Theatre Three consisted of hips and knees, Annabelle discovered when she arrived at Coronation Hospital. Dr Shartles had two hip replacements, then Alex took over for two quite complex knee operations and another hip procedure sandwiched in between, with Dylan assisting. All three were private patients, which meant that Alex would involve himself more thoroughly than he did with public patients having the same surgery.

Dr Shartles's hip replacements went without a hitch, which served as a necessary settling to Annabelle's focus. She enjoyed this aspect of surgery—the fact that there was a standard framework to the whole thing, so that even when something went wrong the surgical staff still had procedures in place for dealing with it.

Today, however, she felt like the meat in a sandwich. As soon as she'd calmed down and dragged her mind away from Duncan, she had time to think about the encounter with Alex which lay ahead. Nice if Dylan hadn't been part of the equation as well!

Dr Shartles left it to his registrar to complete the final procedure, the patient was wheeled out to

Recovery and Annabelle and the other theatre nurse, Barb Thompson, prepped Theatre Three for the next operation. Annabelle was an experienced scrub nurse, gloved and sterile like the surgeons, and worked closely beside them.

Just beyond the swing doors, she heard Alex's voice, and wasn't surprised at the sharpness in it.

'No, not yet. I have some calls to make first. When Calford gets off the phone.'

So they were both here.

Knots tightened in her temples, and she thought, I wish I was on a beach. With Duncan. I wish we *lived* on a beach. On a tropical island. Eating coconuts and mangoes and yams. I don't want to be here.

'Next patient just got cancelled,' Barb reported. 'Don Laycock. Dr Sturgess's patient. Third time. He's…' She glanced over at Annabelle and quickly amended her sentence. 'Not happy.'

'No, he wouldn't be,' Annabelle agreed. She tried to speak calmly and casually, but it didn't quite come off.

Everyone had already heard about the cancelled wedding when she'd got in this morning, although the hospital friends who'd been at the reception had all told her they wouldn't say anything. She wasn't surprised. It was the kind of news that travelled fast, and perhaps Alex himself had told people. Annabelle hadn't had to deliver the little speech she'd prepared for this morning, and which she knew she'd have garbled despite the preparation.

I'm not the only one who's tense, she realised now. Everyone is wondering how this is going to go.

Badly.

They all knew it as soon as the swing doors crashed open.

'Gram positive cocci in his blood sample,' Alex said. A systemic infection, in other words, disqualifying the patient for surgery. 'I don't know why we have to wait until *now* to hear it. Next patient isn't prepped yet, so I'll be back in half an hour.'

He disappeared again before anyone could acknowledge his words in any way, and he hadn't given the slightest sign that he'd known Annabelle was there. He did know it, though. She was in no doubt of that. In his wake, the swing doors vibrated like drum skins.

The knots in her temples grew tighter.

'Take lunch?' Barb suggested.

'Quickly,' anaesthetist Sharon Curtis agreed. 'Because some people's half-hours are shorter than others.'

She meant Alex, although she was careful not to say so.

Until Friday, Annabelle had rather enjoyed the feeling that she was the only one of the theatre staff to know how different Dr Sturgess could be away from this environment. Now, as she left Theatre and headed for the surgical staff tearoom, she suddenly found herself thinking, But this is the environment where he likes to be. Does he like the excuse to terrorise people, and to know that his whims are law? I think he does…

'Dr Calford, you've heard about Don Laycock getting cancelled?' Barb said.

Dylan had just put down the phone, and joined Annabelle and Barb as they headed down the corridor to the tearoom.

'Yes. Third time.' He nodded. 'Poor guy. He's a nervous patient. I think he felt reprieved when he heard—I was checking out another patient in the next bed at the time—but it just prolongs the agony, since he'll have to key himself up all over again once the infection is dealt with.'

He flicked a quick look across to Annabelle and she went hot. Was he thinking the same thing she was? That the same applied to the way she felt about Alex? Keyed up to stand next to him over an operating table. Half an hour's reprieve before she had to key herself up again.

Just before they reached the tearoom, Dylan held her back with a hand on her arm. She wanted to fight his touch, but knew she'd only draw more attention to the way it affected her.

'Wasn't sure if we'd see you today,' he said.

What was it that Mum had said on Friday night? Oh, that's right... 'Life goes on,' she answered.

'As I told my lawyer this morning,' Dylan said, 'when I accepted Sarah's suggested settlement package.'

The cynical drawl didn't suit him, and Annabelle felt an absurd urge to tell him, Don't judge the whole world differently because of a bad marriage. I hate to see you this way.

She kept her mouth firmly shut, of course.

'Alex knocked back my offer of paying for the reception, by the way,' Dylan continued.

'You didn't seriously think he'd accept?'

'No. I didn't.' He added in a low tone, 'Still wondering what I can get *you* to accept. Something, Annabelle.'

'Nothing,' she countered quickly. 'I don't want it. Just forget it.'

'I'm on standby if you change your mind. Meanwhile, I'm at least taking you out to dinner, OK?'

She shook her head. 'Booked up. Sorry.'

'You need some time to yourself. You're stressed out.'

'I know. But there's no time available.'

'Hmm.' He looked at her narrowly for a moment, then went across to the urn and made himself some coffee, turning his back to her as if she wasn't there.

In well-washed theatre gear, his body was impressive in a way she'd never noticed before, and didn't want to notice now. The muscles in his back were clearly defined and solid, although the total impression was one of athleticism rather than bulk. He moved comfortably. A lean and stretch to the left to reach for a mug, an efficient scoop and flick with the spoon in the coffee-can.

His hair was cut short at the back, and was thick enough to hold its shape without being stubbly or spiky. His nape looked soft and sensitive, the perfect place for a woman's fingers to stroke and linger. When he started humming a chart-topping song tunelessly under his breath, and tapping a bar or two of its beat with his fingers on the counter-top, Annabelle turned firmly away and stopped listening.

It was as if Alex's petulant suspicions about an affair between herself and Dylan had changed something in her own perceptions. In some part of her, an invisible line had been crossed. Dylan wasn't just a colleague any more. For good or ill, their relationship was personal now.

When he sat down, she made her own tea and sat as far from him as she could, pretending to read a magazine while she gulped down her sandwich. It was nothing but pretence. In reality, she noticed every time he re-crossed his legs, and every time he brought his mug to his lips and pouted them a little to drink.

Twenty minutes later, she was back outside Theatre Three and ready to scrub, while an orderly talked to the incoming patient, drowsy from her pre-med.

Alex didn't reappear.

'Does he want us to wait?' Barb asked. 'Do you know, Dr Calford? Dr Curtis? I got the impression...'

No one was sure.

Dylan found himself thinking, Whatever we do, it'll turn out to be wrong.

Not for the first time, he wished that Alex's well-deserved reputation as the best knee surgeon in Queensland hadn't wooed him into coming back here last year to work with the man again. If he'd known Sarah had been on the point of calling it quits with their marriage, he might have gone further afield. There were excellent knee surgeons in Sydney and Melbourne, too. Sarah was the one committed to living in Brisbane, with family here and a career in public relations.

When I'm at Alex's level, I'm not going to waste my own energy and everyone else's in terrorising the staff, he thought. I don't believe people perform better when they're on edge the way we all are today.

Aloud, after another two minutes had ticked by with no senior surgeon in sight, he decreed, 'We'll start. Page him, if necessary, but we shouldn't have to.'

He was just going in for the first incision when Alex appeared at last.

'Go ahead, Dr Calford,' he invited at once, but there was something in his drawling tone which signalled clearly to Dylan that he was on trial with this one. Yes, he'd done the procedure numerous times. Yes, he'd been told by Alex himself that his hip replacement technique was excellent. But every patient was different, and when Alex was in the mood to quibble...

He felt Annabelle beside him, her tension communicated in some mysterious way that he couldn't quite pinpoint. The way she was moving, perhaps. It was more abrupt than usual, and the clatter of the instruments in the trays seemed louder, as if she was fumbling. Normally, her hands were neat and efficient and graceful, unconsciously inviting a man to think about other ways in which she'd use them well.

Dylan wanted to tell her to relax but knew that if he did so, he'd be admitting what everyone already knew but no one wanted to say.

Alex has got us walking on knife blades.

'Hold it, James,' Dylan said to the resident, whose main job was to observe and keep the elderly woman's leg where Dylan wanted it. He gave a more technical instruction about position, and James Nguyen nodded then lifted the inert leg higher and rotated it outward.

'No,' Alex said immediately, and made a minute adjustment. It called Dylan's own positioning into question and left James struggling with taking the heavy weight of the woman's leg at an awkward angle.

Annabelle stared down at the table, the bright operating lights shadowing her face, which was already hard to read because of her mask and the cap that came low on her forehead. As a gesture of support, Dylan nudged his leg against hers, but he should have realised it wouldn't be taken as reassurance.

She moved away at once, and he coached himself, Forget it. Concentrate. Do the job.

The nuances of emotion flying across the operating table were like bats. He wanted to fight them off, but it was better to leave them alone.

Alex kept saying, 'No!' And every time they'd all freeze, until he'd dealt with the alleged mistake. Wrong scalpel. Wrong cement mixture prepared. Wrong this, and wrong that. Dylan's scalp tightened with anger and frustration that he had to keep bottled inside while he went doggedly on with the delicate procedure. The patient was elderly, and wouldn't bounce back easily from a botched job or a persistent infection.

'No, Dr Calford,' Alex said again.

Wouldn't it be nice, though, to shoot my whole career down in flames with one well-aimed fist? Dylan decided. A whole raft of reasons held him back, and he knew that control was the stronger and tougher response. His jaw ached.

Beyond the appalling atmosphere, the procedure itself was actually going well, although an untrained observer would have thought they were witnessing a medical disaster.

And then Annabelle opened the wrong hip pack.

Alex exploded. 'You should have known I'd want the new ceramic hip for this patient,' he shouted. 'And if you didn't know, you should have asked! Do you realise you have just ruined over $3000 worth of equipment? Get the right pack, please, someone, and get it now!'

'I'm sorry, Dr Sturgess.' Annabelle's voice shook.

Barb was already looking for the right hip pack, her movements quick and a little clumsy. The error was as much hers as Annabelle's but, in fact, the fault lay most heavily on Alex's shoulders. He should have made his wishes clear. His staff weren't mind-readers. Dylan hadn't known he was planning to use a ceramic hip today either.

While they waited for Barb, Annabelle stood back, her shoulders held high and tight. Alex was becoming more impatient by the second, and didn't try to hide the fact.

'I can't possibly operate under these conditions,' he said in a cold tone.

Nobody pointed out that he hadn't actually been operating at all. The gleaming instruments were all in Dylan's hands. 'I'll expect a report later, Calford, and I'll expect to be paged if you can't handle the next procedure.'

'Fine. No problem,' Dylan said, without moving his lips.

The senior surgeon walked out as if he hadn't heard.

Sharon controlled a sigh, and after a thunderous and lengthy silence said, 'Anyone hear anything about the cricket?'

'All out,' James answered in a thin voice. 'Can't remember the score.'

'All right, everyone, let's take a deep breath and focus, OK?' Dylan said. 'We all have our off-days. Found that hip pack yet, Barb?'

'Yes, finally.'

'It's no one's fault. I hope we're all clear on that.'

The relief he saw in four sets of eyes, above four disposable masks, confirmed his belief that his, not Alex's, was the better way to get results.

Only fifteen minutes late going off, Annabelle noted with relief as she crossed the main hospital foyer in her street clothes. Felt as if she'd been here for about fourteen hours. A spot high on her spine was burning, her shoulders ached and her stomach rumbled.

But three-fifteen was good. She'd have enough time to do a couple of odd jobs at Mum's before they had to leave for her four-thirty appointment. The traffic was still fairly light, and in the short stretches when it wasn't, Annabelle tried the method that Vic always used to urge on her.

'*Visualise* what you want, and it'll happen.'

OK, the three cars ahead are going to turn right at the next light, and I'll be able to overtake that truck…

For Annabelle, at least, it never worked.

At Mum's they made a list of the shopping Annabelle needed to do—some for Mum, some for herself and Duncan—and she watered the plants on the little balcony. She saw Mum's inhaler sitting on the coffee-table…and an open packet of cigarettes on the kitchen window-sill.

She didn't say anything about them, and neither did Mum.

They'd had a huge blow-up on the subject after Vic's death. Mum had given up six years ago, after starting in the swinging sixties and smoking forty a day for the next thirty-two years, but after the news had come about Vic, she'd started again, just a couple a day. Annabelle had exploded when she'd first found the evidence, about three weeks after Vic's funeral.

'I've lost Dad, and I've lost my sister, and now you're doing your best to shorten *your* life, so that I'll lose you, too? Am I the only person with any sanity around here?'

'I lost her, too!' Helen yelled back. 'And I lost Bill. Don't you think that I feel weak and guilty for needing this? But I can hardly get through the days at the moment. Leave me alone!'

Annabelle almost...*almost*...stormed out. A second before slamming Mum's front door, she turned back. They were both in tears. Hers were the first tears she had been able to shed since the news had come. The first tears she'd *let* herself shed, with so much else to do, and in her care a sad, confused baby boy who'd just learned to walk.

She and Helen held out their arms to each other, and sobbed and rocked in each other's embrace for a long time. They were closer from that day on, with a relationship that was richer and deeper, and the closeness gave them a lot of courage.

'We'd better get going, Mum,' Annabelle said at just after four. Then she watched as her mother picked up the inhaler but left the cigarettes where they were.

Dr Badger was on time today. Mum needed her routine appointments with him fairly often these days. He tested her lung function before and after she used the inhaler, and checked for evidence of infection or the dangerous pockets of trapped air which were called bullae.

The news today was mixed. Mum was worried that her inhaler had been losing its effect over the past few days. It contained a bronchodilator which opened her airways as much as her disease allowed.

But Dr Badger shook his head. 'No, I think you'll find that's not the problem.' He was a rather ponderous man in his late fifties, and spoke slowly.

'What do you think is going on, then, Dr Badger?' Annabelle asked. Helen always preferred that she come into the doctor's office too, trusting her to later interpret anything that she hadn't understood.

'You've got a chest infection, Mrs Drew, so we'll treat you for that, and I'll see you again next week.'

He wrote out a script for oral antibiotics, and they made a follow-up appointment with the receptionist. With the prescription to pick up and shopping to do, while Mum waited in the car, Annabelle didn't reach Gumnut Playcare until ten past six.

Duncan was one of just three children left at the child-care centre, and he wasn't playing with the other two, who were a couple of years older, but was slumped on a beanbag, kicking his heels on the floor. Bored? Angry? Lonely? Possibly all three. The afternoon staff were clearing up for the day and paid him no attention.

When he saw Annabelle, he was on his feet in seconds, eager to hurl himself into her arms. Feeling his warm little body against her, and his soft hair tickling her cheek, she hugged him tightly, whispered, 'I missed you today,' and almost cried.

'Go inna pool?' he asked at once, and although it was the last thing she felt like, she promised him they'd have a lovely cool swim as soon as they got home.

CHAPTER FOUR

THE doorbell rang just as Annabelle was poised on the lip of the pool in her colourful bathing suit. Duncan hopped impatiently beside her, ready for his first exuberant leap into the water and into her arms as soon as she'd eased her way down the steps.

'Let's see who that is,' she told him, and hefted him onto her hip so they'd actually have a chance of reaching the front door before the person gave up and left again. Duncan wasn't very goal-oriented about the doorbell.

When she saw Dylan standing there, she wished she hadn't taken the trouble.

'You said you weren't available to go out, so I thought I'd better bring dinner in,' he said, lifting several bulging plastic shopping bags in each hand.

'You're not going to leave this alone, are you?'

'Not yet,' he agreed calmly.

'Even if I tell you that I'm—'

'Stop!' He stepped through the doorway and dumped the shopping bags just inside her tiny entrance hall. 'I warn you, I've prepared for all the excuses. I've brought groceries, in case you had to go shopping.'

Duncan was already examining the contents of the bags.

'No, I've just been shopping.'

'And…' He bent to a vinyl athletic bag at his feet, and she was astonished to see him pull out a hair-dryer, a brush and bottles of shampoo and conditioner.

'What?'

'Classic female excuse number three. If you're washing your hair tonight, I've brought the necessary equipment.'

He grinned a cool, lazy, challenging grin as he flourished the hair-dryer in his hand, and suddenly she was laughing helplessly, laughing until tears flooded her eyes, laughing despite the fact that it wasn't all that funny, laughing just because it was a relief to let go and feel silly for once.

'Sorry, wrong brand of shampoo?' he suggested, as she clung, weak-kneed, to the doorframe.

Duncan, who was still examining the plastic bags, happily announced, 'Chippies! Yummy!' And started laughing, too.

'The girl next door provided the salon supplies for me,' Dylan said.

'I'll just bet she did, Dylan Calford! You're not proving an easy man to say no to. The shampoo is...' Annabelle lifted her hand helplessly '...fine.' It was a far more expensive brand than she ever bought for herself. 'I'm sorry, I think I must have needed that, or something. The laughing, I mean.'

'I can imagine that you did. Are you going to let me all the way in?' He was still poised with his heels on the doorstep.

'I'll have to, won't I?' But it wasn't nearly as belligerent a statement as it could have been in a different tone.

Annabelle began looking around for something on which to wipe her streaming eyes, and realised that all she had on was her bathing suit. She used the heel of her hand instead. 'Um, Duncan and I were just going for a swim.'

'So I see.'

'I'd invite you to join us, only—'

'I don't have a suit.'

'And I don't have any spares.'

'Might not fit, even if you did.'

'I meant spare *men's*.'

She hadn't missed the sweeping glance that trailed over her figure, on show in the sleek, close-fitting swimsuit, and it disturbed her. She knew why he was here. The 'making amends' thing. And she was starting to understand that it was best to let him get it out of his system.

But there was something more, and it wasn't coming from him, it was coming from her. She didn't want to be aware of him like this. Growing hot when he came near. Conscious of her own body—of its curves and its pulse points and its position in space. Enjoying the zestful atmosphere of his company, even when she was angry with him.

Nothing could come of it. It was simply a nuisance, and when she'd already known him for three and a half years without feeling this way she ought to be able to get rid of it quickly.

'Maybe after you've been for yours, and you're getting Duncan dressed, I could skinny-dip for a few minutes,' he suggested. 'It's fairly private out there, if I remember.'

'Yes,' she agreed, *not* thinking about it.

Dylan Calford, naked in her pool, powering through the water like a shark. Water making a glistening film over his skin. Tan lines low on his back and high on his thighs, and between them…

'It's very private,' she went on quickly. 'You can't even see it from inside the house.'

'First, though, I'll get this lot into the kitchen.'

'What on earth have you brought?'

'Take-away Thai, and I didn't know what you liked, so I got a lot of different dishes. And wine. Red and white. Basic groceries to knock the shopping excuse on the head.' He stopped and looked at her. 'Although I think perhaps you're a little less angry with me than you were.'

'I'm not sure who I'm angry with today after the way Alex behaved this afternoon,' she admitted.

Shouldn't have admitted it, and waited, holding her breath uncomfortably, for him to comment. He didn't. Which was nice of him.

She and Duncan had their usual noisy swim. Dylan didn't appear until she'd said, 'Three more jumps, Duncan.'

Standing with his arms resting on the top of the pool gate and a grin on his face, he watched the three jumps, and the 'one more lucky last' that Annabelle always agreed to.

'There are spare towels in the bin, just there,' she told Dylan, and then carried a towel-wrapped Duncan inside to give him a quick rinse in the shower and get him into his pyjamas.

Just before the veranda door closed behind her, Annabelle heard the sound of a resonant splash. Dylan—naked—had just dived in.

The kitchen was an Aladdin's cave of new groceries, she found when she arrived there to heat up some leftover spaghetti and a plate of fruit for Duncan's dinner. Dylan must have brought at least two more loads of shopping bags up from the car, and he'd unpacked it all and wadded the bags together, making it impossible, or at least difficult, for her to say, No, take it back. I didn't need you to do this.

In the pantry, there were cans of tomatoes and soup and corn, packets of spaghetti and biscuits and tea, boxes of cereal, jars of peanut butter and curry sauce. In the fridge there were tubs of yoghurt and blocks of cheese, and in the freezer there were packets of sausages, minced beef, chicken and steak.

In the oven, on a very low heat, he'd stacked the Thai take-away containers to keep them warm. A quick look told her there were dishes enough to freeze later tonight and fall back on for half a dozen meals over the next few weeks, a reprieve from the 'What will we eat tonight?' dilemma that plagued her every evening as she drove home. Duncan liked spicy food.

Annabelle immediately started her usual obsessive, anxious calculations. This will keep us going on basics and freezer supplies for months. I'll halve my food bills. I can pay the credit card bill down. I can take some of this over to Mum's…

Mum could only afford to stay in her unit because it was all paid off, and she had to manage her cash flow as carefully as Annabelle did.

Then she went beyond the initial relief of it and rebelled.

She must not let her immediate need cloud her broader perspective. She couldn't let Dylan think that it was OK to do this. It wasn't. On a practical level, she might need his guilt offerings, but she didn't want them. After the drama of Alex's walkout on Friday night, 'want' was winning over 'need' this week. For once, she would rebel. For once, she would act on selfish feelings and high-minded, *expensive* principles, instead of making a calculated sacrifice.

Without stopping to think, she strapped Duncan into his high chair, gave him a couple of crackers and some juice to tide him over and marched straight out to the pool.

Dylan didn't have a tan line at all. His body—or the back of it, at least—was pale golden brown all over.

'Sorry. Later,' she blurted, and turned on her heel.

'Is there a problem?' he said behind her.

She turned again. It wasn't a very natural movement. Much too slow. Breath held too tightly. He had reached the far end of the pool and was standing up, waist deep, using his hands like a towel to wipe the water off his face.

'It can wait,' she answered.

'Can it? I heard the door slam, and then the pool gate, and you stood there at the edge of the water like my old school swimming coach, about to blow his whistle and yell.'

The water, which had been churning in his wake, began to settle and grow still, and since Annabelle had a very good relationship with the man at the local pool supply shop, its chemical balance was perfect and it was crystal clear.

'Nothing. I just— I wanted to— Um, thank you for the groceries. And the take-away. Don't do it again, Dylan, I mean it. If you were planning to, that is. But please, please, don't.'

Crystal clear. Dylan didn't have a tan line in front either.

'Annabelle—'

'Keep on with your lap swimming, and we'll talk about it later.'

He shrugged. 'If you think there's something to talk about. I put the take-away containers in the—'

'I saw.'

Still and aqua-tinted and completely translucent. Dylan himself probably didn't realise quite how translucent. He had the western sun in his eyes, and the light bouncing into his face off the bright surface of the water.

'Just come inside when you're ready,' she said. 'I'm giving Duncan something else to eat tonight. And I'd better—'

'Yes, go and feed him. I'll be out in a few minutes.'

He launched himself into a strong crawl towards her, his shoulders and arms breaking the water smoothly and his feet making it bubble like a volcanic hot spring behind. In between the shoulders at one end and the feet at the other, she saw the tight curves of the human body's largest muscles. Nope. He really didn't have a tan line at all.

Duncan had finished eating by the time Dylan came in. He was dressed in the smart grey business trousers and shirt he'd been wearing before, but now the shirt-sleeves were rolled to his elbows and he'd left the top two buttons unfastened. His hair was damp, vigorously towelled and uncombed, so that it stood up a little messily on his head.

He didn't seem in a hurry to fix the problem, but Annabelle felt her own fingers itching to do the job. Just a little finger-combing back from his forehead, and a stroke or two down towards the water-cooled nape of his neck.

I can't afford to notice these things about him, she

thought. I can't feel like this. It's stupid. The kind of complication I absolutely do not need!

Duncan yawned, and she looked at the clock. It was after eight, and he was ready for bed.

Dylan read the yawn and Annabelle's glance correctly. 'Yes, go ahead,' he said. 'Put him to bed, and we'll eat afterwards.'

She nodded. 'He's always happy to go, which I'm thankful for after some of the stories I hear from other parents about tantrums over b-e-d.'

'All children have their redeeming features, as I understand it,' he teased.

'He's great. You're great, aren't you, Duncan?' she asked him, and he nodded happily.

He was tucked up in bed, after a story about trucks, ten minutes later.

This left Annabelle alone with Dylan, Thai food and wine at the table he'd set on the back veranda. About the only things missing were candles and flowers, but the lights by the pool, shining back through the tropical greenery and edging the white frangipani flowers with radiance, were a more than adequate substitute. The atmosphere was far more indulgent to the senses than Annabelle wanted it to be.

'Don't do this again,' she told Dylan abruptly. 'Please.'

'You said that,' he answered, 'as if you're worried I'm about to make you my good deed for the month.'

'And aren't you? I can see the evidence right now.'

He laughed. 'You have a point. But if you're telling me not to…'

'I'm telling you not to, Dylan.'

'OK.' He took the lids off the containers, filling her nostrils with the sweet, hot aromas of chilli and lime and coconut and curry. 'Dig in. Since it's a one-off event, we may as well enjoy it to the full.'

Dylan opened the chilled white wine and filled the stemmed glasses with liquid the colour of pale straw, as clear and inviting as the water in the pool. He lifted his glass in a gesture which invited Annabelle to do the same, and they moved to clink them together, eyes fixed on each other. How had that happened? When had she looked up at him?

'To changed plans,' he said, then pulled back and took his glass away at the last second. Annabelle's hand jerked a little, and she felt foolishly deprived, like Duncan if his ice cream dropped off its wooden stick halfway to his mouth. 'Or are you not yet ready to make a toast like that?' Dylan asked.

Annabelle put her glass down hard. 'You're arrogant, aren't you, Dylan Calford? Beyond a bit of guilt at the inconvenience of your timing, you still think you saved me.'

'And you don't agree? Even after today?'

'Of course Alex behaved badly. Anyone would have. It was an emotional situation for both of us. For everyone in the room! I got my head down, and I handled it.'

'You shouldn't have to. You weren't the one who called off the wedding. He's the one who's made a mountain out of a molehill.'

'Easy to dictate how other people should behave when you've never been in a situation anything like that.'

She saw his jaw tighten, heard the staccato hiss of his breath and thought, Good one, Annabelle.

She knew his divorce had rocked him. Everyone knew it, since he hadn't tried particularly hard to hide the fact. She remembered a couple of times when she'd been in the nurse's change-room and he hadn't known anyone was there—or he hadn't cared. There was a wall-mounted phone in the corridor just outside, and she'd heard him talking to Sarah.

Not the words. She'd tried not to listen. But the tone and the cadence of a man's voice gave away a lot. Low and emotional, tight and strident with anger. Once his pager had gone off and they'd both been called into emergency surgery. That time, she *had* heard.

'It's urgent, Sarah, so I have to go. Can we talk about this later? Please? It's a bit unfair, isn't it, to just—? Well, you knew that when we got married. I didn't hide it from you. Look, anyway. Later. No? OK. OK, Sarah, but don't *ever* accuse me of not being prepared to talk!'

When Annabelle came out of the change-room, he was still pacing the far end of the corridor, his capable body angular and tightly wound, and she didn't even think he'd seen her. Ten minutes later, in surgery, he was cool and controlled as always—a team leader, never a whip-cracker.

'I'm sorry,' she apologised now. 'That was overstepping—'

'It's all right. We've started doing that to each other a bit, haven't we?' he agreed, and the way he watched her was like a flood of hot sunshine, or a cloud of fresh scent. 'Minding each other's business instead of our own.'

They both knew why. They didn't need to say it. It was like a secret that only the two of them knew. Linking them together. Pulling them together. Tangling them in sinuous, silky cords of shared awareness. If she'd been doubtful, earlier, about the extent to which he felt this, too, she wasn't doubtful any more. They wanted each other. They desired each other. And she couldn't remember when she'd ever felt like this before.

She must have. Surely. But it didn't feel familiar. It felt unique, and she knew she hadn't felt it for Alex.

Should she have felt it for a man she'd been ready to marry? Or was the quieter, less physical attraction between two people more reliable, stronger and more enduring? She didn't know.

All she did know was that she didn't want to feel this way about Dylan Calford. Not now. Not when it only served to confuse her.

'We can stop,' she said. 'We can stop doing it. Putting our noses into each other's business, I mean. And everything else. Heaven knows, I don't want to. I'm not remotely happy about being in this situation. Without your interference on Friday, none of this would be happening.'

Now, there's an appealing thought, Dylan decided.

He wasn't ready for this either. Didn't want to analyse the whys and wherefores too closely. He just knew he wasn't. Not yet. He was too bruised, too cynical, too battle-wearied. He needed to regain a little of his faith in the human race. And a nice woman like Annabelle Drew didn't deserve to be picked up for a sizzling yet casual affair and then cast aside— which was about all he felt capable of doing at the moment.

The growing chemistry between them suggested she'd be great at the sizzling part. It was the casting aside that wouldn't work.

A week ago, he'd never thought of sex and Sister

Drew in the same breath. Now he wondered how he'd ever be able to separate them again. Across the table, bathed in a light that was far too mellow and golden to be safe for either of them, she had started to eat. She was taking refuge in it, looking down at her plate, as if avoiding eye contact with each other might help.

So far, however, it wasn't helping *him*. The light made her hair shine, and the dipped gaze silhouetted the black satin length of her eyelashes against her flushed cheeks. She lifted a forkful of chicken and rice to her lips and tucked a strand of hair behind her ear, and every movement she made mesmerised him and had him dwelling on the other things that hands and lips and hair could do. The things they could do in bed.

'Mmm, it's good,' she said, and her mouth made a pouting kiss shape on the last word.

Dylan's brain went foggy. She was talking about the meal, not the hot images that filled his mind. He tried to say something helpful, like which restaurant he'd picked it up from, and what this particular dish was called, but neither of those details had stuck. As for something a little more ambitious and intellectual…

'Spicy food really works in the hot weather, doesn't it?' he said at last.

Oh, brilliant!

But she smiled and seized on the topic, although it didn't deserve such zealous attention. 'Yes, like hot tea.'

'Or beer so cold it makes your forehead ache.'

'Or a cold shower. Do you ever do that on a hot night? I don't dry myself, I just stand in front of an electric fan before I get dressed until I'm *freezing*, and then I float around with some actual energy for about twenty minutes until I get sticky again.'

'I swim at night a lot,' he said.

'You have a pool, too?' Brisbane's back gardens were thickly dotted with them, in a climate which permitted outdoor swimming most of the year round.

'Yes, very private, like yours,' he answered, 'only my privacy comes from the courtyard wall, not from jungle greenery like this. I don't really have a back garden, just a landscaped pool surround. I've swum at four in the morning on a hot night. If I can't sleep, or if I get home after a call-out to the hospital.'

'I love swimming at night,' she agreed.

She glanced across at the pool, and he wondered if she'd swim tonight after he'd gone. Would she bother to put on her suit, or would she simply peel off the skirt, the clingy, scoop-necked top and whatever she wore beneath it and slip, seal-like, into the blue water?

He spent the rest of the meal using conversation to fight the vivid pictures in his mind, and they ended up having a rambling talk about a dozen different things that went on for at least an hour and a half.

'Well,' Annabelle finally said.

This was unbelievably nice. Two glasses of wine to cool the pleasurable bite of the spice in her mouth. Coffee, to go with the French apple tart she hadn't spotted in the fridge earlier. The table was a mess of leftovers, but it didn't matter. Whether it was fatigue or wine—probably both—she felt deliciously light-headed.

And happy. Stupidly happy, really, under the circumstances.

Must remind Mum about taking her antibiotic. What if she needs a second course?

'You're *rounder* than I'd thought you'd be, Dylan,' she told him a little unsteadily, to cut off the drone of worries in her head.

'And you've had too much wine.'

'No… Yes,' she admitted. 'A little. Your fault. You kept pouring it. One glass is all I'm good for, especially when I'm tired. I've had two tonight.'

The bottle still had a couple of centimetres left in the bottom of it.

'And I'm round?'

'Rounded, I meant. Orthopaedic surgeons are supposed to be more predictable. Narrower, or something. More focused.'

'Are they?'

'Well, you know, playing the banjo. It's supposed to be golf. Something with networking possibilities.'

'Don't like golf. And there was absolutely no point in me taking up an instrument I had to get serious about. My friends are very generous to let me do the odd practice with their band.'

'And some of that teen stuff you told me about.'

'Running away to try and join the navy when I was fourteen and a half? I was miserable when my father's company first sent him and my mother here. Thought I could jump ship in San Diego or Hawaii and hitch back home to Illinois. Five years later, though, when they got sent home again…'

'You didn't want to go back.'

'I was at university here, and I had a girlfriend.'

'What happened to her?'

'We reached an amicable parting of the ways a year

or two later. Long time ago. Don't know what she's doing now.'

Alex. What was *he* doing now? She should have been with him tonight, enjoying the first week of their marriage, talking about moving more of her things to his place and getting a real estate agent in to look at this house. Instead, she was still here. Alex had had several boxes of her belongings delivered here while she'd been at work, and they were piled in her small third bedroom, awaiting her attention.

And yet she had another man in the house.

Annabelle saw that the watch on Dylan's wrist read ten forty-five, and her feeling of light-headed contentment fled, the way a pleasant dream sometimes fled when her alarm went off, way too early in the morning to be civilised. She stood up.

'Dylan, I'm sorry, I hadn't realised it was getting so late.'

'I had,' he drawled.

He stood up, too, not in a flurry like she had, but lazily, reluctantly.

'Why didn't you say something?'

'I was still debating which thing I should say.'

The dangerous glint in his dark eyes warned her not to ask about what he considered his choices to have been.

'Are you in surgery tomorrow?' she asked quickly.

As an orthopaedic registrar, he usually was. At this stage in his career, he would spend around thirty hours a week performing a wide range of procedures, and that didn't count his extensive periods of time on call for emergencies. If Annabelle managed to move her hours to nights, as she was hoping to do—she

was seeing the unit co-ordinator about it tomorrow—
she would still see Dylan fairly often.

She'd see less of Alex, who only came in at night
when Dylan called on him. She wasn't yet sure how
she would feel about this and, in the greater scheme
of things, it wasn't important. The goal was to have
more time with Duncan and Mum.

'Yes, I'm in surgery,' Dylan was saying. 'I'm not
sure what's scheduled tomorrow.'

'We'll find out. In about eight hours. Which is too
soon.' She stifled a yawn, and saw him touch a hand
to the outside of his hip pocket to confirm that he had
his keys.

'I'll see you in the morning,' he said.

He didn't offer to help clear up, which she was
grateful for. She began to follow him to the door, not
quite shooing him out but close. He didn't resist, but
then, at the last moment, he turned. 'Throw those
empty containers out, OK?'

Annabelle hadn't expected it, and almost barged
into him, bringing herself to a halt on wobbly feet
just a fraction of a second before they made contact.
His hand shot out to her shoulder, heavy and warm,
and he muttered, 'Sorry. I didn't realise you were
right behind me.'

'I'm fine.' He still had his hand on her shoulder,
and her breath felt fluttery.

'Don't wash them out, Annabelle.'

'I'm sorry?' She'd totally lost track of what he was
saying.

'I'm not making sense.' The front hallway was
dark, and his face was shadowy and hard to read.
Only his eyes seemed clear, with fragments of light

from the street reflected deep within them. 'The take-
away containers.'

'Oh, right.'

'Don't wash them out to store Duncan's snacks in,
or something. You were going to, weren't you?'

She nodded ruefully, and he smiled. 'Thought so.
You try too hard. You're too good.'

'I'm not.'

'Yes, you are. I shouldn't be doing this.' He gave
her shoulder a little squeeze, and she felt his other
hand come to rest on her hip, caressing it with light,
slow strokes.

'I'm not too good, Dylan. Don't…make assump-
tions.' They were standing impossibly close now,
looking into each other's faces. His mouth was just a
grey blur in the darkness, his nose and his cheekbones
highlighted by a diffuse streak of light.

Time seemed to stand still. Annabelle heard the
house creak, heard the soft rhythm of Dylan's
breathing.

The possibility of a kiss made the air around them
as thick and sultry as the air before a summer storm.
Her heart throbbed, slow and heavy, and deep in her
stomach there was an ache that was half pleasure, half
pain. She waited, wanting it and not wanting it at the
same time, not yet physically able to tear herself away
from the powerful aura of their awareness.

Almost in a trance, she reached up, wanting to trace
the line of his lips with her fingers. Was his mouth
really as close as it seemed? Was it warm and trembling, as hers was?

'Dylan…' she whispered.

But before she could reach him, his hand captured
hers and closed around it. He stroked her knuckles

with the ball of his thumb, tangled his fingers in hers and made them dance with his—a slow, seductive dance that sent thrills of need flooding up her arm. She could feel his thighs against hers, hard and heavy and warm.

Annabelle shivered, and knew that he would understand exactly what the convulsive movement meant. She ached for him. She wanted him. His touch and his heat, his breath on her skin, and his whispered words, low and husky, filling her mouth as they kissed.

But it didn't happen. Nothing specific or concrete broke the moment. Dylan dropped his hand from her hip, just as she dragged herself deliberately back from the giddy brink of what she felt. They each recognised the decision that the other one had made, and saw the tangled feelings reflected in each other's face.

'I'll see you tomorrow, Sister Drew,' Dylan said lightly, and ducked quickly through the front door he'd just opened, while Annabelle was still struggling for an acceptable, neutral reply.

CHAPTER FIVE

DYLAN's back ached sharply, low in his spine.

A couple of friends had invited him for a sailing weekend and they'd gone down to Stradbroke Island. They'd taken advantage of summer's light evenings to head out straight after work on Friday afternoon and hadn't moored back at the marina until after dark on Sunday night.

Two long days, three late nights, a lot of stretching and pulling on ropes, a lot of bending and twisting in cramped cabins. They'd fished and barbecued, swum off the side of the boat before breakfast and had had a few beers at sunset. Dylan had been looking forward to the trip since Chris had mooted the idea some weeks ago, and he'd begged Chris and David to schedule it for a weekend when he wasn't on call.

It was the first break he'd taken in months, and the first stretch of free time in which his mind hadn't been dominated by painful, repetitive, hostile thoughts about Sarah. It had felt like a celebration, and the marker of a new and better stage in his life. Some of his battle-weariness had healed and faded.

He could look around and see that there *were* happy marriages. David and his wife had been to-gether for fourteen years, and you could hear how much they loved each other just from the way David spoke to Liz on the phone.

But now my back is killing me, Dylan thought. I feel like an old man!

He was annoyed at himself. Firstly, because he'd been so sure he was fit, since he swam almost every day and jogged or hiked when he could. Secondly, because he'd been wrong about his fitness, and now he was paying for it.

The pain was surprisingly sharp, surprisingly intense and extremely inconvenient only a couple of hours into a long day of surgery. He was handling all of Alex's list today, since everything was routine. Alex was getting back a day late from a conference. This placed an added weight of responsibility on Dylan's own shoulders...but at least it spared all of them the moody behaviour Alex was still acting out, four and a half weeks after he'd walked out of his own wedding.

So far, the atmosphere in the operating theatre had been relaxed and pleasant this morning. If their current patient was numbered amongst those rare people who remained aware under general anaesthesia, he would have nothing to complain about. No one yelled. No one swore. No one said anything offensive—no jokes about a patient's cellulite or ugly toenails.

Sharon Curtis talked about a new restaurant. Circulating nurse Barbara Thompson outlined her holiday plans. Dylan asked Annabelle about her weekend. Casually. He always did it casually, and if she guessed that he was still looking for ways to make her life a little easier, she didn't let on.

Why should she? He hadn't succeeded in his mission to any significant extent. Once, during the past three weeks, she had let him buy her lunch—but only because he'd offered to buy Barb's at the same time. Annabelle had also mentioned that her car needed some work, and he'd recommended the place where he had his own vehicle serviced. Later, he had phoned the head mechanic and asked him to look out for her.

'Do me a favour, OK?'

'Tell me what it is first, Dr Calford!'

'If the bill is more than a hundred dollars or so, leave some of the items off her statement and charge them to my account.'

'No problem.'

The invoice he had received a few days later told him he'd saved her a whole thirty-seven dollars and eighty-eight cents.

As a way of easing the economic burden that had fallen onto Annabelle because she hadn't married Alex Sturgess, Dylan was barely making a dent. Should he leave the whole thing alone? Put it down to an over-developed sense of responsibility on his part, and ignore it until it went away?

And what about that moment—that very long, slow, intense moment—four weeks ago, when they'd almost kissed? Where did that fit in?

Today, Dylan could only file it under I for Inconvenient. He didn't want it. Not yet. Not with someone he had to see every day, and the kind of woman he had to take very seriously or not take at all. Life had been a lot simpler four and a half weeks ago, when he hadn't known what Sister Annabelle Drew looked like in a wedding gown and a bathing suit. He wished he'd never found out.

'Want to tell me how we got to this point with this patient?' he asked the resident, in an effort to distract himself from the pain of his back and the unwanted pleasure of watching the way Annabelle's body moved beneath the soft fabric of her green surgical gear.

'You mean the whole history?' James Nguyen said.

'Quick summary, from when he got carried off the rugby field, with his knee packed in ice.'

'OK. Well, I'd guess that was probably some kind of twisting injury.'

'Yep, a high-grade synovial tear.'

'And you would have had him in for pinhole surgery. Fibreoptic instruments inserted into the joint.'

'And what did we do?'

'Shaved the detached tissue and sucked it out,' James said promptly.

'Graphic, but correct.'

'But obviously that wasn't enough?'

'No, we found evidence of a big cruciate tear, quite a mess.'

'So we had to actually open up the knee.'

'Which is what we're doing now. Have a look.' Dylan leaned forward a little, and a fresh spasm of agony attacked him. His hand tensed and shook for a moment, and he hoped no one had seen. 'See how I'm going to shift the leg now? Or rather, get you to shift it and keep it there.'

'That's a better angle, isn't it?'

'Gets to be instinctive after a while.'

In the half-second left before he touched scalpel to flesh to make the cut, Dylan flashed a quick look at Annabelle. If anyone guessed that he was having trouble and pain, it would be her. Nothing to do with the chemistry that had built between them lately, but purely because she was such a cool-headed and experienced theatre nurse.

Her brown eyes met his, but he couldn't read her

expression. She looked as composed as ever. She wasn't frowning. Not that he could see below the blue line of her mask anyway.

His own face felt as tightly screwed up as a piece of unwanted paper and he felt himself sweating. Great! Just great! His body was paying for its excesses just as surely as this patient was paying for his years as a professional rugby player. So much for new beginnings!

But I'm only thirty-three! Dylan thought. The weekend wasn't *that* physical, was it?

The rugby player's knee was a mess, they found. Much worse than Dylan had expected it to be. From the history reported by the patient, he remembered that there had been some knee trouble a few seasons earlier. 'Nothing big. Didn't stop me from playing,' Jason Gregory had said.

Perhaps he should have stopped, however, because playing with the damaged knee had made it a lot worse. There was extensive damage to the bone surface now, with some necrosis—death, in layman's terms—at the ends of both major leg bones.

Dylan glanced at the patient's face, looking peaceful, slack and unaware beneath the uncompromising glare of the overhead lights. Although slightly distorted by the tube protruding from the man's mouth, it was a strong and well-proportioned face, attached to a powerhouse body. Jason Gregory had appeared on magazine covers more than once as sporting hero, hunky pin-up and family man. By all accounts, he was a decent guy, a faithful husband, a keen father and a real team player.

But he would need a complete knee reconstruction, and he would never play professional rugby again.

And I'm going to be the one to give him the news, Dylan realised. How's he going to take it?

At his age, a player of his calibre could reasonably expect another five years in the game. Had he invested his earnings well? Had he considered his future? Not all former players could make it as coaches or commentators. Not all of them had good heads for business, or a second skill they could turn to once their playing days were over.

How did a man deal with having to give up the career he loved, the vocation that had done so much to make him who he was? When it was gone, what was left?

'Here's something that didn't show up during the earlier surgery,' Dylan told the resident. He indicated the extensive areas of bone damage, the necrotic ends and the mess of injuries to the ligaments.

The very young-looking Dr Nguyen whistled. 'What are we going to do?'

'Patch it up for now and plan a complete reconstruction for later. There's no choice. Get in closer and have a look, because it's a degree of damage you might not get to see again for a while.'

Dylan stepped sideways to make more room for the junior surgeon. As he bent over the surgical field, he felt his back burn and spasm with pain once more.

Annabelle *had* noticed something of what he was feeling.

Dylan wasn't certain of this until two hours later, after Jason Gregory had left Recovery to return to his private room in the orthopaedic ward. In the interim, Dylan had done a routine knee replacement on an elderly woman. He felt exhausted from the effort of battling the pain, and more exhausted from the effort of hiding it. It had subsided now, fortunately.

His fears hadn't. He'd chewed painkillers like caramel toffees after Jason Gregory's surgery, and they'd kicked in about an hour ago. Painkillers weren't an ongoing solution, however. What was going on in his body?

'Are you OK, Dylan?' Annabelle fixed him with her big brown eyes as he poured himself a brimming mug of tea. He had the vague notion that the drink would be soothing, and definitely didn't want the stimulant effect of coffee, or its bitter taste in his mouth.

'I'm fine,' he answered.

He *was* fine now, physically, thanks to the painkillers. He'd only taken them for the sake of his performance in surgery. Couldn't risk freezing or doubling up or getting distracted when he had an open knee or hip on the table in front of him and a whole team of people taking their cues from his own performance.

'You looked concerned back there,' Annabelle persisted. 'Was it Jason Gregory's knee? You weren't expecting he would need a total reconstruction, were you?'

'No, I wasn't, but when we opened up the knee and I saw what it looked like, it didn't make sense to consider anything else. You heard what I was saying to James.'

He leaned against the counter-top, partly to get himself safely out of her aura and partly to test whether his back would behave. It did. The painkillers? Or his cautious movement?

Annabelle's aura was another matter. No woman

should smell that good after four hours of surgery. A little steamy, because it was hot and she'd worked hard, but still clean and sweet, like soap and flowers.

'Will he be able to play again?' she asked.

'Realistically? No, he won't,' Dylan answered. 'Not professionally. Some players might get bull-headed about it and try.'

She had her hair twisted into a knot on the top of her head, and a couple of the pins were coming loose. Any minute now it would tumble down to her shoulders, releasing its scent of shampoo. No, OK, she'd felt that it was about to fall. She was reaching up to push the pins back in. The soft green fabric of her top moved across her breasts and he had to fight not to watch. He focused on her face, which wasn't any less attractive than the rest of her body but a lot more acceptable as the object of a man's gaze.

'Playing professionally is all that counts at his level,' she was saying. 'How are you going to tell him?'

'Straight. No ifs or buts. The way I hope someone would tell me if I were in the same position.' A small, distracting throb of fear ran through him. 'I don't want him thinking he's got a chance at one of those one-in-a-million medical miracles they make TV movies about. I'll tell him why, and what would happen if he tried, and why he can't exercise to compensate, and what will happen if there's damage to the other knee as well.'

'And then you'll let him go away and try to put his life back together.'

'Are you saying I should do it differently? Or that I should do more? I think it would be wrong to encourage him to play again. To hold out false hope for him, and risk even worse damage.'

'No, I'm not questioning any of that. But you look as if you want to do more, as if this has hit you quite hard. Is it because he's such a star player?'

No, it's because my back is killing me. Like a sixty-five-year-old man who overdid the pruning and fertilising in his rose garden on the weekend.

It had better not be the start of a pattern! he threatened inwardly, not knowing where to direct his anger. It had better not get any worse!

'When someone's profession is such a big thing in his life, it's always going to be hard,' he answered Annabelle, his voice a little rougher than usual. 'Nothing to do with being a star. It's the ramifications. What if he's…' he cleared his throat '…not good at anything else? What if he's left with no belief in himself?'

Annabelle nodded, moved by the way Dylan spoke with such blunt feeling. She reached for a clean mug, draining upside down on the sink, then watched covertly as he strode across to the fridge, opened the door and hunted for the milk.

He was moving a little stiffly today. His usual animal-like ease with his body seemed to be missing. She remembered the way he'd swum in her pool, tan-line free, and wondered, Is it because of me? I feel as if I move in an unnatural way when I'm around him, too. That stupid moment four weeks ago when I thought we were going to kiss… I think about it—relive it—every time I get within a metre of him, and that happens too often!

Three or four days a week, five or six hours a day, in surgery.

He still had his back to her, standing in front of the fridge. Beneath the hospital green scrub pants, she could see the faint dark shadow of his black underwear—or maybe it was navy—and the edge of a white T-shirt, coming untucked at his waist. It revealed a small, crooked triangle of smooth, beach-brown skin.

He had one elbow propped against the top rim of the fridge, and with the other hand he was probing a spot low on his spine, as if he was testing a bruise. After a few more seconds, he reached cautiously for the milk.

She almost said something, teased him about overdoing it on the weekend, but then he turned and his expression was so preoccupied and closed that she didn't dare to say anything at all.

'Nothing's come up yet,' the unit co-ordinator, Ruth Stacey, told Annabelle half an hour later in her private office. 'You're highly trained and you work in a specialised field, which means it's not easy to move you around.'

'That's what I wanted to say.' Annabelle sat up straighter, then leaned forward. She tried to sound efficient, rather than as if she was begging, although the latter was closer to the truth. 'I'd be willing to switch to night relief work, and just go where I'm needed, for the sake of changing my hours. I know I haven't done general ward nursing or obstetrics for a while, but if you talked to the director of nursing…'

Ruth Stacey shook her head. 'I'm not taking you out of the theatre suite,' she said. '*That's* where you're needed. You know that scrub nurses with your experience aren't thick on the ground. Leave it with me. Something will come up in time.'

'Oh, I'm sure,' Annabelle said, obedient on the outside, rebellious within. 'Thanks for keeping it in mind.'

She appreciated that Ruth had other priorities, and didn't want to push the unit co-ordinator any harder than she already had.

So, change hospitals?

She thought about it as she left Ruth's office. Any other hospital in the city would add at least an hour to her daily commute between home and work and Mum's, but that might be worthwhile for the right timetable.

Although she knew it wasn't Ruth's fault, she hated being put on hold like this. A flat 'No, I can't change your shifts' might have been easier than this 'Be patient and I'll try to work something out for you' message she'd received on both her visits to the unit co-ordinator's office.

Out in the corridor a minute later, she was in no mood to meet Dylan. Both of them were on their way back to the theatre suite for another two or three hours of surgery.

What's Duncan doing right now? Annabelle wondered. Having an afternoon rest, as he's supposed to do? Or pestering the staff, disturbing the other children and trying to escape outside so he can run around? He needs me, and I don't want to be here!

'We've got another sportsman's knee coming up,' Dylan told her as they walked side by side towards the lifts. 'Should start a public awareness campaign. Warning—exercise can be dangerous to your joints.'

Annabelle could tell that the black humour was an

effort. He was feeling the same as she was. 'You don't want to be here today, do you, Dr Calford?' she said.

'Not much.'

'When are you going to talk to Jason Gregory?'

'Tomorrow morning, probably.'

'Tell me how it goes. If you want to,' she added quickly. 'If you need to offload. I mean, I saw that ruined knee, too.'

'Thanks,' he answered, but she had the feeling he had hardly heard.

In the end, Dylan told his sports-star patient the devastating news a little sooner than he'd planned. He needed to see another post-op patient in the two-bed room directly opposite Jason Gregory's private one, and heard the rugby player talking to his wife, Jan, as he crossed the corridor to Jason's room.

'Feels crummy.'

'Ask Sturgess if it's supposed to,' Jan replied.

'Wasn't Sturgess who operated. It was Calford. He's meant to be one of the best. He did Mark Allwood's knee last season, and he was playing again in about six weeks.'

'That's great!'

Yes, it was, Dylan agreed. But Mark Allwood's knee hadn't been anywhere near as bad as Jason's. He'd had a simple, low-grade synovial tear, easily dealt with through pinhole surgery.

Pausing in the doorway, he watched as Jason and his wife both turned to look at him. Their faces were expectant, nervous, hopeful. He took a deep breath.

'Let's have a talk about your surgery,' he said. 'If you're feeling up to it, that is.'

'Still a bit wonky,' Jason answered. 'But go on. Let's hear it. While Jan's here. She's better at coming up with the right questions than I am.'

'Like when will he be able to start training again?' Jan started at once. 'How much physio will he need? How much should it be hurting right now?'

'Let's start at the beginning,' Dylan said.

When he moved to the end of the bed and leaned on the high, wheeled meal tray, his back gave another spasm.

If this was me, hearing this sort of news about my future, how would I take it? he thought, and his stomach felt sick and leaden as he began to speak.

'What did Jason Gregory say?' Annabelle asked Dylan the next day, between operations.

'He's going to get a second opinion.'

'From who?'

'Alex, I expect.'

'Well, Alex is good. And experienced.'

'More so than me, obviously.'

'Yes. He's been doing it longer.'

There was a tiny silence, as if both of them felt uncomfortable about the intrusion of Alex's name into the conversation. Annabelle certainly did. It was like an old injury. You thought it had healed, then it flared up worse than ever after one small bump.

'Gregory's not suggesting you've overreacted to the problem, is he?' Annabelle asked finally.

Dylan looked tired and stressed. As if he hadn't slept, or was fighting off an infection. Somehow, though, the fatigue lines around his eyes and mouth took nothing away from his male appeal. Annabelle

was as strongly caught up in it as she always seemed
to be just lately.

The knowledge nagged at her—taunted her almost.
It was as if some malign voice was whispering in her
ear.

You were going to marry Alex, the voice said.
Would that have made you safe from being so aware
of another man? Could you ever have felt this way
about Alex himself? When are you going to sort out
what's real, what's important, what's fantasy and
what's sheer desperation? When are you going to decide whether you're still furious with Dylan Calford,
or whether you're going to give him the smug satisfaction of knowing that you're grateful because he
was right?

'A mistake?' Dylan echoed. 'No, he and Jan are
both being very good about it, actually. Sensible and
cautious. Asking questions first and leaving decisions
until later. Getting a second opinion is a perfectly
valid thing to do at this stage.'

'But what will Alex tell them?'

'The same as I did, I should hope. And so would
a specialist in Sydney or Melbourne, if they decided
to go further afield.'

Annabelle took a deep breath. 'If that's the case,
Dylan, why do you look so shattered?'

'It's obvious, isn't it? The man's career is over.'
He sounded stiff and prickly and hostile...and something else. 'What exactly are you asking?'

'If you're OK, I suppose. That's all.'

'I'm fine,' he said abruptly, then walked away.

Dylan had told Annabelle that he was fine, and within
a week it was true. The pain in his back eased grad-

ually, until it wasn't there at all, and if he was taking things a little easier than usual, if he was more careful about the way he moved and avoided too much twisting, bending or lifting, then that was only sensible, wasn't it?

It wasn't that he was favouring his back, or that he was afraid.

He swam every day. Twice, when he could. It meant getting up earlier than usual, and plunging into a dark pool late at night when he didn't always feel like it, but if it strengthened his back muscles, then it was worth the effort. He knew of several nurses who'd had to change careers because of chronic back trouble, and he was going to take those cases, coupled with his own recent pain, as a well-timed warning.

Swimming twice a day helped him in one other critical area as well.

Annabelle.

It was the old, tried-and-true cold-shower principle.

Or something.

Work off the need. Go beyond desire, and into total exhaustion. Power through this simmering anger against Alex—thank goodness they'd managed to avoid each other to a large extent over the past couple of weeks—the way he powered through the water. A hundred lengths of his five-metre pool, morning and night. Each of the four major strokes. Bilateral breathing. Tumble turns at each end. By the time he stopped, the water was lapping the sides like storm waves, and his whole body was tingling.

It worked for his back, but he was kidding himself if he thought it did anything for the other stuff. The stuff with Annabelle. Eventually, something—or someone—was going to snap.

CHAPTER SIX

SOMEWHAT to Dylan's surprise, the prime candidate for a major meltdown turned out *not* to be Alex. The start of week six since the non-wedding signalled an abrupt change in the senior surgeon's mood.

Gone was the first week's flagrant bad temper and need to punish. Gone were the avoidance strategies which Dylan had, to be honest, welcomed with as much enthusiasm as Alex had put towards generating them.

Alex stopped scheduling private patients who lived on this side of the city for surgery at a private hospital on the other side of the city, forty minutes' drive away. He stopped delegating almost all the less critical cases to Dylan, and stopped discussing them only via terse phone conversations and abbreviation-laden e-mail messages.

He was breezy and witty during surgery, told a couple of risqué and not particularly good jokes—Annabelle's laugh didn't reach deeper than her tonsils—and remembered to ask Sharon about the birth of her niece.

But there was something about all of it that didn't feel right.

Or am I just a cynic? Dylan asked himself on Friday afternoon. They were doing another hip replacement—private patient, wife of a wealthy Brisbane businessman, the kind of case Alex always made a point of handling himself.

'Now,' he said to Annabelle, his tone affable and almost condescending, 'what kind of hip pack do you think I might be planning to use this afternoon?'

She wouldn't bite, just said in a pleasant, neutral way, 'We have both kinds available, Dr Sturgess. We've anticipated ceramic, but I haven't opened the pack.'

'Not eager to blow the hospital's budget today?'

'I'm never eager to do that.'

'No? Well, let's think, then.' He paused for a quarter of a second. 'Yes, I will use the ceramic hip.'

'Very good, Dr Sturgess.'

Sharon and Barb both glanced at her quickly, just as Dylan was doing. They all saw the way she closed her eyes and chewed on her lip, and they all saw Alex's little half-smile and heard him begin to whistle under his breath.

He drew unnecessary attention to Annabelle at least three more times during the procedure, and by the time it was finished, her cheeks were on fire and her well-washed top was clinging, damp and half-transparent, to her back. If Dylan hadn't known their history, he might almost—only it didn't quite ring true—have thought Alex was flirting with her.

'Annabelle, I'm glad I caught you.' She turned to find Ruth Stacey hurrying up behind her as she crossed the hospital foyer. 'Did you get my message?'

'Yes, I was going to phone your office when I got home.'

'And you're right, I'd still have been there!' the unit co-ordinator said wryly. 'I've got you the shifts you wanted, a regular four nights a week, eleven till seven, covering the weekend. It'll usually be Friday,

Saturday, Sunday and Monday, but occasionally we might have to juggle that a bit.'

'That's great,' Annabelle answered, relief washing over her like a cool breeze. 'When can I start?'

'Next roster goes out on Monday. You're down for two more weeks of days, and then you switch.'

'Thanks so much, Ruth! I really appreciate it.'

'I got the impression you needed it.'

'Oh, I do. Thanks.'

'Have a good weekend.'

'You, too, Ruth.'

Annabelle forgot, for the moment, how uncomfortable Alex had made her feel this afternoon. She floated out of the building on light feet, going through calculations she'd already made in her head at least a hundred times. Eleven-till-seven shifts, four times a week. She'd bring Mum over to stay for those nights. Duncan rarely woke in the night, so it wouldn't be too hard on Mum, and she'd be more than happy to do it. Then she'd be able to give Mum a good breakfast, make sure she took her medication and check her breathing, deliver her home and do her errands and her housework, albeit with Duncan's 'help'.

That would leave three nights a week for Annabelle to get a good sleep herself, plus whatever she could manage in the way of naps while Duncan watched television, or during the early hours of the night before work. She'd join a play-group with him, and maybe a kinder gym, and they'd go to story time at the library…

Outside the hospital's main entrance, the late February day was still bright and hot. To the left, there was a taxi rank and a bus stop, and straight ahead was a set-down zone where cars could park for a few minutes to pick up and let off passengers. To the right, a walkway led past the ambulance entrance and on to the staff car park just down the hill.

Annabelle was just about to head in that direction when she saw a familiar car in front of her. That was Alex's red open-top Mercedes sports, wasn't it? He hardly ever brought that car to the hospital. Normally, he drove his more anonymous and conservative dark green BMW.

Was it Alex's car? It wasn't him at the wheel. She checked the numberplate, which had his initials, followed by the number 007. Definitely, that was Alex's personalised plate, but in the driver's seat there was a woman whom Annabelle didn't know. She was silvery blonde, dressed to match the car, around forty years old, and absorbed in checking her face in a make-up mirror.

Short of openly staring, Annabelle couldn't observe anything more, but a second later she didn't have to. Behind her, as she began to walk on slow and rather numb legs towards the staff car park, she heard Alex's voice, speaking with loud, clear authority. Had he seen that she was just ahead of him? Yes, she was sure of it. That carrying voice was deliberately intended to capture her attention.

'Dylan, I'm not going to operate over the weekend,' he said. 'It's not necessary. Monday will be soon enough.'

'Medically, yes,' Dylan agreed. 'But in terms of the patient's best interests, I'm not so sure. We're talking about a young child and a couple of very anxious parents.'

'Monday,' Alex decreed. 'I'm going away. As you can see.'

'Alex, you're late,' came the woman's voice from the driver's seat of the car.

'Barely!'

'I've had some kind of security guard eyeing me with a black look on his face for the past fifteen minutes, darling.'

I have to sit down, Annabelle thought. *I should just keep walking but I don't know if my legs would get me as far as the car.*

Instinctively, she made a quick, clumsy turn, and headed for the left-most foyer door, but it was locked from the outside—the kind that had push-down bars on the inside and was intended only as an emergency exit. Turning again, she went some metres further along the walkway until she came to a low wall, edging a colourful garden bed, and sat down on that.

Rounding her shoulders and hugging her arms across her chest, she felt exposed and vulnerable and rubbery in her knees. The hot sun pressed on her back, and the light skirt and strappy blue top she'd changed into after finishing in the operating suite seemed inadequate.

Although she didn't look back the way she had come, the position turned out to be a box seat for hearing the scene that was still unfolding, and the cast of three—Dylan, Alex and the unknown blonde—delivered their lines perfectly.

'Ultimately, Alex, it's your call, of course,' Dylan was saying, just audibly.

'Yes, it is,' Alex answered much more loudly. 'And I've made it. We're operating on Monday.'

'If you keep talking shop like this, darling...' The blonde woman's voice carried naturally, without her having to try. 'I'll floor the lovely, responsive accelerator pedal of this gorgeous machine right now, and spend the weekend in Noosa very expensively by myself!'

'Never let a beautiful woman drive your best car, Dylan!' Alex quipped on a laugh. 'Stephanie, move over and give me the keys like a good girl.'

'Thought that would work!' she said, and Annabelle heard a clink as the keys changed hands.

The engine revved up, and they cruised off seconds later. Annabelle cast a quick look and saw Dylan shrug, turn and begin to walk in the direction of the same car park she herself had been heading for.

Only now did he catch sight of Annabelle. He stopped short. Too late, she pretended to be searching for something in her bag, then closed it quickly, got to her feet and said, 'Hi, Dylan!' in a voice so determined to remain steady that it came out more like a bark. 'Have a nice weekend,' she added on a squeak that was even worse, and began to hurry ahead of him towards the beckoning glimpse of her little car.

Please, don't follow me.

Her body language must surely say this to him, although she didn't stop to say it with words. Reaching her car, still shaking and weak-kneed, she took a covert look back the way she'd come, but didn't see him.

She felt sick, and would have leaned her forehead on the car roof if it hadn't been burning hot in the sun. Fumbling for her key, she couldn't get it into the lock because her hand was so tight and shaky. Instead, she just stood there, breathing in car fumes.

Alex, she was quite certain, had engineered that whole scene. Or if 'engineered' was too strong a word, he had at least set the wheels in motion, hoping it would happen. He knew Annabelle's schedule, and her habits, knew that it was highly likely she would be leaving through that exit at just after three on a Friday afternoon.

'Meet me at the front entrance at three, and we'll head off. Here are the keys to the Merc,' he must have said to the blonde. Stephanie. She had a name and a life and feelings, although she looked like she'd come direct from the local franchise of Rent-a-Mistress.

Alex didn't believe in renting when he could buy. He was from a wealthy Brisbane family, and he had connections. Stephanie might be the sister of an old school friend, back on the market after a divorce. Or she might be a regular on the charity circuit, a B-list celeb who could still wangle invitations to the right parties.

She would know about the healthy income that Alex pulled down each year, not just through his work but through his investments, and she would have jumped at him as soon as he'd made his move. She looked like exactly the kind of woman he'd always, and rather smugly, said to Annabelle that he didn't want for his wife—brittle hair and talon fingernails, collagen lips and a metallic laugh like someone sawing on a tin can, dollar signs in her eyes. 'So different to you, Annabelle.'

Future wife or long-term mistress or weekend lover, however, it didn't really matter. They were involved, and Alex had gone out of his way, in public, to make quite sure that Annabelle knew it.

I need to get into my car.

There was still no sign of Dylan, but somehow she was convinced he hadn't gone away. Other cars were leaving the car park, but she hadn't noticed his. She got her door open at last, and left it that way as she slid into the driver's seat. The car was like an oven, robbing her of breath once more.

Why does this feel so bad? she wondered.

She hadn't ever kidded herself that she was rapturously and naïvely in love with Alex Sturgess. On both sides, their decision to marry had been based on other feelings. She'd been aware of his faults, or so she'd thought, and more aware of them after he had walked out of their unfinished wedding. But to discover that he was prepared to punish her like this, over and above his pointed behaviour in surgery lately—it *hurt*!

A shadow fell across the interior of the car, and she looked up to find Dylan standing with his arm resting on the top of her open door. Behind him, she saw his car parked in one of the spots that had opened up as other nurses had ended their shifts and left.

'You were right, OK, Dylan?' she told him in a strained voice. 'You were right about Alex, from the moment you spoke up in the middle of the ceremony. And I understand the point of that meaningless marriage proposal of yours now. You were totally right. It would have been a disaster if Alex and I had gone through with the wedding. I was kidding myself that it would have worked, just because we'd been sensible about it and my family needed it. But that doesn't mean I'm feeling cheerful and happy and let off the hook, so do me a favour and don't—don't…' She stopped, unable to finish.

'I know,' he answered quietly. 'There's a kind of habit builds up, isn't there? A habit of care. You can't just switch it off, even if the other person endeavours to make it easy for you by behaving as badly as possible. It still hurts. It still changes the way you look at the world. And it still makes you wonder what you did to make it happen. Whether, somehow, it *is* your fault, only you can't see straight.'

'Thanks. Yes, that's how it is. Now, go away. I've admitted you were right, and I guess the reason you understand so well is because you've been through it, and I really feel for you about that, but—'

'That's not why I'm here.'

'No?'

'You shouldn't drive when you're feeling like this.'

'I'll be fine in a minute. Stop trying to look after me.' She aimed the key at the ignition.

'No, Annabelle.' His hand swooped down, but she saw it coming and closed her own fingers tightly around the keys. They ended up in three layers, like some odd piece of fruit, with a seed and flesh and skin. Her keys, wrapped in her fist, covered in his hand. The hand was warm, hard, sure of itself. She looked up, still rebellious, and found Dylan leaning over her with narrowed eyes and a steady, determined mouth.

Such a totally kissable mouth, she'd decided several weeks ago. Firm lips, not too full but not thin either. An illogical part of her instantly ached to find out how soft they would be, and how they would move. Demanding or gentle or wickedly seductive? A mix of all three?

Whichever way he kissed, she craved it, beyond her burning disappointment over Alex's behaviour, and knew that a man with Dylan's experience could hardly be in doubt as to how she felt.

'Let me have those keys right now, Belle,' he growled. It sounded like a proposition, not a threat.

Let me have the keys to your bedroom…the keys to your body…the keys to your soul.

'No. I'm fine,' she insisted.

For a moment, his grip tightened and he pulled even closer. She could see a faint mist of sweat in the tanned hollow of his throat, and she could smell the complex and satisfying fragrance of his skin, nutty and fresh.

His body was intimidating in a way that made her breathless and expectant. A huge part of her *wanted* him to take control, make decisions, crush her in his arms and kiss her so thoroughly that she didn't have time to think twice. Not about Alex or Dylan himself, her future, her family or anything else.

Except that it was impossible and wrong. She had to pick up Duncan and go over to Mum's. As she knew from experience, having Duncan with her was likely to make the household chores take twice as long, but her talk with Lauren at Gumnut Playcare recently had gone round and round in circles and hadn't thrown up any solutions.

Duncan had bitten Katie again. Katie's mother wasn't happy.

Understandably.

Duncan needed more attention and more freedom to be his active two-year-old self, but neither of these needs could be met in the structured environment of the child-care centre, without impinging unfairly on the other children. Annabelle no longer left him there for a second longer than absolutely necessary.

Abruptly, she twisted her arm, hoping to loosen Dylan's stubborn grip. She had expected resistance, but he didn't give it. Instead, she pulled her hand away easily, and looked up to find his eyes momentarily closed and his lower lip caught between his teeth as if he were fighting off a spasm of pain. Or was it something else?

'Dylan?' she blurted, her voice suddenly husky.

He opened his eyes, and straightened up. 'Can't stop you if you don't want to be stopped,' he said tightly.

It wasn't true. If he'd been prepared to use his body and his iron grip more forcefully, he could easily have won out.

'Yes, well,' she said awkwardly, then protested for the third time, 'I'll be fine.'

Only she wasn't.

There must have been a hold-up at the traffic lights on the main road just beyond the hospital driveway. Alex and Stephanie were only just coming past now. The attractive blonde was laughing, the lenses of her sunglasses flashing in the bright light. As he drove, Alex took his eyes from the road and shot a long, searching look across towards the car park where Annabelle sat.

Although she was facing the road, she would be hidden from his view behind the glare of her windscreen. Was he hoping to see if her car was still here? To check out the effect of his unpleasant game? What would he have done if their paths hadn't crossed outside the hospital doors as he'd hoped? Repeated the scene in a week's time? Or found another way to rub her nose publicly in his sexual success?

It was so petty, and yet it had worked. She felt exactly as he, no doubt, wanted her to feel.

A mess. As if this were her fault. Sullied and hunted and hurt.

Starting the engine, she reversed out of the space in a series of jerks, then turned the steering-wheel and cruised along the row of parked cars. The space at the end was empty. Turning left, she misjudged the distance, misjudged her speed and felt her hands slipping on the hot steering-wheel. Her left wheel rammed hard against the low concrete marker that edged the final space in the row, and there was a loud, violent sound.

She reversed again, as clumsily as before, then heard the sticky, rubbery noise of a rapidly deflating tyre wobbling over the asphalt.

Dylan appeared in her field of vision before she was out of the car. Annabelle leaned her elbow on the open window and yelled at him with a satisfying lack of control. 'If you say "I told you so," Dylan Calford, I'll reverse my car over your foot!'

'With the driving skill you're showing at the moment, I'm not worried,' he answered. 'You'd miss. Come on. Let's make a rational decision about what we're going to do.'

He strode closer, reached in and flicked up her lock, then opened the door and hauled her out, gripping her upper arm. Her breasts fetched up against the hard plane of his chest, and his mouth was close enough to kiss. Desire rocked her like an earthquake, making her gasp aloud. Their eyes met, and she saw his pupils start to dilate. No doubt—he was feeling this, too.

Then a car hooted, and he let her go. They were blocking the way, and so was her car.

'Got a spare?' Dylan asked.

'Yes.'

'And a jack?'

'Yes.'

'And both are in working order?'

'*Yes*, Dylan!'

'But you're still not.' His eyes narrowed again, and his gaze flicked up and down. 'This is what we'll do. And no arguments this time. I'll park your car and give you a lift back here later on. We'll change the tyre then. Right now, I'll run you wherever you need to go. I'm out of surgery for the day. Technically, I'm still on call, but Brian Collins is here, finishing off some stuff, and he'll cover for me if something comes up. He owes me for when I've done the same for him.'

'I'm not going straight home.'

'Didn't think you were.'

'I mean, even after I've picked up Duncan.'

'I didn't think you were,' he repeated steadily. 'To your mother's, right?'

He took her keys, and this time Annabelle didn't protest at all. Instead, she got lost in wondering how just that one light, brief and slightly ticklish touch, as he'd coaxed the keys from her hand, could have delivered such a jolt of pure, longed-for sensation. She stood there helplessly, watching him ease the crippled car into the empty space, then let him drop his arm around her shoulder.

If she'd turned just a little, if she'd leaned closer against him, she could have rested her head beside his neck and felt his cheek against her hair. He smelt so good. Like soap and coffee and eucalyptus. Comfortable and sexy at the same time.

'Come on,' he said. 'Sit with your eyes closed and make a mental shopping list while I drive.'

'It's not shopping today,' she answered. 'It's cleaning the kitchen and bathroom, changing a couple of light bulbs and paying some bills.'

'Your mother can't do the bills?'

'She gets flustered, and presses the wrong buttons.'

'Does she do them by that new automated phone system, with a credit card?'

'Yes. She was proud of herself originally for mastering it when they first introduced it, but she's been getting less capable lately. The breathlessness just wears her out, and she worries about the future for Duncan and me. She gets very anxious about all sorts of things. Silly things like keying in the right numbers when she's paying bills. Some days, she just goes to pieces about nothing at all.'

'Annabelle, did she push you to marry Alex?' Dylan asked quietly. He slid his arm away again as they reached his car.

'No.' Annabelle shook her head, then added reluctantly, 'She knew his mother, though. Always told me I could trust a man who was Lynette Sturgess's son.'

'I'm sure he wasn't involved with Stephanie before the wedding,' Dylan said, opening the passenger door for her.

'There are other ways to betray someone's trust. It's the pettiness of it that I hate, I think. Or the desire to punish. Oh, I don't want to talk about this any more!'

'Then we won't,' Dylan said simply, as he slid into the driver's seat and started the engine. 'If you want, we'll never talk about it again.'

*   *   *

'Let me do the light bulbs and the bills,' Dylan offered when they reached Helen Drew's building. Annabelle frowned at him and he said, 'Traditional man stuff. Less margin for error.'

She laughed. 'True! OK, I'll show you where the spare bulbs are, and I'll put Mum's credit card by the phone.'

She looked a lot better than she had half an hour ago. The sour taste no doubt left in her mouth by Alex's petty hurtfulness was slowly wearing off. Dylan understood how it felt. He'd been through the same thing with Sarah, but both the divorce and the property settlement were finalised now, and he could see it with a cooler perspective.

As Annabelle had suggested, the nastiness of it was degrading, somehow, to both parties, until the passage of time gave you some relief. He'd spent months wondering what it said about *him* that Sarah was so eager to go out of her way to exact various forms of petty revenge. She had been the one to leave their marriage. He was the one, surely, who should be seeking pay-back!

'You only care about your work,' she had accused him. 'You never have time for me.'

True. Of course it was. Partly. He'd warned her about that—about the fact that you paid a price for such a satisfying career and such a healthy income. And he'd done his best to compensate for it. Phone calls to her every time he had a break from surgery. Great holidays and getaways—expensive and luxurious and with no need for Sarah to lift a finger—whenever he had more than three days off in a row.

He had made the effort to take her out when he was way too tired to want to go. He'd even thought ahead to the distant possibility of kids. 'By then, I'll have my own specialist practice, and more control over my hours,' he'd told her. 'We'll be able to afford a housekeeper and a nanny, so that when I do have to put in long days, you won't be stranded at home with no help.'

Not enough, apparently, despite the fact that Sarah had always spoken so confidently about 'independence' and 'our own lives'. He had come home late one night when he'd been on call to find their townhouse stripped of anything Sarah could claim as hers, and a note reading, 'It's over. You're never here, and I'm sick of it. Sarah.'

That at least had been honest, and necessary, if she'd felt that way.

But did she have to let him know exactly when, and in what circumstances, she'd first slept with the new lover she already had in tow? Did she have to 'accidentally' sell off his small but much-loved collection of old blues record albums at a garage sale for a fraction of what they were worth?

If there was that much bitterness stored up, couldn't she have expressed it earlier, in a way that would have let him at least *try* to take some action?

It was only over the past few months that he'd learned to see all of this as her problem, rather than a reflection on himself. He felt freer now. And he understood Annabelle's current feelings better than she could know.

Meeting her mother, he was a little self-conscious, remembering the circumstances of their first encounter. But all Helen Drew said, in her wheezy voice, was, 'Thank you for driving my daughter here.' She offered him a drink, but he declined. Playing things cautiously.

'The new light bulbs are in the laundry cupboard,' Annabelle told him. 'The one in the bathroom has gone, one in the bedroom and one in the hall.'

'Won't take long,' he said. 'Then I'll take care of the bills.'

'I'll be in the kitchen,' she answered. 'Duncan and Mum are going to read some stories on the balcony.'

It took Dylan five minutes to do the light bulbs, and then he keyed in the pay-by-phone number for the first of Helen's bills. He understood how she could get flustered with this. He'd once calculated that he needed to press over fifty digits to pay his electricity bill—still cheaper and easier than writing and mailing a cheque, however, and he had it down to a fine art now.

Such a fine art, in fact, that he automatically began keying in his own credit-card number instead of Helen's, since hers was with the same company and the first four digits of both cards were the same.

'Damn!' he muttered, then finished the number and waited for the recorded voice to repeat it back to him, ask if it was correct and offer him the opportunity to try again if it wasn't.

Strange that your whole perspective could change in the space of a few seconds, while listening to the meaningful phrase, 'If yes, press 1.'

If yes, press 1.

'Yes' would make things easier for Annabelle and her mother by saving them hundreds of dollars on utility bills which Dylan himself could easily afford. Eventually, when Helen's credit-card bill arrived— assuming she checked it carefully enough—she would realise that the payment hadn't gone through on her card.

'Yes' wasn't just about money, though. In fact, as far as he was concerned, it wasn't about money at all. He knew that Annabelle Drew was a woman he had to take seriously. 'Yes' amounted to a clear and deliberate decision on his part to do exactly that.

His index finger hovered over both digits for a second longer.

If 'Yes' press 1, to re-enter press 2.

When his fingertip touched the 1 button, and the electronic beep sounded in his ear, he suddenly felt very, very good.

Moments later, a voice told him brightly, 'Payment has been accepted.' He scribbled the date and the electronic receipt number on the bill. He dealt with two more bills in the same way, using his own card each time, then saw that Helen and Duncan were still reading on the balcony and went in search of Annabelle.

She was wearing pink rubber gloves, and was squirting an abrasive cream cleanser onto the stove top.

'All done,' he told her, coming across to lean against the adjacent stainless-steel sink. 'Could I take Duncan to the playground, or something?'

'That would be great,' she answered. 'Any second, he's going to get sick of reading and want to "help", and we'll be here forever.'

'Forever sounds good,' Dylan said, then leaned his body and tilted his face, met her slightly—but not very—surprised look in his direction, and kissed her.

CHAPTER SEVEN

ANNABELLE didn't hesitate, or push away. She kissed Dylan back.

Wrapping her arms around his neck and keeping the gloved parts out of the way, she stepped closer so that they were hard against each other. She drank the taste of his mouth like wine, with eager, parted lips. She closed her eyes.

It felt so good. So right. As if it should have happened days ago, and, at the same time, as if now was the perfect moment.

Dylan spread his hands and ran them across her ribs, then up to her breasts. He took their weight and lifted them, searing his thumbs across her hardened nipples. She felt his fingers whisper just above the neckline of her top, then climb to stroke the loose hair back from her hot neck.

She had to stretch up on tiptoe to hold him without getting the wet gloves on the back of his shirt, and she teetered. It was a very satisfying form of unsteadiness, with his solid support against her. He whispered hotly in her ear, 'I've got you.'

'I know.'

'Not letting you go.'

'Don't. Please.' She printed kiss after kiss on his mouth—kisses that were hot and hungry and eager for more. His response swept her away. His kisses were imperious, confident, teasing and meltingly sweet.

'Hold me, Annabelle,' he said fiercely against her mouth. 'I want to feel you.'

'I can't. The gloves...'

'Doesn't matter.' He gathered her more tightly against him, driving the breath high into her lungs. She felt giddy. Just wanted to laugh and cry and kiss him for hours.

'Mummy! Clean a baffroom now?'

She heard Duncan's running feet on the carpet, and Mum's smoke-darkened voice, still on the balcony. 'One more story, Dunc?'

'No. Help clean a baffroom now.'

Annabelle pulled away from Dylan, her breathing still fast and high. Dylan turned to face the sink and grabbed a sponge. There were wet splodges on the back of his shirt.

'I've dripped cleaning stuff on you,' she said.

'I told you, it doesn't matter.'

Duncan arrived, oblivious to the struggle going on in both of them and to the nuances beyond their trivial words. 'I need a sponge,' he announced.

He loved helping to clean the bathroom, because it was such a lovely messy job, and the more enthusiasm he displayed, the messier it was.

'Take him for a walk?' Dylan suggested. 'I'd like to.'

But Duncan was stubborn, and wouldn't go. He was going to help clean that bathroom or collapse in a screaming heap, and that was that.

'I'm not going to push it,' Annabelle told Dylan quietly.

Mum had also arrived in the kitchen now, and she nodded. 'Best not.'

'I'd win eventually—I'm bigger than you,

Duncan!' Annabelle went on. 'But the price is pretty high, late on a Friday afternoon. Can't send him with you, Dylan, if he doesn't want to go, since he doesn't know you that well.'

They got the cleaning done eventually, with Mum in the background berating herself for being so useless.

'Now, about dinner,' Annabelle said to her finally.

'Don't worry. I've still got a couple of those lovely leftover take-away meals you brought me a few weeks ago. I'll thaw one out in the microwave.'

When Annabelle finally reached Dylan's car— Duncan still had a streak of dried cleanser running down his arm—she only wanted one thing. Dylan Calford, holding her in his arms and kissing her silly.

'We have to go back and fix the tyre so I can drive my car. After that, are you...coming back to my place?' she asked him. Didn't even try to pretend it was a casual suggestion.

He glanced across at her, and her heart caught in her throat at the look in his eyes. 'Am I invited?'

'Yes. You are.'

It was still fairly early when they got home. Dylan had followed her all the way from the hospital. Because he was still unsure of the best route, or to check that she was driving safely? After they'd changed the flat tyre, he had commented on a strange noise her engine was making. At the moment, she didn't care about either the noise or Dylan's motivations.

Duncan wanted a swim. 'I'll take him,' Dylan offered. 'I've got a pair of board shorts in the back of my car this time.'

'Want to go in the pool with Dylan, Dunc?'

He nodded energetically, which surprised Annabelle a little. He didn't always take to other people straight away.

While they were swimming, she tossed some salad, heated garlic bread in the oven and made a quick pesto out of a big bunch of mint leaves from the garden, crushed walnuts, parmesan cheese and olive oil. The three of them ate beside the pool at the rickety white plastic table and chairs which Annabelle was desperate to replace but couldn't afford to.

That didn't seem so important any more. There was a satisfaction in knowing that everything around her was her own, and that she was finding ways to manage without the effortless luxury of Alex's wealth.

Alex had never spent more than a few minutes at her house. 'Best if we go to my place.' But that wasn't always true. It wasn't 'best' every single time, even if Alex's pool was twice as big, and his house was cooler, his fridge had more drinks in it and his housekeeper would clean up after them. Eventually, always going to his place created an imbalance.

Dylan doesn't seem to mind coming here, she thought.

By the time they'd finished eating, Duncan was ready for bed. 'Quick as we can tonight,' she promised Dylan.

'I'll still be here when you get back,' he said.

'I hoped you would be,' she answered, a little shyly.

He was still wearing only the pair of baggy, colourful board shorts he'd put on to swim with Duncan, and she had to fight to keep her gaze from lingering on the muscular contours of his tanned shoulders and chest. He seemed casual about it, not showing off.

Too distracted by her own body, perhaps. She recognised the way he was watching her, eyes softly alight, and it made her feel alive, expectant, more sensual than usual. She wasn't used to the feeling, but she liked it.

'Thank you, Duncan, sweetheart,' she whispered to her little boy, when he drifted off to sleep before she'd even finished his story. 'This was a good night for getting sleepy early.'

She kissed his smooth little forehead, brushed back some sweat-dampened tendrils of hair, adjusted the position of the cooling fan that played over him while he slept, and went out to Dylan by the pool.

She went straight into his arms.

'Hello,' he said. He brushed his mouth across hers. 'Nice surprise.' His arms tightened around her.

'Is it?' She looked up into his face, so close to hers. 'Nice, I know, but a surprise?'

'You came right up to me. Didn't break your stride. You held out your arms.' His mouth was a fraction of an inch from hers now as he spoke. 'It was great. I wanted you to do that, but I didn't think you would.'

'Why not, Dylan?'

He smiled. 'Things never happen exactly the way you want them to. I've been having this great scenario playing in my head about standing like this with you in the pool, and slowly peeling your swimsuit from your body.'

'And why can't that happen?'

'Because I'm slowly going to peel your clothes off right here instead.'

'Gee, I walked right into that one, didn't I?'

He just laughed, and began to slide the straps of her top off her shoulders. Annabelle closed her eyes and let it happen. His touch made her throb and pulse all over. At first, she was so overwhelmed by sensation that she couldn't move, but when he slid her top down to her waist, unfastened her skirt and dragged both garments down over her hips, she suddenly wanted to share in his exploration.

How did he feel? Was his skin as hot and sensitive as hers? Or was it still cool and satiny from his earlier swim? How would he react when she touched him? Would he—?

Ah, yes! She felt a delicious sense of power as he groaned. Letting her eyelids flutter open for a few seconds, she saw that his eyes were closed and his head was thrown back. He was dragging his teeth across his bottom lip, as if he'd reached a point where pleasure almost became pain.

Wanting to soothe him, she left his board shorts hanging on his hips, low and precariously positioned, cupped her hands around his jaw and kissed him with soft, tender lips. She loved his hungry response.

Thirty seconds later, they lost their balance, made it worse by clinging to each other too hard and crashed into the pool, still locked in each other's arms. Both of them came up laughing.

'Did you do that on purpose?' he asked.

'No. But I'm glad it happened. It's lovely.'

The water felt good, so milky mild in this temperature that there was no shock, just an invigorating freshness. They stood up together, and he brushed the hair back from her face then reached around and unclipped her bra. 'Don't need this. Or these…'

Her top and skirt were still bunched across her hips.

He slid them down and she wriggled, helping him. His board shorts had lost their last tenuous hold on his hips as they'd hit the water. He kicked his way out of them, then curled himself low in the water to remove her own clothing.

The sight of his wet, dark head so close to her upper thighs made something twist deep inside her. She sank back in the water, floating on her back, and shook skirt and top and underwear off her feet. Dylan scooped his arms beneath her and held her against him, looking deep into her eyes.

'So...' he said.

'So...' she echoed.

'Funny, the way things turn out!'

'Mmm.'

Funny, and a little frightening. She could feel him pressed against her in graphic detail. One full breast was cushioned against his chest, and the other nudged his cupped hand as he held her. Her hip was pressed into his stomach, very low down...

She had slept with Alex, but not until their relationship had already been established and serious, running along in a groove which both of them had already recognised was heading to marriage.

Alex had always been courteous about it, softening her up with a lavish meal and wine, compliments and attention, as if he had to coax her into it, as if they only made love because of his needs, never hers. It seemed incredible to her now that she'd actually responded to that. She'd liked it. Why? Alex had been right. It *had* been about his needs. She'd never felt any urgency of desire for him. Was that why she'd responded to his courteous approach?

With Dylan, it was different. Desire was pulling on

her. Desire was telling her to ignore the fact that they didn't really have a relationship at all. That didn't seem important at the moment. In fact, she preferred it this way.

There was no sense of appropriate transactions taking place, the way there had been with Alex. Dinner in exchange for love-making. Marriage in exchange for her good name and breeding. Security in exchange for wifely support and the creation of heirs. Despite all the problems Alex's proposal had promised to solve, at some deeper level their relationship had hedged her in.

Now she felt free.

Wild, too, in a way she'd never let herself feel before. Vic had always been the wild one. Annabelle had felt constrained to be the opposite—the one who'd given support to Mum, the one who'd pleased Dad by working hard towards a good career, the one who'd set an example in the hope of reining her sister in.

There was no one for whom to set an example tonight, no transactions laid out on the table. There was just her and Dylan, a sultry night and the caress of the water.

Funny, the way things turned out.

Suddenly, she wasn't frightened any more at all. She wanted it, and she wanted it to be like this— open-ended, non-contractual and, above all, *physical*.

'You're beautiful, Annabelle,' Dylan said softly. His black eyes glinted and danced with reflected light from the surface of the pool.

'I'm not,' she answered automatically. 'I—'

'Don't argue. Don't. You're beautiful. Don't know whether to stand here kissing every inch of your wet skin for another hour or whether to take you to bed right now. Help me decide. We're going to bed, right?'

'If we weren't, I wouldn't have let you—'

'Didn't think so.' He smiled. 'Appreciate that about you. No games. I hate games.'

'Then take me to bed now, Dylan.'

He carried her as far as the grass just beyond the pool gate, then set her on her feet and reached for the towel hung over the pool fence. Annabelle didn't want to lose his touch, not for a second. She pulled on his hips, feeling the swift, satisfying brush of his arousal across her stomach. He shuddered and his arm came around her back, anchoring her wet breasts and chill-hardened nipples against his chest.

With the towel left dangling in one hand, he kissed her—kissed her mouth and her neck, her throat and her breasts. They stood entwined together like that for a long time, cool and wet and naked, lost in the taste and feel of each other. When finally he dragged his mouth from hers and wrapped the towel around them both, she was almost dry, and so was he.

'What was this towel for? I've forgotten,' he said.

'To make love on, I presumed,' she teased. 'Like a picnic blanket.'

He didn't answer, but his grin was wicked, and the glint in his dark eyes was even wickeder. One flick of his outstretched arms laid the big, fluffy towel on the grass.

Annabelle gasped. 'Dylan, I didn't mean it.'

'Too bad. You shouldn't say things you don't mean to a man in my condition. A man, what's more, who was anticipating this eagerly enough to think of protection.' Annabelle heard the crackle of a small packet in his hand.

'The neighbours—' she protested.

'Won't see a thing. It's dark.'

He touched her teasingly, his hands light and seductive. Annabelle knew he must have felt the way she shuddered, the way she moulded herself against him and responded.

'Do you mind that I was thinking ahead?' he asked.

'I was, too. But I hadn't...come up with anything. So, no, I don't mind.'

'Good...' She hardly realised what he was doing until he had her on the ground, pinned beneath him and looking up into his grinning face.

He traced the tip of his finger over her lips, along her jaw, down her throat and between her breasts, then he cupped her—so lightly that his touch felt like the brush of some silky fabric.

'Decision time, Annabelle,' he said softly. 'Do you want to go inside?'

'No...'

'Good,' he said again, then propped himself up on his elbows, on either side of her ribs. 'Because neither do I.'

Wild. It was wild. A fever of hands and mouths, pressure and rhythm that caught Annabelle up in a tornado of sensation and didn't let her go until both of them had reached a passionate release. In its aftermath, she lay there on the rumpled towel still throbbing, hot and swollen, clinging to him as if he were her life-raft in a huge black ocean.

She felt shaken by the realisation of how close she'd come to never knowing that a man and a woman could come together this powerfully. The chemistry between herself and Alex had been wrong, and she'd never realised it. Couldn't have realised it until she'd experienced a chemistry that was right.

Suddenly, she felt sorry for the other man. All his wealth and professional success, his sense of control and of his own importance—that fatal combination of character traits which had encouraged him to select her as his future wife and then turn on her the moment he felt she'd let him down. All of that added up to so little that was truly important.

And had Vic, after all, with her flamboyant and headlong dance through life, discovered an essence that Annabelle had overlooked?

After a long interval of lying still, entwined together and saying nothing, Dylan picked up her hand and pressed his lips to her knuckles one by one, and then to each fingertip.

'What are you thinking, Belle? I can hear something ticking in there.' He knocked lightly on her forehead, then turned it into a caress.

'That maybe I'm starting to understand my sister better than I once did.'

'Yeah? Tell me.'

'Only because— I mean— Gosh! Can't explain!'

'Try,' he invited.

'Oh, OK. Um, OK.'

But she was distracted. The unaccustomed heaviness of sated senses felt too good, and when Dylan stretched out his fingers to brush them across her nipples, she was mesmerised by the sight, and by her own response.

She tried again. 'I'm just…thinking about things I've missed out on that Vic instinctively knew.'

'Like what?'

'Oh, being a little selfish occasionally. Responding to what feels good. Not asking too many questions.' She said a bit more, then stopped, wondering if any of it had even made sense, let alone been worth his attention. 'I'm sorry,' she finished.

'You're allowed to talk about her. About anything. Just because my hands like to wander, it doesn't mean my attention is.'

'Maybe it's *my* attention that's wandering.'

'Where's it going?'

'Inside. To somewhere a little more comfortable.'

'Sounds good.'

And it *was* good. It was fabulous, all over again. They fell asleep on her bed, tangled in each other's arms, and Annabelle didn't awaken until the early hours—the darkest hours—when she was jolted from sleep by the sound of glass shattering in her bathroom.

For several seconds, she was disoriented and panicky. Who was there? What were they doing? Where was Duncan? Safe? Her heart was pounding in her ears, and she covered the distance from deep sleep to high alert far too fast. Then she heard Dylan's voice, swearing.

'What happened?' she called.

But he didn't hear.

She rolled clumsily out of bed, still naked and feeling suddenly vulnerable. There was no clothing handy to put on, unless she opened a drawer or wardrobe and scrabbled around in the dark for a T-shirt or a dress.

Heading for the bedroom door, she croaked, 'Dylan?'

'I knocked over a bottle of cough medicine and it broke,' he called. 'I'm sorry. It's a real mess.'

'That's OK, as long as you didn't cut yourself.'

She reached the bathroom, just outside her bedroom and to the left, and at that moment he turned on the light. It blinded and disoriented her afresh, and Dylan had his hand shading his eyes, too.

'I shouldn't have been fumbling around in the dark,' he said. 'Should have turned this on straight away. But I didn't know if the light would wake Duncan up.'

'It wouldn't have. And apparently the breaking glass hasn't either.'

She grabbed a towel, wrapped it around her body and tucked the end down in front, between her breasts. As a covering, it was both uncomfortable and inadequate, and if Duncan did awaken and she had to cuddle him, it would be bound to work loose. Tiptoeing along to his room, however, she saw him still fast asleep.

Back in the bathroom, she found Dylan picking pieces of lethally sharp brown glass out of the puddle of sticky pink syrup that was still spreading wider beside the basin and threatening to drip onto the floor. The mirrored medicine cabinet above the basin gaped open, and several of the bottles and packets were out of place.

'Got somewhere to put this?' Dylan asked, holding out the handful of sticky glass slivers he'd collected.

'Here.' She grabbed one of Duncan's plastic pouring cups from the side of the tub and gave it to him.

'When I've got all the big pieces, we can wash the rest down the sink.'

'What were you looking for in the cabinet?'

'Painkillers.'

'You've got a headache?'

'Uh…yes.' He nodded. Then he frowned.

'I haven't got anything very strong.'

'Just to take the edge off.' He controlled a sigh. 'I should head home, too.'

'Because of the headache?'

'No, because of Duncan.'

'Oh, right.'

'Best, isn't it?'

'I hadn't, um, thought that far ahead. But, yes. You're right. It's best.'

He stopped fishing for bits of glass and looked at her. Looked at her, actually, for the first time since she'd stumbled into the bathroom, blinded by the sudden light. He smiled, too. 'That doesn't mean I can't come back again another night. Quite soon, I'm hoping.'

She relaxed, and wasn't sure why she'd been tense in the first place. Just the shock of thinking for several seconds that she had a violent stranger smashing glass in her bathroom at three in the morning?

'I'm hoping it's soon, too,' she said. 'And I'm sorry about your…your headache.'

Because why would Dylan say he had a headache if he didn't?

'Annabelle, I'm a little bit worried.'

'Yes, Mum?'

'I'm probably just being silly.'

'I'm sure you're not. Tell me.'

'Well, I just got my credit-card statement, and none of this quarter's bills are on it, and it seems as if they should have—' She broke off to cough, and

Annabelle waited. She was standing in the hospital's main foyer, from where she often phoned Mum during her lunch-break. 'Except that I haven't received any reminder notices,' her mother continued. 'But what if they cut off the phone?'

'Let's not worry about that yet,' Annabelle soothed. The phone obviously hadn't been cut off yet, since Mum had phoned from her unit. 'I'm coming over straight after work, after I've picked up Duncan, but we'll be later than usual, because we'll have to get the bus. The garage said the car won't be ready until five.'

'All right.'

The car engine's recent strange noise had turned into an urgent need for replacement parts which Annabelle knew was going to cost hundreds. She'd taken it back to Dylan's car mechanic, since the location was convenient and they'd charged a little less than she'd expected last time.

No more child-care fees after this week, and there's still some room on the credit card...

'But I gave Dr Calford my credit card,' Mum was saying. 'Could he have made a mistake and—? But, no,' she interrupted herself. 'That seems impossible. I just can't understand why nothing's appeared on the statement.'

'I'm sure there's an explanation. Mum, I have to go and get ready for the afternoon list. Just don't even think about it until I get there, OK? I'm sure it'll be something to do with the issue date of the statement, that's all.'

It had only been ten days since the bills had been paid. Dylan wasn't operating today. He'd had a seminar to attend in the morning, and a fracture clinic in the afternoon. They'd seen each other on the week-end, and they were seeing each other tonight, and Annabelle was hugging the whole thing to herself like a big box of chocolates that she wasn't planning to share.

Happy about it. Happy about him. Happiest be-cause she wasn't thinking beyond now, tonight or this week. She was just letting it happen—something she'd never done before in her life. When she got back to the nurses' changing room, there was a note from Dylan in her locker.

'Dropped in but missed you,' he'd written, in his confident doctor's scrawl. 'Was hoping we could grab lunch before my clinic, but Barb mentioned you were running some errands. See you tonight. Dylan.'

The afternoon's list was uneventful, the bus was on time at five past three and Annabelle picked Duncan up just fifteen minutes later than usual. This was his last week at Gumnut Playcare, and every time she saw the way his face changed from glowering frustration to sparkling happiness when she arrived there, she was thankful about it. Today, as icing on the cake, there was another 'incident note' in his pocket. He'd hit Ryan over the head twice with a block.

At Mum's, after another bus ride, he was difficult for much of the time. Wouldn't stop jumping on the couch and running around and around the living room. When Annabelle got angry with him, he got angry back, and shouted a word he certainly hadn't learned in her company.

She ignored it completely, but knew that her voice was tear-filled as she said, 'What am I going to do with him, Mum?'

'He's two, love, and he's active and hungry for life.

If he was growing up on a farm, he'd be fine. You're doing everything right, and we both know he has a loving little heart underneath.'

'Next week…'

'I'm still worried it's going to be too much for you.'

'It's not forever. Just until he settles down. When he starts school, I hope. And I'm worried it's going to be too much for *you*!'

'Nonsense!' Brave words, fragile tone. Then Mum coughed and struggled for breath, needed her oxygen, but was determined to give Annabelle the credit-card statement to look at first.

'Are the bills filed away, Mum?' she asked, when things had settled down a little.

A *little*. Duncan was still jumping on the couch. Annabelle decided to let him do it, this once. Some kids, apparently, never even *thought* of jumping on couches. What would that be like? she wondered.

'No, I got them out again,' Mum said.

'It does seem as if the payments should have appeared on this statement. Let me get their transaction numbers and phone the enquiry lines, see if there's been some kind of a glitch.'

A couple of frustrating phone calls reassured both of them that no phone line or electricity service was about to be disconnected. Everything was in order. The bills had apparently been paid by magic.

No, Annabelle understood finally. It had taken her way longer than it should have done.

Not by magic. By Dylan.

It didn't click until she and Duncan arrived at Dylan's garage to pick up the car.

'So how much will it be?' she made herself ask brightly, dreading the answer.

'Four hundred and ninety-five dollars,' the head mechanic said, then gave her a leering stare. 'Isn't your doctor boyfriend going to pick up the tab for you this time?'

'What did you expect me to say?' Annabelle asked Dylan angrily, an hour later.

'Not much. A small thank-you, maybe.' He looked wary, a little distant, and he was watching her carefully.

He had only arrived at her place a minute ago—with another huge assortment of take-away containers, even though she had already told him she would cook—and she'd launched into her angry interrogation straight away, while Duncan was still safely running around in the back garden.

Had Dylan put those bills of Mum's on his own card?

Yes.

And was he intending to pick up all or part of the tab at her garage, as he'd apparently done before?

Yes to that, too.

Why?

That was obvious, wasn't it?

She paced the kitchen, got distracted for a moment by the sight of him unpacking the twelve…no, four-teen…plastic containers, all of them steaming with hot food, and demanded, 'What am I supposed to do with all that?'

'Eat the dishes we fancy tonight, and freeze the rest.'

'No. You can take it home. I hate this. Why have you started doing this?'

'What's "this"?'

'You know!'

'Helping—'

'No! You were the one who made me see what a horrible, mercenary kind of transaction was going on between Alex and me, and now you're doing the same thing.'

'Annabelle—'

'I'm not your mistress, Dylan. The garage man made it quite clear he thought you were paying for favours received. And I'm not your charity case. I don't want to *need* you. I just want...'

To want you. She didn't quite dare to say it, since the wanting was so strong.

'You don't have to pay for me, or find ways to elevate my lifestyle to your level,' she went on. 'If my lifestyle isn't good enough for you, then *I'm* not good enough for you. And if any part of what's going on here is because you feel sorry for me, you can get out of my house right now.'

'Since none of that applies, I'll stay put,' he answered lightly.

The lightness angered her further. He wasn't taking this seriously. He wasn't taking *her* seriously! Maybe the wanting was only this strong on her side.

'Don't belittle my feelings,' she said. 'This is important.'

'I'm not belittling your feelings. I'm belittling what I did. I paid a few bills for your mother, and set up an arrangement at my garage.'

'Yes, Alex was very willing to take on my family and financial obligations, too. I was happy about that until I realised—until *you* made me see—what he expected in return—a porcelain wife with a saintly aura so extreme it could be permanently damaged, in his eyes, by your outrageous behaviour at our wedding.'

'Hey!' Dylan growled. 'You know I never meant that comment of mine to carry the way it did! Haven't we dealt with that? It's behind us. And as for comparing me with Alex, saintliness is the last thing on my mind when I think of you, Annabelle.'

She ignored the suggestive, caressing lilt in his voice and stood her ground. 'I'm not going to be *kept*. Or helped. I don't want to be dependent on the man I'm…' She hesitated, and searched for the right word. 'The man I'm sleeping with.'

'What if I'm not prepared to build a relationship on those terms?' he shot back at her immediately. 'What if I believe that there's always give and take? That you can't even have a casual fling without need and support going both ways? And anyway, as far as I'm concerned, this isn't—'

She ploughed over him. 'It's not going both ways, the way you've engineered it. It can't go both ways. I've got nothing to give.'

He ignored her.

'I'm not backing down on this, Annabelle. What you're saying is impractical and artificial. You're the one dealing in transactions.'

'Am I? If that's true, then I guess it's over. It is over, Dylan. It has to be.'

She could hardly believe she'd said it. The words had flashed out of her mouth like a knife blade flashing out of its sheath. As soon as they'd been spoken, they settled into place as if they were puzzle pieces.

They fitted. She didn't particularly want them to, but they did.

'It has to be,' she repeated tightly.

She had started this too soon. She had too many issues trailing in her wake. Feelings, obligations, questions. It was very nice to have a man like Dylan in her life—a man who set her on fire, and bossed her around a little bit, with a wicked gleam in his eyes. But she wasn't ready, and she desperately didn't want to fall into the same pattern she'd had with Alex. She didn't trust Dylan's confidence on the issue, didn't trust his belief that he was too different from the senior surgeon to let it happen.

'Oh, for heaven's sake!' Dylan crossed the kitchen in three strides, and pulled her into his arms. His confidence didn't appear to flag.

And maybe he was right to be confident, because she didn't fight him off, just looked helplessly up into his face, melting at his touch the way she always did.

'You don't mean this,' he said.

'I—I do, actually.'

'What, you're turning it off, just like that? One minute we're on fire for each other…' He gave her a graphic verbal sketch about exactly what this had meant to them over the past ten days. Secret heat in the way they looked at each other. An almost painful anticipation about being together. Feverish couplings in her bedroom…and other places. 'The next minute,' he went on, 'you're telling me you've switched off the current. I don't believe it. You still feel it. You *do*!'

The way he was touching her, and the way she responded, proved his point, but she at last managed to flatten her hand against his chest and push him away. At the same time, Annabelle had to bite on her lower lip to stop herself from letting her mouth drift open to receive his kiss.

'That's not the thing that counts for me,' she said. 'I just don't like…the other places where this is going. You shouldn't have paid those bills, or made the arrangement with your mechanic. Not without asking.'

'If I'd asked, would you have let me?'

'No.'

'There you are!'

'*No!* Tricking me into accepting help is worse. I can't explain why this is so important. I'm obviously not explaining. Not well enough. But it is.'

He tried to argue some more, but she resisted. It was painful. Almost impossible. But she managed it, and finally she saw an angry acceptance cloud his eyes.

'You're almost as stubborn as Alex, do you know that?' he muttered.

'Good! It's right to be stubborn sometimes.'

He controlled a sigh. 'I'd better go, then, hadn't I?'

'Yes, I—I think so. Please, take…' Her gesture towards the hot containers on the counter-top died in the face of his laughter.

'Some of the food?' he finished for her. 'Hell, don't be so petty, Annabelle! There's a big picture out there, you know. You're not seeing it, and I can't force you to. So let's leave it at that. I'll see you, OK? Sorry we didn't get a little further than this.'

She mumbled some inept agreement and followed him to her front door. Then Duncan called out for her and she hurried out to the garden, wondering if there was any way she and Dylan could have handled this without making such a mess of it.

CHAPTER EIGHT

THE pain was back.

It came on so gradually that Dylan thought his mind was playing tricks at first. This new hot spot low in his spine wasn't related in any way to the pain he'd had before. Thinking about that first night at Annabelle's, he concluded that making love on a towel on the grass hadn't been such an erotic and inspired idea after all. He'd got a bruise on his spine, or something, from the hard ground beneath them.

Smashing her bottle of cough syrup seemed like proof that he shouldn't be seeking to mask the issue with medication. He left the painkillers alone for the next week or more, and listened helplessly to his nerve-endings telling him, It's getting worse. It's more than a bruise.

Still, he made excuses. A lot of doctors were good at that when it came to their own bodies. Too much swimming, he decided. And the seat-back in his car wasn't positioned correctly. He'd had a couple of difficult operations. He was stressed. All sorts of plausible things.

He definitely felt stressed after Annabelle's meltdown on Tuesday night. He understood what she was saying, but felt that she was coming at the whole thing from the wrong angle. Would have tried to talk to her about it some more, only he didn't know how to say it. There were some missing links in his own understanding as well.

He was sure, though, that her comparing him to Alex was hugely and almost sinfully unfair. So perhaps he'd had a fortunate escape from more tangled perceptions further down the line. Perhaps his experience with Sarah wasn't far enough in the past, after all. At least Sarah had had a single, specific complaint. 'You're never here.'

Some people, on the other hand, had a knack for creating problems in a relationship where none truly existed. If Annabelle was one of them...

And meanwhile, there was the pain in his back.

It started waking him in the night, and he skulked off to a physiotherapist who had a practice at the shopping centre near where he lived. He'd never heard of her. She wasn't on the list of people to whom he or Alex referred their own patients when necessary.

This, of course, was the whole point of seeing her. He didn't want this getting back to anyone else in the profession.

She seemed perfectly competent and pleasant, and had all the right qualifications. He sketched out the problem. She said it was very common, and gave him some ultrasound massage and some exercises. One of the mentholated heat ointments might help, too, she said. He picked some up at the chemist immediately, and slathered it on as soon as he got home.

If it helped, it didn't help much.

He started to notice the pain in surgery again, worse than that first bout after the sailing trip, and thought rebelliously, Why? There's no family history. His parents, in the United States, still maintained an active lifestyle, and his older sister, who also lived there, had never had any back problems that he knew about, even during her two pregnancies.

In addition, his posture was good. He did do a certain amount of lifting and pulling in his profession, but not enough to generate a chronic problem, or so he would have thought.

It had to be the sailing. He'd pulled a muscle or bruised a vertebra without realising it, and he kept unconsciously aggravating the injury before it had fully healed. He just needed to take things easy, do the exercises, get some more massage and be careful.

All this good sense…and none of it worked.

Duncan left Gumnut Playcare for the last time without a backward glance. Each of the staff gave him a hug, raised their voices a little too high to be natural and said they hoped he'd come back for *lots* of visits. Duncan scowled, turned and ran for the car.

I'm going to make the night shifts work! Annabelle vowed.

The first of these was the following night, and she was keyed up for it, aware of the difference. She drove over to pick Mum up straight after dinner, and had her settled in front of television with her oxygen, and Duncan settled in bed with his night-light, by eight. She then dutifully went to bed herself, with the alarm set for twenty past ten. Tonight, she probably wouldn't get any sleep this early, but tomorrow would be a different story.

Sure enough, she spent most of the two hours just lying there, watching the numbers change on the digital clock and thinking circular thoughts about Dylan Calford. She got out of bed before the alarm went off.

The hospital felt different at night, and the theatre

suite even more so. Surgery was limited to emergencies, including Caesarean deliveries, and she arrived in time to hear a newborn crying in its clear plastic cot on its way up in the lift to the maternity ward, one level above.

Occasionally, she might be rostered in Theatre Four for obstetrics, but mostly she'd be across the corridor in Theatre Two or Three, assisting with complicated fractures and closed head injuries, coronary artery by-pass grafts and emergency appendicectomies, and putting people back together after accidents. Sometimes she'd see Dylan.

Not tonight, she hoped.

Tonight, she wanted a nice easy start, with some quiet periods in which to grab some sleep.

Occasionally, it seemed, wishes of this selfish kind did come true. They handled emergency surgery on a fifty-seven-year-old man's bowel obstruction, and sewed up a shallow knife wound in another man's chest. The alleged assailant was in police custody. After this, she slept from three until six, then assisted in another stitching up—glass in a woman's foot this time.

The patient had delayed coming in for some hours, the glass was dirty and she wasn't up to date on her tetanus, so it might not be as simple a recovery as it could have been. At least the surgery itself went smoothly.

'Always makes me think of that prissy little proverb about a stitch in time,' commented fellow nurse, Sue Thorpe, stifling a yawn.

Annabelle pulled off her gloves and threw them in the bin, then helped Sue push the patient, on her

wheeled bed, out to Recovery. She yawned as well. 'You don't think it's true?' she asked Sue.

'Oh, I'm sure it's true! But it's not always helpful. Sometimes you don't get the chance to put in that first stitch. The whole seam is ripped before you notice a problem.'

'Are we talking about needlework here?'

'Life, darling,' Sue drawled.

Perhaps I needed to hear that, Annabelle thought as they tidied up.

She had been wondering what she could have done to stop herself from feeling the way she did about Dylan—full of regret, still wanting him, still angry with him, wondering what her own problem was and if she was just being irrational—but perhaps there was nothing to learn from going over it all. Somehow, it was inevitable that she should have ended up in a mess. Sometimes, as Sue had said, you didn't notice anything was wrong until the whole seam was ripped.

She heard Dylan's voice just then, penetrating through the theatre's swing doors as they opened again. The anaesthetist, Andrew Brockway, had started to leave, but had turned in the doorway. He held the door open with his shoulder as he mumbled a question to Sue. Beyond him, Dylan's words were clearer.

'What's happening?' He sounded alert, and full of authority. 'Is he ready for us?'

Apparently, he was about to operate in this theatre as soon as the place was cleaned and prepared by the incoming staff.

'Not yet,' said a woman's voice. 'He's still in A and E, getting stabilised. And we've got day shift nursing staff coming on.'

'Who else is operating?'

'Kevin Neeley, since the guy has facial injuries,' said someone else. 'Cam Brewer, too, I think.'

Dylan whistled, then said, 'OK, I'll go and—'

The swing doors closed again as Andrew Brockway left, and Annabelle couldn't hear any more. She assumed they had an accident victim with multiple injuries. Dylan and the rest of his surgical team could be here for hours. She finished up some ten minutes later, and didn't see him on her way out.

That night, after a satisfying snooze on the couch while Duncan watched a video, and a two-hour nap in bed between eight and ten, it was a different story. They had a patient flown in by helicopter, having suffered a serious fall while rock-climbing. His injuries were severe and extensive, and it was obvious at once that it would take all night to patch him up. Dylan would be heavily involved, as the twenty-four-year-old had sustained two complicated spiral fractures of each femur—fractures where the broken bone was protruding through the skin, creating a serious risk of infection—and three more simple breaks.

Meanwhile, a gastric lavage had shown a bleeding spleen. The patient's blood pressure was still dropping slowly, despite the replacement blood going into him, and gastro-intestinal surgeon Cam Brewer had been called in to do a life-saving repair before the less critical orthopaedic procedures could take place.

Dylan, already on hand, looked tired in contrast to the way he'd sounded this morning, Annabelle noted, and she wondered how many hours he'd already spent in surgery today. The large team grouped themselves around the patient, and he seemed unusually terse as he outlined what he needed to do and when he needed to do it.

It was out of character, and Annabelle saw that she wasn't the only one to notice it. Sue Thorpe was working again tonight. She'd had years of experience in the operating theatres at Coronation Hospital, and knew everyone. Divorced and with a couple of grown children, she acted like a cross between an interfering mother and everyone's favourite school teacher.

She also found plenty of time to take in exactly what was going on, and Annabelle caught the sharp, assessing glance she shot at Dylan from across the room as he said shortly, 'No, Cam, I've said that shouldn't be a problem, haven't I? His legs are all right for the moment, and they can wait till you're done. I'll stay on hand until then, just in case we get a further complication. Let's get started, shall we? If you don't repair that tear in the spleen, it'll be academic because he'll have lost too much blood.'

They were already transfusing it in as fast as they could.

The atmosphere didn't get better. Annabelle could see that Dylan was trying to stay calm and pleasant—battling to do so, actually. Even when he spoke cheerfully, it didn't sound natural. Why was it such a struggle? Purely because he was tired? That shouldn't be a problem. He wouldn't have reached this stage in his career if he couldn't function under pressure and fatigue.

Finally, it clicked.

He's in pain.

She was more and more sure of it as the long and gruelling operation proceeded. The patient's condition wasn't good. His blood pressure was dangerously low, and Cam Brewer had to work with total concentration to repair the extensively damaged spleen. Only once that was stitched up and the abdomen closed did the patient's condition improve a little.

'This leg is just lovely!' Dylan muttered, when he was able to get to work at last. He listed a long string of equipment he'd need. Plates and pins of different types. 'I'm doing a damned jigsaw puzzle!'

He *was* in pain.

Annabelle remembered the night he'd looked in her bathroom cabinet for painkillers, and his not-quite-convincing agreement when she'd asked if he had a headache.

They had now reached the most difficult part of Dylan's work—the smashed and twisted left leg, through which a jagged and splintered bone still protruded.

He stepped back. 'I want to call Alex Sturgess for this,' he announced.

'Yeah?' said the resident, David Yan.

Cam Brewer looked surprised, too. They had enough doctors here, including a second orthopaedic registrar, Brian Collins, who wanted the experience. This wasn't one of Alex's private patients and, although it was difficult, it wasn't the kind of surgery that he would expect to be summoned for.

Whatever Dylan was suffering, it must be bad—bad enough to put doubt in his mind as to whether he could safely get through the operation.

Sue had already moved to the wall-mounted phone. 'Could we have Dr Sturgess paged at home, please?' she said.

'I'll keep going,' Dylan said. 'Don't want to wait. He can take over when he gets here.'

'Is there a problem, Dylan?' Cam asked.

Dylan gave a technical answer which made enough sense to satisfy everyone—the complex nature of the pinning and plating required, the fact that both legs were involved, the need for fast work.

Satisfied everyone, that was, except Annabelle.

What was it? Migraine? Vision problems?

Pain. Definitely pain. His mouth looked tight and thin, as if he were tasting vinegar. There were grim lines etched around it, his eyes were suffering, and he was sweating. She could see the dampness at his temples and a shine on his upper lip.

But she couldn't ask him about it. Not now. If he wanted people to know, he would have said something. At least Alex would get here as soon as he could. She knew that from personal experience. He could make it out of his house within two minutes of being called in, even at two or three in the morning, and he always took such calls seriously.

'Yes,' he said when he arrived. 'I'm glad you called me, Calford. This is a good one. Brian, you'll get a lot out of this. Now, the way we're going to do it...'

They were in surgery for another four hours.

The change-room felt blessedly cool. Dylan locked the door and pulled his damp T-shirt over his head. Breath left his body on a shudder of exhaustion. The whole long night had been appalling.

At one point, a couple of hours into the operation, he'd looked ahead to what he still had to do, with a patient who was hovering dangerously close to death, and had thought in panic, I can't! The pain's too bad. I don't feel safe. If I made a mistake...

That was when he had asked for Alex to be called in, and he had to be grateful to the other man for not questioning it. The senior surgeon had worked quickly, and had delegated expertly, showing all of the brilliance that, at times like this, excused his worst behaviour. Now the patient was doing better than they had feared.

'But I'm not,' he muttered. 'I'm not doing very well at all.'

He needed to see someone, get some tests done. The self-diagnosis that had taken him off to the physiotherapist for a bit of massage was obviously off base. He was starting to sketch out the more serious scenarios now. Permanent damage. A malignant growth. A pinched nerve that would never settle back where it belonged.

And if the pain continued, then his career couldn't. He couldn't operate if his back went on feeling like this, day after day. Any medication strong enough to numb the agony would hopelessly compromise his mental acuity and his fine motor control.

Dylan shrugged his shoulders into a business shirt and put on the tie that was hanging in his locker. It was Monday morning, and he had rounds. As soon as they were over, he'd phone a colleague—not Alex, spinal problems weren't his area in any case—and ask to be seen.

Kemp McAllister, as first choice. Simon Grant as back-up. This morning, if possible. A professional favour. Now that he'd made up his mind this was serious, he wanted to know the full story as soon as he could.

Annabelle was hovering outside the change-room. Waiting for him? Looked like it. Instantly, there was the usual current of electricity and perception between them. She looked tired, but her eyes were wide and dark, and he was flooded with the warmth of her concern.

'You're in pain,' she said at once. 'I could tell, all through the operation. Where, Dylan? What is it?'

'It's my back,' he muttered. 'Don't let's talk about it here.'

She must have thought he meant, Let's talk about it somewhere else, because she nodded straight away and said, 'Want to grab a quick coffee? I'm a little bit late, but Mum knows that can happen sometimes. Another twenty minutes won't hurt.'

'All right,' he agreed. He wanted it, suddenly. Wanted *her*, sitting across the table from him and listening while he talked it out.

'Just let me change,' she said, and was in and out within three minutes. She'd exchanged the night's limp theatre suit for a pastel top and skirt, and she looked as cool and fresh as a flower.

They found the quietest corner of the hospital's public café, and she set her caffe latte down on the table in front of her, leaned across it and touched his hand. 'Are you afraid it's something serious?'

'I'm— Yes.' He let out a sigh, but kept the worst of his feelings bottled in. No point in admitting to the full range of panicky scenarios that filled his mind. 'It's too soon to think that way,' he said, more decisively. 'I haven't seen anyone yet. But the pain was...pretty bad last night. I didn't want anyone to guess.'

'No one did. Except me. You hid it pretty well. Sue knew something was bothering you, but she shrugged it off, I think. Put it down to fatigue, and the surgery you'd had earlier in the day. Has it been coming on for a while? Was that why you were delving in my medicine cabinet that night?'

'Yes.'

'You said it was a headache.'

'No, I let you say it, and I didn't contradict you. That's not quite so bad, as lies go!'

There was a silence. Dylan thought about the night some more, and was certain that she was thinking about it, too. The first night they'd slept together. One of far too few such nights, full of a promise and delight that hadn't been fulfilled because she'd finished it. She'd had reasons. He conceded that. But should those reasons have been deal-breakers?

Missed connections like this just...*happened* in today's world. At the moment, it seemed like an enormous waste, and he couldn't help feeling angry about it.

'Look, phone me, won't you?' Annabelle said. Her voice wasn't quite steady. Her coffee was already almost gone. She was gulping it down. 'Tell me the news. Or come over to my place. I really mean that, Dylan. If you need to talk.'

To *talk*?

She was leaning forward, her eyes big and warm and her mouth full with compassion. Another inch, and their fingers would have touched. Another six inches, and he could have captured that mouth in a long, deep kiss. Except...

Talking? That was what she was offering?

'No, thanks,' he answered.

'Oh.' She sat back a little, having sensed his rebuff with ease.

Well, good!

Hell, *talking?*

If she was going to reach out, he wanted a heck of a lot more from her than that! He wanted to take hold of that soft, pretty hand and squeeze it. He wanted to feel her fingers lacing through his and stroking his skin. He wanted each touch to contain the erotic promise of sex, and a lot more besides.

Angry with her, he scalded his throat with the last mouthful of his black espresso and stood up.

'Rounds,' he said. 'With the other business, my back, I'll keep you posted.'

'Dylan…' She stood up as well, and followed him. 'If there's anything you need, don't hesitate to ask, OK?'

And that was when he totally lost it.

'Is that the only role you feel safe with, Annabelle? Is it too frightening to have wants and needs of your own? You practically threw me out the door because I gave you a bit of help. Not meant as a transaction of any kind. Just because I cared. And you couldn't take it. But now that you get the chance to be saintly Sister Drew again, you're right at home. What kind of an avoidance strategy have you got going there?'

'I'm not in the least saintly.' She flushed. 'I— And I certainly don't want to be!'

'I used to think that about you—that the title of Sister fitted you, as if there was still that Florence Nightingale aura around you. And I think I was right.'

'That's an insult, Dylan.'

'Is it? Deal with it! For a while, just recently, I thought I was wrong. Alex dropping you at your own wedding jolted you out of your accustomed role for a while, but now you're getting another chance to hide inside it again. No, there's nothing I "need",

OK? Nothing that you're offering, anyway. On the other hand, there's plenty that I want. I think you know what I mean. Let me know if the situation changes, and I might still be interested.'

She nodded slowly. She looked stricken, and he felt a twist of remorse inside him, but she said nothing, and he wasn't going to wait any longer. As he left the café, he didn't give her a backward glance.

'Nothing showed up on the CAT scan, Dylan,' said Kemp McAllister. 'Your spine is in great condition.' He amplified the statement with technical language, because he rightly guessed that Dylan would want full detail. 'Look at the pictures yourself later on.'

He slid the big envelope containing the images from the scan across his desk, then gave the announcement that Dylan had expected.

'I'm going to send you for an MRI. It's still possible there's a tumour that the CAT scan didn't pick up.'

'Pressing on the nerve.'

'That's right. The sailing trip might have caused some temporary, localised inflammation, which increased the pressure on the nerve and caused that first bout of pain. As the inflammation subsided, the pain did, too. But if there is a tumour and it's growing…'

'The pain is back again, and increasing, even without the earlier inflammation,' Dylan finished.

He didn't need to ask any more questions or hear any more explanations from Kemp. He knew as much as the other man did now. Too many ifs. *If* there was a tumour at all. *If* it was operable. *If* it was operable, but so integrally connected to the spinal cord that its removal would leave him with loss of function in his legs...

And before any of those 'ifs' could be eliminated, there was the MRI.

Although he'd never had one himself, he knew exactly what was involved—total immobility for well over half an hour in an extremely confined and painfully noisy cylinder of high-tech machinery, while his back was scanned in minute cross-sections and an image was generated.

The procedure wasn't painful—if you didn't count the assault on the eardrums—but many people found the sense of confinement, immobility and powerlessness quite terrifying. He'd had one patient recently who had shaken so much that the scan had been almost useless.

Dylan wasn't a big fan of confined spaces. For preference, he would have chosen pain.

He cleared his throat. 'When can they fit me in? Any idea?'

'I'll call the imaging centre myself and try to get a cancellation for you. First available chance, Dylan, don't worry.'

'What do you really think, Kemp?'

'Truth? I've seen tumours presenting like this. I've even seen septicaemia presenting like this—abscesses pressing on the spine.'

'I very much doubt it's septicaemia!'

'I agree. That was just an illustration. But let's wait for the MRI before we conjecture any further.'

The wait took four days. Finally, on Friday at seven-thirty in the morning, he got a hurried call from Kemp saying, 'Short notice—I meant to call you last night—but if you can clear your schedule for this afternoon, the imaging centre can fit you in at three.'

'Three today?' Get Brian to cover the last two hours of his fracture clinic. Should be fine. 'Thanks, Kemp.'

Putting down the phone, he turned to find Annabelle emerging from the nurses' change-room in her street clothes after her eleven till seven shift in Theatre Two.

'I'm sorry,' she said. 'I couldn't help— Was that Kemp McAllister you were talking to?' He didn't reply at once, and she went on hurriedly, 'I wasn't eavesdropping. I just heard you say his name. And I was hoping you'd phone, Dylan. I've been…thinking about it…about you…all week.'

'I've got an MRI booked for three o'clock this afternoon,' he told her.

There was no point in prolonging the conversation by trying to duck her interest. They'd slept together. They'd had the beginnings of a relationship. There was still a pull. A *huge* pull, if he was honest, despite the fact that any anger between them definitely went both ways, now. He'd been fairly brutal to her on Monday, and he wasn't sorry about it.

'OK,' was all she said. Those usual big, warm eyes. That usual slow, careful nod. Then she added, 'I'll be thinking of you, Dylan.'

'If you think it'll help,' he drawled, laying the sarcasm on thickly.

'Yes, I think it will,' she retorted, colour warming her cheeks like two ripe peaches.

'Good for you,' he muttered. He turned away down the corridor without waiting to see if she'd heard.

Surprising how much it hurt to be angry with her,

like sandpaper rubbing on sunburned skin. The long morning of surgery he headed into five minutes later came as a relief.

Duncan loved his first morning at playgroup. It was held at a local church hall with plenty of toys, a shady fenced yard, a sand-pit and climbing equipment. He was wary at first, and clung to Annabelle tightly.

She didn't quite know why he was doing it, but relished his need and their closeness. Dylan had hurt her this morning. Angered her, too, the way he'd angered and hurt her on Monday morning with his accusations about saintliness and hiding. Could there be any truth in what he'd said? She had been thinking about it all week, but didn't have any clear answers.

Something to do with her feelings about Vic. She'd known for a while that some of her actions and her decisions were direct responses to how she felt about Vic's way of approaching life.

Vic had lurched from one career path to another—journalism, modelling, web-site design, catering. Although it hadn't seemed to bother her, she'd never stuck at anything long enough to get good at it, or to make any money.

Annabelle herself, in contrast, had enrolled in nursing and had never deflected from her original goals.

Vic had fallen passionately, ecstatically and painfully in love several times a year. On cloud nine while the affair was at maximum sizzle, pit of despair when it ended…until the next exotic and unlikely lover came along. As well as the Greek barman, there had been a surf-shop owner, a garage mechanic, a singer in a band, a TV news cameraman—more men than Annabelle could tally up.

Annabelle, on the other hand, had had a couple of cautious relationships with cautious men, both of which had ended by mutual agreement before anyone had become too deeply involved. Alex's departure from their wedding had been the only romantic event that could have vied for dramatic content with Vic's flamboyant history of affairs.

Vic had been her own woman, answerable to no one, in charge of her decisions and in charge of her life. Independent. Self-sufficient.

Annabelle had always looked to other people—their needs, their approval.

Except…

That was only Vic's perception, she realised as Duncan showed her the star shapes he was making with pink play dough. How independent was Vic really? With everything she did, someone else had to pick up the pieces for her afterwards.

Annabelle had made calls to Vic's catering clients to cancel their bookings and recommend another firm. 'I'm sorry, Belle. I'm rotten at this. I'm losing money hand over fist. And I can't face those people.' She'd cleaned Vic's flat when Vic had broken her lease to go overseas. 'I just don't have time. The best flight deal I could get has me flying out Monday. Getting away is going to give me some perspective, and I really need that right now!'

And Annabelle had inherited Duncan.

Vic hadn't been independent and self-reliant. She'd been lost. She hadn't had a clue what she'd wanted, or what she'd been doing, and if other people hadn't been there to help, her life had fallen apart.

'Mummy staying?' Duncan asked her, still snuggled, uncharacteristically, on her lap as they sat at the play-dough table.

She realised that he thought playgroup was like child-care, and he was expecting—and dreading—her departure. She felt a rush of love, and hugged him tightly. 'Yes, I'm staying,' she told him. 'I'm always going to stay with you at playgroup.'

'Mummy always stay at playgroup,' he said happily. He dropped the play dough at once and ran off outside to explore.

His departure left her free to wonder what any of that stuff about Vic had to do with Dylan's accusations, until she got caught up in conversation with the other parents and carers while they had coffee. One of the mothers looked familiar, and after a bit of speculating and memory-jogging, they finally realised that Gina was the younger sister of one of Annabelle's old school-mates.

'Laurie will want to know all about what you're doing now,' she said, and Annabelle ended up telling everyone much more than she'd expected to about Duncan's difficult start and her own current determination to put his needs first in her life.

'You're crazy, trying to make that schedule work!' one of the women said. 'You'll kill yourself!'

But everyone else was supportive. They talked about sleep disruption with a new baby, and their own decisions about child-care and conflicts regarding working versus staying at home. It felt good. Duncan came up to her frequently—for a hug when he hurt himself, for a push on the swing, for dispute resolution when he and another boy both wanted to ride the same tricycle.

Gina said to Annabelle quietly a little later, 'I don't

agree with Ella that you're going to kill yourself, but you do look tired. Joshie and Duncan seem to be playing nicely together. If you ever want to drop him over for a few hours while you grab a sleep or get some errands done, feel free. We all tend to help each other out that way. This afternoon, if you want to.'

This afternoon, when Dylan had his MRI.

Annabelle hesitated at first. Dylan had been pretty rude, and pretty dampening, about her assumption that she had something of value to give. Why should she show up to hold his hand?

Because no one else would.

He had no family here, and she was sure he'd told as few people as possible about his back pain. He certainly wasn't the kind of man who'd trouble a male friend for support. The mates he'd gone sailing with a few weeks ago would probably be the last people to hear about the problem with his back.

Perhaps we both find it harder to take support than to give it, she thought.

On the face of it, an MRI was a simple, non-invasive test, but she knew one nurse who'd sworn she'd rather 'get eaten by a crocodile' than go through one again.

'Actually, Gina…' Annabelle said, and they fixed it up in a couple of minutes.

She would drop Duncan at Gina's at three-ish, and pick him up again on the way to Mum's at around five. Time for some shopping, some cleaning, a short nap…or a stop at the imaging clinic to see Dylan.

'How did you go?' the receptionist asked.

'It was fine,' the young woman said cheerfully. 'It's a cool machine.'

She leaned on the desk, looking in her backpack for her purse. She wore a black top and skin tight black trousers that rode low on her hips, she had hair the shade of blue food colouring and a very high metal content on various tender parts of her anatomy. On her, the look worked. So did the cheerfulness and the insouciance.

Dylan would have purchased some of it from her, if that were possible. He wondered why she had needed the scan. Something gynaecological? If she was concerned about the result, she wasn't letting it show.

'Dr Calford?' said the technician, appearing in the doorway which led away from the waiting room.

It is ridiculous to feel so nervous!

At the moment, it was the scan itself, but underlying this and strongly colouring Dylan's emotional state was his knowledge that the result could shatter his life. He felt very alone in the face of that knowledge.

It's going to be fine. Cool. Just like the young woman with blue hair had said.

It wasn't.

He hated everything about it. Hated wearing the hospital gown. Hated the antiseptic white of the MRI scanner, inside and out. He hated going in head first, and he hated its tight fit. Heaven only knew how a man with shoulders any broader than his would have squeezed through. He hated the mesh-like cage at his face. He hated the constant white light, and the fact that he wasn't supposed to move a muscle.

Most of all, he hated the noise. Yes, it really was like athletic shoes going round and round in a tumble dryer—a dryer that was tumbling around Dylan himself. As his body was fed slowly, sl-o-owly through the long tube and he ached with the effort of lying still, it felt like time itself had slowed to a standstill.

When he finally emerged, he knew he must be as white as the machine. He felt ill, drained of adrenalin, deafened and off-balance. Getting dressed was such an effort that the technician knocked on the door after a few minutes to see if he was still breathing. She found him sitting there with his shoes in his hand and his head between his knees.

'Are you all right, Dr Calford?'

'Getting there.'

'Yes, it does bother some people.'

Some people, it didn't. The next patient, a frail-looking man of about sixty-five, who seemed completely at ease in his lemon yellow floral hospital gown, poked his head around the door and chuckled at Dylan.

'Doesn't worry me a bit,' he claimed. 'I had one a couple of years ago. Planning to fall asleep in there this time.'

Dylan raised his head and the room tilted and blurred. 'Good for you,' he said.

The man shuffled off, still chuckling.

'Do you have someone waiting for you?' the technician asked.

'No.'

'And you're driving yourself?'

'Yes. I'll be fine.'

'Better wait a while,' she said. 'Have a cuppa. One of the reception staff will be very happy to make one for you.'

'Might do that,' he agreed. He felt dizzy, as if he

himself had been one of the athletic shoes tumbling in the dryer.

Determined not to give in to it, he put his shoes on and walked out to the waiting room. He knew he probably looked like a drunken man—one who was convinced against all evidence that he was walking a straight line. He didn't care.

And then he saw Annabelle.

CHAPTER NINE

DYLAN was scowling at her, Annabelle noted at once.

Or was he just fighting to see straight?

She almost scowled back, not sure now why she had come. She was sure he wouldn't welcome her, even if he fell into the group of people who found MRIs to be difficult. His face told her she was right on both counts. It had been difficult, and he didn't want her. His expression had set hard, and he wasn't smiling.

'Hi,' he said, speaking through a narrow slit in his lips.

'Hi.' She was almost as prickly as he was. 'Looks like I should get you a cup of tea or something. I can drive you home, too, if you like.'

'I'll be fine in a minute. The tech said I could ask at the desk for some tea.'

'I'll ask. Or there's a café next level down if you want brewed coffee and don't mind a styrofoam cup.'

'Whatever. Tea, but I don't care where it comes from.'

She hesitated, then decided to ask at the desk. Styrofoam cups were horrible. She touched Dylan's shoulder, then looked for a sign from him that it was OK to do more. Hug him. Sit down beside him and stroke his thigh for a moment, or lay her head against his chest. But he didn't give her any such sign. Just sat there, doing a very good impression of a man who was feeling perfectly all right.

'When do you get the—?' she began.

He cut in without letting her finish. 'Oberlin—Paul Oberlin, the radiologist—is going to courier the pictures over to Kemp McAllister as soon as he's done his report. If I know Kemp, he'll completely ignore the report anyway, and analyse the images himself. He should phone me by the end of the day.'

'I'll get you that tea.'

He didn't thank her until she put the hot mug in his hand, and even then it was only a grunted word. 'You didn't need to come,' he added.

'I wanted to. But I can't stay long. One of the play-group mums has Duncan, and I'm not sure how it's going to work out. It's the first time he's played there. May I…uh…phone you tomorrow morning, to hear what Paul Oberlin and Kemp McAllister have said?'

He looked at her properly at last, and growled, 'Of course you can, Annabelle. It's not going to stay a secret for much longer, in any case, whatever it is.'

'OK, then.'

She sat down beside him, but didn't touch him the way she wanted to. The space between their bodies felt thick and uncomfortable, and they didn't even talk until he asked, 'How's Duncan?'

'Oh, we've had a great time together this week.'

'You look tired.'

'So I've been told! I'm expecting to look tired for a while. New parents manage it. Plenty of people manage it.'

'Don't let it get to breaking point. You're only human.'

'I know that, Dylan.'

They looked at each other helplessly for a second

or two, then both turned away, unable to bridge the gap. She left a few minutes later.

'Listen, Dylan,' Kemp said on the phone, 'I know you'll want to see these for yourself—'

'Yes, but I also want the bottom line right now, if you can give it to me.'

His stomach was flipping like a fish on dry land, and he hoped it wasn't obvious in his voice. The phone call had come later than he'd expected. The specialist had got caught up in other matters. It was after eight in the evening, and Dylan had spent the past two hours sweating and watching the clock.

'OK, yes, I thought that's what you'd say. Bottom line is that, yes, something showed up. A tumour. From the evidence on the scan, it's not obviously malignant, just a benign nerve tumour a little over a centimetre in diameter, but, of course, we won't know for certain until we've taken it out and had a good look at it. Now, the bad news is—'

Dylan swore. 'That was the *good* news?'

'Well, yes. The thing that concerns me is its position, so close to the nerves. You've got to get it removed, but you may end up with nerve deficits in your legs as a result.'

Nerve deficits in his legs. A polite, technical way of saying that he wouldn't be able to walk properly, or stand for long periods. He wouldn't be able to do his job. You couldn't perform surgery if you couldn't stand.

'If we get Graham Barlow to operate...' Dylan suggested, starting to sweat.

'Yes, that's who I'd recommend. From the way your symptoms have developed, it's growing relatively fast, so we should move forward on the surgery as soon as possible. I've already spoken to Graham, and he can fit you in next Friday. Does that give you enough time to clear your schedule?'

'It'll have to. I don't want to wait on this.'

'Obviously, it's awful for you.'

'I'll get through it. Thanks, Kemp.'

'Get in touch if you have questions. Anything you want to talk about.'

'Thanks,' Dylan said again.

He didn't phone anyone after he'd finished talking to Kemp. Not his parents, or his sister, or his friends. Distantly, he realised that it might be a good idea, but somehow he couldn't do it. Didn't want to have to tell the whole story, or hear the emotional, appalled responses he'd get when he outlined the two worst-case scenarios—malignancy and damaged nerves.

The only person he really wanted to phone was Annabelle. Not to tell her, but to ask her whether he could come round.

Can I bury myself in your body and anaesthetise myself in your arms? Can I take nourishment from the smell of your hair and the sound of your voice? Can I sit beside you in utter silence and feel your care?

He even thought it very likely that she wouldn't turn him away from her bed tonight. She would sense his need, and that would be enough.

Enough for her. Not enough for him.

Annabelle hoped Dylan would phone that night, but he didn't. She went to work at eleven, leaving Mum already asleep in her tiny third bedroom, but she knew Dylan wasn't on call tonight.

Things were fairly quiet until around three in the morning, when they had to call in a cardiothoracic surgeon to perform an emergency coronary artery by-pass, and she got away promptly at seven.

Dylan had told her yesterday that 'of course' she could phone him that morning, but she didn't want to disturb him early. If he'd had a bad night... In the end, she waited until eleven and by then he'd gone out. She didn't leave a message on his machine.

Several more tries over the course of the day got the same result, and she began to wonder if he was screening his calls. It was eight in the evening before she finally reached him, when Duncan was already in bed and Mum was watching her evening television shows.

He knew what she wanted to ask him, and launched into his account straight away. His wooden tone only served to outline his words in darker colours, and she couldn't hold back a stricken cry when he told her the worst possibilities.

'Have you talked to your parents about this?' she asked.

'Not yet.'

'Your sister? Your friends?'

'No. I'll tell Alex, of course. He'll need to know. I've been trying to get hold of him, but he hasn't returned my calls yet.'

'Have you told Sarah?'

He laughed at this. 'No!'

'At some point—'

'I'll tell people after the surgery. When I know. Why tie anyone else in knots with worry when there's nothing they can do? Why have everyone at the hospital buzzing with speculation? My parents would probably fly out—'

'Of course! You should give them that option,' she urged him. 'Don't make their decisions for them.'

He sighed. 'Listen, it's my decision, not theirs. I want to see them. When I know how well I can walk, and whether I'm going to live.' Oh, dear God! 'That's when I want to see them. Until then—'

'You've only got me,' she said softly, her voice catching in her throat.

'Yeah, and you'd get out of my face if you had any sense!'

'Well, maybe I haven't any sense where you're concerned.'

Dylan made a disgusted sound. 'Leave it, Annabelle. I mean that. Leave me alone. Ask yourself why you're only interested now that I'm facing this, now that I'm needy and not so strong.'

'You're still strong, Dylan!'

He ignored her. 'Is it safer for you that way? Does it fit with the way you see yourself? Because it doesn't fit with what *I* want! As you said to me a few weeks ago in a different context, I'm not your charity.'

'No,' she agreed, her voice tight. 'You're not. That's not what this is about.'

He laughed again—the same cynical, dismissive sound she'd heard just now when she'd asked if he'd told Sarah. This link with his ex-wife was, Annabelle knew, anything but flattering. When she put down the phone a minute later, she felt totally shut out of his life.

And she knew fully, for the first time, that she was in love with him.

That was the difference. That was the key. This wasn't about her instinct—too well developed, at times; perhaps he was right about that—to respond to the needs of others and deny what she needed for herself. This was pure selfishness. She loved him, and she wanted to be with him, share this with him, whatever the outcome was. Except that he seemed to be telling her that it was too late.

'How are your shifts now? Busy?' Barb Thompson asked Annabelle.

The two of them had overlapped briefly in the theatre suite. It was Monday morning, and Annabelle was finishing work while Barb was just starting.

'Usually pretty busy,' she answered. 'Sometimes we get a good break. But the pace is hectic, since they're all emergency procedures.'

'Enjoying it, though?'

'Yes, actually. More than I'd expected to. I was really only focusing on the hours. The drama can be satisfying, and when we get a good outcome against the odds it really feels good.'

Good enough to carry her through several tiring days with Duncan, slotted in between her shifts. But only just good enough. She yawned. Now she had three nights in a row in which to get some deep, solid sleep—if she wasn't thinking too much about Dylan.

His own surgery was this coming Friday, but he hadn't wanted her support.

'I just looked at today's list,' Barb said. 'We've got Jason Gregory's knee reconstruction first up.'

'Is Dylan operating?' Annabelle had to ask.

'No, and I was a little surprised about that,' Barb answered. 'Apparently, he's off for the next two weeks. No one seems to know why. Sturgess…that is, Alex…is doing it. In fact, he's already here, somewhere about.'

'It's a difficult operation,' Annabelle said, as neutrally as she could. She knew, of course, why Alex was doing it, but if Dylan didn't want anyone to know what was going on until after his own surgery, she had to respect that.

Barb went back to making her preparations for the morning's list, and Annabelle began to remove her disposable shoe covers, then paused. She could hear Alex's voice, talking to someone on the phone as he waited until the patient was brought down and it was time to scrub.

She didn't need to talk to Alex about the surgery. Jason Gregory was just another patient.

Yes, but he was Dylan's patient, and his professional future mirrored Dylan's own fears about what lay in store for him.

Fighting down her reluctance, she walked across the wide corridor of the theatre suite, to where Alex stood talking on a wall-mounted phone. He replaced the receiver in its cradle just as she neared him, and he would have walked off if she hadn't spoken his name.

'Alex…'

It was the first time she'd used his first name since the day after their cancelled wedding, when she'd phoned him and begged him for a chance to talk.

'Yes?' He turned back to her warily.

'I just heard that you were doing Jason Gregory's surgery this morning.'

'That's right.'

'Are you handling all Dylan's lists over the next two weeks?'

'A couple of them. Brian Collins is doing some. And Keith Shartles's registrar, Lucas North.'

'I know about Dylan's tumour.'

There was a tiny silence. 'Then you're one of the few who does,' Alex said.

'Yes. I—I know that, too.'

'Make sure you keep it that way.'

'I just wanted to say I hope it goes well with Jason Gregory's knee, that's all.'

'He's realistic about what to expect. He's got plans to buy into a tourist development at Port Douglas, apparently.'

'Dylan was concerned about how he'd adjust.'

'Better than Dylan will himself, I expect, if he has the same outcome. A surgeon plans for a longer career than a rugby player.' Alex shifted his shoulders and his weight, as if he was about to walk away, but then he stopped and said quietly, 'About what happened in January... Would you have preferred a divorce further down the track, Annabelle? Because that's what it would have come to. I could suddenly see it, right in that moment after Dylan spoke. I could see it wasn't going to work for us. It was...histrionic of me to blame you and Calford. Then, and later.'

Should I tell him about our affair? Annabelle wondered.

Why, though? It had begun well after Alex had departed from her private life, and it was already over.

'I should apologise for that,' Alex went on. 'I *am* apologising for it,' he amended impatiently. 'The scrub who's replaced you isn't nearly as good. Never anticipates what I want.'

'That's not why I changed shifts, Alex. It wasn't because of us. Or not directly.'

'Yes, well...' He looked at his watch. 'No hard feelings now. Things are OK.'

'Yes.'

'For us, if not for poor Calford.'

She couldn't help protesting, 'There's a chance the tumour can be removed with no damage to the nerves.'

'Yes, but they're not odds I'd take on a horse at the racetrack! No wonder he's taken this week off! I wouldn't like to operate while wondering if it was the last time I'd ever be able to do it.'

'I think he was afraid the pain would compromise his performance.'

'That, too,' Alex agreed.

They both saw the plastic doors open at the end of the corridor at that moment. Jason Gregory had been wheeled down from the ward and was ready for his surgery.

Annabelle spent a good day with Duncan—if a little more active than she really had the energy for—and dropped in for an hour at Mum's. Four days from now, Dylan's surgery would be over.

That night, she was so tired that she slept long and well, from nine in the evening until Duncan's little feet running down the passage woke her the following morning at six. They did laundry, ran errands and swam in the morning, and in the afternoon she had Gina and Joshie over to play.

She and Gina had cool drinks together, talking easily the whole time. At school, so long ago, their age difference of two years had seemed considerable, but now it didn't matter at all. Laurie, who had then been Annabelle's friend, was living on a cattle station in the centre of the state, and she had children, too.

'Which most of my friends don't,' Annabelle said. 'And no one I know who lives close. There are a few kids in this street, but they're school-age.'

'Compatible kids. That's what friendships are based on when you're a parent,' Gina said with a laugh.

'Speaking of which, would you like to leave Joshie here for the rest of the afternoon, and have some time to yourself? I'll feel more comfortable about leaving Duncan with you sometimes if I get to reciprocate.'

'Well, since I did a pregnancy test last week, and it was positive…'

'Oh, congratulations! That's wonderful!'

'It is…and I'm already starting to feel as if I got run over by a bus, so I'll very happily take you up on your offer!' Gina finished.

The two little boys played together with no conflict, after she'd gone, for nearly three hours.

Three days until Dylan's surgery.

On Wednesday, Linda—old friend, financial adviser and thwarted bridesmaid—dropped in for a quick lunch between business meetings.

'Can I do this sometimes?' she asked. She pulled off the tailored jacket of her conservative navy suit and hung it on the back of the kitchen door. 'It's so nice to know you'll often be home during the day!'

She made awkward small talk for a while as they sat on the edge of Duncan's sand-pit, watching him play while they ate ham and salad sandwiches, then suddenly the real reason for her visit came flooding out in a rush.

'I'm seeing someone. It's serious. He wants to marry me. But he wants kids, and I don't know what to say. You know, Rob never wanted them...'

Rob was Linda's previous boyfriend, and he'd never been quite good enough for her, in Annabelle's private opinion.

'And so I kind of got used to thinking I didn't want them either. I don't know *anything* about kids!'

'Nobody does, until they have one,' Annabelle answered. 'Because "kids" in the abstract don't count. It's only *your* kid, and in that area, no matter how the kid is acquired, we all start from square one. So don't let that worry you.'

'But—but—'

'Do you love him, Linda?'

'Uh, yeah, I do,' Linda muttered. 'It's ridiculous, really!'

She was blushing.

'Then make a leap of faith. Marry him, and try for a baby. Life's full of twists and turns.'

'You think so?' The sun came out on Linda's face. 'You think it's that simple?'

Did she? Annabelle wondered. Her turn to talk now. About some of the things she'd been thinking lately about Vic. Vic had believed so completely that she should follow her heart...only her heart had led her on such a wild, erratic dance. Witnessing this, Annabelle had never dared to do the same. But she was starting to see things differently now. Vic hadn't been completely wrong in the way she'd lived her short, flamboyant life.

'Following my heart doesn't have to mean changing lovers and careers and life goals every few months, the way Vic did,' she told Linda. 'It doesn't have to mean messing things up so that other people are left to pick up the pieces. My heart gives steadier signals, I think. Vic did have a lot of courage, in her way. You have to take the leap, and assume you'll have what it takes to follow through when the time comes.'

They couldn't talk about it any more just then. Linda had to put her suit jacket back on and get to her meeting. But their conversation left Annabelle with plenty to think about.

And Dylan was having his surgery in two days.

'Mum, Duncan's in bed and half asleep, already,' Annabelle announced to her mother on Thursday evening at ten past eight.

'Little darling! I'll creep in and kiss him once he's safely off.'

'Would you mind if I head out now? I want to drop in on a friend before I go to work.' Her heart flipped as she said it. Would Dylan consider himself a friend?

'Of course, love. It's nice for you to get out. Is it Linda?'

'No, someone from the hospital.'

She didn't even want to say his name. Wasn't sure why she was doing this. She hadn't seen him all week, and he hadn't phoned. They'd ended their last conversation in anger and distance. Several times, she'd thought of phoning him. Twice she'd keyed in the first few digits of his number, but then she'd stopped. After her talk with Linda today, though...

It was time she took the leap of faith that she'd urged on her old friend.

I was wrong to make such an issue about the bills he paid, and about that leering garage mechanic with his 'doctor boyfriend' line. Dylan caught me on the raw, and I couldn't see it then. Maybe it's too late, but I'll never know if I don't try...

She was dressed casually in jeans and a cotton knit top, ready to change into theatre gear once she got to the hospital at just before eleven. It was tempting to dress up a little, but she resisted it. What would she be trying to prove? And anyway, she didn't have unlimited time. He must be very tense tonight. If he did want to talk it all out...

But when she rang his doorbell, she thought at first that he wasn't even home. After ringing it a second time and waiting in vain, she'd actually turned to leave before she heard the sound of a lock clicking open behind her. He had been in the pool. He wore baggy black swim shorts, water glistened on his skin and there was a towel draped around his neck.

For a moment, neither of them spoke.

'Come in,' he growled at her finally, and stepped back to hold the door open.

'OK,' she bleated, and spent the whole walk through his elegant, masculine townhouse thinking, 'Why am I here? He doesn't want me.'

When they reached the living room, which flowed seamlessly out to a beautifully landscaped courtyard and pool, he offered her something to drink. She chose coffee, thinking of the long night ahead, then added, 'How was your swim?'

'Nice. It's a mild night.'

'Finish your laps. Don't let me interrupt.'

'Time I got out.'

'Get dressed, then. I'll make the coffee.'

Dylan showed her roughly where everything was— this was the first time she'd been to his home—and disappeared into his bedroom, and she was left with the same regret as before. Leaps of faith were all very well in the abstract, but there was no guarantee that you wouldn't make a hard landing.

By the time he returned, Annabelle had the electric kettle boiled and the coffee brewing. He wore jeans and a T-shirt, and hadn't bothered with shoes.

'I suppose you've come to hold my hand,' he said.

Was it a challenge, or just an attack? Either way, it made Annabelle bristle as she poured the coffee into two mugs.

'No, I haven't,' she said.

'So you're not thinking about the fact that I have surgery tomorrow?'

'Of course I am!'

'Then why *are* you here? From the time we've spent together, I'd say there are limited options, and you've just denied the only one that's obvious. I overheard Alex calling me "poor Calford" today.'

It sounded like a *non sequitur*, but Annabelle followed his transition easily—he didn't want anyone's pity. Not Alex's, and not hers.

'You were at the hospital?' she asked inadequately.

'I dropped in to see Jason. He's doing well.' He took the mug she slid across to him, but didn't lift it to his lips. Her own steaming brew was still sitting on the bench-top in front of her as well.

'That's a good omen, I guess,' she said.

He laughed, and it was a harsh, angry sound. 'Do you really think I believe in omens like that?' He swore—a couple of short, pithy words. 'Why are you here, Annabelle? To mouth platitudes? Hell, I hope not! Leave now, if that's the case, because I don't think I could take it tonight.'

'All right.' She took a deep breath. 'You want to know why I'm here?'

Her heart was hammering, and she was angry at how prickly he was, how hard he was making this for her, but she didn't let it sway her. Instead, she deliberately skirted around the protective barrier of the kitchen's black granite bench-top and went up to him. She closed her fingers around his upper arm. The gesture was a demand, but also a caress. His angry prowling ceased.

'*This* is why I'm here,' she said. 'I want you, Dylan. I don't have platitudes, or a hand for you to hold. I just want to be here with you, in the hour and a half before I have to go to work, and if you don't want that, I'll leave.'

His eyes narrowed. 'This is sudden.'

'No! It's not sudden. You know that none of what we felt…none of the desire and the connection…went away when I yelled at you about the garage mechanic and my mother's bills. I overreacted that day. We could have got past it if I'd left the door open. I'm sorry I didn't do that, and I'm here to try again. I'm not thinking of the future. I—I just…want you.'

Love you. Too scary to say it, in case he didn't say it back. She felt it. It burned inside her. But she contented herself with saying the other part.

'I want you, Dylan,' she repeated, on a whisper this time.

He had frozen beneath that one touch of her fingers on his arm, and for a long moment she thought he was going to shake her off and turn away.

'Do you offer this service to all pre-operative patients?' he asked finally. Too silkily.

'No!'

'Then I'm special.'

'Yes. You are. If you don't know that, you're wilfully blind. Do you enjoy making this so hard for me?'

Surely he could *hear* her heart beating by now! How long before he would answer?

Never. He never answered. Or not with words. Instead, a hand dropped to her hip, anchoring her in place as he took one small step, closing the space between them. She looked up into his face and saw the way his dark eyes glittered. Was he still angry?

Surely not. Not when he was about to kiss her. She could see it on his mouth, feel it in the tiny puff of breath that warmed her lower lip. They were only a fraction of an inch apart now. She closed her eyes before his lips touched hers, too churned up with emotion to look at him, and when her eyes were closed, she forgot any thought of his anger.

How could he be angry, when he kissed her like this?

He tasted mint fresh, and his body still felt cool and hard from his swim. His arms wrapped around her, as solid as steel bands. They kissed for a long time, and it felt like magic—like an oasis at the end of a desert journey, like hot food on a wet night, like coming home.

His hands loosened around her body and began to drift, stroking the sensitive skin where her waist curved in, rising higher to brush beneath her breasts then capture them greedily in his hands. He unclipped her bra and they both groaned at the same time as he filled his cupped palms with her weight.

He lifted her top higher and thumbed her hard, exposed nipples, then lowered his head and took her into the warm, wet cavern of his mouth. She shuddered, arched her back and spread her fingers in his hair.

There was no possibility of going slowly now. He gorged hungrily on her breasts and she held onto him like a life-raft in a turbulent current. His capable body seemed like the only fixed point in a swirling, pulsating universe.

'I want to take you to bed,' he muttered. 'This isn't enough, Annabelle.'

'No…'

'*No?*'

'I mean, yes. It isn't enough. Yes, let's go to bed.'

They barely made it. Her top and bra fell onto the living-room floor, and his T-shirt marked the doorway to his room. They stopped there and he pressed her against the wall, his thigh between hers, his mouth on her mouth and his hands everywhere.

She unzipped his jeans and stroked him—warm satin on tempered steel. His ragged response sent her closer to the edge, and she was the one to drag on his naked hips, pulling him to the bed.

Tipping herself backwards, she brought him down on top of her, ready for him, melting and aching for him. He slid inside her and they began to move together, and the coil of tension within her mounted and mounted, threatening to shatter. When she heard him cry out, she thought at first that he'd left her behind, but the sharp sound he made wasn't a sound of pleasure. Frozen in place, he gasped out, 'Stop! Stop!' And she understood.

'It hurts, Dylan?'

'Yes!' He swore. 'Too damn much! I didn't want to take any painkillers tonight. This position. I'm sorry…'

'Roll over. It's OK. Don't stop.'

'I've broken the—'

'No. Don't talk.' She pressed her fingertips to his lips. 'It's OK. It's fine. You haven't broken anything. We'll take it easy. We'll take it differently. Easy is just as good.'

But he shook his head, eased away from her and pivoted cautiously to lie on his back. His mouth was set. In the dim light that stretched into the room from the distant kitchen, she could see him staring sightlessly and silently at the ceiling. There was nothing about his body language that encouraged her to breach the barrier he'd set up.

For a moment, she almost gave up. He was right. The mood was hopelessly broken. He'd shut her out of what he was feeling, and he didn't want her here any more. The love that burned inside her seemed like a useless emotion, incapable of softening him, incapable of getting through to him, incapable of helping him in any way. Certainly it didn't offer her any pleasure for herself at this moment.

What could she say?

Unless…

She began to stroke his chest, her fingertips slow, tantalising, light and very patient. He didn't react. Her fingers whispered across to his nipples and pinched them lightly, then she went lower, finding exquisite pleasure in the contrasts of silky skin and rougher hair, the hardness of his muscles and the careless male beauty of his nakedness.

Propping herself on one elbow, she slid her body half onto his chest. Her nipples brushed his skin, and they were so sensitised now that just this was enough to send pulses clamouring through her whole body.

'Touch me,' she whispered, and lifted his hand to place it on her breast.

For a moment, his fingers felt lifeless, uninterested. She slid a little further, one thigh brushing deliberately across his groin. He shuddered, and this time, once more, it was need. It wasn't pain.

'Touch me, Dylan,' she said again. 'Please?'

A fraction of a second later, she felt his thumb trace the peaked contour of her nipple, while his other hand came up to lift her weight. Sliding even higher, she brought her breasts within reach of his hot mouth, and at last they began to find the rhythm and urgency they'd so nearly lost. When her moving hips brought both of them crashing over the brink, she had tears spilling onto his face and onto the pillow beside him.

He must have felt them, but he didn't say anything. She lay on top of him, her head pillowed on his chest, listening to his heartbeat. It must have been ten minutes before he spoke, and his voice was creaky and stiff.

'Presumably, you have to get to work soon.'

'Yes. What's the time?'

'Clock's just there on the bedside table. I can't see it from this angle.'

'Ten past ten.'

Another silence.

'I'm first on Graham Barlow's list tomorrow,' he said.

'So, no food after midnight?'

'All that stuff. They probably would have admitted me today if I hadn't been a doctor myself. I had the pre-op check-up on Wednesday and everything was OK.'

'It won't be a long procedure, will it?'

'An hour or so, I'd guess. They'll send the tumour to Pathology. Funny, I'm not so concerned about that—the possibility that it's malignant. I'm more concerned about...'

He didn't finish, but she could guess the rest. She waited, then asked, 'When will you be discharged?'

Silence.

'Depends,' he answered at last.

Oh, dear God, of course it did! she realised. How stupid of her to have even asked! It depended on how well he could walk, how much relearning he had to do. How to get out of a chair. How to climb stairs. How to stand without falling. If his nerve damage was extensive, he might be in hospital and rehab for some time.

'You should go, Annabelle.' It didn't take half an hour to get to Coronation Hospital from his place. He meant, I want you to go. I want to be alone. Stare my future in the face, alone.

She didn't argue, just slid away from him awkwardly, aching at once for the lost contact and the lost warmth. Dylan stayed on the bed. He didn't watch her dress. All the same, she felt vulnerable as she reached for the briefs and jeans flung on the floor near the doorway, and her breasts felt swollen and sore—almost bruised. Although it was dark, and there was no one to see, she cupped her hands over them inadequately as she went in search of her bra and top in the living room.

Dylan appeared in the bedroom doorway, fully dressed, hair tousled and still faintly damp, just as she was ready to leave. He cleared his throat and opened his mouth to speak, but then he just shook his head.

'Don't be late for work,' he said finally.

Not the words she'd wanted to hear. He switched on the light, and once they'd both gone past their half-blinded reaction, she could see a potent mix of negative feelings smouldering in the depths of his eyes.

CHAPTER TEN

WHEN a patient was under general anaesthesia, he or she lost the subconscious awareness of time passing that was present in normal sleep. Dylan closed his eyes, began to count backwards from a hundred, as instructed, and woke again a millisecond later, in a bed in the recovery annexe.

Dimly, he knew that his surgery was over. His mouth felt dry, and his eyelids were too heavy to open. His lower back throbbed, and a tiny, wobbly shift in his position, lying on his side, made him aware of the dressing that covered his surgical site. A scratchy sound emerged from his lips, and one of the nurses came over. He knew her. Older woman. Pat Gould.

'Awake, Dr Calford?'

'Bit.'

'Let's check you out.' She took his temperature, blood pressure and pulse. Satisfactory, apparently—he couldn't summon the energy to ask for the exact figures—but he knew he'd be here for another half hour or so, just to make sure.

Can I move my legs?

He was sane enough not to try and answer this question yet. The effect of the anaesthesia was still weighing too heavily on his muscles. 'Barlow?' he asked Pat, just before she left.

'He's going to talk to you after his next procedure is over.'

'Tumour's out?'

'Yes, but that's all I know.'

''Anks,' was all he could manage, and even that was an effort. He closed his eyes and let the anaesthesia win for a while.

'Dylan?' said a soft voice a little later.

No, that wasn't Graham Barlow. He knew who it was.

This time, he got his eyes open. Lids felt a bit lighter now.

'I saw you just as you were getting wheeled in,' Annabelle said. 'There was no time to say anything. We were late finishing this morning, after a peritonitis case.'

'Very late off,' he said. One eye managed to focus on the clock. It was after ten.

'No.' She shook her head. 'I went home. Gave Mum and Duncan breakfast and took Mum home. Dunc's playing with a friend this morning.'

'So you should be asleep.' Tongue was working much better now.

She smiled tentatively. 'Well, I'm not. Not yet.'

Dylan's heart lurched. Lord, he was glad she was here! He was flooded with the feeling suddenly. The ripe beauty of her figure, the richness of her hair, the warmth of her smile. The familiarity of her voice and the radiance of her care.

He would have reached up a hand and touched her, squeezed her, only the hand was still too heavy. He would have said something about what was in his heart, but the only words that filled his mind had too many unanswered questions crowding around them.

Most importantly, did he have the right to say anything at all? And would she want him to? What had she wanted to give him last night, when she'd given him her body in bed? Just that? Just the immediate blessing of oblivion and release? Or much more?

Hell, it was all so woolly in his mind!

'How are you feeling?' Graham Barlow asked, coming up beside Annabelle. He gave her a quick nod, as if she was just a nurse he vaguely knew, not anyone important. Dylan rebelled inside. Annabelle was utterly important.

'Getting there,' he said. 'Tell me, Graham. Annabelle can hear it. I want her to. It's fine.'

'Nothing to tell yet,' the neurosurgeon said. 'We got it out. It's encapsulated, and almost certainly benign but, of course, Anne Smyth in Pathology will have a good look at it to make sure. You won't get the full picture on the extent of nerve damage, if any, until the whole thing has healed and you've had some physio.'

'Damage, if any,' Dylan echoed.

'I did the best possible job I could. There's a slight chance you'll experience no permanent loss of function at all. That's the best I can say.'

'OK. Thanks.' Dylan gave an awkward nod at his colleague, and tried not to let the dread and helplessness show on his face.

'We're going to send you up to the ward now, Dr Calford,' Pat Gould said a few minutes after Graham Barlow had gone.

'I'll come up with you,' Annabelle jumped in at once. She didn't care if Dylan didn't want her. She was here, and she was staying.

He still seemed very groggy, and his body, beneath the heavy white cotton of the hospital sheets, looked so different from the way it had looked last night. There was a strong chance it would never be the same body again. It was just as solid, just as strong, but so heavy and lifeless in his bed. This didn't matter to her, but she was certain that it would matter to him.

It was her own fault. She knew that, too. If she hadn't rebuffed his help, if she hadn't been so afraid of falling into the same unequal partnership that she and Alex had negotiated with each other, and if she hadn't been afraid of following Vic's emotional path as well, things might have been different now. They might have been going through this together.

Dylan had his eyes closed as they went along the corridor, up in the big service lift and into the sixth-floor neurological ward. He opened them as his bed was pushed into position in his private room, and he smiled at her. Her heart jumped and turned over in her chest. If he sent her away... Now, or *ever*.

'When do you have to go?' he asked.

'By lunchtime.' She leaned forward and stroked his shoulder tentatively, ending at the ropy hardness of his forearm.

He twisted his arm a little beneath her touch, and suddenly her fingers were engulfed in his grip. He closed his eyes again, and she just sat there, his touch bringing back powerful images of last night, and the way they'd made love with such urgent intensity.

Was that only because it had been their last chance?

'What are we going to do, Annabelle?' he asked in a scratchy voice.

'Whatever you want.'

Dylan laughed without moving his mouth, eyes still closed. His face looked just as gorgeous and dear to her when it was still and slack as it did when firmed and animated by his work in surgery…or his energy in the pool…or when he kissed her.

'What I want isn't good enough,' he said. 'My career may be over. I may be half-crippled.'

'All right, then we'll do what *I* want,' Annabelle said.

'And what's that?'

'We'll stop this stupid, almost *competitive* game we've both been playing since Alex walked out of the wedding. This game of tallying up which of us needs the other the most, and which of us has the most to give. We've both handled it wrongly. Maybe there was no way to stop that from happening at first, but if we don't change it now…' She stopped.

If we don't change it now, how will we make our love work?

That was what she'd wanted to say, but she still didn't know if he loved her at all, let alone if he was thinking of a long-term future to what he felt. *She* was.

Annabelle watched his face, and saw him nod faintly. Had he understood?

He still had his eyes shut, and his lips were closed and joined by a soft seam. She wanted to kiss them open, and feel his fingers tangling in her hair, the way they had tangled there last night. More than that, she wanted to hear what he would say.

She waited, but nothing came.

'Gone to sleep again?' said one of the ward nurses, a minute later.

Oh, heavens, he had! she realised. Of course he had! He was less than two hours post-op, he was on medication for pain, and sleep would be the best place in the world for him. How could she even have tried to talk to him now?

'I'll come back later,' Annabelle said.

But would he want her when she did?

'Can you drop by on your way to work, Annabelle?'

Dylan was on the phone from his hospital bed, sounding so much stronger and more alert than he had ten hours ago. He sounded a little grim, too, as if phoning her was something he had needed to do—an unpleasant duty—not something he wanted. 'We didn't get a chance to finish our conversation this morning,' he finished.

'No, we didn't,' she agreed. 'So you do remember it, then?'

'No, not exactly,' he admitted. 'But I know it was important.'

'I'll—I'll give you a recap or something.' She could hardly speak.

'So you'll come?'

'Yes, I'll leave here as soon as I can.'

Duncan wasn't in bed yet, but he soon would be. Annabelle didn't know what to think about Dylan's call. Did he want to talk about last night?

Thanks, he might say. It took my mind off things. But don't get the wrong idea.

Or perhaps there was some news about the extent of damage to his nerves.

When she arrived at the hospital forty minutes later, Dylan was sitting up in bed. He looked tired and a little creased, but it suited him…made her want to smooth out those lines around his eyes and mouth with her fingers, and with her lips… And there was life in his face again.

He had his wheeled meal tray beside him, with an open paperback novel sitting on it, as well as a pile of chocolate boxes, and his raised knees had turned the sheet into a tent. Surrounding him, the entire private room was ablaze with flowers.

There were red roses and exotic tropical blooms in yellow and purple and white. There were lilies and carnations and daisies, and *more* roses—pink ones, gold ones, furled buds and open blooms. There were flowers in pots and flowers in Cellophane, and flowers bunched with gold ribbon, and the only thing that could possibly compete with the flowers for her attention were the chocolates…and Dylan.

Annabelle spoke her first thought aloud. 'You've phoned your family!' Surely all these flowers and gifts had to be from them. 'Oh, I'm so glad! Are they coming out?'

He shook his head. 'I haven't phoned them yet. I told you I wanted to wait. These yellow ones are from Alex. You left this box of chocolates, according to the card…'

'Yes, this morning. I went out and came back with them, but you were still asleep.'

'But the rest of the chocolates and the flowers are for you.'

'For…?' It didn't make sense. They were overwhelming, lush and perfect, lavish and expensive and decadent and sweet. They brought tears to her eyes. He really wasn't well enough to have spent half the afternoon on the phone, ordering chocolates and flowers. For *her*.

'From me,' he said softly. 'For everything.'

'Dylan!'

'For *everything*,' he repeated. 'I couldn't wait any

longer to say it, and prove it, and what could I do in this bed all afternoon but order chocolates and flowers? For the way I love you, for the way you gave yourself to me last night, without knowing what was going on between us, and when I was so apprehensive I could hardly see straight. For the words I want to say to you now, which I'm still afraid you'll throw back in my face. I've been a brute to you this past week, not trusting why you were still around.'

'I know why I was still around,' she said softly, sliding onto the bed to sit close to him.

'And I hope I do, too, now. I love you, Annabelle. Marry me!' He took her hands, and warmth flooded up her arms.

'Oh, Dylan!'

'I wanted to wait until I knew…about my legs. The tumour is benign. Graham got the report back late this afternoon. So at least I can promise you my life.'

Dylan's life was more than enough. Annabelle wanted to say it, but her heart was so full she couldn't find the words and, anyway, he didn't give her time.

'But because of the rest—my career, and the question of me being able to walk properly, I was going to wait,' he said. 'Then, though… I think you said something this morning. What was it?'

'You fell asleep!' Annabelle's tears welled again, threatening to brim over.

'I'm very awake now, and I remember it all. It doesn't matter which of us takes and which of us gives. That'll balance out. We can't keep score. It's deathly to do that, in any relationship. I love you, and I'm going to trust that that's enough. Enough for both of us.'

'Oh, it is. I love you, and it *is*. Whatever happens. It's more than enough.'

'No matter which of us has to do the most giving? And what form that giving takes?'

'Yes. No matter. It's not important. I'll marry you, Dylan, as soon as you want.'

He reached up and touched her face, and she bent towards him. Their lips met, and their kiss sealed the moment for both of them—the perfect promise of forever.

'Put me down, Gwanpa!' Duncan protested loudly.

Distracted, Dylan and Annabelle both looked at the little boy, struggling in Dylan's father's arms.

'All right, little guy,' said Mason Calford, in his deep-voiced American accent. 'We'll go for a walk, OK?'

Annabelle watched for another few seconds, to make sure the older man and the little boy were genuinely happy in each other's company, then turned back to her groom. The guests, gathered in the informal garden setting of one of Brisbane's most beautiful public parks, fell silent. The marriage celebrant cleared his throat then apologised and searched in his pocket for a handkerchief. Linda, Annabelle's newly pregnant bridesmaid, gave a nervous hiccup. The best man, Dylan's close friend David, shifted his feet.

'I've just thought of something,' Dylan said quietly in Annabelle's ear. 'We were supposed to get back to the celebrant if we wanted any changes in the standard format of the ceremony, and we never did.'

'You mean the lines about—?'

'Yes. If anyone knows any reason why this couple should not be joined, and so on.'

'Pretty significant lines, those can be. Are you worried?' She smiled at him, and caught his answering grin.

He wore a dark suit which emphasised his broad shoulders, and he was very steady on his feet. It was over three months since his surgery now. The first week had been difficult, as the surgical site had slowly healed. For several days, they had all been afraid that his effortful, hesitant and ungainly walking and standing would be permanent.

Time, however, had proved otherwise. Dylan had worked hard and consistently at his physiotherapy, and there was only a minor numbness remaining in his toes—not enough to compromise his performance during surgery or change his normal gait.

Their June wedding, with his family in attendance from America and the sun shining mild and bright in the afternoon sky, was almost as much a celebration of his health as it was a celebration of their soon-to-be-joined lives.

Almost as much. They were both determined that their marriage would always come first in their shared priorities. They wanted children of their own, in the not-too-distant future, and they both agreed that Annabelle should put her career on hold for the time being. Duncan and Mum both needed her too much. She expected that the coming years would be both full and rich.

'No, I'm not worried at all,' Annabelle answered her groom. 'You can object all you like, and so can anyone else. But *this* time, come hell or high water, Dylan Calford, the wedding is going ahead!'

'You won't get any arguments from me, my darling,' he whispered, and they both joined hands as the celebrant began his opening words.

OUTBACK SURGEON

by

Leah Martyn

Leah Martyn loves to create warm believable characters for the medical series. She is grounded firmly in rural Australia and the special qualities of the bush are reflected in her stories. For plots and possibilities, she bounces ideas off her husband on their early morning walks. Browsing in bookshops and buying an armful of new releases are high on her list of enjoyable things to do.

Don't miss Leah Martyn's exciting new novel, *The Doctor's Pregnancy Secret,* out in August 2007 from Mills & Boon Medical Romance™

For Hilary,
who knows the journey.

CHAPTER ONE

'THANKS, guys. That was terrific!'

Off camera, the television producer favoured his guests with a satisfied grin, his gaze lingering with obvious approval on the female of the pair, Dr Abbey Jones.

Abbey dredged up a dry smile. 'I'm always happy to comment on rural health matters, Rob. You know that. But next time, warn me if I'm here for a debate, will you?' Lifting her chin, she sent a cool, tawny look at her opponent in the debate, Dr Nicholas Tonnelli.

Tonnelli's mouth quirked in a smile that just missed being patronising and she practically had to force herself to accept the hand he extended to formally end their debate.

'You presented an irresistible challenge, Dr Jones.'

Abbey took a shallow breath as her hand vanished inside his. His touch was warm and dry and his green eyes gleamed down at her. 'I enjoyed our encounter,' he added softly.

Disconcerted, she reclaimed her hand as though she feared being burned by the impact, turning away to gather up her hastily scribbled notes. Her lungs heaved in a controlling breath. Her hands, with a mind of their own, began shoving the A4 pages awkwardly into her briefcase.

Chewing her bottom lip, Abbey reluctantly admitted that Tonnelli had been a formidable opponent, his skilled ad lib presentation spurring her on to try to salvage something even halfway credible for her side of the argument.

And it had hardly been fair of Rob, she remonstrated silently, pitting her, a rural GP, against one of Sydney's up and coming spinal surgeons.

Physically, he hadn't been what she'd expected either. But, then, what had she expected? Occasionally, when she'd flipped through the Sydney newspapers, she'd glimpsed pictures of him in the social pages. But now, having met him in the flesh, she had to admit that the black and white images hadn't done him justice. They'd certainly given no indication of the man's almost tangible charisma.

She caught back a huff of irritation. Perhaps he'd won the debate, perhaps he hadn't. But whatever the TV ratings showed, she'd just bet his high-voltage sexy smile had sizzled all the way to the female viewers' little hearts.

But not to hers. Heavens, she wasn't that easily taken in!

A glance at her watch told her she'd have to forego the coffee and cake Rob usually offered and make a quick exit from the studio.

'I'm just off, Rob.' Her professional smile in place, Abbey looked to where the two males were seemingly in close private conversation beside the now-darkened set.

'Already?' Rob Stanton turned, taking several quick strides towards her. 'Thanks again, Abbey, for making yourself available at such short notice. You saved my bacon.'

A chink of wry humour lit her smile. 'A nice fat donation to our hospital funds should be in order, then.'

'Hey, you've got it!' Rob was enthusiastic, as though he'd thought of the idea himself. 'I'll OK it right away.'

'Thanks,' Abbey murmured and shot a level look at Tonnelli. 'Goodbye, Doctor.' She began to turn away and then took a quick breath, her senses clanging when the surgeon moved fast enough to block her way as she made to go past him.

'Do you have to rush off, Dr Jones?'

Abbey glared at him, realising belatedly that now they were not seated, she had to raise her gaze a good six inches to meet his eyes. 'Yes, I do.'

'Let me buy you lunch.'

'No, thank you.'

'What've I done?' The charismatic, mocking face was close to hers and she felt every nerve in her body contract. His mouth, wearing its sexy smile, was getting close to hers, so close she could feel the warm whisper of his breath, take in the clean smell of sandalwood soap on his skin.

Get out of my space, she wanted to tell him calmly and coolly. Instead, she felt her insides grind painfully, as she took an uncertain step backwards, rocking a little on her high heels. 'If you don't mind, Dr Tonnelli, I have a tight schedule today. I just want to get on with my own business.'

'Oh, come on, Doctor... We're off camera now. Can't we bury the hatchet?' he asked, his tone almost an amused drawl.

Abbey tried to fix him with a steely glare and failed

miserably. 'I don't have time to sit around having long lunches, Dr Tonnelli.'

He lifted a shoulder dismissively. 'It needn't necessarily be a long lunch. I know a place where the service is fast and the food actually pretty good.'

'McDonald's?' Abbey parried innocently.

His mouth gave the merest twist of a smile. 'A little more upmarket. Margo's. Heard of it?'

'No.'

When she still hesitated, he added persuasively, 'Surely you usually eat something before you head off on that long drive back to Wingara?'

'I *usually* just grab a sandwich or some fruit to eat in the car.' Abbey began to feel pushed into a corner, almost mesmerised by the subtle challenge in his eyes. And they couldn't stand here much longer. The TV crew packing up their gear were beginning to latch onto the possibility of some gossip. 'Oh, all right, then,' she said, uncomfortably aware her acceptance sounded ungracious, explaining, 'I've a dozen things still to do and a patient to see at Sunningdale rehab centre before I head back west, so I'll need to keep it short, OK?'

'Deal.' He looked pleased. Or rewarded, Abbey thought waspishly, watching him. 'Did you come by cab?' he asked.

Oh, for heaven's sake! Who could afford cabs any more? 'I drove my own vehicle. I'm parked outside.'

'Me too.' Moving smoothly away from her, he opened the heavy glass door to the foyer.

This is crazy, Abbey fretted, her heart fluttering like the wings of a trapped bird as they made their way past the flowering shrubs to the car park. And why did it have to be *him* she'd had to cross swords with and ruin her day? There were any number of registrars at the district hospital Rob could have approached to fill the gap. But, then, they wouldn't have had the impact of Tonnelli.

She sighed and brought her head up, her fair silky bob sliding back from her cheekbones, her thoughts still on the surgeon. It was rumoured in medical circles that he was a genius at just about anything he turned his mind to. A man firmly at the centre of his own universe.

Not to mention his reputation with women...

Well, I don't want him propositioning *me,* she decided through gritted teeth, coming to a stop beside the door of her maroon Range Rover. 'This is me.' Her shoulder brushed against his upper arm, and she found herself staring into his eyes. And taking a sharp little breath. His eyes had the luminosity of an early-morning ocean, she thought fancifully. A kind of wintergreen...

'I'm over there.'

She blinked, following the backward flex of his thumb to the metallic grey Jaguar. It suits him, she decided, having no trouble at all personifying the car's sleek elegance and controlled power and making the comparison with its owner.

'It's probably best if you follow me.' He looked at her from under slightly lowered lids. 'Margo's is rather tucked away, an old house that's been refurbished into a restaurant. But I'm afraid the parking's non-existent—just stop along the street, wherever you can.' He raised the briefest smile. 'See you there in a bit.'

Abbey nodded assent, climbing into her vehicle, tapping her fingers impatiently on the steering-wheel, her gaze following his tall, lithe figure as he strode towards his vehicle on the periphery of the car park.

Her wide, sensitive mouth with its gloss of soft coral firmed into a moue of conjecture. Just what was Nicholas Tonnelli doing here in Hopeton anyway? As far as she knew he didn't operate anywhere outside his own hospital, St Thomas's in Sydney's rather affluent North Shore area. So what had brought him here to a small provincial city in the Central West of New South Wales in the middle of a working week?

He'd almost blown it.

Nick Tonnelli wondered why he'd pushed her so hard. 'Male ego at its worst,' he muttered, grimacing with self-derision, groping in the glove box for his sunglasses. But she *had* accepted his invitation, hadn't he? Yeah, right! Reluctantly, mate. Get real.

A tight little smile drifted around his mouth. Who'd have thought spending a couple of days R and R in his home town and doing a favour for his mate, Rob Stanton, would have led to his meeting someone like the feisty, quite delectable Dr Abbey Jones?

The lady was like a breath of sweet, clean air. And he'd become so bored with the Sydney social scene lately. So utterly, utterly bored.

Abbey glanced across the car park once more. At last! Tonnelli was in motion. In a kind of sick anticipation, she lowered her hand to the ignition switch, her mind simultaneously agonising over what on earth they'd find to talk about over lunch.

Alternatively, she supposed she could save herself the grief and lose him deliberately on the way to the restaurant… A jagged laugh caught in her throat at the very idea.

The journey to Margo's was completed quite quickly, with Abbey keeping Tonnelli's distinctive vehicle in sight as she followed him in and out of several back streets, until he indicated he was about to stop and she glanced sideways and saw the restaurant's sign.

She looked in vain for a parking spot and ended up having to drive further along the narrow street, scattering tiny bits of gravel, when she finally ground her four-wheel-drive to a halt.

Tonnelli gave her an apologetic half-smile when she joined him outside the restaurant. 'The food will more than compensate for the parking hassles,' he promised, guiding her along the flagstone path to the entrance.

Although it was just on midday, the place was already filled with the hushed sounds of patrons dining—a muted hum of conversation, the soft clink of cutlery on china—and an absolutely delicious aroma wafting from the kitchen.

'Oh, it's lovely!' Abbey's comment was spontaneous. Entranced, she looked around her at the walls, papered with a country-style pattern of meadowsweet flowers, and at the framed prints, each one essentially outback Australian, depicting the lifestyles of its drovers, ringers and stockmen.

Told you so, Tonnelli's little nod of satisfaction seemed to imply. 'It's a blackboard menu.' His dark head was turned attentively towards her. 'We'll order

first and then with a bit of luck we'll find a table.'
His green gaze swept over the precincts. 'It's crowded
today. The livestock sales must be on in town.' He
considered the blackboard. 'Ah, it's Italian today.
Fancy some pasta?'

Abbey's teeth caught on her lower lip. 'I think I'll
just have the house salad, thanks.'

'OK.' Nick Tonnelli tapped his fingers on the polished countertop, considering his own choice. 'But
you must try one of their stuffed potatoes,' he insisted. 'And the home-made bread.'

Abbey spread her hands helplessly. 'You must
think I need fattening up.'

'Hardly.' His eyes softened for a moment. 'I'd say
the packaging is perfect as it is.' He added a slow,
very sweet smile then, and it was as though his fingers
played over her skin.

For a split second Abbey registered a riveting
awareness between them. Raw and immediate. Like
an electric current and just as tangible. She swallowed
thickly. 'I'll, um, freshen up while you order, then.'

'Will you have something to drink?' He detained
her with the lightest touch to her forearm. 'White
wine, perhaps?'

Abbey considered her options swiftly. 'A mineral
water, I think. I've a long drive ahead of me.'

'We'll meet at the bar, then.' Two little lines appeared between his dark brows. 'Don't do a runner
on me, will you?'

Abbey felt the heat warm her cheeks as she spun
away. How had he guessed she'd actually considered
it? Perhaps he read minds along with his other talents,
she thought cynically.

In the restroom, she did a quick make-up repair. Taking out her small cosmetic bag, she freshened her lipstick, swiped a comb through her hair and added a squirt of her favourite cologne.

In the mirror with its lovely old-fashioned gilded frame, she looked critically at her reflection, unnerved to see a flush in her cheeks she hadn't seen there in ages.

She was suddenly conscious of her stomach churning. She must have been crazy to have agreed to this lunch, she berated herself for the umpteenth time. She and Tonnelli had nothing in common. For starters, their lifestyles had to be poles apart.

As a senior surgeon in a state-of-the-art hospital, he could have no concept of her world, she reflected thinly. Her little hospital at Wingara was reasonably well equipped, mostly due to the tireless money-raising efforts of the locals. But even so it had to be light years away from what she imagined as Tonnelli's clinical environment.

She hitched up her shoulder-bag, her mind throwing up yet again the question of what on earth would they find to talk about. Heart thrumming, she left the restroom and began making her way back to the bar. She saw him at once, his distinctive dark head with its short cut turning automatically, almost as if he'd sensed her approach. 'Thanks.' Abbey took the drink he handed to her.

'I believe there's a table for us in the garden room.' He began leading the way towards the rear of the restaurant to a cleverly conceived extension like a conservatory, complete with glass walls and ceiling.

He saw her comfortably seated and Abbey took a

moment to look around her. Their table was set with
crisp, palest cream linen, gleaming silver and glass-
ware, and decorating the centre was a trailing arrangement of multicoloured garden flowers. She felt her
spirits lift and decided to make a huge effort. 'I'm
actually looking forward to our lunch.'

'Much better than a sandwich from the deli,' he
agreed. 'Cheers.' Lifting his glass of ice-cold lager,
he took a mouthful. 'I asked for our peasant bread to
be brought first. I don't know about you, but I'm
starving.'

Even as he finished speaking, a smiling waitress
placed the still-warm loaf on the table with the accompanying little pats of butter.

Abbey eyed the crusty, flour-dusted high round loaf
hungrily, feeling her digestive juices begin to react.

'This looks good, hmm?' Without hesitation, Nick
Tonnelli took up the breadknife, wielding it with surgical precision, separating the loaf quickly and effi-
ciently into easily manageable portions.

Watching him, Abbey said faintly, 'You must be a
whiz with the Sunday roast, Dr Tonnelli.'

'Each to his own talent, Abbey,' he responded
blandly. 'And for crying out loud, call me Nick.'.

'Tell me about your patient in the rehab centre.' Nick
Tonnelli's tone was suddenly professional and brisk.

Startled, Abbey looked up from her plate. Was he
just being the polite host? she wondered. Pretending
an interest? Making conversation for the sake of it?
Whatever he was doing, she could hardly ignore such
a pointed demand.

'His name is Todd Jensen. He's a twenty-five-year-old professional rodeo rider.' She looked bleak for a moment. 'Although I probably should be using the past tense here. It's almost certain we won't see him back on the rodeo circuit again.'

Nick's dark brows rose. 'What was it, a workplace accident of some kind?'

'Todd was participating in a buckjumping event. His mount threw him and in its panic struck him on the lower back with its hind hooves.'

The consultant winced and murmured a commiseration.

'It was a dreadful afternoon,' Abbey said quietly. 'Everyone was so shocked. Fortunately, the CareFlight chopper was on standby. Todd was flown straight here to Hopeton.'

Nick's mouth compressed. 'What did the MRI show? That's assuming he had one?'

'Of course he did.' Abbey resented his inference that Todd had somehow received second-class medical attention.

'The new scanning devices for magnetic resonance imaging are ruinously expensive,' Nick clarified. 'I merely wondered whether the district hospital here had managed to install one.'

'They have,' Abbey conceded guardedly. 'Mostly due to the efforts of Jack O'Neal and his committee.'

Nick rubbed a hand around his jaw. 'He's the SR on Kids', isn't he?'

Abbey nodded. 'Jack and his wife, Geena, are tireless fundraisers for the hospital.'

'Commendable.'

'Essential, seeing the shortfall in funding for rural hospitals.'

Nick acknowledged her comment politely. 'To get back to your patient. What did the MRI show?'

'Irreversible nerve damage.'

Nick frowned. 'So, what's his prognosis?'

Biting her lower lip, not sure where they were going with this, Abbey elaborated, 'A wheelchair existence. His accident placed a cloud over our whole community. Todd was well liked, a kind of icon to the young kids. And very good at what he did. The really sad part is he'd had an invitation from one of the rodeo associations in the States. He was about to take off and try his luck in the big time.'

She ran the pad of her thumb across the raised pattern of her glass. 'He's still so angry. Just recently, he told his wife to go and make a new life for herself—that he was only half a man…'

'So he's dropped the ball. That's a fairly normal reaction, Abbey,' Nick pointed out reasonably. 'At the moment his feelings have to be loaded with issues of masculinity and virility so, of course, he's told his wife to get lost. What's more to the point is what's being done presently for your patient? For starters, is his medication up to scratch? How intense is his physio programme? Has there been input from a psychologist? An occupational therapist?'

Abbey lifted her head and regarded him warily. He seemed in his element, rapping out questions. While she, on the other hand, felt as though she were under the microscope, almost an intern again being put through a consultant's wringer.

The silence stretched for a tense moment, until Abbey responded steadily, 'Todd's programme is as good as Sunningdale can provide. And distance-wise, it suits his family to have him there. At least they can make the three-hour drive once a week to see him. But realistically, I'd guess, he's gone about as far as he can go there. Sunningdale will want to discharge him soon.'

'And then what?'

Abbey frowned. 'Well, at this stage his parents are proposing to have him back home with them.'

'In the bush?'

She tilted her chin defensively. 'That's where they live.'

Nick made an impatient sound. 'What's he going to do there, cut wood for the fire from his wheel-chair?' The surgeon shook his head. 'Surely we can do better than that, Abbey? Have you heard of the Dennison Foundation in Sydney?'

Abbey frowned. 'It's a fairly recent concept, isn't it?'

'State of the art in every way. Structured specifi-cally for spinal rehab, with patients being taught how to accustom themselves to the physical realities of being disabled in an able-bodied world. I'm sure you'd see a great improvement in your Todd's ability to cope after a stay there. I'd refer him urgently, if I were you.'

A flush of annoyance rose in Abbey's cheeks. 'Ever heard of waiting lists, Doctor? Besides, his fam-ily couldn't afford those kinds of fees. And I can't imagine the management would be prepared to cut a special deal on a rural GP's referral.'

'What if I referred him?'

Something like resentment stirred in Abbey and she

couldn't let go of it. 'Why should you bother? Todd's nothing to you.'

Nick Tonnelli's expression closed abruptly. 'As professionals, isn't it up to all of us who go under the guise of medical practitioners to assist all humankind where we can? So, Doctor, I suggest you pocket your false pride and face the facts as we have them.

'I'm willing to carry out a reassessment on your patient. Like Todd, I'm good at what I do. Maybe I can help him further. Maybe I can't. But I'm willing to try and if you think my name will help, I'll refer him to the Dennison, if I deem it appropriate. It's up to you.'

Abbey clenched her hands on her lap and stared at them fiercely. He'd given her a terrible dressing-down. All done so quietly and lethally. Dear God! How she would hate to have to work with the man! Thoughts, none of them pleasant, crowded in on her. She should *never* have agreed to this lunch. She should have quit while she was ahead and left him standing in the car park, watching her dust.

She took a deep breath and tried to leave personal issues out of it. Todd's youthful face, stark with hope one minute and dark with despair the next, impinged on her vision. Much as she hated to admit it, Tonnelli was right. Pride had no place here. She would swallow hers, no matter how galling it might be, and ask for his help.

'When could you see Todd?' she asked hesitantly. 'I mean... I don't know your movements... If you have other commitments here...' She broke off help-lessly.

He bit into his bread, his even white teeth leaving

a neat half-circle. 'We could start the ball rolling after our lunch, if that suits you.'

'Fine.' Abbey teased at her lip. She should have known that once the decision was made, he'd want to sweep ahead.

'I would prefer to keep my involvement quite informal, if you don't mind,' he said easily. 'I'll need some time to study Todd's case details and speak with the staff, his physio and OT in particular.

'If I decide the programme at the Dennison will benefit Todd, I'll speak personally with the director, Anna Charles.' At once his expression lightened. 'We trained together. She's done extensive post-grad work at Harvard. A brilliant practitioner. Todd couldn't be in better hands.'

Abbey blinked uncertainly. 'And would she take him—just like that?'

'As a favour to me? Yes, she would.' He smiled, a mere sensual curving of his lips.

Abbey felt her cheeks burn as the possible meaning behind his remark occurred to her. She pulled in a shattered breath. Forget Tonnelli and his women and think of Todd, she told herself with quiet desperation. 'What about the fees?'

Nick lifted a dismissive shoulder. 'I'll arrange something. Nothing in this life is set in concrete, Abbey. Nothing at all.'

CHAPTER TWO

THE main part of their meal was served just after Abbey's capitulation. She looked down at the appetising char-grilled strips of chicken, the crisp salad and accompanying stuffed potato, and despaired.

After the last few minutes, the tense trading of words with Nick Tonnelli, her throat seemed closed, her stomach knotted.

He, on the other hand, she noticed with faint irony, seemed not be suffering any repercussions at all. And after the first few uncomfortable minutes, after which he obviously set out to charm the socks off her, she felt a lessening of tension.

'So, Abbey, what do you do for relaxation at Wingara?' he asked, as they sat over their coffee later. 'No chance of snow sports, I expect?' he added with a touch of humour.

'Hardly.' She laughed, activating the tiny dimple in her cheek. 'I play tennis when I can and we have a sports centre with a pool and quite an active Little Theatre. And I have friends there now, good friends. One couple in particular, Stuart and Andrea Fraser, have quite a large property so I'm able to spend the odd weekend there, picnicking and so on.'

'So, no regrets about opting out of city mainstream medicine, then?' he teased gently, fixing her with his keen, gemstone gaze.

'Often,' Abbey rebuffed him sharply.

He blinked, appearing a little surprised by her answer. 'In what way?'

She lifted a shoulder. 'Broadly speaking, I could give you a dozen examples. But the bottom line is all I can do in a major medical emergency is to stabilise my patient and have them airlifted to the nearest major hospital. And just hope they survive the journey.'

'So what are you saying?' Nick's eyes took on a steely glint.

'Nothing I didn't say in the debate,' Abbey responded bluntly. 'That if a specialist surgeon could be on call to come to us, it would halve the trauma for both patient and family. And would, I dare say, be more cost-effective.'

'Bunkum!' Nick's hand cut the air dismissively. 'Logistics for one thing. Our rural population is so scattered, our distances so vast. All things considered, I believe we, as specialists, do a reasonable job.'

Abbey tossed her head up, throwing into sharp relief the long silky lashes framing the haunting beauty of her tawny eyes. 'When was the last time you conducted a clinic outside St Thomas's, then?'

With a reflex reaction Nick's head shot up, his green gaze striking an arc across the space between them. 'I've considered it but so far the consensus seems to be that it's more appropriate for the patients to come to me than vice versa.' In an abrupt movement, he dipped his head and pulled back the sleeve of his pale blue shirt. His mouth compressed briefly. 'If you've quite finished your coffee, we should be moving, I think.'

So, end of discussion. Abbey curled her mouth into a cynical little moue, bending to retrieve her shoulder-bag from the carpeted floor near her feet. Had she really expected the conversation to go any other way?

While Nick settled the bill, she made her way slowly outside, annoyance with herself shifting and compressing against her ribcage. It wouldn't do to get the man offside. Not now, when it seemed they were about to become involved professionally with Todd's care.

Beside her, a butterfly scooped the air, darting in and out of a border of cornflowers, its pale yellow wings a gauzy haze against the deep blue petals. Her shoulders lifted as she took a calming breath, belatedly registering the near-perfection of the afternoon—the crisp air, the softly falling leaves, the sky an unbroken bowl of china blue…

'Wonderful day.' From behind, Nick softly echoed her thoughts.

Startled, Abbey jerked back. How long had he been standing there? 'I love autumn.' She rushed into speech, embarrassed to be caught mooning like a teenager. 'Especially in this part of the state where the seasons are so clearly defined.'

'Perhaps.' Nick looked unconvinced but he was smiling. 'I still think I prefer the coast. I can well do without all this.' He scuffed a gathering pile of fallen leaves with his shoe.

'Didn't you have fun running through them when you were a kid, though?'

His head went back on a laugh. 'You know, I'd forgotten all that.'

Abbey listened to the small talk threading between them like a line of careful stitches, but at the same time acknowledging she'd have to upset the pattern

and get things rather more settled in her own mind.
'Dr Tonnelli—Nick…' she began awkwardly, 'I hope
you didn't feel obligated to get involved with my patient…'

Nick's gut tightened. She looked so uncertain, so
vulnerable, he wanted to just to hold her, reassure her.
Instead, he shoved his hands into the pockets of his
trousers out of temptation's way. 'Abbey, I want to
do it, OK?'

Her lips parted on a shaky breath. 'Are you sure?'

'I'm sure.' He permitted himself the ghost of a wry
smile. 'Actually, it occurs to me I might have seemed
to have taken over in there, come on a bit strong about
your management of Todd. If I did, I apologise.'

Abbey's senses tightened and she felt confused at
the odd mix of reactions chasing around inside her.
'Honestly, you don't need to.'

'Oh, I think I do.' He gave a taut smile. 'I stormed
all over you. But, then, I have been accused of being
arrogant once or twice. And what's the expression? If
you have to eat crow, it's better to do it while it's
still warm.'

Abbey smothered a laugh. 'Consider the crow
eaten, then.'

She was thoughtful as they made their way down
the path to the street. She guessed it had cost him
something to have placed a question mark over his
earlier behaviour.

But on the other hand, to have put her on the defensive the way he had had probably been nothing
more than a normal reaction from him. Everything
about the man indicated a natural authority, an obvious ability to give orders and have them carried out

without question. There was no doubt about it, Nick Tonnelli was a man of substance and of power.

She stifled a sigh, seeing the stream of professional differences between them widen to a river.

'My time is my own but does it suit you to go across to Sunningdale now?' he was asking.

She nodded, grateful for his courtesy. 'I'll introduce you and stay for a quick visit with Todd. Then I'm afraid I'll have to leave. I've to go and plead for some lab reports I'm waiting on to be rushed through and collect a package of drugs from the pharmacy— What's that noise?' Suddenly, she turned her head up, listening.

Nick frowned. 'I don't— Ah! Motorbike by the sound of it.' Instinctively, he stiffened, stepping in front of Abbey as if to shield her. 'And going way too fast for a built-up area. Hell's bells!' he gasped as the high-pitched roar cut the still of the afternoon and a big black machine shot into view at the top of the street.

'Oh, lord!' Abbey watched in stark disbelief. 'The intersection's too narrow—he'll never take the corner! Nick...' Horrified, she grabbed the surgeon's arm as the bike became airborne.

Nick reacted like quicksilver. 'My car's closer— get my bag!' Wresting his keys from his side pocket, he slapped them into Abbey's hand. 'In the boot— go!' He'd already taken off, running in the direction of the crash, his arms pumping hard into the rhythm of his long strides, even before the final sickening thump of metal could be heard.

Abbey bit back a little sob of distress, her heart hammering, as she pelted along the tree-lined street to Nick's car. Hand shaking, she touched the remote locking button on the keyring and whipped the boot open. She hauled his case out, slammed the boot shut and relocked the car, turning to run back to the accident scene as fast as she could in her high heels.

Hearing the crunching sound of metal, two men had rushed from nearby houses to help.

'Right—let's do it, lads!' Nick took charge and, with muscles straining, they partially raised the heavy bike, bracing it against their legs.

'We need traffic lights or a roundabout there.' One of the men was breathing heavily with the effort.

His companion snorted. 'That won't slow 'em down. 'Struth,' he gasped and they strained again. 'One last heave should do it. You beauty...' he grunted as the motorbike was finally righted.

'Has someone called an ambulance?' Nick rapped, hunkering down beside the prostrate form of the injured rider.

'The wife will have done that.' One of the rescuers flipped his hand towards his house across the street. 'You got first-aid training or something, mate?' he tacked on, watching Nick's hands move with deft swiftness over the accident victim.

'Doctor.' Nick was curt.

'How bad is it?' Panting to a stop, Abbey dropped to Nick's side. She felt her throat dry. Dear God, the youth wasn't even wearing proper leathers.

'Severed femoral artery by the look of it.' Nick looked grim. 'See if you can find a tourniquet, please, Abbey. Step on it! We've got a major problem here.'

Abbey's hands moved like lightning through his

medical supplies. In seconds she'd handed over the belt-like elastic band.

'How's his pulse?' Nick rapped, expertly securing the tourniquet around the youth's upper thigh.

'Rapid and thready. He's not responding to stimuli. I'll get an IV in.' Moments later, she was saying tensely, 'This is a nightmare, Nick—I can't find a vein.'

'Keep trying.'

'OK, I've got it.' Abbey's words came out in a rush of relief. 'IV's in and holding.'

Nick swore, his brow furrowing in concentration. 'BP's dropping like a stone. Come on!' he gritted to the youth's unconscious form. 'Don't shut down on me, sunshine—don't you dare!'

At last the ambulance siren could be heard. The vehicle screamed to a halt beside them, two officers swinging out.

Nick quickly introduced himself and Abbey, adding authoritatively, 'The patient's in shock. We need to run Haemaccel fast. And alert the hospital, please. We'll need a blood specimen and cross-match immediately on arrival.'

Within seconds the officer had passed the flask of blood product across to Nick.

'I found some ID in the kid's saddlebag, Doc.' One of the men who had helped lift the bike flipped open a wallet. 'Bryan Weaver.'

'Give it to the police when they get here,' Nick said grimly. 'It'll be up to them to get hold of the family. But at least we'll be able to give the hospital a name. Thanks, mate.'

'Think he'll make it?' the man asked soberly, as the youth was stretchered into the ambulance.

'Let's be positive.' Nick's response was terse.

'Are you coming with us, Doc?' The ambulance officer was hovering expectantly by the rear doors of the ambulance.

'Yes.' Nick slammed his medical case shut and hitched it up. 'Keys.' He put out a hand and touched Abbey's wrist.

'Oh—sorry.' She fumbled them out of the pocket of her linen blazer. 'He's lost a lot of blood, hasn't he?'

They stared at each other for a brief, painful moment.

Nick lifted a shoulder, the lines of strain etching deeper into his mouth. 'Let's pin our hopes on the Haemaccel keeping him stable until he gets some blood.'

'What about your car?' Abbey blinked uncertainly. 'It's locked but—'

'I'll get a cab back and collect it later.' He looked at her broodingly. 'And I haven't forgotten about Todd. I'll make my own way over to Sunningdale as soon as I can.'

'Yes—OK—thanks.' With an odd feeling of finality, Abbey watched as he swung into the waiting ambulance with all the grace of a superbly fit athlete.

'I'll be in touch,' he called to her before the doors closed and the ambulance was on its way, the chilling sound of the siren pitching into the quiet of the afternoon.

*   *   *

Abbey's thoughts were still scattered as she turned in through the wide gates at Sunningdale. Finding a vacant space in the staff car park, she took it thankfully.

Already she'd decided not to undertake the long drive back to Wingara. It would be quite late by the time she was ready to get on her way and she had no desire to travel the lonely highway on her own at night. Instead, she'd leave at first light tomorrow.

The rehabilitation centre was a pleasant structure with wide verandahs overlooking the well-tended gardens. There was much good work being done here, Abbey thought earnestly, but in Todd's case was it enough?

Her insides twisted. The force of Nick Tonnelli's argument had raised more questions than answers for her patient.

She was relieved to find the nurse manager, Lauren Huxley, still on duty in the Macquarie wing where Todd was a resident. In Abbey's opinion, the bright, vivacious, forty-something nursing sister had great empathy with the patients.

In the first few weeks after Todd's admission Lauren had kept Abbey in close touch with his state of mind, and now the two women had formed an easy friendship.

'We expected you much earlier,' Lauren said warmly, ushering Abbey into her office.

Briefly, Abbey explained about the biker's accident and her involvement.

'Tea, then,' Lauren said firmly. 'You do have time?' Her fine brow rose in query. She was well aware of Abbey's gruelling schedule on the occasions the young GP was able to get into Hopeton.

Abbey huffed a wry laugh. 'I've lost so much time

today another few minutes won't matter. Tea would be lovely, thanks.'

'Good.' Lauren flicked on the electric kettle.

'You've had a face-lift in here since I was in last.' Abbey looked around interestedly, admiring the bright curtains and crisp paintwork. 'It's lovely, Lauren. So cheerful now and comfortable.'

'That was the idea.' Lauren placed the tea-tray on the table between them. 'The new committee's been pretty generous with funding.'

'So they gave you carte blanche?'

'Within reason. But I stuck out for the oval table and upholstered chairs instead of that huge monstrosity of a desk. It's so much less daunting for the families who have to be briefed. I mean, they're down in the pits already in lots of cases. Surely they don't need to be spoken to across a desk like less than bright schoolchildren?'

Abbey smiled, easing off her shoes and wriggling her toes in relief. 'Mmm, the tea's wonderful, Lauren, thanks.' They sat in companionable silence for a moment, until Abbey asked gently, 'How's Todd doing?'

Lauren chuckled. 'Actually, he's had rather a good day. I could even say a riotous day.' She paused for effect. 'He's learning to paint.'

Abbey looked stunned for a moment and then her face lit up with a wide smile. 'But that's wonderful! Who's teaching him? One of the OTs?'

'Mmm, Amanda Steele. She reckons our Todd has real potential.'

Abbey bit the inside of her cheek. 'This may not be the right time to tell you my news, then.'

'About Todd?'

'By a remarkable coincidence I was, uh, introduced to Nicholas Tonnelli today.'

'The *surgeon,* Tonnelli?' Lauren's eyebrows shot up into her long fringe.

'Sounds a bit incredible, doesn't it? I arrived at the TV studios this morning to take part in their usual *Countrywide* programme.'

'And?' Lauren leaned forward, her expression expectant.

Abbey gave a huff of uneasy laughter. 'When I arrived, the producer was hovering. Asked me if I'd mind a slightly different format. In short, what he called an impromptu debate.'

'What?' Lauren squawked. 'And he threw you in against Tonnelli? How did you fare, for heaven's sake?'

Abbey grimaced. 'Actually, I think I did better off camera. But I made sure he got the message on the state of rural health.' She coloured faintly. 'He asked me to lunch. And I found myself telling him about Todd...'

'I get the picture Abbey,' Lauren said with some perception. 'Is Dr Tonnelli suggesting a transfer to Dennison by any chance?'

'He suggested the possibility.' Abbey was cautious. 'And there seems no doubt he could get Todd admitted.' She hesitated, suddenly feeling her relative inexperience in this field of medicine. 'But if Todd's formed a special rapport with his new occupational therapist and is doing better, maybe it's not the right time to move him...'

Lauren shrugged philosophically. 'I think the decision is out of our hands, Abbey. We're all aware

Todd is special but we can't go around with our collective noses out of joint if someone of the calibre of Tonnelli suggests he can be better rehabilitated elsewhere.'

'You all do amazingly dedicated work here, Lauren,' Abbey jumped in supportively. 'But I guess I have to agree with you.'

'I presume Dr Tonnelli will want to see the case notes and talk to us first, before he sees Todd?'

'Oh, yes,' Abbey hastened to clarify. 'He's already mentioned that's the way he likes to work. He wants to be as unobtrusive as possible.'

'Yeah, right.' Lauren snickered. 'Like a tiger going unnoticed amongst the deer.' She got to her feet. 'You'll find Todd on the verandah, I think. I'm off duty in two minutes. Oh—any idea when we can expect the dashing surgeon?'

'Not really.' Abbey explained about Nick's involvement with the biker. 'I have no idea of his movements while he's here in Hopeton. In fact, apart from a courtesy phone call to tell me what he proposes for Todd, I don't expect I'll be seeing him again.'

'I see...' Lauren's eyebrows lifted in mild conjecture. Surely that wasn't a blush on the face of the usually so cool Dr Abbey Jones, was it?

Back in her motel room at the end of the day, Abbey took a shower and then planned what she'd do with the rest of the evening.

Not much, she thought wryly, pulling on a pair of plain denims and a peasant top. Taking up her brush, she scraped her hair back into a casual knot, leaving several strands to feather out in the current fashion. Her motel was only half a block from the hospital so she'd walk over and hopefully find out the condition of the young biker, Bryan Weaver. After that, she'd pick up a take-away meal of some kind.

The hospital was well lit and Abbey drifted inside with a group of early-evening visitors and began making her way towards Reception.

'Hello again, Dr Jones.'

Abbey stopped as if she'd been struck. 'Nick...' Soft colour licked along her cheekbones and she did her best to ignore the swift jolt of pleasure at seeing him. 'What are you doing here?'

'I could ask you the same question.' Slipping a hand under her elbow, he gently drew her aside. 'I imagined you'd have been well on your way to Wingara by now.'

Abbey feigned lightness. 'Oh, it got too late so I decided to stay overnight. I'm really here just to enquire about our biker.'

'Snap.' Nick's eyes seemed to track over her features one by one before he went on. 'I've had a chat with the surgeon. The boy's stable and they're pretty hopeful there'll be no residual damage to his leg.'

'That's good news.' Abbey felt relief sweep through her. 'Did you happen to find out why he was travelling like that, so out of control? I mean there are wheelies and *wheelies*.'

Dark humour spilled into his eyes and pulled a corner of his mouth. 'As a matter of fact, I found his girlfriend waiting like a wilted flower outside Recovery. She told me they'd had a fight and our

Bryan had stormed out minus his leathers. Young idiot. He could have killed himself.'

'Yes.' Abbey's look was sober for a moment, before she began to cast a restive look towards the entrance. 'Well, now I know he'll be OK, I won't bother the staff…'

'Have you eaten?' Nick asked sharply.

'Ah…no.' Abbey felt her throat dry. 'I thought I'd just grab a burger or something and take it back to my motel room.'

'That sounds like a crummy way to spend your evening.' His eyes narrowed on her face and suddenly the intensity of his regard hardened, as though he'd made up his mind about something. 'Why don't we link up, then? Have dinner together?'

In a quick protective movement, Abbey put her hand to her heart. 'I…wasn't counting on a late night.' She heard the slightly desperate note in her voice and winced. 'And you don't have to keep offering to feed me, Nick.'

His made a dismissive gesture with his hand. 'It's no big deal, Abbey. Do you have a problem with two colleagues having a meal together?'

Oh, about a thousand, she thought, with the kind of uncertainty she was feeling around him. 'Put like that, I—guess it would be all right, then.' She shrugged her capitulation. 'But I'm not dressed for anywhere grand.'

'No more am I.' He tipped her a lopsided smile and Abbey blinked, taking in his appearance. He was wearing comfortable cargo pants and a cream lightweight sweater, the sleeves pushed back over his tanned forearms.

'I walked over,' Abbey explained, as they made their way outside to the hospital car park.

'Makes things simple, then.' Nick slowed his strides abruptly. Then, as if it was the most natural thing in the world, he stretched out his hand towards her. 'I'm round the corner in the doctors' car park.'

Feeling somehow as though she was taking a giant leap into the unknown, Abbey slipped her hand into his.

They agreed on a small pub a few kilometres out of town, mainly because Nick said they did a decent steak.

'I have an appointment first thing in the morning at Sunningdale,' he told her as they drove.

Well, he hadn't wasted any time. Abbey turned her head on the car's cushioned leather headrest and addressed his darkened profile. 'I had a chat with the nurse manager, Lauren Huxley, this afternoon. They'll be expecting you.'

He grunted a non-committal reply.

There were only a smattering of patrons at the pub.

'Mid-week,' Nick surmised gruffly, placing a guiding hand on her back as they descended the shallow steps into a sunken lounge-cum-restaurant.

'It's nice,' Abbey said perfunctorily, gazing around her at the exposed timber beams and the rich oaken sheen of the furniture.

Seated, they studied the wine list. 'They serve a nice local red here,' Nick said. 'Like to try it?'

'Fine.' Abbey managed a faint smile.

With their wine served and their steaks ordered, Nick leaned back in his chair, his green gaze travelling musingly over her face and dropping to the soft curve of her throat. 'Life plays strange tricks on us from time to time, doesn't it?'

Abbey swallowed. 'In what way?'

He seemed to think for a moment, before reaching out and taking her left hand. 'Well, when we woke this morning, we hadn't met.' Turning her hand palm up, he stroked the inside of her wrist with his thumb. 'We seemed to have packed quite a bit of getting to know each other in the past eight hours, wouldn't you agree?'

Abbey's heart rate had begun rocketing at the intimacy. 'I suppose,' she conceded, every nerve in her stomach tightening. She wanted to reclaim her hand without appearing like a frightened adolescent. Which was how she felt, she fretted, more than a little unnerved by the arousing effect his stroking was having on her senses.

She took in a fractured little breath, hoping frantically their steaks would arrive so that at least his hands would be occupied with his cutlery.

As if he'd sensed her unease, Nick released her hand abruptly, changing position to fold his arms across his chest. 'What time will you start back in the morning?' he asked, one dark eyebrow arched, the trace of a provocative smile touching his mouth.

'I'll be long gone before you even open your eyes.' Abbey touched the small medallion at her throat. 'I have to be back for surgery at ten.'

'Do you take any special precautions for the journey?'

'I make sure my vehicle is always in good running order. And I let the police sergeant at Wingara know when I'm about to leave. From that, barring mishaps, he's able to gauge my ETA. And why the sudden interest in my lifestyle?' she challenged, lifting her glass and taking a careful mouthful of the deliciously smooth merlot. 'I'm just a rural GP, Nick. I work my tail off with incredibly long hours.'

'Are you suggesting I don't?'

Oh, for heaven's sake! She didn't want to keep getting into these kinds of endless comparisons with him. She looked down at her fingers locked painfully tight around the base of her glass. She wasn't naïve. And she was not about to deny the wild kind of physical chemistry lurking between them—but other than that, they had nothing in common at all.

They each belonged in vastly different areas of medicine. Nick Tonnelli would be like a fish out of water in her world—just as she would in his.

CHAPTER THREE

THEIR steaks arrived, grilled to perfection and accompanied by a huge pile of mixed salad on the side. Abbey's mouth watered at the lushness of three kinds of lettuce, fresh tomatoes, chopped black olives and bits of avocado and red pepper thrown in for good measure. 'This is fantastic, Nick. How come you know all these places?'

His mouth tipped at the corner. 'Hopeton is my home town. I'm here for a few days R and R visiting my *nonna*.'

'Your grandmother?'

'I can see you're surprised.' He grinned and Abbey caught the pulse of deep laughter in his voice. 'Did you imagine I just leapt into life from somewhere? As a matter of fact, I have quite an extended family. Parents, two sisters, brothers-in-law, a niece and two nephews. They all live in Sydney now but my *nonna*, Claudia—' he made it sound like *Cloudia* '—still lives here in the old family home. She's almost eighty-five,' he said proudly.

Abbey thought painfully of her own diminished family and asked quietly, 'Is she in good health?'

'For the most part.' His face softened into reflective lines. 'She's still feisty, demanding when I'm going to find a wife and continue the Tonnelli line.'

Abbey huffed a laugh. 'That's a bit archaic.'

'Hey, she's our matriarch! She's allowed to.'

'Have you ever been in love?' she asked suddenly, prompting raised eyebrows from the surgeon.

'I'm thirty-eight, Abbey. Of course I've been in love. Have you?'

The question hung in the air between them.

'I was engaged once.' Abbey's downcast lashes fanned darkly across her cheekbones. 'He was my trainer. Such an honest, generous man. But when it came down to it, I couldn't set a wedding date. And I realised I didn't feel about him the way I wanted to feel about the man I intended to marry.'

'And how is that?' Nick asked softly. Gaze lowered, he began to swirl the ruby-red wine in his glass.

Suddenly Abbey felt vulnerable. She blamed the wine and Nick Tonnelli's clever probing questions. She came back lightly with, 'Well, if I knew that, life would be a doddle, wouldn't it?'

They went quietly on with their meal.

Nick chewed thoughtfully on his mouthful of prime rump steak. He could hardly believe his luck in running into her again. OK, so maybe they had little in common except their medical training, but he knew enough about himself to realise he had to get to know Abbey Jones better. Though at the moment, how and where seemed insoluble questions.

But he hadn't got to where he was without overcoming a few stumbling blocks. He'd think of something. And it would all be worth it. He had a distinct gut feeling Abbey was as disturbed by his nearness as he was by hers. His gaze lifted, straying momentarily to the enticingly sweet curve of her mouth...

'We'd better exchange phone numbers, hadn't we?'

Nick kept his tone deliberately brisk. 'I imagine we'll need to consult about Todd over the next little while.'

'Oh— OK.'

Nick thought she sounded cautious and hastened to reassure her. 'You have my word I won't steamroller anyone, Abbey.' He placed his knife and fork neatly together on his plate and casually swiped his mouth with his serviette. 'I'll study Todd's case notes and take into account all you've told me before I make an assessment about whether the Dennison can benefit him.'

'But you're reasonably certain it can, aren't you?'

He shrugged a shoulder. 'I truly believe what they can teach Todd there will give him a new lease on life. Granted, not the kind of life he's been used to but, even as a differently abled person, there have to be possibilities for the sports-fit young man he once was.'

The thought of Todd's world being shaken on its axis all over again gnawed at Abbey. He was at such a vulnerable point in his young life. But at least she had Nick's promise that he would act with sensitivity. She could only hope Todd would speak up if felt he was being pressured.

'Time to go?' Nick had seen her quick reference to her watch.

'If you don't mind.' It was only when they walked outside into the foyer that Abbey realised his guiding hand at her back had shifted and now she was warmly pressed to his side. Her nerve ends pinched alarmingly. She didn't want this—an involvement with a big-time surgeon like Nick Tonnelli was crazy thinking. It could go nowhere, lead to nothing.

Yet she couldn't pull away.

'Oh—it's raining!' She held out a hand to the light sprinkle.

'Let's move it, then.' Nick grabbed her hand and they sprinted across the car park and threw themselves into the Jaguar. 'OK?' He arched a questioning eyebrow.

'Hardly damp.' Releasing the scrunchie holding back her ponytail, Abbey finger-combed her hair into a semblance of order and then bent to fasten her seat belt. 'How much longer will you be in Hopeton?'

'Only another day or so.' The engine came to life with an expensive purr and within a few moments he was nosing the car out through the exit and onto the road. 'Basically, I had a few days to call my own and I decided to spend them with Nonna. I like to keep an eye on her.'

Abbey could understand he would. He seemed to care a great deal about people in general. How much more would he care about his own family? His wife? If he had one—

'I have to be back in Sydney on Friday anyway to attend a charity do at the Opera House.'

Probably with one of those women he was always being photographed with on his arm. Abbey's fingers interlinked tightly and she wondered why the mental picture caused her so much anguish.

'It just occurs to me...' He sent her a brooding look. 'What do you do about a locum when you have to be out of the place?'

'Were you thinking of offering?' Abbey shot back with the faintest hint of derision. Run-of-the-mill rural medicine wouldn't interest him at all. He'd really consider himself slumming.

'Think I couldn't handle it?'

Abbey flicked him a puzzled glance, not sure where he was heading. She answered levelly, 'My predecessor, Wolf Ganzer, fills in for me. He retired in the district. And he keeps himself fit and in touch so it suits us both.'

Nick nodded and after a minute enquired softly, 'How about some music to carry us home?'

It seemed to Abbey that the journey back to her motel took very little time. One part of her was thankful, wanting it over. The other part, the silly, romantic part of her, wanted to prolong the evening, the contact with Nicholas Tonnelli.

When he nosed his car in behind her Range Rover in the parking bay outside her unit, she released her seat belt and looked at him. 'Thanks for this evening, Nick. And for agreeing to see Todd.'

'I don't want thanks, Abbey.' His eyes were broodingly intent and he lifted his hand to knuckle it across the soft curve of her cheek. 'But I wouldn't mind a coffee, if you have the makings?'

Abbey stiffened, the faint elusive scent of his aftershave catching her nostrils. She swallowed heavily. 'Um...it'll have to be instant out of those sachet things.'

'Instant's fine.' He sent her a slow, teasing grin. 'I love instant.'

'And my room's a mess.'

'Do I look like I care?'

Abbey could hardly breathe. This was the last thing

she'd expected—or wanted, she told herself. She'd thought he'd just drop her off and—

'Come on, the rain's stopped.' Nick broke into her thoughts, releasing the locks. 'Got your key handy?'

She fished the tagged piece of metal out of the side pocket of her jeans and handed it to him.

'Nick…perhaps this isn't such a good idea,' she backtracked huskily. 'I mean, we should probably just say goodnight and…' She stopped and swallowed, his gravity making her frown. 'Why are you doing this?'

'I don't want the evening to end,' he said simply. 'Do you, Abbey?'

A beat of silence.

Abbey felt she was trying to walk through sand knee-deep. But she couldn't lie. 'No…'

Out of the car, she waited while he unlocked the door of her motel room. Nick ushered her inside and then followed her in.

Abbey had left the standard lamp burning and now its soft glow was drawing the small space into an intimate cosiness. She sent a disquieted glance at the double bed littered with her clothes, and pointedly crossed to the tiny kitchenette on the far side of the unit. 'Coffee won't be long.' Feeling as though her hands belonged to someone else, she filled the small electric jug, and set it to boil.

'I promise I won't keep you up, Abbey.' Nick fetched up one of the high-backed stools and parked himself.

She gave a weak smile. 'The coffee will probably do that anyway.'

'Do you have times when you can't sleep, however you try?' he asked, his voice low.

'Most people do, don't they?' Abbey tore open the sachets and shook the coffee grains into the two waiting cups. 'Especially people in our line of work. Sometimes, when I find it impossible to relax enough to coax sleep, I go outside and look at the stars.'

'I imagine they'd be something special out west.'

'With the sky so clear, absolutely. The stars appear like so many diamonds. Their sparkle is...well, I imagine it's like being in fairyland.' Vaguely embarrassed by her flowery speech, Abbey hastily made the coffee. She passed Nick's black brew across to him, watching as he sugared and stirred it.

'You make it sound wonderful.' His long fingers spanned his cup as he lifted it to his mouth. 'I'll come out and experience it for myself someday.'

Abbey refrained from comment. Instead, her shoulders lifted in a barely perceptible shrug. She poured milk into her own coffee and, beset by a strange unease, took the seat next to him at the counter.

'Don't believe me, do you, Abbey?'

She brought her head up, seeing the crease in his cheek as he smiled, the action activating the laughter lines around his eyes. And quickly lowered her gaze to blot out the all-male physical imprint.

But it took a while for her heart to stop beating so quickly.

Nick couldn't take his eyes off her. He felt his fingers flexing, his arms aching to draw her to him, to touch her hair, feel its silkiness glide through his fingers. The thought of something else far more urgent was enough to set his body on fire.

He raised his cup and took another mouthful of his coffee. Anything to stop the hollow, self-derisive laugh erupting from his throat, he thought ruefully. He cast about for a safer topic. 'Tell me about yourself, Abbey.'

'Oh. There's not much to tell— I'm fairly ordinary.'

'I don't believe that for a second,' he countered, hoping he'd managed to give the wry words the right touch of lightness. 'What about family? Siblings?'

She lifted one shoulder uncertainly. 'One brother, Steven. He's a GP, currently working at a health post in New Guinea.'

Nick's mouth compressed momentarily. 'So not much chance for weekend visits, then?'

'No.' Abbey shook her head. 'But we did manage to catch up last Christmas. I took a flight north and Steve flew south and we met in Darwin. It was good,' she tacked on, an odd little glitch in her voice. 'Really good. More so, because these days we only have each other…'

Nick was startled by the sudden change in her voice. She looked almost…haunted. 'Tell me,' he said quietly.

After a tense moment, she responded, 'Our parents were killed two years ago. One of those tragic road accidents. They were fulfilling their retirement dream of a motoring trip around Australia. They were somewhere west of Adelaide when a petrol tanker ran out of control in front of them and then exploded. They had no chance.'

Nick saw the heart-breaking emotion that froze her face for an instant and recalled how he'd rabbited on about his extended family. What a smug, self-satisfied clod he must have sounded.

He clenched his fists as if he wanted to pound at an unkind fate on her behalf. 'I'm so sorry, Abbey.' He shook his head. 'So sorry you had to go through that...' On an impulse he couldn't explain, he held out his hand, using the action to draw her up from her stool and into his arms.

There was a long moment when they were still. When anything was possible. Abbey took a shaken breath, tilting her face up to his, thinking she should stop this now. But the urge to touch him and to be touched in return was too great. Suddenly all her senses began to stir, unfold, waken. Her heart did a back flip in her chest. And she was waiting, expectant when Nick leaned forward to claim her mouth.

Nicholas. She said his name in her head, closing her eyes, revelling in the subtle warmth of his body as he held her closer. He made her feel wildly sensual, as if she wanted to go on tiptoe, take him to her, absorb the very essence of his maleness.

She made a little sound in her throat, waves of heat sweeping over her as she opened fully to the demanding pressure of his lips.

It was much too soon when Nick broke away from her. He turned his head a little, smudging kisses across her temple, her eyelids and into the soft curve of her throat, sending erotic visions to her mind, searing heat along each vein.

Abbey clung to him, clung and clung, her cheek hard against the warmth of his chest, while his arms cradled her as though she was infinitely precious.

She had no clear idea how long they stood there.

Finally Nick's chest rose and fell in a long sigh and he slowly untwined the hands she'd looped around his neck and pulled back from her. 'Abbey…this is a hard call but I have to go—while I still can.'

She lifted weighted eyelids to look at him, realising he was right. If he didn't leave now, there was only one way they could go from here and she wasn't about to let that happen. She shivered when his thumb touched her full lower lip.

'Don't forget me, will you?' His voice sounded raw.

She swallowed jerkily, wondering how her legs were still holding her up.

'I…don't know where any of this is leading, Abbey.' He sent her a strained look. 'But let's not shut the door on the possibilities…please.' Then, as if he couldn't bear to leave her, he kissed her again. Just briefly but hard. 'I'm going…'

'Take care,' Abbey whispered, her eyes wide and dazed-looking.

'I'll see you.' He placed the softest kiss at the side of her mouth. 'Somehow.'

Abbey waited until she heard the throb of his car engine fade away before she trusted her legs to move. Was he saying he wanted a serious chance at some kind of relationship?

She lifted her shoulders in a shaken sigh, crossing to the bed. The idea was impractical. And totally impossible.

It took only a few minutes to pack her small suitcase for her return to Wingara in the morning.

Her head was spinning, and already there was a giant gnawing emptiness in the region of her heart.

* * *

On the other side of town, Nick sat sprawled on the old swing-seat on his grandmother's back porch, his lean fingers cradling a glass of neat bourbon. He felt dazed, as though he'd gone a round or two with a heavyweight boxer.

Hell's bells.

The ice cubes rattled as he rolled the whisky glass between the palms of his hands. Abbey Jones. A grunt of self-derision left his throat. 'Turned on like a randy adolescent, Tonnelli,' he muttered, downing the rest of his drink, feeling the spirit scorch his insides like a ridge of fire.

Impatiently, he put the glass aside and then shot out of the seat, leaving the swing rocking. Leaning against the railing, he lifted his hands, tunnelling them through his hair and linking them at the base of his neck.

His gaze narrowed on the old pear tree, his body attuned, hearing the stillness, and he faced the fact that emotionally he'd fallen headlong into the deepest water of his life.

But what to do about it?

Abbey's alarm work her at five a.m. Blinking her eyes wide open, she stared at the ceiling. 'Oh, no,' she groaned, as the events of last night enveloped her.

She felt the sudden heat in her cheeks, waiting to feel shocked at how she'd opened herself to Nick Tonnelli. But it didn't happen. Instead, she remembered the way he'd held her, the tenderness of his kisses before he'd left...

But how could they share any kind of future? she

fretted, throwing herself out of bed and under the shower.

How?

Ten minutes later, dressed in the jeans she'd worn last night and a plain white shirt, Abbey swallowed a hastily made cup of tea. She'd get breakfast along the road somewhere, she decided. After she'd put some distance behind her.

Hitching up her bits and pieces, she left the motel quietly and only seconds later she'd reversed into the forecourt and nosed her four-wheel-drive out onto the road.

After almost an hour into her journey, Abbey suddenly realised she'd completely forgotten to call Geoff Rogers, Wingara's police sergeant. Well, there was a first time for everything, she thought dryly. Slamming the Range Rover into second gear to cut back on her speed, she pulled to a stop at the edge of the road.

Picking up her mobile phone, she activated the logged-in number, her gaze thoughtfully assessing the dun-gold grass of the paddocks on each side of the road. There was still something so untouched about Australia's wide open spaces, she thought philosophically. Something fearless.

It had had the hottest kind of sun blasting down on it for thousands of years, had seen drought, bushfires and floods but, despite all that, the country still came up smilingly defiant. It didn't surprise her that its stark beauty created a kind of spiritual awakening for many of the tourists who frequented the region…

'Wingara Police.' Geoff's voice came through loud and clear.

Abbey blinked a couple of times as though she'd been in a trance. 'Geoff, it's Abbey Jones. I'm just through Jareel township.'

'Abbey! You OK?'

'Fine. Sorry, I forgot to call earlier.'

Geoff chuckled. 'You're forgiven. Wild night out, was it?'

More like a wild night *in*. Abbey pursed her lips and scrubbed a pattern on the steering wheel with her thumb. 'I should be home by eight, Geoff.'

'OK, Doc. It'll be good to have you back. Ah…how's young Todd? Did you manage to see him?'

'Yes, I did.' Abbey hesitated. Literally everyone in Wingara was going to ask about Todd. 'There may be some better news about his progress in the not-too-distant future, Geoff. I can't say any more just now.'

'Understood. You always give us your best shot, Abbey. And it's not just me reckons that.'

Abbey closed off her mobile, Geoff's remarks warming her through and through.

It was a few minutes to eight when she coasted down a slight incline and glided into the township. But this time the familiar skip in her heart as the quaint wooden shopfronts with their old-fashioned awnings came into view was missing.

Why did she feel she'd left a part of herself back in Hopeton? The question buzzed around in her head and she bit off a huff of impatience at her crazy thinking.

Deciding she'd get herself sorted out before she went into the surgery, she took a side street to the rambling old house she called home. The place was far too big for her needs and she used only a tenth of its space, but it came with the job so the matter of where she lived had been largely taken out of her hands.

Almost absent-mindedly, she hauled her luggage out of the boot and made her way inside. For some reason, today the house seemed almost eerily quiet. How odd, she thought, catching the edge of her lip uncertainly. It had never seemed that way before.

A curious, unsettled feeling swamped her as she pulled stuff from her suitcase and piled her used clothing into the hamper in the laundry. 'For heaven's sake!' she muttered. You'd better get your mind back on your practice, Abbey, she told herself silently. Nick Tonnelli and his kisses are history!

But her body still tingled in memory.

Half an hour later, she'd freshened up and changed into a longish dark green skirt and pinstriped shirt. Stifling a sigh, she left the house quickly. Her surgery list was probably a kilometre long and she'd never felt less like work.

'You're back nice and early.' Meri Landsdowne, the practice manager-cum-everything greeted Abbey warmly. 'Good trip home?'

That word again. Abbey sent the other a wry smile. 'No dramas.' She took the few steps and joined Meri behind Reception. 'How have things been here?' Abbey pulled the desk diary towards her.

'Fairly quiet, actually. Wolf even managed to get his mid-week game of bowls in.' Meri made a small grimace. 'Frankly, I think everyone's been holding off until you were back. Ed Carmichael for starters.'

'Again!'

'First cab off the rank,' Meri commiserated. She gave a snip of laughter. 'Perhaps we could get a moat built around the surgery to keep him out.'

'He can probably swim like a fish,' Abbey surmised dryly. 'But he's a lonely man, Meri. He misses his days as a shearers' cook. We shouldn't be too hard on him.'

'Oh, Abbey, we both know half the time he only comes in for a yarn. And there are plenty of things he could be involved in. For heaven's sake, he's barely sixty!'

'I've had lengthy chats with him about what he could do to fill in his time.' Abbey flicked through the list of appointments. 'But nothing seemed to appeal to him. He reckons he's read every book in the library.'

'Oh, please!' Meri turned away to activate the answering-machine. 'Come on, let's have a cuppa before the hordes arrive. Did you get breakfast somewhere?'

Abbey gave a rueful grin. 'I meant to…'

'So, what distracted you, Doctor?' Meri sent her a laughing look as they made their way along the corridor to the kitchen. 'Or, should I say, who?' The practice manager cocked her auburn head at a questioning angle. 'You look…different, somehow.'

'New shirt,' Abbey dismissed, feeling her cheeks warm. Meri's green eyes were filled with curiosity.

A few minutes later, they were settled companionably over a pot of tea and the still-warm banana bread

Meri had brought in. 'Heaven,' Abbey sighed, as she took a slice and bit into it with obvious enjoyment. 'Much nicer than anything I could've eaten at some greasy-spoon café along the highway.'

Meri raised an eyebrow. 'You never skip breakfast, Abbey. How come?'

Abbey felt goose-bumps break out all over her. 'Just preoccupied, I guess. Um...there may be some changes with Todd Jensen's rehab coming up,' she deflected quickly, and then stopped. There was no getting away from it. She'd have to fill Meri in to some degree about Nick Tonnelli's involvement. Meri was the first point of contact at the surgery and would need to be put in the picture when Nick began liaising about Todd. But her manager would be discreet. And in a small-town medical practice, that was always a great bonus.

'That's fantastic,' Meri responded softly, after she'd heard what Abbey had to say about the surgeon and the Dennison clinic. 'Audrey and Keith will need careful handling though,' she added thoughtfully, referring to Todd's rather fearful parents. 'They won't want him moved to Sydney.'

Abbey lifted a shoulder. 'That'll be up to Dr Tonnelli. And I don't imagine he'll have much trouble convincing them if he decides the Dennison is the place for Todd.'

'Charmer, is he?'

Abbey felt the flush creep up her throat. 'Not bad...' She hiccuped a laugh, her embarrassed gaze going to the floor. 'For a surgeon.'

CHAPTER FOUR

As Meri had indicated, Abbey's first patient for the day was Ed Carmichael.

'What can I do for you today, Ed?' Abbey looked up expectantly as her patient made himself comfortable, stretching out his legs and folding his arms across his chest. Abbey noticed that as usual he was dressed very neatly in a bush shirt and jeans and the inevitable riding boots.

'It's my right eye, Doc. Just noticed it getting dry and a bit uncomfortable, like.'

Abbey nodded. 'How long since you've had your eyes properly checked?'

'Earlier this year. I got new specs, bifocals this time.'

'No problems with them?'

Ed shook his head and then asked gruffly, 'Could it be a cataract?'

'That would have been picked up when you had your eyes examined. And cataracts don't just happen, Ed. You'd be noticing a clouding of your vision over many months or even years.'

'So I'm not likely to be going blind, then?'

'No, Ed. I think that's very unlikely.' Abbey blocked a smile, but really it wasn't a smiling matter. She sobered. Her patient's real problem was having so much time on his hands that he'd begun to imagine that every twinge signalled a medical crisis of some kind. She got to her feet. 'Pop over here to the couch now, and I'll have a look under some light. Just to make sure there's no infection that could be causing the dryness.'

Ed Carmichael obliged and, with as little fuss as possible, Abbey settled him under the examination light. 'Your eye looks fine,' she said, scanning the eyeball for anything untoward. 'Some dryness is fairly common as we age, though, but drops can help with that.

'Now, these will just help to make tears.' Back at her desk, Abbey scribbled the brand names of several appropriate eyedrops. 'Any one of these will be suitable and they don't contain an antibiotic so you can get them over the counter without a prescription. Use the drops several times a day if you need to.'

'And that'll help, will it, Doc?' Ed's pale blue eyes regarded her seriously. 'Not that I'm doubting you,' he added hastily, taking the folded piece of paper and shoving it into his shirt pocket.

Abbey smiled. 'It should. And as I said, this kind of thing is usually age-related. But as well as the drops, you could try holding a warm flannel briefly against your eye, say, three times a day. The gentle heat will give all those little nerves and blood vessels a wake-up call and a reminder to make some moisture.'

'Thanks, Doc.' Ed pulled himself up from the chair. 'I'll give it a go.'

Abbey worked conscientiously through her patient list, but felt somewhat relieved when Meri popped her head in to announce, 'Last one. Natalie Wilson, new patient with a bub.'

'Which one is the patient?' Abbey threw her pen down and stretched, rotating her head to ease the muscles at the back of her neck.

Meri placed the new file on the desk. 'Mrs Wilson didn't make that clear, actually. Just said she's recently moved to the district and wondered whether she could have a word with the doctor.'

'Better trot her along, then.' Abbey flashed a faintly weary smile at the practice manager.

'After that, I'll lock the door and put the kettle on,' Meri announced firmly.

'Come in, Natalie, and have a seat,' Abbey invited warmly, as the young mother stood uncertainly in the doorway.

'Thanks.' Natalie Wilson dipped her fair head and took the chair beside Abbey's desk. 'This is Chloe,' she said proudly, her arms tightening around the pink-clad chubby infant on her lap.

'She's gorgeous.' Abbey's look was soft. 'How old is she?'

'Four months.' Natalie swallowed unevenly. 'We're…um, new in town. Ryan, my husband, has just been appointed manager for the organic growers co-operative.'

Abbey nodded. 'So, how can I help you?'

'I— That is, we wanted some advice, really.' She hesitated. 'About immunisation for Chloe. Are there any natural alternatives?'

Abbey took her time answering. Whether or not to immunise their children was every parent's choice, of course. But in her paediatric rotation Abbey had seen the needless pain and suffering little ones had been put through as a result of not being properly immunised against what amounted to killer diseases.

'Natalie, I have to say, the short answer is no.' Abbey looked levelly at her patient. 'Is there a reason why you don't want your baby immunised?'

The young mother nibbled on her bottom lip. 'It's just you hear of such terrible things happening afterwards—like brain damage...'

'Those cases are extremely rare,' Abbey discounted. 'In fact, I've never seen one in all the years I've been practising medicine.'

A smile nipped Natalie's mouth. 'That can't have been so long. You don't look very old.'

'Sometimes I feel about a hundred.' Abbey gave a low, husky laugh, warming to the other's light humour. 'But there's no problem with Chloe, is there? She's in good health?'

'Oh, yes,' Natalie was quick to answer. 'And I'm breastfeeding her.'

Abbey's gaze grew wistful. The little one did seem utterly content. 'You know, Natalie, on the whole, most vaccines cause minimum side effects. And it's a sad fact that some of the crippling diseases that were around in our grandparents' time are making a comeback.'

'And that's because parents are not having their children immunised, isn't it?' Nevertheless, the young mother still looked doubtful.

'Look...' Abbey swung to her feet and went across to her filing cabinet. 'Why don't I give you some relevant stuff to read, the latest statistics and so on, and you and your husband can make up your minds? I certainly wouldn't want to pressure you. In the end the decision has to be yours. If you decide you want Chloe done, pop her back in and we'll take care of it, OK?'

'Thanks so much, Dr Jones.' Natalie took the printed matter and tucked it into her big shoulder-bag. She stood to her feet, carefully cradling her daughter in the crook of her arm. 'You've been really laid-back about all this.'

'You sound surprised.' Abbey held the door open for her.

Natalie's mouth turned down comically. 'I really thought I'd be in for a lecture,' she admitted wryly.

'No lectures here,' Abbey said with a smile. 'I can guarantee it.' She touched a finger to Chloe's plump little cheek. 'Take care, now.'

Abbey's afternoon surgery kept her busy with a trail of small emergencies, one of which was the situation of two lads from the high school who needed stitches after clashing heads during a game of rugby.

'How on earth can they call it a *game*?' Meri shook her head in bewilderment, watching the two walking wounded leave the surgery in the care of their teacher.

'Rugby depends on skill,' Abbey said knowledgeably, recalling her own brother's brilliance at the game when he'd been at university. 'The more skill you have, the better you can keep out of trouble on the field.'

Meri sniffed. 'I'm just glad I have daughters. At least they can't get into too much strife with their ballet.'

Abbey pulled across a couple of letters that were waiting for her signature. 'Except ballet dancers quite often suffer horrendous problems with their feet,' she pointed out evenly.

'Do they?' Meri looked appalled.

'Well, some of the professional ones appear to. It's all that stuff on points they have to do.'

Meri lifted a shoulder. 'Oh, well, Cassie and Georgia haven't advanced to that stage yet. And by then perhaps they'll be into something sensible like tennis,' she said hopefully.

Abbey chuckled. 'Or kick-boxing?'

'Don't!' Meri pretended to shudder and then smiled a bit grimly. 'When you have kids, there's such a minefield of decision-making involved, isn't there?'

Thinking of her earlier discussion with Natalie Wilson, Abbey could only silently agree. But as yet I don't have to concern myself with that kind of responsibility, she thought broodingly. And until the right man came along, the subject of having children was hardly up for discussion...

'Oh— Wolf phoned earlier.' Meri deftly creased the letters into neat folds and slipped them into the waiting envelopes. 'Did you want him to do a late ward round? If not, he's off gallivanting somewhere.'

'I'll give him a call and let him off the hook.' Abbey blocked a yawn, edging off the tall stool behind Reception and standing to her feet. She glanced at her watch. Almost five o'clock. 'It won't take me long to pop over to the hospital and do a round. Then, barring further emergencies, I'm off home.'

'You must be out on your feet after that long drive,' Meri commiserated. 'And you haven't stopped all day. Who'd be a rural GP, eh?' She turned aside to answer the ringing telephone. Several seconds later she was holding out the receiver towards Abbey. 'For you. It's Dr Tonnelli.'

Abbey felt her heart slam against her ribs. 'I'll take it in my room, thanks, Meri,' she instructed quickly. 'And you pop off home to the girls now. I'll lock up and set the alarm.'

'If you're sure?'

'Go.'

''Night, then.' Meri waggled her fingers, her look faintly curious as she watched Abbey almost skip towards her consulting room.

Abbey entered her office, her heart pounding sickeningly. Then, blowing out a long, calming breath, she reached out and picked up the cordless receiver.

'Nick, hello!'

Tonnelli curled a low laugh. 'Hello, yourself, Dr Jones. How are things?'

Personally—crazy, mixed up, scary. Take your pick. 'Fine. And with you?'

'Oh, can't complain.' A heavy beat of silence. 'I thought of you the moment I woke this morning, Abbey. Did you think of me?'

He'd spoken quietly, his voice so deep it made her shiver. Not only had she thought of him, she'd still had the smell of him on her clothes, the taste of him on her mouth. 'Nick…'

'I'm here.'

Another silence.

'Do you want me as much as I want you, Abbey?'

Her eyes closed. 'Nick—this is all a bit unreal.'

'What part of it? Our kisses seemed pretty real to me,' he said with a wicked chuckle.

'That's not what I meant.' Sounding strangled, she

tried to block out the memory, the sweet shock when
their mouths had met for the first time. When he'd
leaned forward and teased her lips apart—and had
kissed her as she had never been kissed in all of her
thirty-one years.

'Not very experienced, are you, Abbey?' he asked
gently.

Not with men of his calibre, certainly. With the
phone still clamped to her ear, she swung up from
her chair and went to the window, as if fighting
against the sensual cocoon he'd begun weaving
around her. 'Where are you?' she asked, desperate to
normalise the conversation.

'Not where I want to be, that's for sure.'

Abbey's heart raced, thudded, missed a beat.
'Please, could we not talk about this?'

'We have to talk about this—*us*,' he went on doggedly. 'Surely it was more than just a momentary...*attraction*?'

'Perhaps it was,' she agreed tightly. 'But, Nick,
we're hundreds of miles apart. Our *lives* are hundreds
of miles apart!'

'So you're baling out without even giving us a
shot? Turning your feelings off like a tap? You dis-
appoint me, Abbey. I took you to be a far more gutsy
lady than that.'

Abbey's fingers tightened on the phone. She
wouldn't let him get to her. 'This kind of conversation
is pointless, Nick, and if that's all you called for—'

'It isn't,' he emphasised almost roughly. 'I've seen
Todd.'

Immediately, Abbey felt on safer ground. She swallowed. 'And?'

'I think the Dennison can help him. I've already begun liaising with Anna Charles and lined up an ambulance. Todd should be installed by next Monday. I'll have my secretary fax my findings to you.'

'Oh, Nick, that's brilliant.' Hardly aware of what she was doing, Abbey turned from the window and began to pace her room. 'And what about Todd's parents? It could be a bit sticky.'

'I've already spoken to them. They'll be in Sydney on Monday to help him settle in.'

So he had everyone eating out of his hand. Abbey felt the ground sliding out from under her. She gave a brittle laugh. 'When you decide to move, you really move, don't you?'

'There's no point in procrastinating, Abbey—about anything.'

Abbey's throat tightened. 'Don't go on as though we have some kind of future together, Nick. Tell me more about Todd's situation,' she sidetracked quickly. If she could keep him to medical matters, maybe she could cope—just. 'What about the fees?'

'It's sorted.' He sounded irritated. 'And to make Todd feel really at home, his OT is going to continue working with him.'

'Amanda? She's going to Sydney with him?' Abbey could hardly contain her disbelief. 'Just like that?'

'No, Abbey, not just like that.'

'What did you do,' she cut in harshly, 'bribe her?'

'Don't be extreme. At Anna's request, of course, I offered her an increase in salary. It's rather more expensive to live in Sydney than in Hopeton.'

It sounded like they were all closing ranks around

her patient and leaving her out. Big-time specialists pulling professional strings, as though they were controlling puppets. 'Well, isn't that just typical?' she snapped, fighting against a sick kind of resentment.

'What?'

'Do you enjoy stripping expertise from rural health, Dr Tonnelli? Amanda Steele is one of the best occupational therapists Sunningdale has had in years. Her methods are nothing short of inspirational to the residents—'

'Abbey, you're putting the wrong spin on this.'

'The hell I am...' Abbey felt her throat close. 'I was right about you from the beginning, Nick. You just steamroller over everything to get your own way. Well, you've shot all your ducks now, so I hope you're happy!'

'Abbey, listen—'

'No, Nick, you listen. You said you were disappointed in *me*,' she went on, her words echoing with hurt and disillusionment. 'Well, I'm disappointed in you—more than I can say. I'll expect your fax!' She ended the call abruptly and promptly burst into tears. Her heart was shattering, destroyed just like the trust she'd foolishly built around him.

Nick felt as though his insides were tied in a thousand knots. And it wasn't a condition he was used to, he admitted uncomfortably. For the most part he had always been in control of his life. Now his thoughts were jumbled, too incoherent to organise rationally.

Thanks to Abbey Jones.

In an abrupt movement, he threw himself out of his armchair and prowled across the room to stare through the big picture window, his gaze reaching beyond the canopy of trees. Early evening mist hung across the mountains and already the sharpness of winter was in the air.

He stifled a sigh, turning and retracing his steps to the fireplace. Hunkering down, he carefully placed a new log on the fire and then eased the fireguard back into place.

'You have problems, Nikkolo?'

Claudia Tonnelli's snow-white head was lowered intently over her needlework but Nick knew his grandmother in her wisdom had missed nothing of his agitation. For an instant he was tempted to blurt everything out, as he'd done when he'd been much younger, and wait for her advice. Because she'd be bound to offer it, he thought dryly, uncurling to his feet.

'Nothing you need worry about, Nonna.'

'Come.' The elderly lady patted the space beside her on the sofa. 'Talk to me.'

Nick pushed his hands roughly through his hair. 'Not just now, Nonna. In fact, I think I'll go for a long run.'

During the days following her phone conversation with Nick, Abbey pushed all thoughts of him to the back of her mind. It was the only way she could cope.

His fax had arrived, together with a penned footnote from Nick himself telling her that Todd had been persuaded to let his wife visit and at least they'd begun to talk. Which is more than *we* are doing, Abbey thought bitterly, adding the faxed information to Todd's already thick file.

Nevertheless, every time the phone rang, she'd foolishly hope it would be Nick but, of course, it never was. Well, who could blame him? The pain in her heart welled up again, and again she beat it back. Why would he bother to call, when she'd told him off in no uncertain manner?

Had she been too hasty in judging his actions over Todd? Abbey shook her head. I just would have liked to have been consulted, she rationalised for the umpteenth time. Surely that hadn't been too much to ask?

Heavens, she'd have to stop this!

Resolutely, she made a notation on the file in front of her and placed it aside. Spinning off her chair, she moved to the window, absorbing the stillness, her gaze going to the distant low hills and then drawing back to the tangle of vivid bougainvillea that wound itself in glorious abandon across the roof of the pergola in the surgery's back garden.

'With such a beautiful view from my window, why on earth am I wishing I was somewhere else?' she whispered to the late afternoon air, almost absently glancing at her watch and realising it was Friday again.

And remembering it was two weeks and two days since Nick had kissed her. And held her as though he'd never wanted to let her go. She sighed, her thoughts becoming so bleak it seemed almost a relief to let the anguish engulf her momentarily.

Closing her eyes, she began to relive it all, losing herself in hopeless longing.

Reality came back with a snap when her door opened and was softly closed again.

Abbey spun round, coming to a shocked halt, her

eyes snapping wide in disbelief. 'Nick…' His name came hoarsely from her throat.

'Your secretary said it was all right to come in.' He raised an eyebrow in query and waited.

Abbey's wits deserted her. She didn't know what to do. But all her instincts were screaming at her to bolt. To pretend he wasn't there. But that wouldn't work, he was blocking her exit. And not looking entirely friendly.

In fact he looked…*intense*, for want of a better word. Almost as if she'd never seen him before, she stared at the imposingly broad-shouldered physique, delineated by the close-fitting black ribbed jumper, his jaw jutting almost arrogantly over its poloneck. Blinking, she met the brunt of his gaze with its sea-green luminosity…

Her heart skittered. 'What—what are you doing here?'

'I've taken a month's leave.' He stood very still, the fingers of his left hand hooked into the collar of a leather jacket he'd slung over one shoulder. 'Do you think we can pick up where we left off, Abbey?'

Nick watched her eyes cloud and cursed himself for the ambiguity of his question. He allowed himself a small smile. 'Not from where you put the phone down on me, obviously,' he clarified.

Abbey winced at the memory, crossing her arms over her chest, her fingers kneading her upper arms. 'I don't believe any of this—that you've come all this way…' Breaking off, she stilled and gave a little frown. 'What am I going to do with you for a month?'

Green eyes regarded her levelly. 'Put me to work.' With a smile Abbey wasn't sure she trusted, he continued smoothly, 'You could do with some help, couldn't you?'

Well, of course she could. Abbey felt almost sick with vulnerability, and tried telling herself she wasn't feeling what she thought she was feeling, that her insides hadn't turned to mush, that his closeness wasn't making her nerves zing like the strings of a violin gone mad. She shook her head, asking throatily, 'Why, Nick?'

'You must know why, Abbey.' There was a slight edge to his voice and suddenly he seemed to come to a decision. Moving purposefully towards her desk, he unfurled the leather jacket from his shoulder and hooked it over the back of a chair.

As though he was staking some kind of claim. Abbey bristled. 'Being an MO here is light years away from your brand of high-tech medicine,' she pointed out, fighting to regain her poise.

'I'll adapt.'

Her heart skipped a beat. It could never work. Could it...? She looked at him warily.

'What, no comeback, Dr Jones?' Nick's mouth tightened fractionally. He moved a few paces to park himself on the edge of her desk and gazed at her broodingly. 'I scare the daylights out of you, don't I?'

Snapping her chin up, she huffed forcefully, 'Of course not!'

His mouth folded in on a smile. 'Then that has to be a start.' In one easy movement, he straightened from his perch, taking the two steps necessary to gather her into his arms.

'Nick…' Her voice sounded breathy. 'You're taking a lot for granted.'

'Really, Abbey?' He brought her a few centimetres closer. 'Then let's make it worthwhile…'

His lips ravished her, seduced her then teased her lightly, exquisitely until she shivered and arched against him.

She sighed against his mouth, her hands seeking out the solidness of him, her fingers digging into his shoulders, moving to shape the muscles at the base of his neck, going higher to run through the silky tufts of hair at his nape.

And then slowly he lifted his head.

Breathing hard, he tilted her face, one hand sliding among the strands of her hair. Scooping them up gently, he let them fall away in a cascade of gold and light. 'I could eat you, Abbey.'

Her insides heaved crazily. Locking her hands around his neck, she mustered a shaky smile. 'How would you explain that to my patients?'

His chuckle was warm, as rich as cream on apple pie. 'You're lovely,' he murmured deeply, his hand gliding to her breast and cupping it through her silk shirt.

'Nick…' She melted back into his arms.

And then abruptly pulled away.

'What is it?' A frown touched his forehead.

'Meri could walk in at any minute.' Quickly, Abbey finger-combed her hair into place. 'And speaking of Meri, if you're going to be working here, you'd better come out to Reception and meet her properly. And who knows? She'll probably find you the occasional chocolate biscuit if you bat that sexy smile at her now and again.'

'Really?' Grinning, he placed his hands on Abbey's shoulders, his thumbs stroking the soft hollow at the base of her throat. 'Do I have a sexy smile, then?'

'Stop fishing for compliments, Doctor.' She gave a strangled laugh, unfastening his hands and stepping back. After a moment she asked carefully, 'Was it difficult, getting time off?' She still felt amazed and slightly panicked at the lengths he'd gone to to be with her.

'The hospital needed a bit of persuasion,' he admitted. 'But they owed me the time anyway. They've appointed an excellent locum to cover my caseload, so in the end everyone's needs were met.'

Abbey felt riddled with guilt. 'I hope you won't be bored rigid here.'

'How could I be?' He sent her a dry look. 'I expect you to keep me very busy, Dr Jones.'

Abbey flushed. 'I…can't pay you much,' she deflected quickly. 'There is some extra funding to cover a locum but nothing like your normal salary.'

He shook his head. 'Abbey, the money isn't important. I wanted—*needed*—to spend this time with you. End of story. Now, where should I stay? I noticed several pubs on the way here.'

Abbey made a face. 'The Sapphire's the best but you don't need to shell out money to stay in a pub. I'm rattling around in a huge house that comes with the job. You can live with me.'

His mouth kicked up in a crooked smile. 'Live as in *live*?' he inquired softly.

Abbey felt the heat rising, warming her throat,

flowering over her cheeks. She knew he was teasing her—well, she hoped he was. But she couldn't help wondering just what he expected from this month he was proposing to spend here.

And whether or not she was going to be able to meet those expectations.

'I meant to say, you can share my home—if that suits, of course...'

Nick's heart somersaulted. She looked even more lovely than he remembered and he suddenly knew without a shadow of a doubt he wanted to test the strength of this relationship as far as it would go. And despite the frustration ripping through him, he knew he'd have to tread very softly around Abbey Jones. Very softly indeed.

'Thanks.' He rubbed the back of his neck. 'That will suit me very well.'

CHAPTER FIVE

'I'LL give you the tour,' Abbey said, as they went out, closing the door on her consulting room. 'Then I'll take you home to my place and you can get settled in while I do a hospital round.'

'Why can't I come to the hospital with you?'

Well, no reason, Abbey supposed, nibbling at the corner of her bottom lip. 'It's all pretty basic medicine,' she warned.

Nick's eyes clouded slightly. 'Abbey, I'm on your patch now. I'm keen to learn about rural medicine.'

She opened the door of the second consulting room. 'I was just pointing out that there'll be none of the drama associated with Theatres.'

'I'm quite looking forward to the change of pace.' His voice was carefully neutral. 'But who knows?' He raised an eyebrow just slightly and grinned. 'You kind of lose the feel of general medicine when you detour into a speciality. I might turn out to be a real dud at your brand of medicine.'

As if! Abbey angled her gaze quickly away from the lively intelligence of those amazing eyes. 'This will be yours.' She led him into the reasonably sized surgery. 'Wolf uses it when he covers for me. Feel free to move things around if they don't suit.'

'I'll bear that in mind. But on first glance it seems fine.'

'Treatment room through here. It's quite large,' she

said, pulling back a screen to reveal an identical set of equipment. 'Once upon a time there were several doctors working here.' Her mouth moved in a rueful little moue. 'But not for some years now.'

They moved on to the staff kitchen and walked onto the outdoor deck leading off it.

'Oh, boy,' Nick breathed in obvious approval, placing his hands on the timber railings. 'This is really something…' His gaze went towards the hills and the magic of a vividly pink and gold sunset. 'The last time I saw something like this was in Bali.'

'Have you travelled a lot?' Abbey came up to stand beside him.

'Some.' He lifted a shoulder. 'Dad took us over to Italy when we were youngsters and I've been back a couple of times. Done most of Europe. I worked in the States for a year, Canada for six months.'

She sent him a strained little smile, feeling like a real country bumpkin. Sadly, she realised she'd hardly travelled at all outside her own country. But there'd scarcely been time—or money, she reflected ruefully, considering the whopping great study loan she'd had to repay.

'Is your family very wealthy, Nick?'

A smile nipped his mouth. 'We never wanted for anything, I suppose. My grandparents established a vineyard outside Hopeton when they migrated from Italy. They never looked back. It just went from strength to strength.'

And brought in lots of money obviously. 'Is it still in your family?'

'Oh, yes. But they put in a manager some years ago, when we moved to Sydney. My parents run the sales and promotional side of things from there. Anything else you'd like to know?' he drawled with his slow smile.

'Sorry.' Embarrassed, Abbey looked away. 'I didn't mean to sound as though I was interrogating you.'

'You weren't,' he denied blandly. And then he frowned slightly, his eyes on her face with the intensity of a camera lens. 'Abbey, stop looking for the differences between us. This will work,' he said with conviction. 'We'll be good together.'

'Well, let's hope the patients think so,' Abbey waffled, feeling the warmth of his regard all over her. 'End of tour.' She turned abruptly from the railings. 'Let's put Meri in the picture and then we'll be on our way.'

'I'll follow you,' Nick said, as they left the surgery and made their way to their respective vehicles. 'How far is it to the hospital?'

'About five minutes.' Abbey waggled her bunch of keys until she found the one for the ignition. 'Seven if it's a foggy morning.'

Nick grinned. 'Perhaps I should invest in a push-bike? Save on petrol.'

'Or a sulky,' Abbey shot back impishly. 'That would go quite well with your new rural image. And there happens to be a beauty on display at the heritage village. Maybe they'd let you borrow that. I'm sure we could round up a nice fat pony to pull it.'

'And perhaps you could rustle up an old-fashioned Gladstone bag and a jar of leeches while you're at it?' Nick's eyes were full of laughter.

He'd never felt so light-hearted. And he was still wearing a smile as he tailed Abbey's Range Rover through the town proper and across the disused railway line. As she had predicted, they were at the hospital within a few minutes.

Nick got out of his car and looked around him. The hospital was a low-set building of weathered brick with several annexes at various points. There was a strip of lawn, faded to winter-brown, around the perimeter. And further over again, a windsock flapped gently in the breeze at the end of a large unfenced paddock.

'We do have the odd emergency,' Abbey explained, coming to stand beside him. 'The strip's regularly maintained for the CareFlight chopper to land.'

He shook his head. 'It's so quiet.'

'Mmm.' Abbey's gaze stretched to the shimmering water of a lagoon in a farmer's adjoining paddock and the wild ducks resembling tiny specks swimming serenely on its surface. 'It kind of folds in on you, especially at night.'

'You're not lonely?'

'For a while at first. Not now. But living here is vastly different from living in the city. In every way.'

'Yes.' Nick's reply was muted.

After a minute, they turned and began making their way across to the hospital entrance. 'Like me to fill you in about the staff?' Abbey flicked him a brief smile.

'Please.'

'We've a husband-and-wife team, Rhys and Diane Macklin, as joint nurse managers. They're terrific. Keep the place ticking over. Usually one of them is on duty. And we have a regular staff of RNs. They're rostered parttime as necessary. And there are two youngish aides, Zoe and Tristan. They're really just getting the feel of working within a hospital to see if they'd like to go ahead and train as registered nurses.'

Nick nodded. 'That sounds remarkably innovative.'

'Well, in a small place like Wingara, it can work quite well. And Rhys and Diane have the necessary accreditation to be their preceptors.'

'Who's the cook?' His grin was youthfully hopeful.

'I wondered when we'd get to that.' Abbey lifted her gaze briefly to the sky. 'Bella Sykes provides the meals at the hospital and also does for me.'

'Does?' Nick lifted an eyebrow.

Abbey chuckled. 'She looks after the doctor's residence which means she comes in a couple of times a week to clean and keep the place looking reasonable. She's an absolute gem.'

Nick looked thoughtful. 'The local community obviously values your presence enormously, Abbey. How will they respond to me being here, do you suppose?'

'Thinking of backing out, Doctor?'

Nick's jaw jutted. 'With you to hold my hand? No way.'

Diane Macklin was just coming out of her office as they approached the nurses' station. 'Abbey!' The nurse manager's dark head with its smooth bob tilted enquiringly. 'Three times in one day. Are you concerned about a patient?'

'With you in charge?' Abbey laughed. 'Not a chance. Um, Diane, this is Dr Nick Tonnelli.' Abbey turned to the man beside her. 'He'll be giving me a hand for the next few weeks.'

'Welcome aboard, Doctor.' Diane extended a hand across the counter. Her gaze skittered curiously from Nick to Abbey. 'I'll just bet you're old friends from medical school. Am I right?'

Nick tipped a sly wink at Abbey. 'I was a few years ahead of Abbey,' he deflected smoothly. 'Wasn't I?'

Abbey almost choked. 'Ah...yes.' Well, she supposed he would have been. He was several years older than her after all. 'And Nick's here for a holiday as well,' she added boldly.

'My first trip so far west,' he admitted, keeping the patter going but flicking Abbey a dry look.

'Oh, you'll love it,' Diane enthused. 'And I'm sure we'll keep you busy.'

Abbey stole a glance at her watch. 'Diane, we'd best get on. I'll just give Nick a quick tour of the hospital so he can find things.'

'Good idea. But do yell if you need anything, Dr Tonnelli.'

'It's Nick, Diane.'

The RN beamed. 'OK, then—Nick. Oh, Abbey, before you go...' Diane gave an apologetic half-smile. 'There was something. I wonder if you'd mind just having a word with young Brent.'

A frown touched Abbey's forehead. 'I've signed his release. He's going home tomorrow. What seems to be the problem?'

'Oh, nothing about his physical care,' Diane hastily reassured her. 'But he's seemed terribly quiet for most of the afternoon and he's asked me twice if I thought he was ready to go home.'

'That's odd.' Nick stroked his chin in conjecture. 'Most patients can't wait to get shut of us.' He raised a brow at Abbey. 'What was he admitted for?'

'Snakebite.'

'Oh—excuse me, folks.' Diane spun round as a patient's buzzer sounded. 'That's old Mrs Delaney.' She made a small face. 'Poor old love probably needs turning again.'

'You go, Diane.' Abbey made a shooing motion with her hand. 'I'll certainly pop in on Brent. See if there's something needs sorting out.'

'Thanks.' Diane flapped a hand in farewell, looking smart and efficient in her navy trousers and crisp white shirt, as she hurried away to the ward.

'You know, he may just need to talk.' Nick backed himself against the counter and folded his arms. 'And, just for the record, I've never seen a case of snakebite.'

'That's not so surprising,' Abbey said, moving round beside him so that their arms were almost touching. 'Although these days, more and more snakes are being found in city environs and most of them are now being placed on the potentially lethal list.'

'Charming.' Nick's response was touched with dry humour. 'So, is it still the same treatment we were taught in med school? Compression, head for the nearest hospital and combat the poison with an anti-venom?'

'Mmm.' A smile nipped Abbey's mouth. 'Much more civilised than in the old days. They used to pack the bite puncture with gunpowder and light the fuse.' Seeing the horror on Nick's face, she elaborated ghoulishly, 'You can imagine what it did to the affected part of the body.'

'You're kidding me!'

'Go look it up in the local history section at the library. It's all there. And there was another method—'

'Stop, please!' Nick raised his hands in mock surrender.

Abbey chuckled. 'Put you off your dinner, did I? Better get used to it, Doctor. You're in the bush now. Um, what did you mean about Brent?' She changed the tenor of the conversation quietly. 'That he might need to talk…'

'Just a thought. Give me the background.'

'Brent is sixteen,' Abbey began carefully. 'He's left school, works on the family property about seventy kilometres out. He was bitten on Monday last.'

'So he's been hospitalised all this week.'

'It seemed the best and safest option. To make sure there were no residual effects. And don't forget, if I'd released him too early, it would have been a round trip of a hundred and forty K's if his parents had needed to get him back in.'

'So you erred on the side of caution,' Nick said. 'I'd have done the same. Was it a severe bite?'

'It was a blue-bellied black snake.' Abbey identified the species with a shudder. 'And it got a really good go at Brent's calf muscle. Fortunately, he was near enough to the homestead to be found fairly quickly and he didn't panic.

'Out here kids are indoctrinated about what to do in case of snakebite. I remember when I'd been here only a few weeks, the principal of the school rang and asked when I'd be available to do "the snake talk".' She gave a low, throaty laugh, lifting her hands to make the quotation marks in the air.

Nick tore his gaze away from her smiling mouth. 'You said Brent didn't panic?'

'Ripped up his T-shirt, used it as a tourniquet and stayed put. He was visible from the track to the homestead and it was late afternoon. He knew his dad would be along within a reasonable time and he could hail him. It worked out that way and Tony and Karen brought their son straight in.'

'So, given all that, how calmly he appeared to handle things, is it just possible young Brent is now suffering from PTS?'

Abbey looked taken aback. 'Post-traumatic stress?'

Nick shrugged, palms out. 'It happens as a result of dogbites and shark attacks.'

Was it possible? Her hand closed around the small medallion at her throat.

'How's he been sleeping?'

'Not all that well, actually. But I put it down to the strangeness of being in hospital for the first time.' Abbey felt the nerves in her stomach tighten. Had she been less perceptive than she should have been where her young patient was concerned? She shook her head. 'He hasn't seemed to want to talk especially. In fact, I've been flat out getting two words out of him.'

'Well, there could be a reason for that.' Nick sent her a dry smile. 'He's sixteen, Abbey. His testosterone is probably working overtime and you're a beautiful lady doctor. The kid was probably struck dumb.'

Abbey felt the flush creep up her throat but then her chin rose. 'That's crazy!'

'Is it?'

'So I should try and talk to him, then?' Her hand clutched at her cloud of fair hair in agitation. 'Is that what you're saying?'

'Why don't you let me?'

'You?'

'I'm on staff now,' he reminded her. 'And your Brent may just open up to another male. This is how we'll handle it.'

Brent Davis was the only patient in the three-bed unit. Clad in sleep shorts and T-shirt, he was obviously bored, his gaze intermittently on the small television screen in front of him.

Abbey braced herself, going forward, her greeting low-key and cheerful. 'Hi, there, Brent. Just doing a final round.'

Colour stained the boy's face and he kept his gaze determinedly on the TV screen.

'This is Dr Tonnelli.' Abbey whipped the blood-pressure cuff around the youth's left arm and began to pump. 'He's from Sydney. Going to spend some time with us here in Wingara.'

'Hi, Brent.' Nick extended his hand. 'Dr Jones tells me you crash-tackled a death adder recently.'

Brent looked up sharply. 'Don't get adders this far west.' He sent Abbey an exasperated look. 'I told you it was a black snake.'

'So you did.' Abbey smiled, releasing the cuff.

'How did it actually happen, mate?' Casually, Nick parked himself on the youngster's bed and raised a quizzical dark brow.

Almost holding her breath, Abbey watched Brent's

throat tighten with heartbreaking vulnerability, before he made faltering eye contact with the male doctor.

'I...was just walking through the grass. This time of year it's pretty long and it's dry, tufty kind of stuff. I must have disturbed the snake—maybe it was sleeping.'

'Don't they usually sleep on logs?' Head bent, Abbey was making notes on Brent's chart.

'Not always.'

'So, you disturbed it...' Nick folded his arms, and gave the boy an encouraging nod to continue.

'Bastard gave me one hell of a fright.' Brent made a sound somewhere between a snort and a laugh. 'It went straight into a strike pattern—like an S.' The boy flexed his hand and forearm to illustrate.

'Hell's teeth...' Nick grimaced. 'And then it struck and bit you?'

'Yeah. Quick as a flash.' Brent's demeanour had suddenly lightened with the enthusiasm of recounting his tale. 'I almost wet myself.'

'Hmm, lucky you didn't do that.' Nick's grin was slow. 'And Dr Jones tells me you kept your head and did all the right things until you were able to get here to the hospital. I don't know whether I'd have been so cool.'

Brent lifted a shoulder dismissively. 'Out here, you have to learn to take care of yourself from when you're a kid. Otherwise you're dead meat.'

Over their young patient's head, Nick exchanged a guarded smile with Abbey. This response was just what they'd hoped for. And, it seemed, once started, Brent couldn't stop. Aided by Nick's subtle prompting, he relaxed like a coiled spring unwinding as he continued to regale them with what had happened.

Finally, Nick flicked a glance at his watch. 'So, it's home tomorrow?'

'Yeah.' Brent's smile flashed briefly.

'What time are your parents coming, Brent?' Abbey clipped the medical chart back on to the end of the bed.

'About ten. Uh—thanks for looking after me.' He rushed the words out, his gaze catching Abbey's for the briefest second before he dipped his head shyly.

'You're welcome, Brent.' Abbey sent him a warm smile. 'And better wear long trousers out in the paddocks from now on, eh?'

'And watch where you put those big feet,' Nick joked, pulling himself unhurriedly upright. 'Stay cool, champ.' He touched a hand to the boy's fair head.

'No worries, Doc. See you.'

'You bet.' Nick raised a one-fingered salute.

Out in the corridor, he turned to Abbey. 'Told you we'd be a good team.'

Abbey's smile was a little strained. '*You* were good, Nick. Thanks.'

'Hey, you.' As they turned the corner, he tugged her to a halt. 'You look as though you've just hocked your best silver.'

She smiled weakly. 'I don't have any silver.'

'You know what I mean.'

Her mouth tightened momentarily. 'Why didn't I see Brent needed to unload all that stuff? He was relaxed as cooked spaghetti when we left.'

'And he'll probably sleep like a baby tonight. It's what's called getting a second opinion, Abbey, and I imagine they're a bit thin on the ground out here. Am I right?' he tacked on softly.

She nodded feeling the pressures of being a sole practitioner close in on her. 'But I would have sent him home still all screwed up—'

'Stop it!' Nick's command was razor sharp. 'You can't second-guess everything you do in medicine, Abbey. Imagine, as a surgeon, if I did that. I'd be residing at the funny farm by now. You do the best you can. None of us can do more than that.'

'But—'

He gave an irritated 'tsk'. 'Abbey, physically, your patient is well again. He's young and resilient. He'd have sorted himself out—probably talked to his parents about it, or a mate.'

'I suppose so…'

'I know so.' Nick's eyes glinted briefly. 'Now, come on, Dr Jones.' He took her arm again. 'You promised to show me through the rest of this place.'

Wingara hospital was old but beautifully maintained. Nick looked around with growing interest, deciding the wide corridors and carved wooden panelling over the doorways could have easily graced a fine old homestead. 'It's got a long history, obviously,' he remarked.

'Oh, yes.' Abbey nodded, regaining her equilibrium. 'Built in the days when Wingara was a thriving centre. In those days there was a permanent senior reg on staff and always a couple of residents, plus several GPs in private practice as well.'

'So, what happened?'

'The usual things.' Abbey's mouth turned down. 'The sapphire mine gave out, the rail line closed, the

sawmill went into liquidation and people had to relocate to get work. Suddenly, it was the domino effect
at its worst. Money leaves the town so shops lose
business or fold. The pupil numbers at the school di-
minish so a teacher is lost, and so it goes on. But
there's talk of the mine reopening and the local coun-
cil has embraced tourism, so there's a bit of a revival
happening.' She smiled. 'Things are looking up
again.'

'What's the bed capacity?' They'd stopped and
looked into one of the spacious private rooms.

'Only ten now. And, thank heavens, we've never
had a full house since I've been here.'

'Do you have an OR?' Nick began striding ahead,
his interest clearly raised.

'We have a *theatre*,' Abbey emphasised. 'You're
not in the States now, you know.'

Nick laughed ruefully. 'Force of habit. Makes more
sense to say OR when you think about it, though.'

Abbey looked unimpressed. 'Here we are.' She
turned into an annexe and opened the door to the
pristine operating theatre. Her mouth had a sad little
droop. 'It's hardly used any more but Rhys insists the
instruments are kept sterilised.'

Nick shook his head slowly. 'It's brilliant—for a
rural hospital, that is…' His mouth compressed. He
could comprehend more clearly now Abbey's underlying anger and frustration at the bureaucracy's continued neglect of rural medicine. Although he'd assumed things were improving…

He strode into the theatre then, as if to better ac-
quaint himself with its layout, his movements sure
and purposeful as he gauged the angle of a light here,

stroked the tips of his fingers over a stainless-steel surface there.

'Do you want me to leave you here to play while I go home and start dinner?' Abbey queried dryly from the doorway.

Nick's head came up and he grinned a bit sheepishly. 'Be right with you.'

CHAPTER SIX

THE doctor's residence was next door to the hospital with a vacant block between. Again, like the hospital, it was of brick, a sprawling old building with a bay window at the front and with a large veranda on the eastern side, positioned to catch the morning sun in the winter and to offer shade during the hot summer afternoons.

As Abbey led the way inside, she had the strangest feeling a whole new chapter of her life was about to begin.

'Ah—sure there's enough room?'

Abbey wrinkled her nose at Nick's mocking look, her heels tapping as they walked along the polished hallway. 'There are four bedrooms, all quite large. You can take the one with the bay window, if you like. Bella keeps them all aired—don't ask me why.' She opened the door on the freshness of a lemon-scented furniture polish. 'What do you think?'

There was something very homely and intimate about it, Nick thought. His gaze swept the room, taking in the fitted wardrobes, the dark oak dresser and bedside tables with their old-fashioned glass lamps. 'It looks very comfortable,' he said, his mouth drying as he looked across at the double bed with its plump navy blue duvet and lighter blue pillowcases.

He took a breath that expanded the whole of his diaphragm. 'Thank you, Abbey.'

Abbey's heart did a tumble turn. She swallowed. 'For what?'

'For inviting me to share your home.'

Suddenly the atmosphere changed, the light-hearted harmony disappearing, replaced with tension as tight as a trip wire.

Her startled eyes met his and widened, and her lips parted to take in a soft little breath.

It was too much for Nick. With a muted sound of need, he drew her into his arms. Raising his hands, he cupped her face, his thumbs following the contours of her cheekbones. She looked so beautiful, he thought, looking down at the little flecks like gold dust in her eyes.

Lowering his head, he tasted the fluttering pulse at her throat, before catching her lips, threading his fingers through her hair to lock her head more closely to his.

On a little moan of pleasure Abbey welcomed his deepening kiss, shivering at the intensity of her feelings the like of which she'd never experienced with any other man. Winding her arms around his waist, she urged him closer, closing the last remaining gap between them, tasting heaven.

But surely this shouldn't be happening.

With a tiny whimper, she dragged her mouth from his, her breathing shallow. 'Nick...' Her hand flew up to cover her mouth.

'Abbey?' He stared down into her wide, troubled eyes.

She held his gaze for a searing moment and then looked away, taking a step back as if to separate herself from the physical boundary of his arms.

In a show of mild desperation, Nick brought his hands up, locking them at the back of his neck. Did she expect him to apologise? Well, he was damned if he was going to. She'd kissed him back, hadn't she?

'I...think we need some ground rules.' Abbey wound her arms around her midriff to stop herself trembling. She licked her lips, tasting him all over again.

His jaw tightened. 'Are you trying to tell me you don't like me touching you?'

She flushed. 'That's not the point. This is a small community. We both have a professional standard to uphold.'

'You're having second thoughts about having me here?'

'No.' Abbey took a shallow breath. 'I'm just saying we need to be aware of how things look.'

A grim little smile twisted his mouth. 'In other words, to use the vernacular, you don't want it to appear as though I've come here merely to shack up with you.' And then he looked at her wary, troubled expression and his gut clenched. 'Look.' He pressed his palms against his eyes and pushed out a gust of breath. 'I'll get a room at the pub.'

'You don't have to do that!' Abbey shook her head and wondered why she was trying so hard to keep him under her roof. 'Just...as I said. We need to talk a few things through.' Seeing how his expression darkened at that, she added hurriedly, 'But we could do that later, perhaps—over a glass of wine or something...'

'Fine,' he agreed heavily. 'Is it OK if I take a few

minutes to unpack? It's been a long day. I'd like to get squared away.'

'Of course,' she said quickly, almost breathlessly in her haste to try and normalise things between them. In a brief aside, she wondered if Nick was obsessively neat about the house. Oh, lord. She wasn't a particularly messy person but she did like to kick her shoes off the minute she walked in the door and she'd been known to leave empty coffee-mugs in odd places.

But I won't keep looking for the negatives between us.

She rallied, even dredging up a passable smile. 'I'll, um, grab a shower and see you in a bit, then. My bedroom has an *en suite* bathroom so feel free to use the main one.' She heard herself babbling and stopped. 'See you in a bit,' she repeated and hurriedly left the bedroom.

Barely forty-five minutes later, Nick joined Abbey in the kitchen, showered, his suitcase unpacked and his gear more or less sorted.

'That was quick.' She gave a stilted smile. 'I've just been checking the fridge. There's nothing very interesting for dinner and I wouldn't insult your ancestral palate by offering you a supermarket-brand lasagne.'

'I've eaten worse things.' His mouth folded in on a smile and he hooked out a chair to sit back to front on it, his arms folded along the top. 'Honestly, Abbey, I'm not pedantic about food. But I do like to choose what I eat, if that makes sense.'

It did. 'I usually do a shop on Saturday after I've finished surgery.' Abbey met his mild look neutrally, before her eyes darted away again. 'I guess we could make a list of the kinds of things we like…' She paused, as if waiting for his approval.

'Sure. That's fine with me.' He rolled back his shoulders and stretched.

Her expression lightened. Perhaps sharing living arrangements would work out after all. 'The Sapphire does a nice roast on a Friday,' she offered tentatively.

'The pub it is, then.' Nick kept his tone deliberately brisk. 'But I might make it an early night, if you don't mind.'

She suppressed a tight smile. 'And there I was imagining you'd want to hang about for the karaoke.'

'Maybe next Friday.' As if he was trying hard to regain his good humour, Nick's return smile was wry and crooked. Spinning off his chair, he placed it neatly back at the table. 'Let's go then, if you're quite ready.'

They took Abbey's four-wheel-drive. 'And while you're here, Nick, we split living expenses down the middle. OK?' They'd crossed the old railway line and were re-entering the town proper.

'Whatever you say, Abbey.'

She sent him a quick enquiring look. His remark had sounded as though he was humouring her. She frowned slightly. Suddenly the outcome of this month he proposed spending here with her seemed very blurred and uncertain.

'Be prepared to be well looked over,' she warned him. She'd parked neatly opposite the hotel and now they were making their way across the street to the beer garden.

'So, I shouldn't try holding your hand, then,' he interpreted dryly.

Abbey's heart thumped painfully. If he didn't lighten up, she'd jolly well send him home to eat that awful lasagne.

The beer garden was not overly crowded for a Friday evening and Abbey breathed a sigh of relief, scattering a smile here and there to several of the townsfolk who were obviously enjoying a meal out.

Seeing her action, a flash of humour lit Nick's eyes and he mimicked her greeting.

'Cheeky,' Abbey murmured, hiding a smile and taking the chair he held out for her.

'I always say, start as you mean to go on and at least now the locals will know I'm a friendly soul. I must say this all looks very civilised,' he sidetracked, looking around the precincts. And suddenly, he felt a lift in his spirits. Already he was sensing something special here in Abbey's world, not least the slower pace. His expression closed thoughtfully and he sat back in his chair, the better to take in his surroundings.

Fat candles on the wooden tables were giving out an atmosphere of light and shadow. And there was a sheen on the leaves of the outdoor plants dotting the perimeter of the raised timber platform, the fairy lights strung between them twinkling like so many diamonds. Or stars, he substituted, slightly embarrassed at his attempt at poetic language.

Tipping his head back, he looked up, his gaze widening in awe. The slender winter moon looked almost like an intruder amongst the canopy of stars, some of which looked close enough to touch, bright, like welcoming windows of light in a vast darkened abyss, while the myriad of others were scattered far and wide like so much fairy dust in the swept enormous heavens.

'Stunning.' Nick's voice was hushed.

Wordlessly, Abbey followed his gaze and felt her heart contract. 'Yes,' she agreed in a small voice, and didn't object when his fingers sought hers and tightened.

'You…haven't mentioned Todd.' The words slipped a bit disjointedly from Abbey. They were halfway through their roast dinners, their glasses of smooth merlot almost untouched beside their plates.

Nick gave her a brief, narrowed look and then dropped his gaze. 'I wasn't sure if the subject was taboo. But to answer the question you're probably burning to ask, he's going great guns. Even talking of getting involved in the sporting wheelies. In fact, I believe Ben Bristow, one of our champions from the Sydney paralympics, has been to see him.'

'Oh, that's fabulous. Sunningdale couldn't have managed anything like that for him,' Abbey said with quiet honesty. 'I imagine Todd would take to any kind of sporting challenge like a duck to water.'

'And Ben's influence will be invaluable.' Nick picked up his glass unhurriedly and took a mouthful of wine. 'His own story is not dissimilar to Todd's. Ben was a brilliant athlete, training for a triathlon event, when his spinal column was damaged after a road accident. It happened about five years ago. But he picked himself up, and now his list of sporting achievements would put an able-bodied athlete to shame. Consequently, he's become a bit of a hero,

especially to disabled kids. He and Todd would seem
to have that in common as well.'

Nick put his glass down and went quietly on with
his meal, leaving Abbey feeling less than proud of
how she'd berated him about his handling of Todd's
care. 'I should apologise,' she said, and Nick arched
an eyebrow.

'About how I reacted, when you told me what had
been decided about Todd.' Her downcast lashes
fanned darkly across her cheekbones. 'I—I know it's
no excuse, but I felt, as his GP, I'd been left entirely
out of the consultative process.'

His mouth compressed. 'I never in a million years
would have wanted you to feel I'd put you down in
some way. So that's why you let loose on me.' He
smiled a bit crookedly, as if recalling the conversation. 'I must admit I was confused about your reaction.'

Abbey picked absently at her food. 'Perhaps I was
feeling a bit…*intense* about things when you called.'

'Perhaps we both were,' he concurred quietly.

An awkward silence descended over them, until
Nick rescued the situation smoothly. 'You know you
were way off the track about Amanda Steele, Abbey.
I didn't hijack her to the detriment of Sunningdale.
Her moving to the Dennison was a reciprocal arrangement with one of the OTs there. And it's only a temporary arrangement until Todd gains enough confidence in his ability to cope.'

'Now I feel doubly foolish,' Abbey wailed. 'And
on the phone, I must have sounded so…'

'Insecure?' Nick prompted with a smile.

'All right—insecure,' Abbey echoed in a small voice but nearly smiling.

'So...' He put his hand out towards her. 'Have we sorted that out now? Put an end to your... insecurities?'

She held her breath, looking straight into his eyes, feeling the sensual charge of his thumb tracing the top of her hand. Every nerve in her body was singing with sensation. Her heart thumped against her ribs and she wondered starkly whether, instead, her insecurities around this man were just beginning...

When she woke next morning, Abbey couldn't shake off the feeling of unreality.

But within seconds the soft closing of Nick's bedroom door and his muffled footsteps along the hall put paid to any fanciful idea that she may have dreamed his presence under her roof.

But where on earth was he going at this ungodly hour? She frowned at the clock-radio on her bedside table and stifled a groan. The man's mad, she decided, turning over and pulling the duvet up to her chin.

She was in the kitchen and dressed for work when she discovered the reason for him disappearing so early.

'Morning, Abbey.' He surged into the kitchen via the back door.

Her eyebrows lifted. 'You've been out running!'

Nick gave a warm, rich chuckle. 'Give the lady a prize for observation.' He'd obviously discarded his trainers in the adjoining laundry. He padded across the tiled floor in his thick sports socks. Looking thoroughly at home, he helped himself from the jug of orange juice Abbey had squeezed earlier and left on the counter. 'May I?' The glass was already halfway to his lips.

She nodded, suddenly utterly aware of the very essence of him. Heavens, he stripped well. She swallowed against the sudden dryness in her throat. He was wearing black shorts and a black and white striped football jersey that had obviously seen better days, but that only served to make him look deliciously rumpled and as sexy as—

'Where did you go?' She held tightly on to her tea-mug, trying not to notice the ripple of his thigh muscles and the faint sheen of healthy male sweat in the shallow dip of his collar-bone where the neck of his jersey had fallen open.

'Someone's paddock, I think.' He drained his glass and refilled it halfway. 'I did a couple of laps of the helipad and then I climbed through the fence near the lagoon.'

'That would be the Dwyers' place.' Abbey slid off the tall stool and rinsed her mug at the sink.

He turned to her with a grin. 'They wouldn't have mistaken me for a wallaby and taken a shot at me, would they?'

Abbey made a click of exasperation. 'The farmers don't go round shooting randomly at anything that moves! Besides, you're way too tall for a wallaby,' she reproved, and he grinned, propping himself against the counter and crossing his ankles.

'Do you run every day?' she asked.

'When I can. And when I can't manage it, I use the air walker at home.' He raised his glass and swallowed the rest of his juice. 'I work long hours in Theatre. I need to be fitter than most.'

Abbey blinked. She'd never thought of it quite like that, but she guessed he was right. He certainly would need excellent physical stamina to stay alert and on top of his very demanding speciality. 'There's a sports track at the showgrounds,' she told him. 'I believe the early-morning joggers use that. I'll show you where it is later, if you like.'

'Thanks, but I think I'll stick to the paddocks. I like the sense of freedom running alone gives me.'

In a nervous gesture Abbey ran her hands down the sides of her tailored trousers. She couldn't help thinking Nick Tonnelli was one dangerous, potent mix and with no surgical list to keep him occupied for the next month, all that latent masculinity and coiled physical energy was going to need an outlet.

Just the thought that it all could be directed at her made her say, jerkily, 'Um, if you want breakfast, there's muesli in the pantry. And low-fat milk in the fridge.'

'I can't stand that stuff!' He shot her a rueful grin. 'Better add whole milk to the shopping list, hmm?'

Abbey gave him a pained look. 'I take it wholemeal bread is acceptable?'

'Very.'

'And canola spread? Or do you indulge in lashings of butter for your toast?'

He tapped her on the end of her nose with the tip of one finger. 'Canola's fine. Are you going across to the surgery now?'

'Shortly.'

'Like me to do a hospital round, then?'

Her mouth kicked up in a smile. 'Dressed like that? Hardly, Doctor. Even in Wingara, we like to observe some semblance of respectability for visiting medical officers.' With a quick twist of her slim body, she dodged the teatowel he threw at her.

Giving release to a wry chuckle, Nick turned to the sink to rinse his glass and then put the jug of juice in the fridge. 'I'll shower and make myself respectable first. That do?'

'Nicely. And when you've finished your hospital round, you may like to come over to the surgery. I'm sure Meri will be more than happy to clue you in about our style of paperwork and anything else you'll need to know about how the place runs. And don't forget I'll need your help with the grocery shopping this afternoon.'

'So bossy,' he grumbled, turning to refill the kettle at the sink, but Abbey could see the smile hovering around the corners of his mouth.

'I like to be organised,' she defended herself lightly, quite unable to stop her own smile. And five minutes later, as she made her way out to the carport, she was conscious of an absurd sense of light-heartedness.

Flipping open the door of her four-wheel-drive and settling in behind the wheel, she was suddenly over-whelmed with a rush of feeling. Oh, heck! Leaving aside the undoubted physical attraction Nick's body presented, was it just possible she was beginning to actually *like* the man?

*　　*　　*

Abbey's last consultation was over by eleven o'clock and Nick had joined her in the staff kitchen for a coffee-break.

'Do you normally finish about this time?' He took another slice of the apple cake he'd bought from the local bakery. 'This isn't half-bad.' He grinned, tucking in unabashedly.

'The way your eyes lit up when Meri mentioned chocolate biscuits and now this.' She pointed to the crumbly mess on his plate. 'I'm beginning to wonder if you've a shocking sweet tooth,' Abbey said laughingly.

'No worries, Doc.' Nick sprawled back in his chair, looking smug. 'This baby will run it off easily. Now, what about your Saturday surgery?'

Abbey became serious. 'I usually start at eight, earlier if it's necessary. Some of the rural workers have special needs, like a limited timeframe when they get into town. So I do my best to accommodate them. But normally I'm through by noon.' She twitched a wry smile. 'Meri books only what's essential, otherwise I'd never be out of the place.' She tilted her head in query. 'So, what about your morning, then? How was your ward round?'

'Different.' They exchanged smiles of understanding. 'Rhys was on duty so I made his acquaintance, and Brent's parents turned up early so I had a word with them as well.'

'And Brent seemed eager to go home?'

'Oh, yes.' Nick grinned. 'Quite an air of self-importance about him.'

'Mainly thanks to you,' Abbey said softly.

'Abbey, don't labour this. We're…' The rest of

Nick's words were lost when Meri popped her head in the door.

'We have an emergency, folks.' She darted a quick worried look from one to the other. 'Rhys Macklin's on the line. They've had a call from a mobile at Jumbuck Ridge. One of a party of climbers is in strife.'

'I'll speak,' Abbey said briskly. 'Could you put the call through to my room, please, Meri?'

Nick shot her a sharp look, as they simultaneously sprang to their feet. 'How far is it to this place?'

'About twenty K's out.' Abbey pushed open the door of her consulting room, sensing his presence close behind. 'But we've no ambulance available to-day. We've only the one and it left this morning to transport a patient to Hopeton for kidney dialysis.'

'So we're it?'

'Looks like it.' Abbey picked up the phone.

Arms folded, Nick took up his stance against the window-ledge, listening with scarcely concealed impatience as Abbey fired questions into the mouthpiece. He could hardly comprehend the implications of having no ambulance available.

But surely to heaven they had an alternative procedure they followed in emergencies like this—or was it in the end all down to Abbey? He shook his head, the realisation of the terrifying uncertainties she probably faced on a regular basis shocking his equilibrium like the chill of an icy-cold shower on a winter's morning.

'Fine. Thanks, Rhys.' Abbey replaced the receiver and snapped her gaze to Nick. 'Right, we have a clearer picture now. Apparently, it's an abseiling group from the high school—seven students, one PE teacher, one parent.'

'And?' Instinctively, Nick had moved closer.

'The last one of the student team to descend pushed out too far. He came back in at an angle instead of front-on to the cliff and appears to have come up against some kind of projecting rock and knocked himself out. Fortunately, his locking device has activated and that's saved him from further injury.'

Nick's breath hissed through his teeth. 'So, we can assume he's still unconscious.'

'Would seem so.'

'Then we'd better get cracking.'

'We'll take my vehicle.' Abbey began locking drawers and cabinets. 'And we'll need to stop off at home and change into tracksuits and some non-slip footwear and then swing by the hospital. Rhys will have a trauma kit ready for us.'

'I've been on to Geoff Rogers.' Meri was just putting the phone down as they sped through Reception. 'The police sergeant,' she elaborated for Nick's benefit. 'He'll do his best to round up an SES crew. But it's Saturday—the guys could be anywhere.' She bit her lip. 'Want me to stay here at the surgery in case…?' Meri drew to a halt and shrugged helplessly.

'Lock up and go home, Meri.' Abbey was firm. 'There's nothing further you can do here. We'll coordinate everything through the hospital.'

Meri nodded. 'OK. Mind how you both go.'

'So, apart from the injured student, do we know what kind of scenario we're facing when we get to this Jumbuck Ridge?' Nick asked. They'd left the town proper behind and were now travelling as fast as Abbey dared on the strip of country road.

'The rest of the youngsters plus the parent have already made their descent and are at the base of the cliff. The teacher, Andrew Parrish, is at the top. But he's more or less helpless until help arrives.'

'In the form of you and me.' Nick scraped a hand around his jaw, considering their options.

'Yes.' Abbey's eyes clouded with faint uncertainty. 'Can you abseil?'

'I've done a bit. But not for a while,' he qualified. 'You can, I take it?'

'Steve urged me to get the gist of it when I'd signed the contract to come out here. I learned the basics at one of those artificial walls at the gym first and then Andrew kindly gave me a few practical lessons after I'd taken up residence.' She sent him a tight little smile. 'I didn't want to appear like a wimp and have to stand on the sidelines every time something like this happened.'

'As if abseiling would come under your job description,' Nick growled, his eyes on the brush of flowering red and yellow lantana that flanked the roadside. 'And how many times have you had to *throw* yourself into your work like this?' he asked pithily, clamping down on his fear-driven thoughts for her safety.

'A few, but it doesn't get any easier.' Abbey gunned the motor to take a steep incline. 'This is the first time we've been without an ambulance, though.'

'Then let's hope the State Emergency lads will get there before too long. I take it they'll make their way to the base of the cliff and wait for us?'

'Yes.' Abbey felt the nerves of her stomach screw down tight at the thought of the logistics involved in the retrieval of the injured youth, let alone without the back-up of an ambulance at the end of it. 'It's a pretty rough track but they have a kind of troop-carrier vehicle. And they'll be able to improvise so we'll end up with an ambulance of sorts.'

They were quiet then, each occupied with their own very different thoughts.

Physical education teacher Andrew Parrish was waiting for them at the clifftop. 'This is a real stuff-up,' he said grimly, after Abbey had skimmed over the introductions.

'So, do we have a name and how far down is the boy?' Nick demanded, already beginning some warm-up arm and shoulder stretches for the physical demands of the descent ahead.

'The lad's name is Grant Halligan,' Andrew said. 'Aged sixteen. By my estimation, he's about twenty metres down.' He looked at Nick as if sizing up his capabilities. 'Uh…I don't know how savvy you are with any of this, Doc…'

'I've abseiled enough to know what I'm doing.'

'OK, then.' Andrew looked at him keenly. 'Grant obviously needs medical attention so one of you will have to drop down to him—'

'We'll both go,' Abbey cut in, her raised chin warning Nick not to argue.

'I'll organise a harness for each of you, then.' The teacher looked relieved to be getting on with things. 'Doc, you're obviously physically stronger than

Abbey so, as well as your normal sit-harness, I'd like you to wear the special retrieval harness.'

Nick's dark brows flexed in query.

'It's a full-body harness.' Andrew pointed out the sturdy shoulder straps and leg loops. 'If Grant's out of it, and it looks as though he is, you're going to have to attach his harness to yours to get him down safely.'

Abbey bit her lip. 'That doesn't sound like it's going to be terribly easy, Andrew.'

'We'll cope,' Nick snapped. 'Now, could we move it, please?'

Silently and quickly, they climbed into the borrowed abseiling gear. Automatically tightening the waist belt above his hips, Nick felt the unmistakable dip in his stomach. Suddenly the smooth order of his operating room seemed light years away. And much, much safer.

'Now take these clip-gates,' Andrew instructed, handing Nick the metal locking devices. 'They're the best and easiest to operate in case you happen to have only one hand free. And when you've secured Grant to your harness, you can cut his line away.'

'With this?' Nick looked dubiously at the instrument Andrew pressed into his hand, no more than a small piece of sheathed metal.

'Don't worry. It's sharp enough to skin a rabbit,' Andrew said knowledgeably. 'So watch how you handle it.'

Nick grunted and slid the knife into an accessible pocket.

'Abbey, you set?' Andrew touched her shoulder.

'Yes.' She swallowed the dryness in her throat,

checking the trauma kit's bulk which she'd anchored at the rear just below her bottom. 'If we're ready, then?' Her eyes met Nick's and clung.

'Ready.'

'Don't forget, now, Nick, you'll have Grant's extra weight on your line.' Andrew issued last-minute urgent instructions. 'So be aware of the sudden impact when you cut the line away. But I'll have you firmly anchored and it'll be fairly smooth sailing from where he's stuck right down to the base. Just steady as she goes, OK?'

'Fine.' Nick's teeth were clamped. Adrenalin was pumping out of him and already the tacky feel of sweat was annoyingly obvious down the ridge of his backbone.

Minute by minute his respect for Abbey's dedication to her responsibilities as a doctor in this isolated place had grown.

Along with his fears for her.

How the hell did she cope, living with this insidious kind of pressure? How? She was one gutsy lady—that went without saying. But surely enough was enough!

Whatever means he had to use and however he had to use them, he resolved he'd take her away from it all.

And sooner rather than later.

CHAPTER SEVEN

BOUNCING down the granite face of the cliff, Nick felt his skill returning. Cautiously, he cast a look downwards, just able to glimpse their patient in his bright yellow sweatshirt. 'We're nearly there,' he called to Abbey, who was slightly above him and to his left. 'Slacken off.'

'I hear you.' Abbey paid out her rope little by little, moving on down the rockface until she was alongside him.

'Right—this'll do us.' Nick signalled and together they swung in as closely as they could to the boy. 'And the gods are surely with us...' Nick's voice lightened as they landed on a ledge of rock and he began testing its viability. Finally, he managed to position his feet so that he was more or less evenly balanced. 'This should hold both of us, Abbey. Close up now.'

'I'm with you...' She edged in beside him.

Nick's gaze swung to her. She looked pale. A swell of protectiveness surged into his gut. 'You OK?'

'Piece of cake.' Her brittle laugh jagged eerily into the stillness.

Grant Halligan was hanging in space, quite still. But the top part of his inert body had drooped so far forward he was almost bent double into a U-shape.

Nick swore under his breath. 'Another couple of

centimetres of gravity and he'd have turned completely upside down. OK, Abbey, let's reel him in.'

'Can you reach him from there?'

'Just about…'

With sickening dread, she watched as Nick edged perilously along the ledge, making the most of his long reach to grip the boy's waist harness and guide him in close to the cliff face. Lord, were they already too late?

Grant's colour was glassily blue. If they didn't act fast, he would be in danger of going into full cardiac arrest. And how they would begin to deal with that, suspended as they were on the side of a cliff, was something Abbey didn't want to contemplate.

Gingerly she positioned herself to receive Grant's torso and support his head. 'Right, I've got him!' Immediately she began to equalise the position of his head and neck, which would automatically clear his airway. 'How's his pulse?'

Nick's forehead creased in a frown. 'It's there but it's faint. And no breath sounds. Damn.' He dragged in a huge breath and in one swift movement bent to deliver five quick mouth-to-mouth breaths into their patient.

'Bingo…' Abbey let her own breath go in relief as the boy began to splutter and then cough.

'Best sound in the world.' Nick's voice roughened. 'But he's still well out of it. Grab me the torch, Abbey!' Automatically, he took Grant's weight so Abbey could access the trauma kit.

Tight-lipped, she leant into her sit-in harness and almost in slow motion slid her hand down, feeling around for the pocket containing the pencil torch.

Convulsively, her fingers wrapped around it but then she fumbled getting it out, almost dropping it.

'Oh—help!' Her stomach heaved and she could feel the sudden perspiration patch wetly across her scalp under her safety hat. 'Here…' She swallowed jerkily and handed the torch to Nick.

Nick's face was set in concentration as he flicked the light into the boy's eyes. 'Equal and reacting,' he relayed, feeling the tightness in his temples ease fractionally. But they still had a mountain of uncharted territory to traverse before anyone could begin to relax.

So, no bleed into the brain, Abbey interpreted Nick's findings silently. She gnawed at her lip. 'His knee seems to be at an odd angle.'

'I had noticed.' Nick began feeling around for the clip-gates attached to a runner looped over his shoulder. The injured knee was an added complication. The sooner they got the kid down and treated, the better. He lowered his gaze to where Grant's injury was just visible below the coloured leg-band of his shorts. The scraped skin was of little importance but his instincts were telling him that the puffy state of the student's knee and the blood seeping from the wound the rock had inflicted were matters for concern.

'He's obviously hit the rock with some force,' Nick surmised. 'Possibly after he banged his head and lost control. I can't do much from here. I'll look at him properly when we get him down.'

Watching Nick clench his fingers across the special clips that would anchor Grant to his harness, Abbey felt a swirl of nervous tension in her stomach. 'Are we about to try and hitch him to you now?'

'We can't hang about—sorry, joke,' he said heavily. 'But this could be tricky. I'm going to have to try to align Grant's body to mine, chest to chest. That's the only way I can anchor him to my harness.'

Abbey's nerves tightened. 'In practical terms, how do you want to work it, then?'

Nick gave an irritated snort. 'Like I do this for a living!'

In other words, your guess is as good as mine. Charming! She knew he was uptight but there was no need to snap her head off. Swallowing a sharp retort, she beat back a sudden wave of nausea, the result of inadvertently looking down.

'Abbey?' For a moment they looked at each other and Nick's mouth twisted with faint mockery. 'Sorry for my lapse just then.' His hand tightened on her shoulder, his gaze winging back to their patient. He took an obviously deep controlling breath. 'We'll manoeuvre Grant upright now. I'll help as much as I can, but I'll have to concentrate on getting him adjacent to my own body so I can secure the clip-gates to both our harnesses. OK, let's do it. But keep it slow and steady...'

It was useless. Abbey shook her head in despair. It was like trying to steady a ton-weight balloon with a piece of string. Grant was a well-built young man, his unconscious state only adding to their difficulties. And in their precarious position, it was well nigh impossible to co-ordinate the lift so the two harness belts were close enough to link.

'This isn't going to work.' Nick's lean, handsome face was stretched tautly. His shoulders slumped and he shook his head.

Abbey sensed his anguish. But they couldn't give up now. Grant's life could well depend on their teamwork. She pushed down her fears. 'Give me the clipgates, Nick.'

His head went back as though she'd struck him. 'Are you mad? Grant's way too heavy and you're not wearing the right harness—'

'Stop trying to be a hero,' she snapped. 'And anyway, I didn't mean I'd try to take him. But we have to get a resolution here, Nick. It's not working—when you're steady, he's either too high or too low.'

'Well, I'd gathered that, Abbey,' he spat sarcastically.

She squeezed her eyes shut for a second and counted to ten. 'Could you link your hands under his behind and try to lift him to your waist? Then I could make a grab for his harness and snap you together.'

Nick's jaw tightened. 'Hell!' he spat the word between clenched teeth. 'I hate not being in control of this situation. I hate it!' But nevertheless he did what Abbey had suggested, gripping Grant, lifting him as high as he could, his muscles straining with the effort.

Abbey was pale and tight-lipped, knowing she had only the barest window of opportunity to hitch the two harnesses before Nick's hold on the boy would of necessity have to slacken. She steadied her breathing, conscious of almost choreographing her movements.

'I…can't hold him much longer.' Nick gasped, pulling his torso back so Abbey could use what little access there was between him and the injured youth. 'Now!' he yelled. 'Quick—or I've lost him!'

In a flash and remembering everything she'd been

taught, Abbey used her feet in a technique called 'smearing', where most of the climber's weight was positioned over one foot to reduce the overall load on the arms. Twisting slightly, she turned her upper body so that her arm closest to the rockface could counterbalance her movement and give her other arm maximum extension…

'Now! Abbey…' What the hell was taking her so long? The muscles of Nick's throat and around his mouth were locked in a grimace and sweat pooled wetly in his lower back. His mind was so concentrated he hardly felt the nudge of Abbey's fingers as she secured one then quickly two more clip-gates to link the two men.

'Done…' Her voice was barely above a whisper.

Abbey hardly remembered how they'd got down. She only remembered the relief she'd felt when Nick had cut Grant's rope and they could begin their descent.

And there were plenty of hands to help them once they were safely on the ground. A subdued cheer had even gone up. Grant was released from his harness and placed on the stretcher provided by the State Emergency Service personnel.

Abbey divested herself of her own harness, dimly aware her legs felt as unsteady as a puppet's.

'I'll take that, Abbey.' Terry French, the leader of the SES team, hurried to her side to unclip the trauma kit and heft it across his shoulder. 'You did a great job.'

'Thanks, Terry, but I couldn't have made it without Dr Tonnelli.'

'He did well.'

Abbey gave in to a tight little smile. That, from the usually laconic SES leader, was high praise. She must remember to tell Nick—that's if they were still speaking…

'But it's the last time young Parrish pulls something like today's effort,' Terry said forcefully.

'Oh?' Abbey's eyes widened in query.

'He should've checked the ambulance was available, and when it wasn't he should've cancelled the abseiling. *And* he had no business taking that many kids without another trained adult. I'll have something to say at the next P and C meeting, I can tell you.'

Well, the Parents and Citizens committee could sort all that out later, Abbey thought wearily. All that mattered now was Grant's welfare.

Quickly, she pulled her thoughts together. She removed her safety hat, shook out her hair and began making her way across to where Nick was already leaning over the stretcher to attend to their patient.

Abbey could see Grant had begun to come round but he seemed confused and emotional. 'It's OK, Grant.' She bent to reassure him. 'You'll be fine,' she murmured over and over, rubbing warmth into his hands.

'Could we have the portable oxygen unit over here, please?' Nick began issuing orders, a deep cleft between his dark brows. 'And a space blanket.'

'Anything presenting yet?' Abbey watched as he palpated the boy's stomach.

'Feels soft enough so no spleen damage. Check his breath sounds, please, Abbey.'

'Bit raspy.' Abbey folded the stethoscope away. 'Could be a lower rib fracture. What about his knee?'

Nick was gently manipulating the swollen joint, his look intense. 'Fractured kneecap,' he said shortly. 'No doubt about it. But I can fix that.'

Abbey's gaze widened in alarm. 'You'll operate here at Wingara?'

'I thought that's what you wanted, Abbey.' His voice was suddenly hard. 'A specialist to come to the patient.'

Abbey bit her lips together. Nick's arbitrary decision had literally taken control right out of her hands.

Again.

Her mind flew ahead. Was their little operating theatre up to it at short notice? Given that it could be, this was still her practice and her patient. So, didn't that make her the MO in charge? But surely it would be petty in the extreme to start pulling rank when Nick's suggestion made perfect sense?

She had only a few seconds to decide on a course of action. Terry was already liaising with the CareFlight base. The sharp prongs of indecision tore at her and wouldn't let go.

'We'll run normal saline.' Nick was inserting the cannula in Grant's arm as he spoke. 'We don't want him shocking on us. And would you draw up twenty-five milligrams of pethidine, please? That'll hold him until we can get him to the OR.'

Abbey hesitated.

'What?' Nick's brow darkened ominously. 'Don't we have emergency drugs with us?'

Abbey took a thin breath. Grant's eyes had fluttered open again, dulled with pain, expressing all the heart-breaking youthful uncertainty of his situation.

'Abbey!'

She seemed to come back from somewhere.

'Do you need my instructions written on a white-board?' Nick shot the words at her with the lethal softness of bullets from a silenced gun.

Stung by his air of arrogance, Abbey jerked, 'Just who made *you* the boss here, Dr Tonnelli?' As soon as the words were out, she regretted them, for his expression darkened and his mouth tightened into a grim line.

She shook her head, biting the soft inside edge of her bottom lip. This was totally unprofessional behaviour. Why on earth did Nicholas Tonnelli bring out the worst in her?

And the best, another saner, kinder voice insisted.

Smothering her resentment, she drew up the required dose and shot the painkiller home.

'That's more like it.'

His growled patronising response infuriated Abbey all over again. She drew a deep breath, almost grateful for the diversion of Terry calling her name.

'Hey, Abbey!' Terry's tone was urgent. He jogged across, his face set in concern. 'The CareFlight chopper can't get here for a couple of hours. Three-car pile-up just south of Jareel. What do you want to do?'

Click! In an instant, Abbey knew the decision regarding Grant's surgery had been made for her. She took a steadying breath before she spoke, keeping her voiced instructions low. 'Cancel our request for a chopper, please, Terry. Dr Tonnelli's a surgeon. He's offered to operate on Grant's knee here.'

The SES leader beamed. 'Well, that's a turn-up. I'll get onto CareFlight and let them know we don't need 'em this time.'

Meanwhile, *she'd* better get on to Wingara hospital. Her mouth drying with apprehension, Abbey pulled out her mobile phone. Co-ordinating everything was going to be the ultimate test of their staff's abilities to deal with an emergency. And she could only pray that Rhys would be co-operative and back the decision to open the theatre for Grant's procedure.

'It'll be fantastic to have the theatre in use again!' Rhys's enthusiastic response shot Abbey's doubts to pieces. 'What will Nick want to do?'

'He's going to be wiring Grant's patella. He can't be sure of the degree of complexity until he goes in, of course.'

'OK. I'd like to be involved and I'll do a ring-around for a couple of extra hands. Carmen and Renee should be available. They'll be glad of the chance to hone their theatre skills, I'm sure,' Rhys said confidently.

Abbey brushed a fingertip between her brows, thinking quickly. 'We'll need to cross-match blood on arrival and X-ray as necessary. Especially, we'll need some pictures of his chest. There's evidence of a fractured lower rib. And could Diane come in and hold the fort while we're in Theatre?'

'Absolutely,' Rhys confirmed. 'No worries. What's your ETA, Abbey?'

Abbey ran through the logistics in her head, casting a quick look to where Nick was supervising the stretcher lift into the emergency vehicle. The improvised ambulance would have several kilometres of slow travel over rough terrain out to the road but then they should be able to pick up speed... 'Forty-five minutes maximum, Rhys.'

'Fine. That'll give me enough time to get prepped. See you in a bit, then.'

'Oh, Rhys.' Abbey spoke urgently. 'Andrew Parrish will have contacted Grant's parents. They'll probably turn up at the hospital to wait for the chopper.'

'I'll have someone look out for them,' Rhys said calmly, 'and explain the change of plan. Tea and sympathy until either you or Nick can speak to them?'

'Thanks, Rhys.' Abbey felt a sliver of responsibility slide from her. 'That would be brilliant. See you soon.' Switching off her mobile, she moved swiftly to Nick's side.

'Ah, Abbey.' He inclined his head, his eyes gleaming with determination. 'We're about to go. I'll travel with Grant, if that's OK with you?'

'You mean you're actually asking me?' she acknowledged thinly.

His hand flew out, clamping her wrist, his dark brows snapping together. 'Don't turn territorial on me again, Abbey. This isn't the time.'

Abbey's heart thumped. Had she gone too far? 'I'll grab a lift back up to the top and collect my car,' she said throatily, feeling relief when his hand returned to his side.

'See you back at the hospital, then.' Nick's expression gentled. 'Uh...' He snapped his fingers. 'About anaesthetising Grant for the op—I forgot to ask. Can you help out? I can guide you if—'

'That won't be necessary,' she cut in. 'I did my elective in anaesthesiology at John Bosco's in Melbourne.'

'You wanted to specialise?'

Abbey stiffened. 'Is that so strange?' She turned away before he could answer.

Abbey could scarcely believe how smoothly the hospital was coping. She was still basking in a sense of real pride as she finished scrubbing.

The sound of the door swinging open sent her spinning away from the basin, and by the time Nick had begun scrubbing beside her, she was drying her hands and asking sharply, 'What size gloves do you need?'

He sent her an abrupt look from under his brows. 'Eight and a half, if the stocks can manage it. But I can get by with nine.'

'Rhys will have everything under control.' Abbey forced lightness into her tone. 'Even glove sizes, I imagine. Since the alert went out that you were going to operate, he's apparently been beavering away like you wouldn't believe.'

'I'm extremely grateful for his flexibility over this.' The tightening of Nick's mouth suggested her own compliance had been hardily won.

Abbey opened her mouth and closed it. This wasn't the time to start sniping at one another. They had a job to do on a vulnerable young patient and for that they needed calm and total professionalism.

Abruptly, she turned and left the little annexe and crossed to the theatre. Rhys had prepared the anaesthetic trolley perfectly and Abbey felt a rush of adrenalin she hadn't experienced for the longest time.

She'd do a brilliant job for Grant. And perhaps at the end of it, she might have actually appeased Nick as well. At the thought, warm colour swept up from her chest to her face, but there was no time now to consider why it mattered so much to have the wretched man's approval. But somehow it did.

An hour and a half later, the procedure was all done.

'Thanks, team. Fantastic effort.' Nick inserted the last suture in Grant's knee and signalled for Abbey to reverse the anaesthetic.

'Are this lad's climbing days over, do you think?' Rhys handed the surgeon the non-stick dressing to seal the site, and then waited with the bulky padding that would be placed over Grant's repaired kneecap.

'Not at all.' Deftly, Nick secured the wide crêpe bandage that would hold the padding in place. 'Does Wingara boast the services of a physiotherapist?'

Rhys nodded. 'Fran Rogers, the sergeant's wife, runs a practice from the sports centre.'

'She's good,' Carmen, one of the nurses assisting, chimed in. 'Sorted out the crick in my neck in a couple of sessions.'

'Sounds like we'll be in business, then.' Above his mask, Nick's eyes lit with good humour. 'OK, guys, that's it.' He stepped back from the operating table, working his shoulders briefly. 'I'd like Grant's leg elevated on pillows for the next twenty-four hours, please. And I'll write him up for some antibiotics and pain relief to be going on with.' His green gaze shifted from the nurses to Abbey. 'Would you mind finishing up in here? I don't want to keep Grant's parents waiting any longer than necessary for news.'

'I don't mind at all.' Abbey paused and then added huskily, 'That was a fine piece of work, Nick.'

Nick's eyes met hers and held. 'You made it easy,

Dr Jones. We make a good team.' With that, he turned on his heel and left the theatre.

There seemed nothing more she could do at the hospital, so Abbey made her way home. Letting herself in, she acknowledged a feeling of vagueness, as if her body and mind were operating on autopilot.

It had been the oddest kind of day.

Walking into the kitchen, she looked around, registering her and Nick's breakfast dishes neatly stacked in the drainer.

A soft breath gusted from her mouth and she shook her head. Had it been only this morning they'd stood here fooling about like teenagers, exchanging light-hearted banter?

Absently, she turned on the tap and got herself a glass of water. Peering through the kitchen window as she drank it, she noticed that already the afternoon was rapidly drawing to a close, the sunset throwing huge splashes of dark pink and gold into the sky.

She lingered, watching several wood doves flutter in and out of the shrubbery before settling for the night. What was it about this time of the day that made her feel so introspective, so lonely, so strangely vulnerable?

'Mind sharing the view?'

Nick's soft footfall and equally softly spoken question had Abbey spinning round, a hand to her heart. She swallowed jerkily. 'I didn't realise you were home.'

'Have been for some time.'

His smile left a lingering warmth in his eyes and Abbey felt her heart lurch.

'I reassured Grant's parents and left a few post-op instructions with Diane. There didn't seem much else you needed me for. There wasn't, was there?'

She faltered, 'No—not really.' She desperately needed a hug but she couldn't tell him *that*. Her eyes flew over him. He'd obviously showered and changed into comfortable cargo pants and a navy long-sleeved sweatshirt.

Nick tilted his head, his eyes narrowing. 'You look shattered.'

'Thanks!' She lifted her chin, spinning back to the window, putting her glass down with a little thump in the sink. Was he saying she wasn't up to it? That she couldn't cope with one medical emergency? 'That's real music to my ears, I don't think!'

Nick clicked his tongue. 'Don't go all huffy on me, Abbey. I'm trying to help, dammit. Why don't you let me? For starters, are you hungry? I know I am.'

Abbey half turned to him. She supposed she was. They'd had nothing since his apple cake at morning tea. Perhaps it was hunger that was making her feel so hollowed out, so on edge around him. She nibbled the edge of her lower lip. 'We—we didn't get round to doing our grocery shopping, did we? And the supermarket will be closed by now.'

'I'm sure the pantry will yield up something edible.' His eyes captured hers. 'If not, I'll improvise.'

'You'll cook?'

'I don't just wield a knife in the OR, you know.' He flashed her a heart-thudding grin. 'I'll knock up some kind of pasta to delight your palate, OK?'

'Very OK.' Abbey felt her gastric juices react in expectation. 'There's bound to be a can of tomatoes in the pantry,' she said, warming to the idea. 'And I'm almost certain there's pasta of some description in a glass jar—'

'I'll find everything.' Nick's hands dropped to her shoulders to give her an insistent little nudge towards the door. 'Go and have a relaxing bath or whatever.'

Abbey made it to the doorway and turned back. 'There are a few herbs in pots at the bottom of the back steps—'

'Out, Dr Jones!' Nick waved an arm to get rid of her. 'I'm doing this. Go and have your bath.'

She sent him a wide-eyed innocent look. 'I prefer showers.'

He sighed audibly. 'Then have a nice relaxing shower, for Pete's sake. Now, scoot, before I lose all control and join you there.'

That did it. 'Consider me gone.'

Nick waited until he heard the soft click of her bedroom door, then lowered his head, bracing his arms against the bench. Hell, it was taking all his will-power not to follow her. But that was not the way. Every instinct was telling him that.

Ruefully, he looked down at his white-knuckled grip on the edge of the benchtop. It would be the death knell to his hopes if he rushed her. But holding back was hard—harder than anything he'd ever had to do.

CHAPTER EIGHT

ABBEY got out of the shower knowing she was in a state of wild anticipation of the evening ahead.

Oh, for heaven's sake, get a grip! Giving herself the silent admonishment, she padded through to the bedroom. It was merely going to be a quiet evening at home with a colleague, accompanied by an impromptu meal. And perhaps said colleague was a dud cook anyway and the food would be awful...

Who was she kidding? She gave a jagged laugh, throwing her softest, sleekest pair of jeans across the bed, then collected lacy underclothes from the bureau drawer.

The evening wasn't about colleagues or food, good or bad. It was about a man and a woman. And they both knew it!

With an effort, she managed to get her thoughts under control, dressing quickly in her jeans and a close-fitting red V-necked pullover. The colour gave her a sense of power, she decided. Besides, it went well with her complexion.

She took in a calming breath and then picked up her brush, stroking it almost roughly through her hair. In a final dash of bravado, she coloured her mouth expertly with a rose lipstick and fluffed on a light spray of perfume. After one last glimpse in the mirror, she left her bedroom and made her way along the hallway to the kitchen.

Nick was bent over the cook top. The pasta was boiling merrily and he was stirring something in a saucepan on another hotplate. 'Something smells good,' she said, sniffing the appetising aroma as she peered over his shoulder.

'It's getting there.' Grinning, he turned his head and kissed her, a sweet undemanding little smooch that took her by surprise. 'What about setting the table?'

'So, does this concoction have a name?' Abbey got down some large bowls for their pasta.

Nick gave the pot a final stir. 'Officially, Tortiglioni alla zingara. But this version has sweet potato instead of aubergine, otherwise it's pretty much authentic.' He drained the pasta with a flourish and gave it a shake. 'I've left the Parmesan separate— not everyone cares for it.'

Her mouth watering, Abbey watched as he swirled the pasta into a large bowl and then folded the rich red sauce through it. 'It's hardly Italian fare without it, though, is it?'

'Probably not.' Lifting a hand, he playfully ran the tip of his finger down her nose and across the top of her cheek. 'I found some oregano as well in one of your pots. I haven't managed to prepare it yet.'

'I'll do that.' Her heart gave a sideways skip and she gave an off-key little laugh, stepping away from him to the worktop. She took up the rather scraggy-looking bunch of leaves. 'Should I chop it or tear it?'

'Roughly chop, please.' Nick was precise. 'And then chuck it over the pasta.'

They ate with obvious enjoyment. 'How did I do,

then?' Nick gave her a look so warm that Abbey caught her breath.

She coloured faintly. 'You did so well I might just keep you.' She laughed. 'Honestly, Nick, this is wonderful.'

He lifted a shoulder modestly. 'But, then, we were both starving, weren't we? Probably bread and cheese would've seemed like a feast.' Something flickered in his gaze, something Abbey couldn't immediately define, and then he looked away.

'It's still very early, isn't it?' They'd come to the end of the meal and Abbey cast around for something to say, and in the process sent a distracted look at the quaint little cuckoo clock on the wall.

'Meaning what, exactly?' Nick's gaze shimmered over her face and then roamed to register the gleam of lamplight in her hair and on the ridge of her collarbone. Hell's bells, he could almost taste her...

Abbey felt panic-stricken. What on earth were they to do with the long evening ahead? What did Nick expect to do? Her teeth caught on her lower lip as she drummed up an awkward smile. 'Meaning, do you play Scrabble—or Trivial Pursuit?'

His gaze went briefly to the ceiling. 'I've a much better idea. Let's make some coffee and take it through to the lounge. Is it cool enough for a fire, do you suppose?'

'Oh, yes, I should think so.' Glad of something to do, Abbey shot to her feet. 'The kindling's all there. If you'd do that, I'll make the coffee.'

She took as long as she dared. Finally, when it was obvious she couldn't delay any longer, she picked up the tray of coffee and walked through the arched doorway to the lounge room.

Nick had the fire going and he'd lit one table lamp at the end of the comfortable old sofa. He was sitting under the light, leafing through one of her *Town and Country* magazines, and when she walked in he looked directly at her, his face still in shadow. 'I thought you must have gone to Brazil for the coffee beans,' he said blandly.

Abbey felt herself beginning to flush. 'Sorry if I was a bit long. I stacked the dishwasher as well.'

He raised a dark eyebrow. 'I didn't know we had one.'

'It's in the laundry for the moment.' She placed the tray on the mahogany chest in front of the fire. 'We're still waiting for the plumber to do the necessary adjustment so it can go in the kitchen,' she lamented. 'It certainly would make things a lot easier.'

'Well, don't look at me!' Nick raised his hands in mock horror. 'My mechanical skills stop a long way short of anything to do with plumbing.'

'Surely you can replace a tap washer?' she teased.

He looked baffled. 'Taps have washers? That's news to me.'

Abbey's mouth tucked in on a grin as she sent down the plunger on the coffee. They were shadow dancing again—fooling about, as if it was obvious to both of them that if their conversation became too serious, too personal, it would all be too confronting.

And because anything else would have seemed ridiculous, she took her place beside him on the sofa, feeling his gaze on her as she leant over and poured his coffee.

'Thanks.' Nick's fingers brushed hers as she handed him the steaming brew. 'That smells wonderful.' His mouth quirked in the faintest smile. 'Well worth the trip to Brazil.'

Abbey hiccuped a laugh and their gazes met and clung. His look was warm and heavy and on reflex she moistened parched lips. His gaze dropped to her mouth, almost burning her with intent.

With fingers that shook, Abbey poured her own coffee, taking several deep breaths to steady herself.

'How long does your contract have to run?' he asked.

She swallowed the sudden dryness in her throat. Where on earth had that sprung from? 'Six months or thereabouts. Why?'

'Just wondered.' He took a careful mouthful of his coffee. 'Any plans to come back to the coast?'

At his question, their gazes swivelled and caught and Nick's eyes held hers for a long moment, before he looked down broodingly into his coffee-cup.

'I...hadn't actually thought about it.' Leaving her coffee untouched on the tray, Abbey wrapped her arms around her midriff, as if warding off his question. 'It would be very difficult to find a replacement. The people had been waiting for over a year for a full-time medical officer when I came.'

'So, what are you saying?' Nick's jaw hardened. 'That you're bound here by some kind of emotional and ethical blackmail?'

Abbey's sound of disgust indicated what she thought of that. 'Does it occur to you I might like it here?'

'It sure looked like you were having a barrel of

laughs coming down that cliff today,' he growled. 'I hate the thought of you taking those kinds of risks, Abbey.'

She bristled. 'For heaven's sake, Nick! It's not like Wingara has a team of paramedics on call. Attending the scene of an accident is my job!'

The silence fell thickly between them.

Jerkily, Abbey picked up her coffee, taking several quick mouthfuls. 'You can't tell me what to do, Nick,' she said quietly. 'It's none of your business anyway.'

'What if I were to make it my business?'

'And how would you do that?' More composed now, although her heart was rattling against her rib-cage, she turned her head towards him, leaning back into the softness of the sofa, her coffee balanced high against her chest.

'Convince you to come back to Sydney with me.' His eyes locked with hers, dark in shadow, caressing, powerful.

'You're asking me to dump my patients?' She barely controlled the accusation in her voice. 'I'd have to find your offer pretty damned irresistible to make me even consider that.' Their eyes skittered away from each other and then reconnected and all of a sudden, once again, it was dangerous territory.

'Perhaps you will.'

Abbey opened her mouth and closed it and then opened it again. 'So, the chase is on, then?' she blurted, almost unable to believe they were having this conversation.

He sent her a dry smile. 'If you want to put it like that, yes, Abbey Jones, the chase is on.'

His meaning was quite clear and her response was instinctive. 'This is insane, Nick. But much more fun than Scrabble, I have to say.' She finished her coffee slowly and placed her cup back on the tray. 'So, what would you like to do now?' She tilted a slightly challenging look at him, letting her shoes drop to the floor and curling her legs beneath her.

Nick's sudden action made her jump.

'What are you doing?' she gasped, as he swung her feet around and then lifted them onto his lap.

'Just this...' With strong, supple hands, he began to massage the soles of her feet.

Abbey felt like purring. No one had ever massaged her feet before. She'd had no idea anything could be so seductive and, in a way, so liberating... 'I shouldn't be letting you do this.'

'Indulge me, hmm?' His dark head came up, his mouth curling slightly, as his hands moved up and down her feet and ankles, first her left and then right. 'Good?'

Abbey took a shaken breath then smiled, false brightness covering a multitude of mixed emotions. 'It's fantastic.'

As he'd known it would be.

'I could go to sleep,' she murmured a bit later. Her head had dropped back on the cushions and her whole body felt like liquid silk.

'I'll help you to bed,' Nick promised softly.

'No, you won't.' His words had her shooting determinedly upright, bracing her hand against the back of the sofa and preparing to lever herself off.

But Nick was quicker. Before she could properly make her move, his arms had cradled her and scooped her up. 'Bed for you, Dr Jones,' he murmured into her hair. 'It's been a very long, very full day.'

'It's not that late.'

'Maybe it's later than you think.'

'Nick, put me down!' But her outrage was muted and only half-hearted.

'Don't argue, Abbey.' He carried her easily as if she weighed no more than an armful of roses.

She made a tiny sound in her throat. It felt so good in his arms... So safe. Safe? Now, that was odd... She was aware of him opening the door to her bedroom and carrying her inside.

The moon was out in earnest now, striping the walls and the white bed cover with soft light.

'Nick...?' Abbey reached up to stroke his face, and felt him stiffen. 'Will you start the dishwasher?'

His mouth twitched. 'You're a real romantic.'

'You're trying to seduce me...'

'Of course I am.' She felt his smile on her temple as he pressed a kiss there. 'But not tonight.' He lowered her to the bed. 'Sleep well.'

'Mmm.' Her eyes were already closed.

Abbey rose earlier than usual next morning but it was obvious Nick had risen earlier still. She found him in the kitchen, his hands wrapped round a mug of tea.

'Oh...' Her gaze ran over his attire. 'You've already done your run.' Her tone showed her disappointment. She'd been hoping some exercise would have helped chase away the inner turmoil she'd felt from the moment she'd woken. 'I was going to come with you.'

'You have to be up early to catch me.' The sides of his mouth pleated in a dry smile. 'Sleep well?'

'Yes, thank you,' she murmured, her throat suddenly dry. Jerkily, she turned her back on him, helping herself to a cup of tea from the pot he'd made.

'You had a phone call last night.'

'Was it the hospital?' Abbey spun round, cup in hand.

Nick shook his head. 'Your friend, Andrea Fraser. I introduced myself, said you'd turned in early. She's invited us out to their place today. I accepted. I hope that's all right?'

'It's fine.' Abbey swallowed some of her tea. 'And it'll be nice. I haven't seen the Frasers in a while,' she remarked with a tiny frown. 'You'll like their property, Risden. There's a lovely expanse of river and places to picnic. What time do they want us?'

Nick lifted a shoulder. 'As soon as we'd like. I said we'd need to do a hospital round and so on first.'

'I'll do that.'

'I prefer to check my own post-op patients,' he said evenly.

So, thanks but, no, thanks. Abbey could have let it go but didn't. 'Don't you trust me to know what to look for?'

He made an impatient click with his tongue. 'It's not like we're swamped, Abbey. Lighten up.' He swung to his feet, brushing her arm as he emptied the dregs of his mug into the sink.

She moved away as if she'd been stung, his scathing tone negating any closeness she'd felt towards him last night. She brought her chin up. 'We should arrange an on-call roster, then. I certainly don't want to be treading on your precious toes every time I open my mouth.'

'Now you're being childish,' he said mildly. Dumping his mug in the sink, he walked out.

'I know who's childish!' she flung after him. 'Nick…' She went after him, catching up with him in the hallway opposite his bedroom. 'Why are you being like this?'

He folded his arms, leaning back against the wall and looking big and determined. 'Like what?'

She raised a shoulder uncertainly. 'So…cross.'

'Cross?' The word seemed to amuse him.

Abbey sucked in her breath. 'You know what I mean.' Her gaze steadied on him. The faint shadows under his eyes were obviously a residue of a restless night. Could that mean…? She felt weak suddenly, too near him. 'Didn't you sleep well?'

His shoulders lifted in a long-suffering sigh. 'I slept fine, thanks.' He rubbed a hand through his hair, his mouth compressing on a wry smile. 'I promise I'll be more reasonable after a shower and some breakfast.'

Abbey's thoughts were churning. 'I'll, um, make something, then. I'm quite good at scrambled eggs…'

Several expressions chased through his eyes. 'I know for a fact you're good at any number of things, Dr Jones,' he said, his voice not quite even. 'See you in a bit.'

They left for the Frasers' property just after ten.

'We'll take my car,' Nick said. 'Roads OK?'

'Fine.' Abbey's felt her nerves tighten. Dipping her head, she slid into the passenger seat as he held the door open for her. 'It's about fifty K's out and we'll be travelling in the opposite direction to Jumbuck Ridge,' she told him. 'The country is much more pleasant, softer.'

'So, fill me in about your friends.' Nick was obviously enjoying himself, gunning the Jag along a straight stretch of country road.

'Stuart's a born and bred local. Risden's been in his family for ever. But he's the new-breed grazier. Been away to university and all that stuff. He's a lovely guy. And Andrea and he are just so well suited. Where he's rather considered in what he does, she's all bubbly and spontaneous.'

'Do they have children?' Nick asked interestedly.

'Two. Michael who's eleven and Jazlyn who's nine, I think. They do school at home. Andi was a teacher so she's able to see to all that.'

Nick raised a dark eyebrow. 'How did they meet?'

'Andi was transferred to Wingara Primary. They met at a fundraiser for the hospital.'

For a while then there was silence, until Nick said quietly, 'It really is something special out here, isn't it?' He silenced a self-deprecating laugh, a little amazed at how some inner part of him had begun to respond almost unconsciously to the rich, bold colours of this huge landscape. The true deep blues and rusty reds were stuff from an artist's palette. And the stillness was so intense, he could almost hear his own heartbeat.

'It all kind of takes you over.' Abbey's eyes glowed. 'The landscape seems so pure and clean. And everything seems so incredibly *still*.'

He swung his head towards her and lifted an

eyebrow. 'How did you know that's what I was thinking?'

'Just did,' she answered on a half-laugh, and saw a frown notch his forehead. Now what? Was it all right for him to guess her thoughts but not the reverse? Turning her head, she stared out through the side window, her eyes following the distant line of trees that marked the river.

Her thoughts began spinning this way and that. He'd set out deliberately to spend this time with her. Was he now in a way being hoist with his own petard—being made vulnerable by the same physical closeness he'd orchestrated?

The breathtaking thought sent a wild ripple through her veins that powered to a waterfall when his hand reached out, found her fingers and carried them all the way to his lips.

'Well, aren't you the dark horse?' Andrea's blue eyes were alight with conjecture.

'Who, me?' Abbey pretended innocence. She was helping her friend stack the dishwasher after a delicious barbecue lunch of best Risden-produced steaks, potatoes cooked in their jackets in the coals and heaped helpings of salads.

'Yes, you.' A muted 'tsk' left Andrea's mouth. With brisk precision, she slotted the dinner plates into their racks in the dishwasher. 'How long has this been going on?'

Abbey felt warm colour flood her cheeks. 'Nick and I met a few weeks ago in Hopeton—at the TV station of all places. Over a medical debate scheduled for the *Countrywide* programme.'

'Oh, my gosh!' Andrea's hand went to her heart. 'That's brilliant!'

'You wouldn't have thought so if you'd been me,' Abbey said with feeling. 'Anyhow...' she lifted a shoulder expressively '...Nick kind of followed it up.'

'Followed *you* up, you mean!' Andrea was blunt. 'It's obvious something's clicked between you. He can't take his eyes off you. Are you just as keen?'

Abbey groaned. 'Andi, it's early days and it's complicated.'

'He's not married, is he?'

'Of course not!'

'Divorced with dependent children?'

'No!'

'Then, ducky, if you've fallen for him, go for it!' Andrea gave an odd little laugh. 'Not that *I'm* an expert on matters of the heart...'

Abbey looked closely at her friend. All through lunch she'd seemed unlike herself, a bit brittle—especially around her husband. Which was peculiar to say the least. Abbey frowned. Andi and Stuart had always appeared so happy together, their marriage strong...

'OK, that's all done.' Andrea set the cycle, bringing her head up and agitatedly pushing a strand of dark hair away from her face. 'Now, while Stu and the kids are giving Nick the short guided tour of Risden, let's open another bottle of wine and take ourselves out onto the veranda for a while.'

'Um, I'll just have some of your homemade lemonade, thanks, Andi.' Abbey felt a small twinge of unease. Andi was a very moderate drinker at the best of times. But today she'd had several glasses of wine with lunch, and now she was proposing to start on another bottle. But it wasn't Abbey's place to say anything...

'You're giving me your doctor's look.' Andrea's mouth tipped in a crooked smile. 'And you're probably right to stay with the soft stuff. So I'll be good and join you in a lemonade. I've the beginnings of a rotten headache anyway.'

Abbey put her hand on the other's shoulder. 'Can I get you something for it? I brought my bag.'

'I'll take a couple of paracetamol.' Andrea pressed a hand across her eyes. 'And perhaps a cup of tea might be helpful.'

'I'll make it.' Abbey turned to fill the kettle. 'Go and dose yourself and put your feet up. I'll bring the tea out in a jiffy.'

Something was definitely out of kilter here. Two little lines pleated Abbey's forehead as she filled the china teapot and placed two pretty cups and saucers on the tray. Somehow she'd have to get Andrea to open up, because Abbey's trained eye was telling her that her friend was under stress of some kind. She could only hope Andi would let her help.

They sat on the veranda in comfortable old wicker chairs and looked down over the home paddock.

'It's so peaceful here,' Abbey sighed, leaning back in the plump butter-yellow cushions.

'On the surface, yes.' Andrea's throat convulsed as she swallowed. 'I think Stuart's having an affair,' she said in an abrupt way, as if this was what had been simmering in her mind all day.

Abbey's mouth opened and closed. She shook her head. 'That's ridiculous!'

'Is it?' Andrea looked directly at Abbey and her chin lifted defensively. 'We haven't made love in weeks. All he wants to do at night is to sit in front of that bloody computer screen.'

'And that constitutes an affair?' Abbey was in total disbelief. 'Have you asked him what's going on?'

Andrea looked bleak. 'He says he's checking out the market price of beef on the internet.'

'Well, that's feasible, isn't it? It's your livelihood after all.'

'How come he logs off the second I go into his office, then? As though…' Andrea paused and bit her bottom lip. 'As though he's got something to hide?'

Oh, lord. Abbey swung off her chair and went to stand at the railings. She needed to think. Something didn't add up here. Being devious was just not in Stuart's character. Something deeper was happening. She turned her head, her eyes running over her friend's taut face. 'So, are you saying he's *met* someone on the net and it's developed into an on-line affair?'

Andrea put her cup down carefully on its saucer. 'I know it sounds a bit off the wall for Stuart—but what else could it be?' She palmed the sudden wetness away from her eyes and gave a choked laugh. 'He's certainly gone off me…'

'Honey, that's crazy talk.' Abbey stepped back quickly from the railings, pulling her chair close to the other woman's. She took Andrea's hands and held them firmly. 'It's obvious something is going on with Stu, something he can't talk about. But I'd bet my last dollar he's not been unfaithful—even in cyberspace.'

Andrea's shoulder lifted in a long sigh. 'I'm at my wit's end. That's really why I asked you to come today—I had to talk to someone and I couldn't get into Wingara. It's all been hectic here and the kids have had exams to prepare for—'

'Shh.' Abbey tightened her grip and squeezed. 'I'm glad you called. You and Stu are my friends. And, for whatever reason, I'm always happy to come to this beautiful place, you know that.'

Think. Abbey's troubled gaze left her friend's for a minute and she looked out across the dun-gold grass of the paddocks to the blue-green of the eucalyptuses that lined the stretch of river away in the distance. Suddenly, her fair head came up in query. 'Could Stuart be ill?'

Andrea looked shocked. 'Surely I would've known? I mean, he's still working all the hours God sends…'

'Well, that's what he would do,' Abbey reinforced softly. 'Keep on keeping on, pushing his fears into the background. Pretending everything was normal.'

'Oh, my God…' Andrea's hands came up to press against her cheeks. 'But why wouldn't he have gone to see you? Surely—'

'Andi, listen,' Abbey came in forcefully. 'In the first place, I'm female. Not all men are comfortable with women doctors, especially if it's something highly personal. And in the second, Stu is like every other male in rural Australia. Their health is the last thing they concern themselves with. They're indestructible, as they see it.'

'Could that be it?' Andrea pushed her hair back from her face, pleating a strand as if it helped her think. 'But if he's ill...' Her eyes widened in sudden panic. 'What should I do? Confront him or— Oh, heavens, look! They're back!'

Abbey's gaze swivelled to where the battered Land Rover was coming up the track towards the house. 'Leave it with me,' she counselled quietly. 'Nick's here for a while and he'll be in the surgery each day. Somehow, between us, we'll get Stuart in to see him for a check-up.'

CHAPTER NINE

As it turned out, Abbey found the delicate matter of persuading Stuart to see a doctor was taken right out of her hands.

On their way back to Wingara township, she chatted to Nick about their day. 'Did you enjoy your tour of the place with Stuart?' she asked.

'Immensely. The whole experience has given me a new perspective. Oh, by the way, remind me to have Meri clear a longer than usual appointment time for Wednesday next. Stuart wants a word about a few symptoms he's experiencing.'

Abbey's heart skittered. So her guess had been right. 'Then I hope to heaven he's going to tell Andrea about his appointment with you.'

Nick frowned and then said slowly, 'I didn't realise he'd been keeping things to himself. That's not good.'

'No.' Abbey sighed, letting her head go back on the seat rest. 'She's up the wall with worry—Stuart's begun distancing himself from her emotionally. Andi thinks he's having an affair.'

'Good grief...' Nick muttered, and shook his head.

After a while, Abbey asked, 'Should I say anything to Andi, Nick? I mean, I did point out the possibility that Stuart could be ill—'

'Don't start playing go-between, Abbey.' Nick was firm. 'If you've planted the seed, Andrea can approach her husband. After that it's up to Stuart as to

137

whether or not he wants to open up and express his fears. With the best will in the world, no one, not even his wife, can force him.'

'But that's so infantile!' Abbey exclaimed. 'And so unfair to Andi.'

'Abbey…' Nick warned. 'It'll sort itself out in time.'

Next morning, Abbey went to the surgery early, leaving Nick to do the ward round at the hospital. As she began putting things to rights on her desk, she realised she was on tenterhooks. She'd been hoping with all her heart she would have heard from her friend by now. But Andrea had not been in touch.

Abbey shook her head. Obviously, Stuart hadn't confided in his wife. Instead, he'd probably given her some lame excuse for his trip to town on Wednesday—like having to buy feed for the cattle or go the bank!

Sighing, she moved across to the window of her consulting room and looked out, not registering the beautiful crispness of the morning.

Anxiety for the Frasers' well-being was eating her alive.

She stayed at the window another minute longer and then, determinedly pushing aside her misgivings, returned to her desk, buzzing Meri for her first patient, Rachel Petersen.

'Good morning, Rachel. Are you playing hookey?' Abbey smiled. Rachel was the deputy principal at the primary school.

'I am, actually. But someone's covering for me— at least I hope so.'

Abbey could see at a glance that Rachel was not her usual calm self. She waited until her patient was comfortably seated and then asked, 'So, what can I do for you this morning, Rachel?'

'My hair's falling out.'

Abbey frowned briefly. 'In handfuls or have you just noticed it coming away when you've brushed it?'

The teacher lifted a shoulder. 'It's been a general loss, I suppose—but enough to make me panic. What could be wrong, Abbey?'

'Any number of things.' Abbey was cautious. 'Are you feeling unusually stressed at the moment?'

The woman's shoulders lifted in a heavy sigh. 'Well, as a working single parent, I'm used to keeping all the balls in the air, but just at the moment it's a real effort catching them.

'And teaching is hardly a doddle these days,' she went on ruefully. 'When I first began, it was so much more creative. Now...' She shook her head. 'There are so many rules and regulations. And the calibre of families has changed. For instance, I heard the other day that several of my pupils had been seen foraging from the rubbish bins at the back of the pub. They were hungry, poor little mites, and that's terrible, Abbey! Sorry.' She chewed her lip and gave a wry smile. 'I'm going on and I don't mean to waste your time.'

'You're not.' Abbey was firm. 'But there are two separate issues here, Rachel. First, we'll deal with your health and then I want to hear more about these children. Perhaps if we liaise, something can be done for them. But for the moment, your health is my concern.'

'Well?' Rachel asked a few minutes later, as she pulled herself up from the examination couch and slid her feet to the floor.

'You do appear a little tense.' Abbey said cautiously, washing her hands at the basin. 'And it may be just a case of everything catching up with you and depleting your energy stores, both physically and mentally. But in view of your hair loss, we'll run a check to rule out any thyroid imbalance.'

'How will you do that?' Rachel slipped her shoes back on and took her place back at Abbey's desk.

'A blood test is the most accurate. If your thyroid is under-active, it can certainly cause premature hair loss. Fortunately, simple replacement medication can soon put things right.'

Rachel's hands interlocked on the desktop. 'And if it's not that causing the hair loss?'

Abbey heard the thread of anxiety in her patient's voice and sought to reassure her. 'There are several options we can try. A multimineral tablet containing zinc can be helpful and there've been good results from a new lotion that can be rubbed into your scalp to help hair growth. Of course, don't neglect the obvious.' Abbey smiled. 'Regular shampooing and massage.'

'Massage…' Rachel managed a wry smile. 'That sounds like a recipe for relaxation.'

'We'll start with the lotion while we're waiting for the result of your blood test to come back.' Abbey pulled her pad towards her. 'And you'd probably benefit from some actual relaxation therapy.' She looked up, her eyebrows raised in query. 'Isn't something happening at the sports centre along those lines?'

'We received some flyers at the school about it.' Rachel looked uncertain. 'I could perhaps try that, couldn't I?'

'Absolutely.' Abbey smiled. She handed the prescription across. 'Now, I'll take some blood and while I'm doing that, you can tell me about these children.'

When her last patient for the morning had gone, Abbey sat on at her desk, her head lowered, her fingers gently massaging her temples.

It had been one of those mornings when she'd been expected to be all things to all people. She sighed, considering her own emotional state.

Everything always came back to Nick Tonnelli—large as life, a man waiting for some kind of sign from her that they could move forward. But to where? And to what? Abbey made a little sound of frustration, suddenly at odds with the emotional games people were forced to play.

She looked up as a rap sounded on her door.

'Come in.' Abbey hurriedly schooled her expression.

'Got a minute?' Nick's dark head came through the opening.

'If you've come bearing coffee, I've probably got several.' Abbey forced a wry smile and brought her gaze up to meet his.

'Ah…' Nick looked rueful. 'I've already had some. Could I—?'

'No, it's OK.' Abbey waved him in. 'I'm just feeling the aftermath of a heavy morning. I'll buzz Meri to bring some. Could you manage another?'

Nick shrugged. 'If Meri doesn't mind.'

'Of course not,' Abbey said dismissively. 'We look

after each other here.' Reaching out, she pressed a button on the intercom.

'Tough list?' Nick parked himself in the chair opposite her.

'I'm not complaining.' In a nervous gesture, Abbey caught up her hair from her collar and let it go, for the first time noticing he was carrying a patient file.

'Stuart Fraser doesn't seem to have much of a medical history with us.' Nick tossed the notes to one side and sent her a quizzical look.

'He probably doesn't.' Abbey shrugged. 'I think I've only seen him once, when he needed a tetanus jab. In the past he may have seen Wolf.'

'Obviously just for routine stuff,' Nick said. 'Minor farm accidents and so on.'

'Here we are!' Meri announced cheerfully, as she arrived with a pot of coffee and a plate of chocolate biscuits. 'Energy hit for you. And I'd guess much needed. Patients coming out of the woodwork this morning,' she lamented. 'But probably half of them only came to get a look at Nick.'

'They don't still do that, do they?'

'With bells on.' Abbey felt a bubble of laughter rise in her chest at his look of disbelief. 'Thanks, Meri.' She sent the receptionist a warm smile. 'This will really hit the spot.'

'You're welcome,' Meri responded cheerfully, and turned to leave. 'Oh, Nick…' She paused at the door. 'Some emails have come through for you.'

'Excellent. I wasn't expecting to hear back so promptly.'

'I'll print them out and leave them on your desk,' Meri offered obligingly, fluttering a wave as she left.

'I shot off a couple this morning to colleagues in Sydney,' Nick explained, spinning his hands up behind his neck. 'I want to cover all the bases before I see Stuart.'

Abbey felt her stomach twist at the implication. 'What do you suspect?'

'Prostate.'

'He's only forty-two.'

Nick looked tensely back behind her to the startling brilliance of blue sky. 'And his father died of prostate cancer at sixty-eight.'

'Oh, lord.' Abbey closed her eyes for a second and then opened them, staring down at her hands clasped on her lap. She looked up, her eyes meeting Nick's with a plea. 'If Stuart has prostate cancer, what are his options? From my knowledge, they're few and fairly radical.'

'Abbey, don't go there, all right?' Nick's eyebrows jumped together in sudden irritation. 'At least, not yet. We'll know more on Wednesday after Stuart's been in.' His mouth tightened. 'I urged him to come and see me this morning, practically pleaded with him. But apparently he had to do something with his bloody cows!'

'Stu's a farmer, Nick,' Abbey explained patiently. 'His cows will always come first. And you beating yourself up for not persuading him to come in immediately won't change his mindset. By the way, he's booked for eleven o'clock.'

At fifteen minutes to eleven on Wednesday, Meri rang through from Reception. 'You've no one else booked for today, Abbey, but Andrea Fraser's here with her husband. He's just gone in to see Nick and she wondered if you'd have time for a word.'

'Of course.' Abbey's mind flew into overdrive. 'I'll be right out, Meri.' Her hand shaking, she put the receiver down, a new foreboding shadowing her thoughts.

She found Andrea standing stiffly beside the reception counter, her face pinched-looking, her hair uncombed and sticking out at odd angles, as though her appearance had been the last thing on her mind when she'd left home. Abbey looped a comforting arm around her friend's shoulders. 'Let's go out onto the back deck where we can talk,' she said quietly.

'He told me this morning,' Andrea said without preamble, shredding the tissue she was winding in and out of her fingers. 'It's his prostate for sure. He hasn't been able to pee properly.' Tears suddenly welled in her eyes. 'The awful part is his dad died from prostate cancer.' She stopped and took a shuddering breath. 'Stuart's been sick with worry and that's what he's been doing on the net, trying to find out about the symptoms and treatment. Oh, Abbey…I don't know what I'd do if anything happened to Stu…'

'Andi, you're getting way ahead of yourself,' Abbey cautioned firmly. 'Self-diagnosis is a dangerous thing. We have to wait for Nick. But in view of his family history, Stuart is right to seek medical help. Difficulty in passing urine is the first symptom something is amiss.'

Andrea's eyes widened momentarily in apprehension. 'What will Nick do first, then? And what will he be looking for?'

'He'll do a physical examination, which will tell him if the prostate gland is enlarged.'

Andrea shook her head. 'It's all such gobbledegook. I mean, I don't even know exactly where the prostate *is,* for heaven's sake!'

'The prostate gland is about the size of a walnut and it's situated at the base of the bladder,' Abbey explained gently. 'So, of course, when it begins to enlarge, as it seems to have done in Stu's case, it puts pressure on the urethra. That's the clinical name for the urine-carrying tube.'

'It's very much a male thing, isn't it?'

'Yes.'

'Oh, lord, Abbey.' Andrea laughed, a strange little tragic sound. 'What if he—if we can't ever—'

'Stop it, Andi.' Abbey homed in exactly on her friend's scrambled thoughts. 'Your mind's running too far ahead.'

Andrea dabbed at her eyes. 'C-can you blame me?'

'No, of course not. Stuart has always been well and strong. It comes as a great shock to any of us when illness suddenly makes us vulnerable. But come on, now,' she said bracingly. 'Let's cheer up. I have a feeling Nick will want to speak to you and Stuart together after he's done Stu's medical.'

'I should fix myself up a bit, then.' Andrea gave a shaky smile. 'I don't remember whether I even washed my face this morning. And my hair must look like it's been shoved in the microwave.'

'Well, Doc, what do you reckon?' Stuart began zipping up his trousers.

'First things first, Stuart.' Nick stripped off his

gloves and went to wash his hands. 'As a matter of urgency, we need to get your urine moving again.'

'Tell me about it.' Stuart sank wearily into his chair. 'What do I have to do?'

Nick's mouth clamped as he took his place back at the desk. 'It's more what I have to do, mate. But I think you'd be more comfortable over at the hospital for the procedure.'

'You mean you have to cut me?' Stuart looked alarmed.

'No surgery.' Nick shook his head. 'Not at the moment anyway. But for starters I'll have to do some fancy stuff with a flexible tube to drain your bladder.' His dark head bent, Nick scribbled something on Stuart's card. 'How would you be placed to make an immediate trip to Sydney?'

Stuart's eyes clouded. 'How immediate?'

'Tomorrow?'

'I'd have to think about it, Doc.'

'Stuart, we can't wait on this.' Nick was frank. 'You need to be under the care of a urologist. I'd willingly stay as your doctor but it's not my field.'

Stuart chewed on his bottom lip. 'Could I maybe see someone in Hopeton?'

Nick lifted a shoulder. 'You could, but the regular guy isn't due to take a clinic until next month.'

'And that's not soon enough?'

'Not from my information, no.' There was moment of intense silence and a creak of leather as Nick leaned back in his chair and steepled his fingers under his chin. 'To begin with, the specialist will want to do an ultrasound of your prostate or a biopsy or both.

He'll follow this up with a PSA—a diagnostic prostate-specific antigen blood test.'

''Struth!' Stuart's large hand clenched on the desktop. 'Now you're sounding like the vet around one of my cows.' He gave Nick a very straight look. 'Does all this stuff have to be done because of my dad's history?'

'It would be remiss of me not to refer you.' Nick was guarded. 'Do you have brothers?'

'One. He lives in Hopeton.'

'Then he should get himself along to his doctor and have this test done as well.'

Stuart looked shell-shocked, as if the seriousness of his situation had just begun to sink in. 'I've a wife and two young kids, Nick.' His throat jerked as he swallowed. 'If I've got it—the big C, I mean—what are my chances?'

Nick's mouth pursed thoughtfully. 'No one's going to rush you into anything, Stuart. And if you're comparing your situation with your father's, don't. You told me he was in his late sixties when he was diagnosed and the cancer spread swiftly. You're a much younger man and you'll have options your dad didn't have. But look…' Nick spread his hands across the desktop '…don't let's jump the gun. Let's just get you over to the hospital and made more comfortable for a start.' He glanced at his watch. 'But first we'd better get Andi in here and tell her briefly what's going on. Then I suggest we schedule a proper talk for a bit later on today. Suit you?'

'Guess so.' Stuart rubbed a knuckled hand along his jaw, sending Nick a beseeching blue look. 'Does she have to know everything?'

Nick swung out of his chair and crossed to his patient's side, propping himself on the edge of the desk. 'I understand you want to protect your wife, Stu, but for both your sakes, Andrea needs to know what's going on. Besides...' Nick's mouth crimped at the corners in a dry grin '...Abbey would skin me alive if I let you off.'

Later that afternoon arrangements for the Frasers were discussed and clarified. And then things began moving swiftly.

As it was the larger of the two, they'd all gathered in Abbey's consulting room.

'OK.' Nick opened Stuart's file and began to refer to it. 'I've got you in to see James Ferguson on Friday morning, nine o'clock, Stuart. Is that going to give you enough time to get to Sydney and settle in?'

Stuart looked at his wife. 'Should do, shouldn't it?'

'We fly out on the noon plane from Hopeton tomorrow and it's only an hour's flight so, yes, that sounds good, Nick.'

'What about the children?' Abbey asked.

'Oh, we'll take them with us.' Andrea was unequivocal. 'We need to stay together as a family through this.' She sent a brave little smile around the assembled company. 'Don't we, Stu?'

For answer, Stuart reached across and took his wife's hand, bringing it across to rest on his thigh. 'This Ferguson chap, Nick...' Stuart looked uncertain. 'He won't be all stiff and starchy, will he?'

'Not at all.' Nick's pose was relaxed as he leaned back in his chair and folded his arms. 'I play squash with him. He's about your age, wife and kids. Laid-back kind of guy. You'll find him easy to talk to.'

'How did you get us in so quickly?' Andrea still looked a little bemused at the speed with which everything had been arranged. 'I mean, sometimes it takes months to see a specialist.'

Nick's hand moved dismissively. 'We exchange favours from time to time. It's no big deal.'

Andrea dropped her gaze. 'I thought perhaps Stu's case was desperately urgent or something…'

'It is in a way,' Abbey came in guardedly. 'For your peace of mind, you both need to know what's going on, rather than waiting in limbo until Stuart can be seen some time in the future. Wouldn't you agree?'

The Frasers' nods of agreement synchronised and they clasped their hands more tightly. 'Thanks, both of you.' Andrea's voice came out huskily and she bit her lips. 'And thank God you were here for my man, Nick—that's all I can say.'

'Fair go, love,' Stuart protested mildly. 'I would've got my act together eventually and consulted Abbey. I was just…'

'Chicken?' supplied his wife with a grin.

Everyone laughed, breaking the tense nature of the consultation.

'Well, if that's all you need us for, I think we'll get home.' Andrea looked expectantly at her husband who nodded and looked relieved that the taxing day was almost over.

'Right. Here's your letter of referral.' Nick handed the long white envelope over to his patient. 'I'll email Jim anyway so he'll have your history in advance. And we'll be in touch, Stu, when you get back.'

'You betcha.' Stuart held out his hand. 'Thanks, Nick. I don't know what else to say. And, Abbey...' His face worked for a minute. 'Thanks for the support. You don't know how much it means to us...'

When they'd seen the Frasers out, Nick closed the door and stood against it. He lifted his gaze and looked straight at Abbey.

Her mouth opened on a little breath of sound, glimpsing something in the sea-green depths of his eyes that alarmed her. 'You're worried, aren't you?'

Nick's mouth tightened. 'It shows, huh?' He shovelled both hands through his hair, moving across to stand with his back against the window-ledge.

'What did you find?' Abbey felt a curl of unease.

'Enough to wish Stuart had got himself checked out long before this.'

'Oh, no...' She sank down on the edge of the desk. Everything Nick was saying indicated that Stuart and Andrea could be facing some agonising decisions. 'Traditionally, we were taught that prostate cancer was a tortoise,' she said bleakly. 'So slow-growing that something else was likely to kill a man off first. Now...' She stopped and shook her head.

'Now we find it's a whole new ball game,' Nick picked up flatly. 'Traditional thinking is out the window. Heart attacks and strokes have lost some of their first-strike capacity and prostate cancer is right up there as a possible killer.'

Abbey's throat lumped. 'If it's bad news, how are the Frasers going to cope?'

Nick returned her stricken look without flinching.

'They'll cope, Abbey. They'll have to. And we'll do everything we can to support them.'

'We shouldn't pre-empt the outcome of the tests, though,' she pointed out logically, clinging to the thread of hope.

Nick's mouth compressed into a straight line. 'We could be more optimistic if the father's medical history wasn't staring us in the face.'

Sweet heaven. Abbey tamped down the sudden dread in her heart. 'Poor Andi and Stu,' she said faintly. 'It makes you realise just how tenuous life is. How precious.'

'Hell, yes.' Nick sent her a searching look and felt a fullness in his heart he couldn't deny. Almost defensively, as if he needed to hide his emotions, he turned away and looked out of the window. A beat of silence. 'Did you have anything planned for the rest of the day?' he threw back over his shoulder.

Abbey looked blank for a moment and then rallied. 'I have a meeting over at the school. It seems we have a batch of "new poor" in Wingara—families who through no fault of their own are finding life very difficult.'

'Surely that's a matter for the social security people?'

'More often than not, it's the long way round a problem,' she pointed out with a sigh. 'Where possible, we prefer to handle things like this on a community level. And with that in mind, the deputy principal is liaising with several relevant organisations and yours truly to try to see if we can get a breakfast group going at the school, feed any child who's hungry for one reason or another.' Abbey stopped, her

teeth biting into the softness of her lower lip reflec-
tively. 'Although getting someone to run it might be
a problem. Everyone's so busy with their own lives
these days.'

'Mmm...'

Abbey looked at him sharply. Had he heard anything she'd said? His attention seemed to have dis-
sipated like leaves in the wind. She straightened off
the edge of the desk and stood upright. 'What about
you?' she asked, taking the few paces to join him at
the window.

He drew in a deep breath that came out as a ragged
sigh. 'If you don't need me for anything, I think I'll
go for a long run, slough off some of this gloom.
After sending Stuart off to face who knows what, I
feel carved up inside.'

'Oh, Nick...' She shook her head in slight disbelief. Nicholas Tonnelli feeling vulnerable? How
wrong could you be about people? She'd had no idea
the Frasers' situation would have got to him like this.
With his kind of professional experience, she would
have thought he'd have had objectivity down to a fine
art—be, at the very least, case-hardened.

He gave a huff of raw laughter. 'Pathetic, isn't it?'

'No, it's not,' she came back softly. 'It's just being
human.' She took a tentative step towards him. 'How
can I help?'

'Just let me hold you.'

Her heart gave an extra thud. 'A medicinal hug?'

'Yes, please, Doctor.' Wearing a faintly twisted
smile, Nick drew her unresisting body against his.

Pressed against the hardness of him, Abbey made
a little sound in her throat, the clean familiarity of his

scent surrounding her. After a long time, she pulled back and said shakily, 'I…should get to my meeting.'

'Should you?' His dark head swooped towards her, his mouth teasingly urgent against her lips, the corner of her mouth. 'Off you go, then,' he said, regret in his gruffness. 'I'll come out and see you off.'

They walked out to Reception together. 'Mind how you go.' Opening the outer door, he ushered her through.

Abbey sent him an old-fashioned look. 'I'll be sure to watch out for the teeming masses at the intersection. Enjoy your run.'

Nick's eyes glinted with dry humour. Propping himself against the doorframe, he watched her drive off with a fluttered wave in his direction. He huffed a frustrated sigh as he turned back inside. Hell, he was missing her already.

Wandering through to his room, he collected his bag and set the alarm. Was it possible to fast-track love? It must be. He certainly had a king-sized dose of it!

'Abbey…' He said her name softly. Already she'd stirred such powerful feelings in him, imbued him with a zest for the ordinary things of life, the precious, simple things that he'd all but forgotten.

CHAPTER TEN

AT THE meeting, Abbey tried to pay attention. But every now and again she was conscious of her thoughts wandering, becoming way too fanciful for comfort.

Was she in love with Nicholas Tonnelli? Colour whipped along her cheekbones at the mere thought. Was this how it felt—wild for the sight of him, the touch of him? Merely thinking about the possibility made her remember the night he'd massaged her feet. The night he'd carried her to bed...

Dreamily, she propped her chin on her hand. Just recalling the way they'd batted the loaded suggestions back and forth was doing crazy things to her insides, fuelling the slow crawl of nerves in her stomach—

'What do you think, Abbey? Feasible?'

'Uh...' Abbey snapped back to reality, surveying the expectant faces of the newly formed committee around her. She'd heard Rachel Petersen's voice but her question had become lost in the fog of Abbey's introspection. Hastily, she picked up her pen and twirled it, gaining time. 'Just run that past me again.'

Rachel raised a finely etched eyebrow. 'Are you OK, Abbey? You look a bit hot.' She gave a 'tsk' of irritation. 'It's probably this blessed air-conditioning again. It's never been adjusted properly.'

'I'm fine.' Abbey took a mouthful from the glass of water in front of her. 'Just a bit of a headache starting.' She drummed up a quick smile. 'You were saying?'

'I suggested we use the facilities at the school tuck shop for this breakfast club. It's just had a major re-vamp and, as it's on school property, we could keep an eye on things.'

'It sounds ideal.' Abbey linked the assembled group with a questioning look. 'If everyone is happy about that?'

Sounds of agreement echoed around the table. 'What kind of tucker would you suggest we serve the kiddies?' Geoff Rogers asked practically. 'It's winter now. Poor little blighters need something to warm their insides.'

'Porridge?' Fran, Geoff's wife, suggested.

'Not all kids like porridge,' Abbey said thought-fully. 'But, of course, we could still offer it. Perhaps cereal and warm milk? Toast with a nourishing spread?'

'I'm sure we could manage fruit when so much is grown locally.' Rachel's voice bubbled with enthu-siasm. 'We could even run to grilled tomatoes or scrambled eggs.'

'And what about a nice thick vegetable soup at lunchtime?' Fran suggested. 'Then, if the parents can't provide much for supper, at least the little ones will have something in their tummies.'

'It's not just the poorer families of the town who need the facility,' Rachel said earnestly. 'Some of the children who come on buses from the outlying dis-tricts have to leave home very early. I'm sure half of them aren't up to eating much breakfast, even if it's put in front of them. But by the time they get here to school, they're ravenous.'

'How are we going to judge numbers, then?' One of the members of the P and C committee came in for the first time.

'I do have some knowledge of this kind of venture from an inner-city practice where I worked once,' Abbey said, and realised everyone was looking speculatively at her. 'We may err on the side of ordering too much at first but things usually even out after a while. And basically...' she rocked a hand expressively '...if the leftovers are stored properly, there won't be much loss.'

'There's just one tiny thing.' Rachel sent a hopeful look around the table. 'Who's going to run it? We need someone who's used to catering for numbers but who can order economically at the same time. Funding is available but we certainly can't waste it.'

There was a beat of silence while everyone thought, and then the obvious solution hit Abbey like a bolt of lightning. Looking pleased, she snapped her diary shut. 'What about Ed Carmichael?'

There was a momentary hush. And then a babble of excited voices. 'I must say, I'd always thought in terms of a woman running the scheme.' Geoff stroked his chin thoughtfully. 'But crikey! Ed's a natural when you think about it. He's been a camp cook for the shearers. And there's no doubt we could rely on him to do the right thing by the kids.'

'I often see him around the town.' Someone else sought to have their say. 'He always looks very neat and clean.'

'And I know Ed would do a wonderful job.'

Abbey's eyes were lit with warmth. 'Plus I'm almost sure he'd want to give this service to the children on a voluntary basis.'

There were smiles of satisfaction and little nods of approval. 'I'll approach Mr Carmichael officially, then.' Rachel positively beamed. 'We could have our children eating properly within a matter of hours. Thank you, everyone, for coming. A most gratifying result.'

Abbey drove home slowly. It was almost dusk and she wondered whether Nick was back from his run. Her stomach tightened. She *needed* him to be back, she realised with a little jolt. Switching off the engine, she climbed out of her vehicle and went into the house by the back door.

A wonderful aroma drifted out from the kitchen. 'Nick?' She walked quickly through the laundry, not believing the joy she felt. He was planted firmly at the stove, cooking.

'Hi.' He turned his head as she came through and they shared a tentative smile. 'Good meeting?'

Abbey nodded. 'Very productive. Looks like you've been productive as well. What are you making?'

'Vegetable curry.' He went back to his stirring. 'I'll do the rice now you're home.'

Home. Abbey's heart slammed against her ribs. If only she and Nick were sharing a real home together. As a couple. In love...

'Oh—OK. I'll just, um, get a shower, then.' Heart pounding, she slipped past him, her thoughts whirling. So what am I going to do about you, Nick? she fretted, stripping off her work clothes and stepping under the jets of warm water.

'Oh, lord,' she whispered, feelings of apprehension rushing at her. How could this have happened? In so short a time and with her hardly realising it, she'd come to depend on him so much. In all the ways that counted. But he had a life in Sydney. A life in the fast lane.

A life she could never be a part of.

The week dragged to a close.

On Friday at four o'clock, Nick poked his head into Abbey's consulting room. 'I'm off to do a ward round.'

'Fine,' she responded dispiritedly. She'd been hoping against hope there would have been some word from Andrea by now. But apart from James Ferguson's brief advice to Nick that Stuart had been seen and that the specialist had put a rush on the test results, there'd been nothing.

'It's too soon to have heard anything definite, Abbey.' Nick homed in on her worries accurately. He came in and closed the door.

'I know.' She lifted a shoulder. 'Are you releasing Grant today?'

'I thought so, yes. He's made a very quick recovery.' Nick parked himself on the corner of her desk. 'I've begun liaising with Fran Rogers about some physio for him. I gather she's already been in for a chat and told Grant what he can expect by way of rehab.' He arched an eyebrow. 'What's the status of the flu jabs for Wingara's senior population?'

'Down on last year.' Abbey looked taken aback at his abrupt change of conversation. 'Why do you ask?'

'There's been a procession of elderly folk going down with flu right throughout the district, according to Rhys and Diane. Some are being cared for at home by their relatives, but the hospital's receiving its fair share of patients as well.'

Abbey dropped her gaze. Nick had placed himself on ward rounds for the entire week so she hadn't been near the hospital.

'Ideally, they should all have had their flu vaccinations way back.' Nick spun off the desk and paced to the window. Turning, he folded his arms and frowned. 'What kind of preventative campaign did you run?'

Abbey's chin came up. What did he think she was running here, the World Health Organisation? And surely he wasn't blaming her for people's failure to take responsibility for their own health? 'We had the usual reminders around the surgery and I put a piece in the local paper advising folk that the vaccine was here and it was time to get their shots,' she snapped defensively. 'It's up to individuals, Nick. It's not as though they can be corralled like cows and given a jab.'

His dark brows drew together. 'I'm not so far removed from grassroots medicine that I'm unaware of that, Abbey. But perhaps it's time to think ahead and see what we could do for next year.'

Next year? Abbey felt as if all her muscle supports had suddenly let go. Where was Nick Tonnelli coming from? He wouldn't be here next *month*—let alone next year!

'What did you have in mind?' she asked in a tone of controlled patience.

He took a few steps to spin out a chair and drop into it, leaning forward earnestly. 'I thought I'd have a word with Rob Stanton, get a couple of his documentary team out here.'

'In what capacity?'

'We could film a segment for the *Countrywide* programme.' Nick's gaze lit up with the enthusiasm of his plan. 'Feature several of the locals who have come down with flu, speak to them now, when they're recovering, and have them recount how debilitated they've felt and how they'll be sure to have their flu shots in future. We could get Rob to put it to air— say, March, April next year. What do you think?'

Abbey had to admit the idea had merit but nevertheless voiced her reservations. 'People may not want cameras and microphones in their faces, though.'

'Naturally, we'd need their permission.' Nick remained undaunted. 'But I'm sure Rob would do a sensitive, folksy piece that would have the right amount of impact. And he certainly owes you big time for that business over the debate,' he ended darkly.

Abbey avoided his eyes, her mouth trembling infinitesimally at the mention of that particular day. The day her life had been altered for ever. 'All right.' She picked up the phone as it rang beside her. 'But I want to see the film clip before it goes to air. I don't want any of my patients being made to look like yokels. If Rob can work with that...'

Nick shrugged. 'I'll run the idea past him and get back to you.'

*   *   *

They did the grocery shopping on Saturday afternoon, bickering lightly over the menu for the coming week. 'We could have a cooking session tomorrow,' Abbey suggested, stopping by the meat cabinet. 'Cook enough food for the week and store it in the freezer.'

'Not on your life!' Nick's mouth turned down. 'I've got more to do with my Sunday that spend it in the kitchen, thank you.' Gently, he prised her fingers off the large tray of beef cuts.

'Nick!' She grabbed his hand to stop him and was startled by the wild shiver of electricity that ran between them. Flustered, she met his eyes and saw an answering flare before he doused it.

'Let's have a picnic tomorrow instead,' he suggested, his voice slightly uneven. 'I'll grab a couple of these T-bone steaks. We could find a spot by the river and barbecue them. How does that sound?'

Abbey's heart wrenched. It sounded wonderful.

By mid-week, Abbey was beginning to feel that as far as the Frasers were concerned, no news was definitely not good news. And when Nick took a phone call during their lunch-break and didn't return, her nerves began gathering and clenching like fine wires.

She glanced at her watch. Heavens, he'd been gone for ages. Hastily, she rinsed the crockery they'd used for their simple snack and then, as if compelled by forces outside herself, went along to his consulting room and knocked.

'Come in and close the door, Abbey.' Nick looked back from his stance at the window and beckoned her inside. He pulled a couple of chairs together and they sat facing one another. Silently, he reached out and took her hands, rubbing his thumbs almost absently over her knuckles. 'I'm afraid it's not good news about Stuart.'

Her mouth dried. 'Was that Dr Ferguson on the phone?'

'Yes. Stuart's been advised to undergo a radical prostatectomy.'

Abbey paled and whispered. 'Oh, no…'

'Jim called in a second opinion, Magnus Nahrung from the Prince Alfred. He agreed with Jim's findings.'

'When will they do the surgery?'

'He's down for tomorrow morning.' At Abbey's little gasp, Nick continued flatly, 'Apparently, Stu didn't want to hang about.'

Abbey was aghast. 'He could be left impotent, Nick!'

'Or dead within ten years if the cancer gets into his bones and he doesn't have the surgery.' Nick's response was brutally frank. 'Optimistic inaction certainly isn't an option. And whatever it takes, Stuart wants to stay with his family, Abbey. He told me that much.'

Abbey took a shaken breath. 'Have they had counselling? Of course they have…' She grimaced, answering her own question. She swallowed the tears clogging her throat. 'Did Dr Ferguson say how Stuart and Andi are handling things?'

Nick allowed himself a lopsided smile. 'With amazing calm and stoicism, he said. Whatever their own misgivings, they're putting a positive spin on things for the kids' sakes.'

Abbey bit her lip. 'That sounds like them, doesn't it?' She spun up off the chair, wrapping her arms around her midriff. 'I wonder why Andi hasn't called?'

'She'll have all her thoughts focused on her husband at the moment, Abbey. Frankly, outside the hospital staff, I doubt she'd have the energy to talk to anyone right now. But she'll know our thoughts are with her and Stuart.'

'Yes.' Abbey swallowed hard and nodded. 'Yes, she will...'

That night, Abbey woke from a dream with her heart pounding and a scream in her throat.

In seconds Nick was in the doorway. 'Abbey— what's up? Are you ill?'

She sat upright and snapped the bedside lamp on. 'I must've had a bad dream.'

'More like a nightmare.' Nick's voice was gruff and he came further into the room.

Abbey pushed a strand of hair away from her face. 'It was about Andi and Stuart...'

'You're trembling.' The mattress gave under his weight, and then his arms were around her, cradling her against his chest. 'You can't let it get to you like this,' he murmured throatily. 'What happened to objectivity?'

'Pie in the sky.' Abbey gave a shuddery little breath, snuggling into the hollow of his shoulder. 'You haven't been to bed,' she said, feeling the soft stuff of the track top he'd put on earlier, after his shower.

He gave a hard laugh. 'I'm too wired to sleep. Stuart's been on my mind, too.'

'What happened to objectivity?' She brought a hand up and stroked his face, loving the smooth sweep of his skin against her palm.

'Out with the bath water.'

'We're a fine pair, aren't we?' She smoothed back his eyebrow with the side of her thumb. 'What've you been doing?'

'I tried to read. Ended up watching a late movie on TV.' His arms tightened. 'Try to get back to sleep now, OK?'

'I don't think I can,' she sighed. Beside which, his scent was too disturbing. So was the warmth of his body against hers.

'What should we do, then?' His voice was low, deeper than deep. It sought out hidden nerve ends, whispered along blood vessels and right into her heart.

'We could make some cocoa,' she said throatily.

'I hate cocoa.'

Abbey could hardly breathe, arching against him as strong fingers touched where she so longed to be touched. 'Bedtime story?'

'Mmm. About a man and a woman…' he said huskily, drawing her to her feet.

Safe in his arms, Abbey closed her eyes, feeling every sense spring alive, the drugging drift of the sandalwood soap on his skin swirling around her like so many strands of silk.

Her hands, with a mind of their own, smoothed over him, from the hardness of his shoulder muscles to curve lower, then round by the hollow of his hip, then on, dragging a primitive groan from his throat.

'Abbey—enough!'

'I'm sorry...' Stung by the reprimand, she pulled back, inflamed by the response of her own body.

'God, no! That's not what I meant.' Nick spoke as if the air was being pushed out of his body. Tipping her face up, he stared down into her eyes. 'I want you,' he said deeply. 'I think you're wonderful. And beautiful. And perfect...'

'I'm not perfect,' she countered softly, her hair glinting silver in the lamplight as she shook her head.

'Perfect for me...' With a long shudder, he dragged air into his lungs. 'Do you want me as much as I want you?'

Drawn by something in his voice, her gaze came up slowly, meeting such a naked look of longing it took her breath away. Desire, fierce and unrelenting, tore through her, annihilating at a stroke any doubts she might have had.

'Don't you have too many clothes on?' Her huff of laughter was fractured, nerves gripping her insides like tentacles.

With fingers that were not quite steady, he slid the lacy strap of her nightie off her shoulder. 'I wondered when you'd notice.'

Abbey took a shaken breath, held captive by the look in his eyes. The first touch of his mouth on hers shattered the last slender threads of her control as he gathered her in.

Their clothes seemed to fall away.

He's beautiful. Abbey's breath lodged in her throat.

Strong, lean, powerful, the sprinkle of dark hair tangling across the centre of his chest, arrowing down...

In the warm glow of the lamplight, she touched him, her fingertips sensitised as they travelled over his body, his gasp of pleasure fuelling her own desire.

And then it was Nick's turn. Using his hands like a maestro, he raised her awareness to fever pitch, his lips following with a devastating intimacy that left her reeling, a jangle of senses, of touch and taste and feeling.

When they arrived at the moment when all was trust, she looked right into his eyes, the moment so tender, so precious. 'Sweet Abbey,' she heard him whisper, before they closed their eyes and the pleasure of giving and receiving claimed them, the intensity whirling them under and then as they reached flashpoint, rolling in long, flowing waves to envelop them.

Afterwards, they lay for a long time just holding each other. Abbey could hardly believe it. She'd become Nick Tonnelli's lover. Oh, lord, she thought.

She must have spoken the exclamation aloud for Nick frowned suddenly. 'Not regretting anything, are you, Abbey?' Lifting his head slightly, he smudged a kiss over her temple. 'It was beautiful—wasn't it?'

'Beautiful,' she echoed. There was no point in saying otherwise. It would have been a lie. But what in real terms did being lovers mean? And where did they go from here? Abbey closed her eyes, her face warm against his naked chest. 'Nick...' Her voice was hesitant. 'We, um, didn't use anything.'

He went still. 'I assumed—expected you to say something if it wasn't all right.'

She placed a finger across his lips. It probably was all right. She was as regular as clockwork. 'It should be OK. I'm in a safe time.'

Not two minutes later the phone rang. Nick swore. 'Stay there—I'll get it.' He reached for his track pants and dragged them on. He wasn't away long.

'Well?' Struggling upright, Abbey pulled the sheet up to her chin.

'MVA, sole occupant. ETA ten minutes. Doesn't sound too serious. I'll handle it. Curl up now and try to get some sleep, OK?'

She took an uncertain breath. 'Yes…all right. Mind how you go.'

He leaned over and knuckled her cheek. 'Always do.'

Not always, Nick. The sobering little thought stayed with Abbey until she finally fell into a dreamless sleep.

Next morning she was up and dressed and in the surgery before Nick had even surfaced. Her excuse was that she had paperwork to get up to date, scripts to write…

She worked for nearly an hour and then put her pen down. She'd have to see Nick the moment he got in. At the thought of what she had to ask him, her stomach somersaulted. And when, shortly after, she heard his steady footfall outside in the corridor, the soft closing of his surgery door, her heartbeat quickened alarmingly, almost choking her.

The walk to his consulting room seemed endless.

She paused for a moment outside his door then, taking a deep breath, she knocked and went in.

'Abbey…' Nick wanted to spring from his chair and gather her in but something in her expression held him back. 'Meri said you'd left a note not to be disturbed.'

'Reams of paperwork to catch up on.' She gave the semblance of a smile. 'How was your MVA?'

Nick made a dismissive movement with his hand. 'Suspected drunk driver. Silly young kid still on his provisional licence. Geoff Rogers wanted a blood alcohol reading.'

'Much damage?' Immediately Abbey's caring instincts were aroused.

'Whiplash, gash to his head. I've just been over to check on him. He's a bit sick and sorry for himself. It's to be hoped he's learned his lesson about drinking and driving.' Abruptly, Nick stood to his feet, his eyes raking her face. 'Are you OK?'

'Fine,' she lied. 'I just need you to—that is, I wondered if you'd mind signing this.' She slid her hand into the side pocket of her skirt and withdrew a slip of paper. 'It's a script,' she elaborated, handing it across to him.

'Yes, I can see that.' He frowned down at the computer printout. 'It's made out to you.'

She gave a strangled laugh. 'It's not ethical to sign one's own prescription, Nick. You must know that.'

'It's for the morning-after pill.' His voice had risen and tightened. He looked up, his eyes unguarded. 'Why, Abbey?'

Thoughts, all of them confused, clawed at her. 'Because I don't want to take any chances,' she said wretchedly.

'You said you were safe.' He dropped back into his chair, as if his strings had been cut.

'I'm as sure as I can be that I'm safe, but who can ever be that sure? I mean, we're both fit and healthy. There's every reason to think we could...' She stopped and faced him with uncertainty and wariness clouding her eyes.

Nick felt something cold run down his backbone. He flicked at the piece of paper in his hand. 'Are you sure you want to go this road, Abbey? I mean, if we've made a baby together—'

She interrupted him with a humourless little laugh. 'Nick, you're a free spirit. You don't want a baby. You like the unencumbered lifestyle you've chosen, otherwise you'd have changed it long ago.'

His dark brows shot together. 'Don't presume to know how I want to live *my* life, Abbey,' he countered with dangerous calm. 'Are you sure this isn't about you and your own misgivings about parenthood?'

Abbey was appalled. 'I love children,' she defended herself hotly. 'But I'd prefer to have them when the time is right and with a man I love and who l-loves me. A man I can *rely* on!'

Nick recoiled as if she'd slapped him. For several moments he just sat there. Then with a savage yank he hauled his pen from his top pocket and added a bold signature to the prescription. 'There you are, Dr Jones.' He stood abruptly, as if to physically distance himself from what she'd asked him to do. Moving to the window, he reached out like a blind man towards the sill, gripping it with both hands, staring out.

Shakily, Abbey picked up the slip of paper. Her composure was shattering. 'I'm just trying to be responsible, Nick.' She fluttered the words accusingly at his back and left quietly.

Oh, God, why was his throat tightening like this? 'How could she *think* I wouldn't want a child?' he rasped under his breath. '*Our* child.' He pressed his fingers across his eyes, as if staving off pain. What the hell was last night about then? His gut wrenched. How dumb can you be, Tonnelli? Obviously their love-making hadn't stopped her world the way it had stopped his!

Abbey sat frozenly at her desk, her head buried in her hands. She felt sick to her stomach. Nothing she'd said to Nick had come out right. Remembering, she felt her heart lurch painfully. It had taken her under five minutes to completely destroy everything precious between them. *Everything.*

When her phone rang, she reached out groggily and picked it up. 'Yes, Meri.' Her voice came out cracked and she swallowed thickly.

'The Wilsons are here.' Meri kept her tone pitched confidentially low.

'Who?' Abbey tried to concentrate.

'Ryan and Natalie. They want their baby immunised.'

'Oh, I remember now.' Abbey massaged a hand across her forehead, as if to clear her thinking process. 'We could probably fit them some time today, couldn't we?'

'Actually, they wondered if you'd see them now. They're a bit edgy. I gather it's been quite a big decision for them.'

'Oh, OK...' Abbey's brow furrowed. 'Give me two minutes and then show them in.' She replaced the receiver slowly.

She'd have to pull herself together somehow. She had a full list of patients and the world could not be shut out indefinitely. As Meri knocked and showed the Wilson family in, she whipped her prescription off the desk and into her top drawer. Before the day got much older, she'd have to find a minute to nip out to the chemist.

About eleven o'clock, Nick called through on her intercom. 'I thought you'd like to know, Jim Ferguson just called,' he said crisply. 'Stuart's surgery went well. He's in Recovery.'

Abbey felt relief rush through her. 'That's wonderful news. Thanks,' she added after a second, but he'd already hung up.

Somehow they managed to avoid each other for most of the day. Only once did she encounter Nick, when she'd gone out to Reception and he'd been seeing off a young couple with their toddler. A cute little boy with a thatch of dark curls.

The young mother was smiling disarmingly at Nick. 'Keiran was so good today. You must have a way with kids, Dr Tonnelli. Could we book to see you for his next shot?'

His mouth a tight line, Nick shook his head. 'Dr Jones will look after you, Mrs O'Connor.' He looked up and stared mockingly at Abbey. 'I won't be here.'

Abbey turned on her heel and almost ran back to

her room, the drum-heavy thud in her chest almost suffocating her. Damn! Sick with hurt and disillusionment, she stabbed the computer off and shaded her eyes.

All day long, she'd allowed herself to nurture the faintest hope that somehow she and Nick could put things back together. But he couldn't have made it more clear that it was over. *Over.* She blinked through a blur of tears. Oh, Nick, what have I done?

CHAPTER ELEVEN

How on earth were they to go on from here? How?

Abbey stretched her time in the surgery for as long as she could and then went across to the hospital. Pinning a bright smile on her face, she went through the motions, doing a ward round slowly and methodically.

Anything to delay going home. Except how could she think of it as home any longer? She and Nick would be stepping round each other like strangers. She bit her lips tightly together, smothering a bitter smile. The only time she'd fallen headlong in love in the whole of her life—and it had ended in disaster and heartbreak.

There was no feeling of warmth in the house when she opened the back door. No comforting aroma of a meal being lovingly prepared. But the lights were on so Nick must be home. Perhaps there was still hope...

Her breath caught and shuddered in her throat and her lips parted softly as she called, 'Nick?'

'In here.'

Abbey took a breath so deep it hurt, then on rubbery legs she made her way through the archway into the lounge. Nick was there, standing by the fireplace, his bags packed and set neatly against the wall beside him. Staring at him, the tight set to his mouth and jaw, Abbey felt her heart was splitting in two. She closed her eyes briefly and then forced herself to look at him. 'You're leaving.'

'There's no point in me staying.'

'But you came for a month!'

He made a rough sound of scorn. 'Just gives weight to your perception of my unreliability, then, doesn't it?'

'That wasn't what I meant to say!' She defended herself raggedly. 'It just came out that way...'

'The hell it did.' Pretending not to see the raw look of hurt on her face, he hardened his gaze even further. 'I wish I could say it's been worth it, Abbey, but we both know I'd be lying. I was an arrogant fool to have come here at all.' Their gazes locked for a long time, before he stooped and picked up his bags. 'I won't ask you to think of me sometimes,' he stated bitterly, and then he was gone, leaving her alone.

Except she wasn't alone.

The house was full of reminders of him. From the stoneware he'd bought to make his special lasagne to the bottles of wine he'd chosen so carefully and which they'd never opened.

Dull depression settled on her like a cloud, but resolutely she went through to her bedroom, stripping off the sheets and pillowcases and stuffing them into the washing machine.

And she'd be darned if she'd use this particular bed linen ever again—not with the scent of him still clinging to it and swathing her in a heartbreaking mist of remembering...

'Nick not coming in today?' It was the next morning and Meri had just put a mug of coffee on Abbey's desk.

'No…' Abbey sighed, daunted by the need for explanation. 'Actually, Meri…he's left Wingara.'

The two women stared awkwardly at each other, and then Meri took the initiative. 'I'm really sorry to hear that, Abbey. But I've been around the traps long enough to know neither of you would have made the decision lightly.'

Except the decision for him to leave hadn't been hers at all. 'Thanks, Meri.' Abbey's voice shook fractionally. 'We'll just have to soldier on, won't we?'

Meri looked wry. 'Women have been doing it since time began.'

The next month brought no relief to Abbey's pain and deep sense of loss. On the lighter side, the Frasers were home and quietly optimistic that Stuart would have no residual effects from his surgery.

'I'm just so happy to have him beside me at night,' Andrea confessed during a flying visit to Abbey for a pap smear. 'Just to hold each other. And if that's all we can have…' Her eyes misted over.

'Andi, it's early days yet.' Abbey swabbed the specimen onto a slide. 'And you said the specialist's last report was very encouraging. Let's just concentrate on things working out wonderfully for you and Stuart.'

'Amen to that.' Andrea settled herself back in the chair. 'Do you want to talk about what happened between you and Nick?' she asked with the easy frankness of friendship. 'You were so right for each other, Abbey.'

'Oh, please…' Abbey went to wash her hands. 'It

didn't work out, Andi,' she said wearily. 'Can we leave it at that?'

Andrea bit her lip. 'You look awful, Abbey—so strained. Couldn't you…?' Andi waved her hands about helplessly.

'No.' Abbey's answer was unequivocal. 'I should have the results of your test back in a week,' she sidetracked professionally. 'I'll ring if there's anything untoward.'

Another month went by.

'Meri, I have to go to Hopeton next week.' Abbey pushed the desk diary aside and pocketed her ballpoint. 'Could you call Wolf and see if he's available to provide cover? I'll need Wednesday and Thursday.'

'Sure.' Meri made a note on her pad. 'Regional meetings again?'

'Mmm.' Amongst other things, Abbey thought sombrely.

'You have a visitor.' Meri was all smiles when Abbey arrived back during the late afternoon from her trip to Hopeton.

Abbey came to a halt, her lungs fighting for air. Was it Nick? Had he come back?

'Go on,' Meri insisted in her best managing voice. 'He's waiting in your office.' She reached out a hand and swept up the post. 'I'm just off. See you both in the morning.'

Afterwards, Abbey had no clear idea how her legs had carried her along the corridor to her office. Heart trampolining, she turned the knob and pushed the door slowly open. And gave a tiny gasp, as the tall male figure turned from the window.

'Steve!' She dropped her bag and ran into her brother's outstretched arms. And promptly burst into tears.

'Have you missed me that much, little sis?' Steve seemed amused.

'Must have, mustn't I?' With a watery smile, Abbey eased herself away.

He gave her an astute brotherly glance. 'Don't think so, Abbey. You look like you've just come from Heartbreak Hotel.'

Abbey sniffed and gave a funny little grimace. 'Very droll. Are you writing an agony column these days?'

'Not me.' He shook his fair head. 'But I know the signs, kiddo, and my doctoring instincts tell me my little sister is in need of some TLC. Come on.' He looped an arm around her shoulders. 'Let's get you home and fed.'

It was lovely to be cosseted. Tucked up on the sofa in the lounge room, Abbey sipped gratefully at the big mug of scalding tea, replete from the helping of fluffy scrambled eggs Steve had magically produced in record time.

Watching her fork up the meal hungrily, he'd demanded, 'Why aren't you eating properly?'

'I am.'

'Not from what I saw in the fridge.'

Abbey had shrugged uninterestedly. 'There's stuff in the freezer.'

She looked up now as he sauntered back into the room and asked, 'All squared away?'

'Yep.' He looked at her narrowly. 'More tea?'

'No, thanks. But that was lovely, Steve.' She leaned over to place her empty mug on the side table.

Steve seemed to hesitate and then, as if coming to a decision, bounded across to the sofa. 'Shove up a bit, hmm?' Obediently, Abbey drew her knees up and he plonked down beside her, his head resting on the cushioned back, his legs outstretched and crossed at the ankles. He glanced across at her. 'OK, let's have it, Abbey.'

Abbey sighed and closed her eyes. 'Do you have all night?'

'If necessary. Come on.' His hand covered hers, hard and strong. 'Roll it out. It's probably not half as bad as you think.'

Abbey swallowed and swallowed again and made a tentative beginning. 'There's a man...'

'Does this man have a name?'

'Nicholas Tonnelli.'

'Hell. How did you get hooked up with him?'

So she told her brother the whole sad story.

When she'd finished, Steve rolled his head across the cushioned back to look at her. 'So you're going to contact him, right?'

'How can I?' she said bleakly. 'He hates me.'

'Rats! How could he hate you? You've both got your wires crossed, that's all.'

If only it was that simple.

'You have to see Nick and talk to him, Abbey,' Steve repeated. 'Or I will.'

She snatched her hand back. 'Don't you dare! Keep out of it, Steve.'

'No, I won't. These are lives we're talking about here, Abbey, yours and—'

She let out a wail and he stopped and hugged her close. 'Come on, kid. You can do it. Remember the courage you found when Mum and Dad died? Through all the stuff we had to do?'

She met his eyes, her own troubled. 'It's not the same.'

'Yes, it is. Trust me, I'm a doctor.'

That old cliché brought a wobbly smile to her mouth. 'Will you come with me?'

'Uh-uh. But I'll hold the fort while you're gone.'

'How long are you down for?'

He lifted a shoulder. 'As long as I need. My contract's finished.'

Abbey perked up. 'So you're going to settle back in Australia?'

'Eventually. Actually…' He looked at the floor, faintly embarrassed. 'I've met a girl, Catherine. She's a surgeon.'

'And?' Abbey prodded him with her toe.

He looked sheepish. 'We, uh, got married.'

'Oh, my God! That's fantastic!' She took both his hands in hers, for the first time noticing his gold wedding band. 'So, what are you doing here? Why aren't you with your wife?'

'I came down to see you. To tell you about the marriage and take you back for a holiday with us. But I guess there's no chance of that now, is there?'

Abbey shook her head slowly, pushing a strand of hair back from her face. 'How long had you and Catherine known each other?'

'Couple of months. But we just knew it was right

between us, Abbey. As right as it will be for you and Nick.'

If only she could believe that.

Steve insisted she take a few days off work and rest. 'I'll muddle along with Meri's help. And I promise I won't kill off any of your patients. Well, not intentionally.' He grinned.

She gave him a shaky smile. 'Thanks, Steve. I owe you one.'

He reached out and cuffed her chin. 'Just be nice to Catherine when you meet her.'

'Of course I'll be nice to Catherine. When is she coming down?'

Steve made a face. 'As soon as she can. Her contract still has another few weeks to run. Hopefully, there'll be a suitable practice somewhere we can invest in. We've managed to save a bit. But back to you,' he said softly. 'When are you going to see Nick?'

Abbey's stomach heaved alarmingly. 'You're not going to give up, are you?'

'Nope.'

'Day after tomorrow, then. I'll drive to Hopeton and get a flight to Sydney from there.' And pray to heaven Nick would see her.

Abbey had travelled barely thirty minutes from Wingara when her mobile phone rang. She rolled her eyes. It was probably Steve again, checking on her. He'd already rung once. Automatically, she reduced her speed and pulled her car to a stop. Activating the speak button, she put the phone to her ear. 'Hello.'

'Abbey, don't hang up!'

Abbey felt as though her heart had flown into her mouth. Her lungs, starved for air, felt crushed. For a second she feared she was about to pass out. 'Nick?'

'Yes. I'm on my way to Wingara to see you.'

'But I'm on my way to see *you*!' She heard his swift intake of breath. 'I've only just left town.'

'All right...' He seemed to be thinking. 'I'm about an hour away. Turn round and head back, Abbey. I'll meet you at home.'

Home. Abbey swallowed. Had she heard right?

'Abbey, did you get that?'

'Yes.' Silly tears clumped on her lashes and she swiped them away. 'I'll be waiting for you...'

Abbey leaned back on the headrest until she felt calm enough to restart the Range Rover. But first she should call Steve, she supposed, and tell him what had happened.

'So, I'll steer clear for the next day and a half, then, shall I?'

'Idiot brother.' But she was smiling.

Abbey had steeled herself for a great deal of awkwardness when they met, running over little speeches in her head. But the reality turned out to be very different from what she'd imagined.

Nick drove in slowly and parked around the back of the house. His heart was clamouring. Switching off the engine, he sat for a moment looking into space. Suddenly his hand clenched on the wheel, the sharp edge of need ripping through him. He swallowed against the sudden constriction in his throat. Just don't mess this up, Tonnelli, he cautioned himself silently. Or you'll lose her for ever.

And why was he still hanging about here? He threw open the door of the Jag and swung out.

And Abbey was standing there. Waiting.

'Hello,' she croaked.

'Hello, yourself.' Nick's gaze snapped over her. 'You've lost weight.'

'And you need a shave,' she told him candidly.

He smiled slightly, lifting a hand and scrubbing it over his jaw. 'I've been on the road since four o'clock this morning.'

'You've driven all the way from Sydney?'

'Yes, Abbey.' His eyes burned like emeralds. 'To ask you to marry me.'

'Oh.' Abbey thought she might have fallen in a heap if his arms had not gone around her, holding her as if he'd never let her go.

After a long time he pulled back, lifting his hands to bracket her face, his entire heart in his gaze. 'This feels so right, doesn't it? You and me?'

Abbey nodded, tears welling up and overflowing.

'Don't cry, sweetheart!' Nick took her hands and curled them over his heart. 'I love you!'

'Now he tells me…' Abbey hiccuped a laugh. 'After I've spent the loneliest weeks of my life.'

'It's been hell for me, too.' His voice shook. 'You should never have allowed me to walk out the way I did, Abbey.'

'How was I supposed to stop you?' flashed Abbey, dazed by the brush of his lips against hers. 'Let the air out of your tyres?'

'Might have worked.' Smiling, Nick felt the knot in his chest begin to unravel. It was going to be all right. His arms went around her again, wrapping her against him, his mouth claiming hers as if he was dying of thirst.

A whimper rose in her throat and, breaking the kiss, Nick scooped her into his arms and carried her inside to the lounge room, making a beeline for the sofa. He sat down, settling her on his knee. 'So, what's your answer, Abbey?' he asked softly, his throat working. 'Will you marry me?'

'Of course I'll marry you.' Shakily, she stretched out a hand, touching his hair, the outside edge of his ear, the soft hollow in his throat. 'But I don't want to put any pressure on you.'

He lifted his head and looked at her in puzzlement. 'How could you possibly do that?'

She looked into his eyes, reading the sincerity and, unmistakably, the love. Joy, clear and pure, streamed through her. She dropped her gaze shyly. 'I have to tell you something, Nick.'

'That you love me?' His voice was gentle.

'Of course that.' She burrowed closer. 'I— That is—we…' She hesitated and blinked rapidly.

'You've got me worried now, Abbey.' Nick gave her a little shake. 'Just tell me.'

'I'm pregnant.'

A beat of absolute silence.

'Pregnant!' Nick sat back hard in the sofa. 'You mean you didn't take the—?'

'No.' Abbey shook her head. 'It was such a terrible day and the patient list was endless.' She stopped and took a long shuddering breath. 'And by the time I realised I hadn't had the script filled, it was late and we'd had that awful fight. Well, I just wanted to die and—'

'Oh, Abbey. My poor sweet darling.' His arms went around her and he was rocking her. 'You should've thumped me. I behaved so selfishly, so ego-driven. But a baby?' His gaze clouded and he turned her head and looked into her eyes. 'Are you sure?'

'Yes.' She choked on a laugh. 'I've had it confirmed.'

'Whew!' Nick let the air out of his lungs in a long hiss. 'We're having a baby.'

'Are you pleased?' Abbey's voice was suddenly thin with unshed tears.

'Oh, God, yes!' His hand smoothed over her tummy, as though already he hoped to find there might be changes. 'Oh, this is something, isn't it? But how have you managed on your own?' A frown touched his eyes. 'Have you been sick?'

'A bit queasy,' she confessed with a grimace. 'But something wonderful happened.' Excitedly, she told him about her brother's unexpected arrival and the support he'd offered.

'Then thank heaven for Steve.' Nick held her more closely. 'I'd better buy him a beer.'

Abbey chuckled. 'He'll want several, I should think. And he's recently married.' She filled Nick in about Catherine.

'Good grief,' he grumbled. 'I leave the place for five minutes and all this happens.'

'Then you'd better stick close to me in future, hadn't you?' Abbey pressed her forehead against his.

'Depend on that.' Nick caught her hand and began kissing her fingers one by one. 'Will you mind living in Sydney?' His mouth twisted with faint irony. 'I don't think it would be practical for me to relocate here.'

Abbey wriggled closer. 'As long as we're together, I don't mind where we live.'

'But knowing you and how much you care about your patients, I imagine you'll want to find a replacement before we can make any firm wedding plans?'

'Actually…' She made a little moue of conjecture. 'It's just occurred to me Wingara might be the ideal set-up for Steve and Catherine.'

They smiled like a pair of conspirators and Nick raised a dark eyebrow. 'So we could get married soon, then?'

'Soonish. I'd like to wait for Catherine to be here.' Thoughtfully, Abbey ran her finger down the front of his shirt. 'I don't have much family…'

'Silly girl—of course you do,' he murmured unsteadily. 'You have me—and our baby.'

A slow, radiant smile lit her face. 'I do, don't I? I love you, Nicholas.'

His eyes closed and when he opened them, the message shone clear. 'And I love you, Abbey Jones.'

And the way he kissed her then convinced Abbey, as no words ever could, that he certainly did.

0507/05a

MILLS & BOON®

In June 2007 Mills & Boon present
two bestselling collections, each featuring
three classic romances by three of your
favourite authors…

Blind-Date Grooms

Featuring
The Blind-Date Bride by Emma Darcy
Marriage by Deception by Sara Craven
The Blind-Date Proposal by Jessica Hart

On sale 1st June 2007

Available at WHSmith, Tesco, ASDA, and all good bookshops
www.millsandboon.co.uk

0507/05b

MILLS & BOON®

City Heat

Featuring
The Parisian Playboy by Helen Brooks
City Cinderella by Catherine George
Manhattan Merger by Rebecca Winters

**Don't miss out on these
superb stories!**

On sale 1st June 2007

Available at WHSmith, Tesco, ASDA, and all good bookshops
www.millsandboon.co.uk

MILLS & BOON

MODERN

On sale 1st June 2007

THE RUTHLESS MARRIAGE PROPOSAL
by Miranda Lee

Billionaire Sebastian Armstrong thinks he knows his
housekeeper inside out. But beneath her prim exterior
Emily's a passionate woman trying to forget she's fallen
in love with her handsome boss…

BOUGHT FOR THE GREEK'S BED
by Julia James

When Vicky Peters agreed to become Mrs Theo Theakis,
she knew that the marriage would be purely convenient!
But Theo decides that her presence in his bed will be
money well spent…

THE GREEK TYCOON'S VIRGIN MISTRESS
by Chantelle Shaw

Supermodel Anneliese Christiansen seems to have it all – but
Anna is an innocent, and she has her own reasons for resisting
Greek billionaire Damon Kouvaris's ruthless seduction…

THE SICILIAN'S RED-HOT REVENGE
by Kate Walker

After one night of passion with Vito Corsentino,
Emily Lawton never expected to see him again. But the
brooding Sicilian has tracked her down and if Vito finds out
Emily's having his baby he'll want more than revenge!

Available at WHSmith, Tesco, ASDA, and all good bookshops
www.millsandboon.co.uk

MILLS & BOON

MODERN

On sale 1st June 2007

THE ITALIAN PRINCE'S PREGNANT BRIDE
by Sandra Marton

Tycoon Prince Nicolo Barbieri wasn't expecting what would come with his latest acquisition: Aimee Black – who, it seemed, was pregnant with Nicolo's baby!

KEPT BY THE SPANISH BILLIONAIRE
by Cathy Williams

Incorrigible playboy Rafael Vives instantly resolves to keep beautiful Amy as his mistress of the moment. But she longs to be much more than *just* the billionaire's playmate...

THE KRISTALLIS BABY
by Natalie Rivers

Billionaire Nikos Kristallis is shocked when he learns that his orphaned nephew – and the only heir to the Kristallis fortune – is being cared for by Carrie Thomas. Nik has a plan... he'll take her innocence and then claim her as his bride!

MEDITERRANEAN BOSS, CONVENIENT MISTRESS
by Kathryn Ross

Charlotte Hopkirk is instantly attracted to her new boss, gorgeous Italian doctor Marco Delmari. They agree on a relationship based on convenience rather than love, but Charlie is a hopeless romantic, and before long she realises she's in love...

Available at WHSmith, Tesco, ASDA, and all good bookshops
www.millsandboon.co.uk

0507/03a

MILLS & BOON
MEDICAL
On sale 1st June 2007

SINGLE FATHER, WIFE NEEDED
by Sarah Morgan

Nurse Evanna Duncan and single father Dr Logan MacNeil
work together at the Glenmore surgery. Although Evanna has
always been in love with Logan, he thinks of her only as a
friend. As Evanna finally decides to move on Logan starts
to see her in a different light…

THE ITALIAN DOCTOR'S PERFECT FAMILY
by Alison Roberts

The gorgeous new Italian doctor, Toni Costa, is making
Pip Murdoch feel things she has never imagined, though Pip
has responsibilities that won't allow her to give in to her
heart. Toni knows he can help Pip and persuade her
that together they can be a real family.

A BABY OF THEIR OWN
by Gill Sanderson

There is an undeniable spark of attraction between
Dr Carly Sinclair and the enigmatic Dr Alexander Braikovitch.
Carly can see the deep emotions Alex hides from the
outside world. If she can overcome his past, perhaps
they can have a future together…

Available at WHSmith, Tesco, ASDA, and all good bookshops
www.millsandboon.co.uk

0507/03b

MILLS & BOON
MEDICAL
On sale 1st June 2007

HIS VERY SPECIAL NURSE
by Margaret McDonagh

Dr Kyle Sinclair is devastatingly handsome – and nurse
Alex Patterson cannot help but be drawn to her new boss!
Kyle hasn't looked at a woman since his marriage fell
apart – could Alex be the one to heal his heart and
help him love again?

THE SURGEON AND THE SINGLE MUM
by Lucy Clark

City surgeon Trent Mornington has shut off his emotions –
until a howling storm sweeps him into the lives of rural
GP Aracely Smith and her little son. Warmed by the beautiful
seaside town of Port Wallaby, it's not long before Trent is
thinking of Aracely and Robby as his family-to-be...

THE SURGEON'S LONGED-FOR BRIDE
by Emily Forbes

Anaesthetist Abby Jackson has come home and is reunited
with her best friend, surgeon Dan Dempsey. Dan's a constant
in her life – someone to make her smile. She just hasn't
thought of him as anything more – until now...

Available at WHSmith, Tesco, ASDA, and all good bookshops
www.millsandboon.co.uk

MILLS & BOON
Romance
On sale 1st June 2007

A MOTHER FOR THE TYCOON'S CHILD
by Patricia Thayer

Morgan finds love with gorgeous single father Justin as she
battles with the legacy of her past. Don't miss the final
instalment of the heartwarming *Rocky Mountain Brides*.

THE BOSS AND HIS SECRETARY
by Jessica Steele

This is a classic office romance from a much-loved British author.
When Taryn takes a job with handsome millionaire Jake she's
determined not to mix business and pleasure…

BILLIONAIRE ON HER DOORSTEP
by Ally Blake

Be swept away to sunny Australia. Maggie never expected to find
love in sleepy seaside Sorrento, but one day she opens her door…
and knows her life will never be the same again.

MARRIED BY MORNING
by Shirley Jump

In the makeover Bride and Groom duet, playboy Carter's
practical employee Daphne is certainly surprised when she
finds out her boss has his eye on her…

Available at WHSmith, Tesco, ASDA, and all good bookshops
www.millsandboon.co.uk

MILLS & BOON

Blaze

On sale 1st June 2007

TWO HOT!
by Cara Summers

Having affairs with two men – both incredible lovers with
very different styles – Zoe McNamara's in over her head.
But the truth is more exciting than Zoe could
ever have imagined…

DARING IN THE DARK
by Jennifer LaBrecque

Simon Thackery has a great life. Except he doesn't have Tawny
Edwards…who is engaged to his best friend. After a
twenty-four-hour blackout, can he prove he's the better man?

MIDNIGHT OIL
by Karen Kendall

Landlord Troy Barrington is determined to close down the
After Hours Salon. As part owner, masseuse Peggy Underwood
can't let him win. So she'll have to use the tools of her trade
to change his mind!

THE HONEYMOON THAT WASN'T
by Debbi Rawlins

Tony San Angelo and Dakota Shea have a sizzling chemistry.
So when they have the opportunity to hijack a honeymoon,
Tony and Dakota jump at the chance of hot days
and steamy nights…

Available at WHSmith, Tesco, ASDA, and all good bookshops
www.millsandboon.co.uk

0507/04a

MILLS & BOON
Historical

On sale 1st June 2007

Regency

A SCOUNDREL OF CONSEQUENCE
by Helen Dickson

William Lampard, distinguished military captain,
kept London abuzz with scandal. Against his better judgement,
he made a wager to seduce Miss Cassandra Greenwood.
But despite her provocative ways, and the impudent sway
of her skirts, he quickly realised that her innocence and
goodness put her above a mere dalliance…

Regency

AN INNOCENT COURTESAN
by Elizabeth Beacon

Caroline Besford was forced her into marriage with a
man who refused to share her bed. In making her escape,
Caro became Cleo – an untouched courtesan! Amazingly,
the husband who ignored his plain bride is now pursuing her!
But what will the Colonel do when he discovers that his
darling Cleo is his dowdy wife, Caroline?

Available at WHSmith, Tesco, ASDA, and all good bookshops
www.millsandboon.co.uk

MILLS & BOON Historical

On sale 1st June 2007

Regency

THE RAKE'S PROPOSAL
by Sarah Elliott

Katherine Sutcliff would bring a scandalous secret to the marriage bed. She needed a suitable match – so why was she distracted by her most unsuitable attraction to the disreputable Lord Benjamin Sinclair?

THE KING'S CHAMPION
by Catherine March

With Eleanor's reputation compromised, the King commands her to marry. Ellie is overjoyed to be tied to her perfect knight. But Troye is desperate to resist the emotions she is reawakening in him…

THE HIRED HUSBAND
by Judith Stacy

Rachel Branford is intent on saving her family's name. And handsome Mitch Kincaid may be the answer! Abandoned in an orphanage, Mitch has struggled to gain wealth and power. Until he finds himself tempted by Rachel's money… then Rachel herself!

Available at WHSmith, Tesco, ASDA, and all good bookshops
www.millsandboon.co.uk

0607/25/MB093

*What lurks beneath the surface
of the powerful and prestigious
Chrighton Dynasty?*

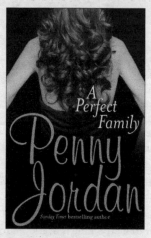

As three generations of the Chrighton family
gather for a special birthday celebration, no one
could possibly have anticipated that their secure
world was about to be rocked by the events of
one fateful weekend.

One dramatic revelation leads to another
– a secret war-time liaison, a carefully concealed
embezzlement scam, the illicit seduction of
somebody else's wife.

And the results are going to be explosive…

Available 1st June 2007

www.millsandboon.co.uk

0406/10/QUEENS 07

Queens of Romance

An outstanding collection by international bestselling authors

16th March 2007

20th April 2007

18th May 2007

15th June 2007

Collect all 4 superb books!

www.millsandboon.co.uk